LAST ACT IN PALMYRA

Also by Lindsey Davis

THE SILVER PIGS
SHADOWS IN BRONZE
VENUS IN COPPER
THE IRON HAND OF MARS
POSEIDON'S GOLD

LAST ACT
IN
PALMYRA

LINDSEY DAVIS

THE MYSTERIOUS PRESS

Published by Warner Books

A Time Warner Company

First published in Great Britain in 1994 by Century, Random House UK Limited, London.

Copyright © 1994 by Lindsey Davis

 Mysterious Press books are published by Warner Books, Inc., 1271 Avenue of the Americas, New York, NY 10020.

 A Time Warner Company

The Mysterious Press name and logo are registered trademarks of Warner Books, Inc.

Printed in the United States of America

First U.S. printing: March 1996

10 9 8 7 6 5 4 3 2 1

Library of Congress Cataloging-in-Publication Data

Davis, Lindsey.
    Last act in Palmyra / Lindsey Davis.
       p.   cm.
    ISBN 0-89296-625-4
  1. Falco, Marcus Didius (Fictitious character)—Fiction. 2. Rome—History—Vespasian, 69-79—Fiction. 3. Private investigators—Rome—Fiction. I. Title.
PR6054.A8925L37 1996
823'.914—dc20
                                       95-1612
                                         CIP

For Janet
("Six o'clock; first there bags a table . . .")
with neither gunshots nor simulated rape
—and only one insult to lawyers!

Last Act in Palmyra

"*There comes a time in everyone's life when he feels he was born to be an actor. Something within him tells him he is the coming man, and that one day he will electrify the world. Then he burns with a desire to show them how the thing's done, and to draw a salary of three hundred a week. . . .*"

Jerome K. Jerome

"*And let those that play your clowns speak no more than is set down for them; for there be of them that will themselves laugh, to set on some quantity of barren spectators to laugh too; though, in the mean time, some necessary question of the play be then to be considered . . .*"

William Shakespeare

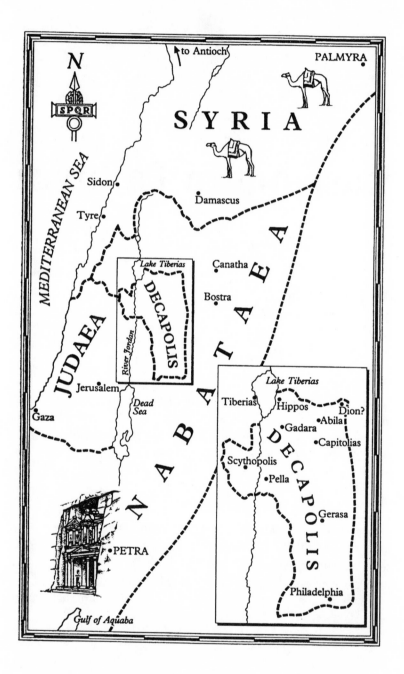

Principal Characters

Sophrona	a missing musician, looking for love
Khaleed	not looking for love, though it's found him all right
Habib	an elusive Syrian businessman
People pretending to be Habib	(there's big money in elusiveness)
Alexander	a backward-facing goat; an unsuccessful freak
Alexander's owner	sensibly looking for early retirement

Dramatis Personae

From the Orchestra

Ione	a tambourinist	}
Afrania	a tibia-player	} not a trio to mess with
Plancina	a panpipe girl	}
Ribes	a lyre-player who hasn't found his muse	

From The Spook Who Spoke
"Moschion"   a prototype

Prologue

The scene is set in Rome, in the Circus of Nero and in a small back room at the Palace of the Caesars on Palatine Hill. The time is A.D. 72.

SYNOPSIS: *Helena,* daughter of *Camillus,* is a young girl disappointed by *Falco,* a trickster, who seemed to have promised her marriage. He now claims he has been let down by *Vespasian,* an Emperor, his patron. In the nick of time *Thalia,* a high-class entertainer, and *Anacrites,* a low-class spy, both suggest ways in which Falco may escape from this predicament, but he must prevent Helena discovering what he is up to, or a Chorus of Disapproval is bound to ensue.

LAST ACT IN PALMYRA

One

"Somebody could get killed here!" Helena exclaimed.

I grinned, watching the arena avidly. "That's what we're meant to be hoping for!" Playing the bloodthirsty spectator comes easy to a Roman.

"I'm worried about the elephant," she murmured. It stepped tentatively forwards, now at shoulder height on the ramp. A trainer risked tickling its toes.

I felt more concern for the man at ground level who would catch the full weight if the elephant fell. Not too much concern, however. I was happy that for once the person in danger was not me.

Helena and I were sitting safely in the front row of Nero's Circus, just across the river outside Rome. This place had a bloody history, but was nowadays used for comparatively staid chariot racing. The long circuit was dominated by the huge red granite obelisk that Caligula had imported from Heliopolis. The Circus lay in Agrippina's Gardens at the foot of the Vatican Hill. Empty of crowds and of Christians being turned into firebrands, it had an almost peaceful atmosphere. This was broken only by brief cries of "Hup!" from practicing tumblers and rope dancers and restrained encouragement from the elephant's trainers.

We were the only two observers allowed into this rather fraught rehearsal. I happened to know the entertainment manager. I had gained entrance by mentioning her name at the starting gates, and was now waiting for a chance to talk to her. Her name was Thalia. She was a gregarious character, with physical attractions that she did not bother concealing behind the indignity of clothing, so my girlfriend had come to protect me. As a senator's daughter, Helena Justina had strict ideas about letting the man she lived with put himself in moral danger. As a private informer in an unsatisfactory job and with a shady past behind me, I suppose I had asked for it.

Above us soared a sky that a bad lyric poet would certainly have called cerulean. It was early April; midmorning on a promising day. Just across the Tiber everyone in the imperial city was twisting garlands for a long warm springtime of festivals. We were well into the third year of Vespasian's reign as Emperor, and it was a time of busy reconstruction as burned-out public monuments were rebuilt after the civil wars. If I thought about it, I was in a mood for some refurbishment myself.

Thalia must have despaired of proceedings out in the arena, for she threw a few harsh words over a barely decent shoulder, then left the trainers to get on with it. She came over to greet us. Behind her we could see people still cajoling the elephant, who was a very small one, along the ramp that was supposed to bring him to a platform; from this they had hopefully stretched a tightrope. The baby elephant could not yet see the rope, but he knew he did not like what he had discovered about his training program so far.

At Thalia's arrival my own worries became wilder too. She not only had an interesting occupation, but unusual friends. One of them lay around her neck like a scarf. I had met him at close quarters once before, and still blanched at the memory. He was a snake, of modest size but gigantic curiosity. A python: one of the constricting species. He obviously remembered me from our last meeting, for he came reaching out delightedly, as if he wanted to hug me to death. His tongue flickered, testing the air.

Thalia herself took careful handling. With commanding height and a crackling voice that cut right across this huge arena, she could always make her presence felt. She also possessed a shape few men could take their eyes off. Currently it was draped in silly strips of saffron gauze, held in place by gigantic jewelry that would break bones if she dropped any of it on your foot. I liked her. I sincerely hoped she liked me. Who wants to offend a woman who is sporting a live python for effect?

"Falco, you ridiculous bastard!" Being named after one of the Graces had never affected her manners.

She stopped in front of us, feet planted apart to help support the snake's weight. Her huge thighs bulged through the flimsy saffron. Bangles the size of trireme rowlocks gripped tightly on her arms. I started to make introductions, but nobody was listening.

"Your gigolo looks jaded!" Thalia snorted to Helena, jerking her head at me. They had never met before but Thalia did not trouble with etiquette. The python now peered at me from her pillowing bosom. He seemed more torpid than usual, but even so something about his disparaging attitude reminded me of my relatives. He had small scales, beautifully patterned in large diamond shapes. "So what's this, Falco? Come to take up my offer?"

I tried to look innocent. "I did promise to come and see your act, Thalia." I sounded like some stuffed green fig barely out of his toga praetexta, making his first solemn speech in court at the Basilica. There was no doubt I had lost my case before the usher set the water clock.

Thalia winked at Helena. "He told me he was leaving home to seek employment taming tigers."

"Taming Helena takes all my time," I got in.

"He told *me*," Helena said to Thalia, as if I had never spoken, "he was a tycoon with big olive vineyards in Samnium, and that if I tickled his fancy he would show me the Seven Wonders of the World."

"Well, we all make mistakes," Thalia sympathized.

Helena Justina crossed her ankles with a swift kick at the embroidered flounce on her skirt. They were devastating ankles. She could be a devastating girl.

Thalia was giving her a practiced scrutiny. From our previous encounters Thalia knew me to be a low-life informer, plugging away at a dismal occupation in return for putrid wages and the public's contempt. Now she took in my unexpectedly superior girlfriend. Helena was posing as a cool, quiet, serious person, though one who could silence a cohort of drunken Praetorians with a few crisp words. She also wore a stunningly expensive gold filigree bracelet that by itself must have told the snake dancer something: even though she had come to the Circus with a dried melon seed like me, my lass was a patrician piece, backed up by solid collateral.

Having assessed the jewelry, Thalia turned back to me. "Your luck's changed!" It was true. I accepted the compliment with a happy grin.

Helena gracefully rearranged the drape of her silken stole. She knew I didn't deserve her, and that I knew it too.

Thalia gently lifted the python from her neck, then rewound it around a bollard so she could sit down and talk to us. The creature, which had always tried to upset me, immediately unraveled its blunt, spade-shaped head and stared balefully with its slitted eyes. I resisted the urge to pull in my boots. I refused to be alarmed by a legless thug. Besides, sudden movement can be a mistake with a snake.

"Jason's really taken to you!" cackled Thalia.

"Oh, he's called Jason, is he?"

An inch closer and I was planning to spear Jason with my knife. I was only holding off because I knew Thalia was fond of him. Turning Jason into a snakeskin belt was likely to upset her. The thought of what Thalia might do to a person who upset her was even more worrying than a squeeze from her pet.

"He looks a bit sick at the moment," she explained to Helena. "See how milky his eyes are? He's ready to shed his skin again. Jason's a growing boy—he has to have a new outfit every couple of months. It makes him go broody for over a week. I can't use him in public appearances; he's completely unreliable when you're trying to fix up bookings. Believe me, it's worse than operating an act with a troupe of young girls who have to lie down moaning every month—"

Helena looked ready to reply in kind, but I interrupted the women's talk. "So how's business, Thalia? The gateman told me you've taken over the management from Fronto?"

"Someone had to take charge. It was either me or a damned man." Thalia had always taken a brutal view of men. Can't think why, though her bedroom stories were sordid.

The Fronto I referred to had been an importer of exotic arena beasts, and an organizer of even more exotic entertainment for the smart banqueting crowd. He met with a sudden indisposition, in the form of a panther who ate him. Apparently Thalia, a one-time party-circuit dancer, was now running the business he left behind.

"Still got the panther?" I joked.

"Oh yes!" I knew Thalia saw this as a mark of respect for

Fronto, since parts of her ex-employer might still be inside the beast. "Did you catch out the grieving widow?" she demanded of me abruptly. In fact, Fronto's widow had failed to grieve convincingly—a normal scenario in Rome, where life was cheap and death might not be random if a man offended his wife. It was while investigating the possible collusion between the widow and the panther that I had first met Thalia and her collection of snakes.

"Not enough evidence to bring her before the courts, but we stopped her chasing after legacies. She's married to a lawyer now."

"That's a tough punishment, even for a bitch like her!" Thalia grimaced evilly.

I grinned back. "Tell me, does your move into management mean I've lost my opportunity to see you do your snake dance?"

"I still do my act. I like to give the crowd a thrill."

"But you don't perform with Jason because of his off days?" Helena smiled. They had accepted one another. Helena for one usually gave her friendship reluctantly. Getting to know her could be as tricky as mopping up oil with a sponge. It had taken me six months to make any headway, even though I had wit, good looks, and years of experience on my side.

"I use Zeno," said Thalia, as if this reptile needed no other description. I had already heard that Thalia's act involved an immense snake that even she spoke of with awe.

"Is that another python?" Helena asked curiously.

"And a half!"

"And who does the dancing—him or you? Or is the trick to make the audience think Zeno is taking a greater part than he really does?"

"Just like making love to a man . . . Smart girl you've picked up here!" Thalia commented drily to me. "You're right," she confirmed to Helena. "I dance; I hope Zeno doesn't. Twenty feet of African constrictor is too heavy to lift, for one thing."

"Twenty feet!"

"And the rest of it."

"Goodness! So how dangerous is it?"

"Well . . ." Thalia tapped her nose confidentially, then she seemed to let us in on a secret. "Pythons only eat what they can get their jaws around, and even then in captivity they're picky eaters. They're immensely strong, so people think they're sinister. But I've never known one to show the slightest interest in killing a human being."

I laughed shortly, considering my unease over Jason, and feeling conned. "So this act of yours is pretty tame, really!"

"Fancy a dance with my big Zeno yourself?" Thalia challenged me caustically. I backed down with a gracious gesture. "No, you're right, Falco. I've been thinking the act needs pepping up. I might have to get a cobra, to add a bit more danger. Good for catching rats around the menagerie too."

Helena and I both fell silent, knowing cobra bites to be generally fatal.

The conversation took a turn in a different direction. "Well, that's my news!" Thalia said. "So what job are you on now, Falco?"

"Ah. A hard question."

"With an easy answer," Helena joined in lightly enough. "He's not on any job at all."

That was not quite true. I had been offered a commission only that morning, though Helena was still unaware of it. The business was secret. I mean not just that it would involve working under cover, but that it was secret from Helena because she would strongly disapprove of the client.

"You call yourself an informer, don't you?" Thalia said. I nodded, though with only half my attention on it as I continued to worry about keeping from Helena the truth of what I had just been offered.

"Don't be shy!" Thalia joked. "You're among friends. You can confess to anything!"

"He's quite a good one," said Helena, who already seemed to be eyeing me suspiciously. She might not know what I was hiding, but she was beginning to suspect that there was something. I tried to think about the weather.

Thalia tipped her head on one side. "So what's it about, Falco?"

"Information mostly. Finding evidence for barristers—you know about that—or just listening for gossip, more often than not. Helping election candidates slander their opponents. Helping husbands find reasons to divorce wives they've grown tired of. Helping wives avoid paying blackmail to lovers they've discarded. Helping the lovers shed women they've seen through."

"Oh, a social service," Thalia scoffed.

"Definitely. A real boon to the community . . . Sometimes I trace stolen antiques," I added, hoping to impose an air of class. It sounded merely as though I hunted down fake Egyptian amulets, or pornographic scrolls.

"Do you look for missing persons too?" Thalia demanded, as if she had suddenly had an idea. I nodded again, rather reluctantly. Mine is a job where I try to prevent people getting ideas, since they tend to be time-consuming and unprofitable for me. I was right to be wary. The dancer exploded gleefully. "Hah! If I had any money, I'd take you on for a search-and-retrieve myself."

"If we didn't need to eat," I replied mildly, "I'd accept the tempting offer!"

At that moment the baby elephant spotted the tightrope and realized why he was being taken for a walk up the ramp. He began trumpeting wildly, then somehow turned around and tried to charge back down. Trainers scattered. With a mutter of impatience, Thalia rushed out into the arena again. She told Helena to look after her snake. Evidently I could not be trusted with the task.

Two

Helena and Jason watched keenly as Thalia strode up the ramp to comfort the elephant. We could hear her berating its trainers; she loved animals, but evidently believed in producing high-class acts by a regime of fear—in her staff, that is. Like me, they had now decided the exercise was doomed. Even if they could entice their ungainly gray acrobat out over the void, the rope was bound to snap. I wondered whether to point this out. No one would thank me, so I stayed mum. Scientific information has a low rating in Rome.

Helena and Jason were getting on well. She had had some practice with untrustworthy reptiles, after all; she knew me.

Since nothing else was required, I started to think. Informers spend a lot of time crouching in dark porticos, waiting to overhear scandals that may bring in a greasy denarius from some unlikable patron. It's boring work. You are bound to fall into one bad habit or another. Other informers amuse themselves with casual vice. I had grown out of that. My failing was to indulge in private thought.

The elephant had now been fed a sesame bun, but still looked dismal. So did I. What was on my mind was the job I had just been offered. I was thinking up excuses to turn it down.

Sometimes I worked for Vespasian. A new Emperor, sprung from a middle-class background and wanting to keep a canny eye on the nasty snobs of the old élite, may need the occasional favor. I mean, a favor of the kind he won't be boasting about when his glorious achievements are recorded in bronze lettering on marble monuments. Rome was full of plotters who would have liked to poke Vespasian off the throne, so long as they could make the attempt with a fairly long stick in case he turned round and bit them. There were others annoyances, too, that he wanted to be rid of—dreary men fastened into high public positions on the strength of moldy old pedigrees, men who had neither brains nor energy nor morals, and whom the new Emperor intended to replace with brighter talent. Somebody had to weed out the plotters and discredit the idiots. I was quick and discreet, and Vespasian could trust me to tidy up loose ends. There were never repercussions from my jobs.

We first took each other on eighteen months ago. Now, whenever I had more creditors than usual, or when I forgot how much I loathed the work, I agreed to imperial employment. Though I despised myself for becoming a tool of the state, I had earned some cash. Cash was always welcome in my vicinity.

As a result of my efforts Rome and some of the provinces were more secure. But last week the imperial family had broken an important promise. Instead of promoting me socially, so I could marry Helena Justina and appease her disgruntled family, when I had called to claim my recompense from the Caesars they kicked me down the Palatine steps empty-handed. At that, Helena declared that Vespasian had given me his last commission. He himself failed to notice that I might feel slighted by so small a thing as mere lack of reward; within three days here he was, offering me another of his diplomatic trips abroad. Helena would be furious.

Luckily, when the new summons to the Palace came, I was heading downstairs from our apartment on my way to pick up gossip at the barber's. The message had been brought to me by a puny slave with coarse eyebrows joined together above hardly any brain—up to standard for Palace messengers. I managed to grab the back of his short tunic and march him down to the ground-floor laundry without Helena seeing him. I paid a small bribe to Lenia, the laundress, to keep her quiet. Then I hurried the slave back to the Palatine and gave him a stern warning against causing me domestic inconvenience.

"Stuff you, Falco! I'll go where I'm sent."

"Who sent you then?"

He looked nervous—with reason. "Anacrites."

I growled. This was worse news than being asked to attend Vespasian or one of his sons.

Anacrites was the official Chief Spy at the Palace. We were old antagonists. Our rivalry was the most bitter kind: purely professional. He liked to see himself as an expert at dealing with tricky characters in dangerous locations, but the truth was he led too soft a life and had lost the knack; besides, Vespasian kept him short of resources, so he was beset by pathetic subordinates and never had a ready bribe to hand. Lack of small change is fatal in our job.

Whenever Anacrites bungled some sensitive commission, he knew Vespasian would send me in to put his mistakes right. (I provided my own resources; I came cheap.) My successes had aroused his permanent jealousy. Now, although his habit was always to appear friendly in public, I knew that one day Anacrites meant to fix me for good.

I gave his messenger another piece of colorful career advice, then stomped in for what was bound to be a tense confrontation. Anacrites' office was about the size of my mother's lamp store. Spies were not accorded respect under Vespasian; he had never cared who might be overheard insulting him. Vespasian had Rome to rebuild, and took the rash view that his public achievements would sufficiently enhance his reputation without the need to resort to terror tactics.

Under this relaxed regime Anacrites was visibly struggling. He had equipped himself with a folding bronze chair, but sat crushed up in one corner of the room in order to make space for his clerk. The clerk was a big, misshapen lump of Thracian sheep's fat in a flashy red tunic that he must have stolen off a balcony parapet while it was hanging out to air. His huge feet took up most of the floor in their ungainly sandals, ink and lamp oil spilled on their thongs. Even with Anacrites sitting there, this clerk managed to suggest that *he* was the important person visitors ought to address.

The room gave off a faintly unprofessional impression. It had an odd scent of turpentine corn plasters and cold toasted bread. Scattered all around were crumpled scrolls and wax tablets that I took to be expenses claims. Probably claims by Anacrites and his runners which the Emperor had refused to pay. Vespasian was notoriously tight, and spies have no sense of discretion when requesting travel refunds.

As I went in, the master of espionage was chewing a stylus and staring dreamily at a fly on the wall. Once he saw me, Anacrites straightened up and looked important. He hit his knee with a crack that made the clerk wince, and me too; then he sank back pretending to be unconcerned. I winked at the clerk. He knew what a bastard he worked for, yet openly dared to grin back at me.

Anacrites affected tunics in discreet shades of stone and buff as if he were pretending to merge into backgrounds, but his clothes always had a slightly racy cut, and his hair lay oiled back from his temples so precisely I felt my nostrils curl. The vanity in his appearance matched his view of himself professionally. He was a good public speaker, able to mislead with easy grace. I never trust men who have nicely manicured fingernails and a deceitful way with words.

My dusty boot knocked into a group of scrolls. "What's this? More poisonous accusations against innocent citizens?"

"Falco, just you attend to your business, and I'll look after mine." He managed to imply that his business was deeply relevant and intriguing, while my motives and methods smelled like a barrel of dead squid.

"A pleasure," I agreed. "Must have received the wrong message. Someone claimed you needed me—"

"I *sent* for you." He had to act as if he were giving me orders. I ignored the insult—temporarily.

I pressed a small copper into his clerk's hand. "Go out and buy yourself an apple." Anacrites looked furious at me interfering with his staff. While he was still thinking up a countermand, the Thracian skipped. I slumped onto the clerk's vacant stool, spreading myself across most of the office, grabbed a scroll to look through nosily.

"That document is confidential, Falco."

I carried on unrolling the papyrus, raising an eyebrow. "Dear gods, I hope it is! You won't want this muck being made public . . ." I dropped the scroll behind my stool, out of his reach. He went pink with annoyance at not being able to see which secrets I had been looking at.

Actually, I had not bothered to read it. Nothing but nonsense ever came through this office. Most of the sly schemes Anacrites was pursuing would sound ludicrous to the average stroller in the Forum. I preferred not to upset myself by finding out.

"Falco, you're making my office untidy!"

"So spill the message and I'll go."

Anacrites was too professional to squabble. Pulling himself together, he lowered his voice. "We ought to be on the same side," he commented, like a drunken old friend reaching the point where he wants to tell you just why he shoved his elderly father over the cliff. "I don't know what makes us always seem so incompatible!"

I could suggest reasons. He was a sinister shark with devious motives who manipulated everyone. He received a good salary for working as little as possible. I was just a freelance hero doing his best in a hard world, meanly paid for it, and always in arrears. Anacrites stayed in the Palace and dabbled in sophisticated concepts, while I was out saving the Empire, getting filthy and beaten up.

I smiled quietly. "I've no idea."

He knew I was lying. Then he hit me with the words I dread to hear from bureaucrats. "Time we made it all up, then! Marcus Didius, old friend, let's go out for a drink. . . ."

Three

He hauled me off to a thermopolium the Palace secretaries use. I had been there before. It was always full of ghastly types who liked to think they ruled the world. When secretariat papyrus beetles go out to socialize they have to burrow among their own kind.

They can't even find a decent hole. This was a shabby stand-up wine bar where the air smelled sour and one glance around the clientele explained it. The few pots of food looked caked with week-old crusts of gravy on their rims; nobody was eating from them. In a chipped dish a dry old gherkin tried to look impressive beneath a pair of copulating flies. A misshapen, bad-tempered male skivvy flung herb twigs into pannikins of hot wine boiled down to the color of dried blood.

Even halfway through the morning, eight or ten inky blots in dingy tunics were crammed up against one another, all talking about their terrible jobs and their lost chances for promotion. They swigged drearily as if someone had just told them the Parthians had wiped out five thousand Roman veterans and the price of olive oil had slumped. I felt ill just looking at them.

Anacrites ordered. I knew I was in trouble when he also settled the bill.

"What's this? I expect a Palace employee to dash for the latrine door whenever a reckoning hoves into view!"

"You like your joke, Falco." What made him think it was a joke?

"Your health," I said politely, trying not to sound as if actually I wished him a plague of warts and Tiber fever.

"Yours too! So, Falco, here we are . . ." From a beautiful woman slipping out of her tunic, this could have been a promising remark. From him it stank.

"Here we are," I growled back, intending to be somewhere else as soon as possible. Then I sniffed at my drink, which smelled like thin vinegar, and waited in silence for him to come to the point. Trying to rush Anacrites only made him dawdle more.

After what seemed like half an hour, though I had only managed to swallow a digit of the awful wine, he struck: "I've been hearing all about your German adventure." I smiled to myself as he tried to insinuate an admiring tone into his basic hostility. "How was it?"

"Fine, if you like gloomy weather, legionary swank, and amazing examples of ineptitude among the higher ranks. Fine, if you like to winter in a forest where the ferocity of the animals is excelled only by the bad mood of the trousered barbarians who are holding spears to your throat."

"You do love to talk!"

"And I hate wasting time. What's the point of this fake banter, Anacrites?"

He gave me a soothing smile, meant to patronize. "The Emperor happens to want another extraterritorial expedition—by somebody discreet."

My response may have sounded cynical. "You mean he's instructed you to do the job yourself, but you're keen to duck? Is the mission just dangerous, or does it involve an inconvenient journey, a foul climate, a total lack of civilized amenities, and a tyrannical king who likes his Romans laced on a spit over a very hot fire?"

"Oh, the place is civilized."

That applied to very few corners outside the Empire—the one thing these tended to have in common was a determination to *stay* outside. It led to an unfriendly reception for our envoys. The more we pretended to arrive with peaceful intentions, the more certain they felt that we had their country earmarked for annexation. "I don't like the sound of that! Before you bother asking, my answer's no."

Anacrites was keeping his face expressionless. He sipped his wine. I had seen him quaff fine fifteen-year-old Alban, and I knew he could tell the difference. It amused me to watch his strange, light eyes flicker as he tried not to mind drinking this bitter brew in company he also despised. He asked, "What makes you so certain the old man instructed me to go myself?"

"Anacrites, when he wants me, he tells me so in person."

"Maybe he asked my opinion, and I warned him you were unreceptive to work from the Palace nowadays."

"I've always been unreceptive." I was reluctant to mention my recent kick in the teeth, though in fact Anacrites had been present when my request for promotion was turned down by Vespasian's son Domitian. I even suspected Anacrites was behind that act of imperial graciousness. He must have noticed my anger.

"I find your feelings perfectly understandable," the Chief Spy said in what he must have hoped was a winning way, apparently unaware he was risking several broken ribs. "You had a big investment in getting promoted. It must have been a bad shock being turned down. I suppose this spells the end of your relationship with the Camillus girl?"

"I'll handle my own feelings. And don't speculate about my girl."

"Sorry!" he murmured meekly. I felt my teeth grind. "Look, Falco, I thought I might be able to do you a favor here. The Emperor put me in charge of this; I can commission whoever I want. After what happened the other day at the Palace, you may welcome an opportunity to get as far away from Rome as possible. . . ."

Sometimes Anacrites sounded as though he had been listening at my doorlatch while I talked life over with Helena. As we lived on the sixth floor, it was unlikely any of his minions had flogged up to eavesdrop, but I took a firmer grip on my winecup while my eyes narrowed.

"There's no need to go on the defensive, Falco!" He could be too observant for anybody's good. Then he shrugged, raising his hands easily. "Suit yourself. If I can't identify a suitable envoy I can always go myself."

"Why, where is it?" I asked, without intending to.

"Nabataea."

"Arabia Petraia?"

"Does that surprise you?"

"No."

I had hung around the Forum often enough to consider myself an expert in foreign policy. Most of the gossipmongers on the steps of the Temple of Saturn had never stepped outside Rome, or at least had gone no further than whichever little villa in central Italy their grandfathers came from; unlike them I had seen the edge of the Empire. I knew what went on at the frontier, and when the Emperor looked beyond it I knew what his preoccupations were.

Nabataea lay between our troubled lands in Judaea, which Vespasian and his son Titus had recently pacified, and the imperial province of Egypt. It was the meeting point of several great trade routes across Arabia from the Far East: spices and peppers, gemstones and sea pearls, exotic woods and incense. By policing these caravan routes the Nabataeans kept the country safe for merchants, and charged highly for the service. At Petra, their secretively guarded stronghold, they had established a key center of trade. Their customs levies were notorious, and since Rome was the most voracious customer for luxury goods, in the end it was Rome who paid. I could see exactly why Vespasian might now be wondering whether the rich and powerful Nabataeans should be encouraged to join the Empire and bring their vital, lucrative trading post under our direct control.

Anacrites mistook my silence for interest in his proposal. He gave me the usual flattery about this being a task very few agents could tackle.

"You mean you've already asked ten other people, and they all developed sick headaches!"

"It could be a job to get you noticed."

"You mean if I do well, the assumption will be it can't have been so difficult after all."

"You've been around too long!" He grinned. Momentarily I liked him more than usual. "You seemed the ideal candidate, Falco."

"Oh come off it! I've never been outside Europe!"

"You have connections with the East."

I laughed shortly. "Only the fact my brother died there!"

"It gives you an interest—"

"Correct! An interest in making sure I never visit the damned desert myself!"

I told Anacrites to wrap himself in a vine leaf and jump head first into an amphora of rancid oil, then I derisively poured what remained in my winecup back into his flagon, and marched off.

Behind me I knew the Chief Spy wore an indulgent smile. He was sure I would think over his fascinating proposition, then come creeping back.

Anacrites was forgetting about Helena.

Four

Guiltily I recalled my attention to the baby elephant.

Helena was looking at me. She said nothing, but she gave me a certain still, quiet stare. It had the same effect on me as walking down a dark alley between high buildings in a known haunt of robbers with knives.

There was no need to mention that I had been offered a new mission; Helena knew. Now my problem was not trying to find a way of telling her, but sounding as if I had intended to come clean all along. I disguised a sigh. Helena looked away.

"We'll give the elephant a rest," Thalia grumbled, coming back to us. "Is he being a good boy?" She meant the python. Presumably.

"He's a treat," Helena answered, in the same dry tone. "Thalia, what were you saying about a possible job for Marcus?"

"Oh, it's nothing."

"If it was nothing," I said, "you wouldn't have thought of mentioning it."

"Just a girl."

"Marcus likes jobs involving girls," Helena commented.

"I bet he does!"

"I met a nice one once," I put in reminiscently. The girl I once met took my hand, fairly nicely.

"He's all talk," Thalia consoled her.

"Well, he thinks he's a poet."

"That's right: all lip and libido!" I joined in, for self-protection.

"Pure swank," said Thalia. "Like the bastard who ran off with my water organist."

"Is this your missing person?" I forced myself to show an interest, partly to insert some professional grit but mainly to distract Helena from guessing I had been called to the Palace again.

Thalia spread herself on the arena seats. The effect was dramatic. I made sure I was gazing out towards the elephant. "Don't rush me, as the High Priest said to the acolyte . . . Sophrona, her name was."

"It would be." All the cheap skirts who pretended to play musical instruments were called Sophrona nowadays.

"She was really good, Falco!" I knew what that meant. (Actually, coming from Thalia it meant she *was* really good.) "She could play," Thalia confirmed. "There were plenty of parasites taking advantage of the Emperor's interest." She was referring to Nero, the water-organ fanatic, not our present endearing specimen. Vespasian's most famous musical trait was going to sleep during Nero's lyre performances, for which he had been lucky to escape with nothing worse than a few months' exile. "A true artiste, Sophrona was."

"Musicianship?" I queried innocently.

"A lovely touch . . . And looks! When Sophrona pumped out her tunes men rose in their seats."

I took it at face value, not looking at Helena, who was supposed to have been politely brought up. Nevertheless I heard her giggling shamelessly before she asked, "Had she been with you long?"

"Virtually from babyhood. Her mother was a lanky chorus dancer in a mime group I once ran into. Reckoned she couldn't look after a child. Couldn't be bothered, more like. I saved the scrap, fostered her out until she was a useful age, then taught her what I could. She was too tall for an acrobat, but luckily she turned out to be musical, so when I saw that the hydraulus was the instrument of the moment I grabbed the chance and got Sophrona trained. I paid for it, at a time when I wasn't doing so well as nowadays, so I'm annoyed at losing her."

"Tell us what happened, Thalia?" I asked. "How could an expert like you be so careless as to lose valuable talent from your troupe?"

"It wasn't me who lost her!" Thalia snorted. "That fool Fronto. He was showing some prospective patrons around—Eastern visitors. He reckoned they were theatrical entrepreneurs, but they were time-wasters."

"Just wanted a free gawp at the menagerie?"

"And at female tumblers with no clothes on. The rest of us could see we hadn't much hope of them hiring us for anything. Even if they had done it would have been all sodomy and mean tips. So nobody took much notice. It was just before the panther got loose and munched up Fronto; naturally things grew rather hectic after that. The Syrians did pay us another hopeful visit, but we pulled down the awnings. They must have left Rome, and then we realized Sophrona had gone too."

"A man in it?"

"Oh bound to be!"

I noticed Helena smiling again as Thalia exploded with contempt. Then Helena asked, "At least you know they were Syrian. So who were these visitors?"

"No idea. Fronto was the man in charge," Thalia grumbled, as if she were accusing him of seedy moral habits. "Once Fronto ended up inside the panther, all we could remember was that they spoke Greek with a very funny accent, wore stripy robes, and seemed to think somewhere called 'the ten Towns' was the tops in civic life."

"I've heard of the Decapolis," I said. "It's a Greek federation in central Syria. That's a long way to go looking for a musician who's done a moonlight."

"Not to mention the fact that if you do go," said Helena, "whichever order you flog around these ten gracious metropolitan sites, she's bound to be in the last town you visit. By the time you get there, you'll be too tired to argue with her."

"No point anyway," I added. "She's probably got a set of twins and marsh fever by now. Don't you have any other facts to go on, Thalia?"

"Only a name one of the menagerie-keepers remembered—Habib."

"Oh dear. In the East it's probably as common as Gaius," said Helena. "Or Marcus," she added slyly.

"And we know *he's* common!" Thalia joined in.

"Could the girl have gone looking for her mother?" I asked, having had some experience of tracing fostered children.

Thalia shook her head. "She doesn't know who her mother was."

"Might the mother have come looking for her?"

"Doubt it. I've heard nothing about her for twenty years. She might be working under a different name. Well, face it, Falco, she's most likely dead by now."

I agreed the point somberly. "So what about the father? Any chance Sophrona heard from him?"

Thalia roared with laughter. "What father? There were various candidates, none of whom had the slightest interest in being pinned down. As I recall it, only one of them had anything about him, and naturally he was the one the mother wouldn't look at twice."

"She must have looked once!" I observed facetiously.

Thalia gave me a pitying glance, then said to Helena, "Explain the facts of life to him, dearie! Just because you go to bed with a man doesn't mean you have to look at the bastard!"

Helena was smiling again, though the expression in her eyes was less charitable. I reckoned it might be time to halt the ribaldry. "So we're stuck with the 'young love' theory?"

"Don't get excited, Falco," Thalia told me with her usual frankness. "Sophrona was a treasure and I'd risk a lot to get her back. But I can't afford the fare to send you scavenging in the Orient. Still, next time you have business in the desert, remember me!"

"Stranger things have happened." I spoke with care. Helena was watching me thoughtfully. "The East is a lively arena at present. People are talking about the place all the time. Since Jerusalem was captured, the whole area is opening up for expansion."

"So that's it!" Helena muttered. "I knew you were up to something again."

Thalia looked surprised. "You're really going to Syria?"

"Somewhere close, possibly. Proposals have been whispered in my direction." For a moment it had seemed easier to break the news to Helena with a witness who was strong enough to prevent me from being beaten up. Like most of my good ideas, I was rapidly losing faith in this one.

Unaware of the undercurrents, Thalia asked, "Would I have to pay you if you did some scouting for me?"

"For a friend I can be commissioned to be paid on results."

"What about your fare?"

"Ah well! Someone else may be persuaded to come up with the fare—"

"I thought so!" Helena exclaimed, breaking in angrily. "This will be someone called Vespasian?"

"You know I was intending to tell you—"

"You promised, Marcus. You promised to refuse the work next time." She stood up and stalked out across the arena to pat the elephant. The set of her back implied it was safer not to follow her.

I watched her go, a tall, dark-haired girl with a straight carriage. Watching Helena was as pleasant as hearing Falernian glug into a winecup, especially when it was my own cup.

Mine she might be, but I still had serious second thoughts about upsetting her.

Thalia was eyeing me shrewdly. "You're in love!" People always said this with a mixture of wonder and disgust.

"You have a keen grasp of the situation!" I grinned.

"What's the problem between you?"

"There's no problem between us. Just other people who think there ought to be."

"What other people?"

"Most of Rome."

Thalia raised her eyes. "Sounds as if going somewhere else could make life easier!"

"Who wants an easy life?" She knew I was lying about that.

To my relief, once her temper cooled down Helena strolled back, leading the elephant, who was now devoted to her. I assumed he realized he would have to shift me before it could do him any good. He nuzzled her ear in a way I liked to do myself, while she bent her head away resignedly, just as if avoiding annoying attentions from me.

"Helena doesn't want you to leave her," observed Thalia.

"Who said anything about leaving her? Helena Justina is my partner. We share danger and disaster, joy and triumph—"

"Oh very nice!" Thalia commenced, with a skeptical rasp.

Helena had listened to my speech in a way that at least allowed me to make another: "At the moment I wouldn't mind putting myself a long way from Rome," I said. "Especially if the Treasury pays for it. The only issue is whether *Helena* wants to go."

She accepted my gaze quietly. She too was searching for ways we could live together without interference or pressure from others. Travel was one method we had found that sometimes worked. "So long as I do have a say in the decision, I'll go where you go, Marcus Didius."

"That's right, dearie," Thalia agreed with her. "Always best to trot along and keep an eye on them!"

Act One
Nabataea

About a month later. The scene is set initially in Petra, a remote city in the desert. Dramatic mountains dominate on either side. Then on rapidly to Bostra.

SYNOPSIS: *Falco*, an adventurer, and *Helena*, a rash young woman, arrive in a strange city disguised as curious travelers. They are unaware that *Anacrites*, a jealous enemy, has transmitted news of their visit to the one man they need to avoid. When an unpleasant accident befalls *Heliodorus*, a theatrical hack, their help is enlisted by *Chremes*, an actor-producer, but by then everyone is looking nervously for a quick camel ride out of town.

Five

We had been following the two men all the way to the High Place. From time to time we heard their voices ringing off the rocks up ahead of us. They were talking in occasional short sentences, like acquaintances who kept the politeness going. Not lost in a deep conversation, not angry, but not strangers either. Strangers would have either walked along in silence or made more of a sustained effort.

I did wonder if they might be priests, going up for a ritual.

"If they are, we should turn back," Helena suggested. The remark was her only contribution so far that morning. Her tone was cool, sensible, and subtly implying that *I* was a dangerous idiot for bringing us here.

A staid response seemed called for; I put on a frivolous manner: "I never intrude on religion, particularly when the Lord of

the Mountain might demand the ultimate sacrifice." We knew
little of the Petrans' religion, beyond the facts that their chief god
was symbolized by blocks of rock and that this strong, mysterious deity was said to require bloodthirsty appeasement, carried
out on the mountaintops he ruled. "My mother wouldn't like her
boy to be consecrated to Dushara."

Helena said nothing.

Helena said nothing, in fact, during most of our climb. We
were having a furious argument, the kind that's intensely silent.
For this reason, although *we* heard that the two men were toiling
up ahead of us, *they* almost certainly failed to notice that we
were following. We made no attempt to let them know. It
seemed unimportant at the time.

I decided that their intermittent voices were too casual to
cause alarm. Even if they were priests they were probably going
routinely to sweep away yesterday's offerings (in whatever unlikable form those offerings took). They might be locals making the
trip for a picnic. Most likely they were fellow visitors, just pant-
ing up to the sky-high altar out of curiosity.

So we clambered on, more concerned about the steepness of
the path and our own quarrel than anybody else.

There were various ways to reach the High Place. "Some joker
down by the temple tried to tell me this route is how they bring
the virgins up for sacrifice."

"*You've* nothing to worry about then!" Helena deigned to utter.

We had taken what appeared to be a gentle flight of steps a little to the left of the theater. It rapidly steepened, cutting up beside a narrow gorge. We had the rock face on both sides at first,
quarried intriguingly and threatening to overhang our way; soon
we acquired a narrow but increasingly spectacular defile to our
right. Greenery clung to its sides—spear-leafed oleanders and
tamarisk among the red, gray, and amber striations of the rocks.
These were most eye-catching on the cliff face alongside us,

where the Nabataeans had carved out their passage to the mountaintop taking their normal delight in revealing the silken patterns of the sandstone.

This was no place for hurrying. The twisting path angled through a rocky corridor and crossed the gorge, widening briefly into a more open space where I snatched my first breather, planning several more before we reached the uppermost heights.Helena paused too, pretending she had only stopped because I was in her way.

"Do you want to get past me?"

"I can wait." She was gasping. I grinned at her. Then we both turned to face out across Petra, already a fine view, with the widest part of the gravelly road in the valley below snaking away past the theater and a bunch of tasteful rock-face tombs, then on towards the distant town.

"Are you going to fight with me all day?"

"Probably," growled Helena.

We both fell silent. Helena surveyed the dusty thongs of her sandals. She was thinking about whatever dark issues had come between us. I kept quiet too, because as usual I was not entirely certain what the quarrel was about.

Getting to Petra had been less difficult than I had feared. Anacrites had taken great pleasure in implying that my journey here posed intolerable problems. I simply brought us by sea to Gaza. I had "hired"—at a price that meant "bought outright"— an ox and cart, transport I was used to handling, then looked around for the trade route. Strangers were discouraged from traveling it, but caravans up to a thousand strong converged on Nabataea each year. They arrived in Petra from several directions, their ways parting again when they left. Some toiled westwards to northern Egypt. Some took the interior road up to Bostra, before going on to Damascus or Palmyra. Many crossed straight to the Judaean coast for urgent shipment from the great port at Gaza to the hungry markets in Rome. So with dozens of merchants trekking towards Gaza, all leading immense, slowly moving strings of camels or oxen, it was no trouble for me as an ex-army scout to trace back their route. No entrepôt can be kept secret. Nor can its guardians prevent penetration of their city by strangers. Petra was essentially a public place.

Even before we arrived I was making mental notes for Vespasian. The rocky approach had been striking, yet there was plenty of greenery. Nabataea was rich in freshwater springs. Reports of flocks and agriculture were correct. They lacked horses, but camels and oxen were everywhere. All along the rift valley was a flourishing mining industry, and we soon discovered that the locals produced pottery of great delicacy, floral platters and bowls in huge quantities, all decorated with panache. In short, even without the income from the merchants, there would be plenty here to attract the benevolent interest of Rome.

"Well!" Helena let slip. "I reckon you can report back to your masters that the rich kingdom of Nabataea certainly deserves inclusion in the Empire." She was insultingly equating me with some mad-eyed, province-collecting patriot.

"Don't annoy me, lady—"

"We have so much to offer them!" she quipped; beneath the political irony was a personal sneer at me.

Whether the rich Nabataeans would see things our way might be a different cask of nuts. Helena knew that. They had guarded their independence with skill for several centuries, making it their role to keep the routes across the desert safely open and offer a market to traders of all kinds. They were practiced in negotiating peace with would-be invaders, from the successors of Alexander to Pompey and Augustus. They had an amiable monarchy. Their present king, Rabel, was a youth whose mother was acting as regent, an arrangement that seemed to be non-controversial. Much of the routine workload of government fell to the Chief Minister. This more sinister character was referred to as The Brother. I guessed what that meant. Still, so long as the people of Petra were flourishing so vibrantly, I daresay they could put up with somebody to hate and fear. Everyone likes to have a figure of authority to mutter about. You can't blame the weather for all of life's ills.

The weather, incidentally, was fabulous. Sunlight streamed off the rocks, melting everything into a dazzling haze.

We continued our climb.

The second time we stopped, more desperately out of breath, I unhooked a water flask I was carrying on my belt. We sat side by side on a large rock, too hot to fight.

"What's the matter?" Something Helena had said earlier had struck a nerve. "Finding out that I'm acting for the Chief Spy?"

"Anacrites!" she snorted with contempt.

"So? He's a slug, but no worse than the other slime lovers in Rome."

"I thought at least you were working for Vespasian. You let me come all this way thinking that—"

"An oversight." By this time I had convinced myself that was true. "It just never came up in conversation. Anyway, what's the difference?"

"The difference is, Anacrites when he's acting independently is a threat to you. I don't trust the man."

"Neither do I, so you can stop erupting." Hauling her up here had been an inspired move; I could see she had lost her energy for bickering. I gave her more water. Then I kept her sitting on the rock. The soft sandstone made a tolerable backrest if your back was muscular; I leaned on the rock and made Helena lean against me. "Look at the view and be friends with the man who loves you."

"Oh him!" she scoffed.

There was one good thing about this argument: yesterday, when we left the outer caravanserai and entered Petra itself down the famous narrow gorge, we had been squabbling so bitterly none of the guards gave us a second glance. A man listening to his woman complaining about him can ride pretty well anywhere; armed retainers always treat him with sympathy. As they had waved us along the raised causeway and into the rocky cleft, then hurried us on under the monumental arch that marked the way, little did they know that at the same time as she harangued me Helena was reconnoitering their fortifications with eyes as sharp and a mind as acute as Caesar's.

We had already passed enough rock-hewn tombs, free-standing blocks with strange, stepped roofs, inscriptions, and carved reliefs to strike a sense of awe. Then had come the forbidding gorge, along which I noticed sophisticated systems of water pipes.

"Pray it doesn't rain!" I muttered, as we lost sight of the entrance behind us. "A torrent rushes down here, and people get swept away . . ."

Eventually the path had narrowed to a single gloomy track where the rocks seemed ready to meet above our heads; after that the gorge suddenly widened again and we glimpsed the sunlit facade of the Great Temple. Instead of exclaiming with delight Helena muttered, "Our journey's superfluous. They could hold this entrance against an army, using just five men!"

Emerging through the crack in the rocks, we had drawn up abruptly in front of the temple, as we were intended to. Once I got my breath back from gasping with awe, I commented, "I thought you were going to say, 'Well, Marcus, you may never have shown me the Seven Wonders of the World, but at least you've brought me to the Eighth!' "

We stood in silence for a moment.

"I like the goddess in the round pavilion between the broken pediments," said Helena.

"Those are what I call really smart entablatures," I answered, playing the architectural snob. "What do you think is in the big orb on top of the goddess's pavilion?"

"Bath oils."

"Of course!"

After a moment, Helena carried on where she had left off just before we reached this fabulous spectacle: "So Petra lies in a mountain enclave. But there are other entrances? I had the impression this was the only one." Dear gods, she was single-minded. Anacrites should be paying her instead of me.

Some Romans get away with treating their womenfolk like mindless ornaments, but I knew I stood no chance of that so I answered calmly, "That's the impression the cautious Nabataeans like to give. Now gape at the opulent rock carving, sweetheart, and try to look as if you just popped this side of the mountain to buy a pair of Indian earrings and a length of turquoise silk."

"Don't mix me up with your previous trashy girlfriends!" she rounded on me crossly, as a Nabataean irregular who was obviously checking for suspicious faces wandered past. Helena took my point. "I may buy a bale in its natural state, but I'll have it bleached a good plain white at home . . ."

We had passed muster. Easily fooled, these guards! Either that, or they were sentimentalists who could not bear to arrest a henpecked man.

There had not been, yesterday, much time for me to sort out what lay behind Helena's wrath. Nervous about how long we could keep up our act as innocent travelers, I had taken us very hastily into town along the dry dirt track that curved away past numerous cliffside tombs and temples. We noticed that although this was a desert, there were gardens everywhere. The Nabataeans possessed spring water, and made the most of conserving rainfall. For people still close to their nomadic roots, they were surprisingly fine engineers. All the same it *was* a desert; when it did rain on our journey, a shower had covered our clothing with fine reddish dust, and when we combed our hair, black grit had worked in right to the scalp.

At the end of the track lay a settlement, with many fine houses and public buildings as well as a tightly packed lower-class habitation full of small square dwellings, each set behind its own walled courtyard. I had found us a room, at a price that showed the Petrans knew exactly what a room was worth in the middle of the desert. Then I spent the evening scouting the walls to the north and south of the city. They were nothing spectacular, for the Nabataeans had long preferred to make treaties rather than physically resist hostility—a trick made easier by their custom of offering to guide invading troops through the desert, then taking the longest, most difficult route so that the troops arrived at Petra too exhausted to start fighting. (Most armies lack Helena's stamina.)

She was looking at me now in a way that made her considerably more attractive than most armies. She was completely wrapped in stoles against the heat, so she looked cool, though I could feel her warmth as I held her against me. She smelled of sweet almond oil.

"This is a wonderful place," she conceded. Her voice had dropped a murmur. Those rich dark eyes of hers still flashed, but I had fallen in love with Helena when she was angry; she was well aware of the effect it still had on me. "I certainly see the world with you."

"That's generous." I fought back, though with a familiar sense of imminent surrender. At even closer quarters our eyes met. Hers were not scathing at all when you knew her, but redolent of good humor and intelligence. "Helena, are you following the local rule of suing for peace?"

"Better to safeguard what you have," she agreed. "It's a good Petran system."

"Thanks." I favor the laconic in negotiation. I hoped Helena had not heard of the Nabataeans' other political custom: sending away their won-over opponents with large quantities of treasure. The Falco purse, as usual, was not up to it.

"Yes, you can skip the exorbitant gifts." She smiled, though I had said nothing.

Asserting my rights, I slid my other arm around her. It was accepted as a term in the treaty. I started to feel happy again.

The sun beat down on the glowing rocks, where huge clumps of dark tulips with dusty leaves clung tenaciously. The voices ahead of us had passed out of earshot. We were alone in the warm silence, in what seemed a not unfriendly place.

Helena and I had a history of friendly relations near the tops of famous mountains. Taking a girl to see a spectacular view has only one purpose, to my mind, and if a man can achieve the same purpose halfway up the hill, he saves some energy for better things. I gathered Helena closer and settled down to enjoy as much playful recreation as she was likely to allow us alongside a public footpath that might be frequented by stern-visaged priests.

Six

"Anyway, was it really an oversight?" Helena asked sometime later—a girl not easily deflected. If she was thinking that letting me kiss her had softened me up, she was right.

"Forgetting to mention Anacrites? Certainly. I don't lie to you."

"Men always say that."

"Sounds as if you've been talking to Thalia. I can't be held responsible for all the other lying bastards."

"And usually you say it in the middle of an argument."

"So you reckon it's just the line I use? Wrong, lady! But even if that were true, we do need to preserve a few escape routes! I want us to survive together," I told her piously. (Frank talk always disarmed Helena, since she expected me to be devious.) "Don't you?"

"Yes," she said. Helena never messed me around playing coy. I could tell her that I loved her without feeling embarrassed, and I knew I could rely on her to be equally frank: she thought I was unreliable. Despite that she added, "A girl doesn't come this far across the world with a mere Thursday-afternoon dalliance!"

I kissed her again. "Thursday afternoons? Is that when senators' wives and daughters have free run of the gladiators' barracks?" Helena wriggled furiously, which might have led to more playfulness had our baking rock seat not lain right alongside a well-beaten track. A stone fell somewhere. We both remembered the voices we had heard, and were afraid their owners might be coming back. I did wonder if I could take us off up the hillside, but its steepness and stoniness looked unpromising.

I loved traveling with Helena—except for the frustrating series of small cabins and cramped hired rooms where we never felt free to make love. Suddenly I was longing for our sixth-floor tenement apartment, where few interlopers struggled up the stairs and only rooftop pigeons could overhear.

"Let's go home!"

"What—to our rented room?"

"To Rome."

"Don't be silly," scoffed Helena. "We're going up to see the mountaintop."

My only interest in the mountaintop had been the possibilities it offered for grappling Helena. Nevertheless I put on my serious traveler's face and we continued uphill.

The summit was announced by a pair of unequal obelisks. Perhaps they represented gods. If so, they were crude, mysterious, and definitely alien to the human-featured Roman pantheon. They appeared to have been created not by transporting stones here, but by carving away the entire surrounding rock bed to a depth of six or seven meters to leave these dramatic sentinels. The effort involved was staggering, and the final effect eerie. They were unidentical twins, one slightly taller, one flared at the base. Beyond lay some sort of strongly built building that we preferred not to investigate in case it was occupied by priests honing sacrificial knives.

We climbed on, reaching the ceremonial area by a steep flight of steps. This brought us out onto a windswept promontory. On all sides the high, airy rock offered staggering views of the circlet of harsh mountains within which Petra lies. We had emerged on the north side of a slightly sunken rectangular court. Around it had been cut three benches, presumably for spectators, like the triple couches in a formal dining room. Ahead of us lay a raised platform on which were displayed offerings that we tactfully ignored. To the right, steps led to the main altar. There a tall column of black stone represented the god. Beyond him lay another, larger, round altar like a basin cut from the living rock, connected by a channel to a rectangular water tank.

By now my imagination was working at a hairy pace. I hoped I was impervious to awe-striking locations and sinister religions, but I had been to Britain, Gaul, and Germany; I knew more than I wanted about unpleasant pagan rites. I grasped Helena's hand as the wind buffeted us. She walked fearlessly out onto the sunken court, gazing at the spectacular views as if we were on some balustraded vista provided for the convenience of summer tourists above the Bay of Surrentum.

I was wishing we were. This place gave me a bad feeling. It aroused no sense of reverence. I hate ancient sites where creatures have long been slain for the grim delight of monolithic gods. I especially hate them when the local populace like to pretend, as the Nabataeans did with great relish, that some of the creatures they sacrificed could have been human. Even at that point I felt alert, as if we were walking into trouble.

There was trouble at Dushara's shrine all right, though it did not yet directly involve us. We still had time to avoid it—though not for much longer.

"Well, this is it, my darling. Let's go back now."

But Helena had spied some new feature. She pushed her hair back out of her eyes and dragged me over to look. To the south of the ceremonial area lay another rectangular reservoir. This one apparently drained the summit to provide an ample supply of fresh water for the rites of sacrifice. Unlike the rest of the High Place, this cistern was occupied.

The man in the water could have been taking a swim in the sunlight. But as soon as I spotted him I knew that he was not floating there for pleasure or exercise.

Seven

If I had had any sense I would still have convinced myself he was just bathing peacefully. We could have turned away without staring too closely, then a rapid stroll downhill would have taken us back to our lodging. We should have done that anyway; I should have kept us out of it.

He was almost submerged. His head was under water. Only something bulky, caught under his clothing, was holding him afloat.

We were both already running forwards. "Unbelievable!" Helena marveled bitterly as she scrambled down from the sacrificial platform. "Just two days here, and look what you've found."

I had reached the rock-formed tank ahead of her. I lowered myself over the edge into the water, trying to forget I couldn't swim. The water came above my waist. The chill made me gasp. It was a large cistern, about four feet deep: ample to drown in.

The swirl of water as I entered caused the body to move and start sinking. I managed to grab at the garments that had helped buoy him up. Arriving a few moments later, we could have avoided this trouble. He would have been lying out of sight on the bottom as the drowned do—assuming, of course, that drowning was the real cause of his death.

Slowly I pulled my burden to the side. An inflated goatskin floated out from under his tangled cloak as I maneuvered him. Helena leaned down and held his feet, then helped me haul him half out of the water. She had the nice manners of any senator's daughter, but no qualms about helping out in an emergency.

I climbed out again. We completed the operation. He was heavy, but together we managed to remove him from the cistern and flop him face down. Without more ado I turned his head sideways. I leaned on his ribs for a respectable period, trying to revive him. I noticed my first shove seemed to expel air rather than water. And there was none of the froth I had seen with other corpses who had drowned. We get plenty in the Tiber.

Helena waited, at first standing above me with the wind blowing her clothes against her body while she gazed thoughtfully around the high plateau. Then she walked to the far side of the cistern, examining the ground.

As I worked I was thinking things through. Helena and I had been climbing quite slowly, and our pause for recreation had taken up time. But for that, we would have arrived at the crucial moment. But for that, we would be sharing the fabulous windswept views with two men, both alive.

We had come too late for this one. I knew even before I started my efforts would be useless. Still, I gave him the courtesy. I might need to be resuscitated by a stranger myself one day.

Eventually I rolled him over on his back and stood up again.

He was fortyish. Too fat and flabby. A wide, berry-brown face with a heavy chin and thuggish neck. The face looked mottled under its tan. Short arms; broad hands. He had not troubled himself with shaving today. Lank, rather long hair merged with coarse black eyebrows and dripped sluggishly on to the rock floor beneath him. He was dressed in a long, loose-weave brown tunic, with a more sun-bleached cloak tangled wetly around him. Shoes knotted on top of the foot, a toe-thong apiece. No weapon. Something bulky under his clothes at the waist, however—a writing tablet, not written on.

Helena held out something else she had found beside the cistern—a round-bottomed flask on a plaited leather cord. Its wicker casing, stained brown with wine, made me pull out the stopper: wine had been in it recently, though only a couple of drops shook out onto my palm. Maybe the goatskin had contained wine too. Being tipsy could explain how he came to be overpowered.

His attire was Eastern, protecting him from the burning heat. Those swaths of cloth would have impeded his movements if he had been struggling to escape an attacker. I had no doubt he had been attacked. His face was grazed and cut, probably where he had been pushed bodily over the edge of the water tank. Then someone must have jumped in alongside, probably not to hold his head under; marks on his neck looked more like strangulation to me. Helena showed me that in addition to the ground that had been soaked when I clambered out, beside the tank on the far side was a similar wet area where the killer must have emerged sopping wet. The sun had made his tracks faint already, but Helena had found them leading back towards the ceremonial platform.

We left the body and recrossed the summit in front of the altar. The trail petered out, already evaporated by sun and wind. To the north we found a moon god's shrine with two crescent-crowned pillars flanking a niche; beyond that lay a wide staircase leading downwards. But now we could hear voices approaching—a large number of people, intoning a low ceremonial chant. This was plainly a major ceremonial route to the High Place. I doubted whether the killer could have rushed down that way, or the procession now winding up the stairs would have been disturbed.

Helena and I turned away and climbed back by the same steps that had brought us up. We scrambled down as far as the priests' house or guardpost. We could have knocked and asked for help. Why take the easy way? Still loath to encounter anybody with a sharp implement who might view me as an easy catch for the altar, I convinced myself the murderer would have crept past anonymously too.

Now I noticed a second path. This must be the one he had taken; he had certainly not passed us while we were canoodling. Helena was a senator's daughter after all; she was supposed to know the meaning of modesty. We had been alert for voyeurs.

I never know when to leave well alone. "Go down," I commanded Helena. "Either wait for me near the theater, or I'll see you back at the lodging. Go down the same way we came up."

She made no protest. The sight of the dead man's face must have stayed in her mind. Anyway, her attitude mirrored my own. I would have done this in Rome; being a visiting flea on the rump of civilization changed nothing. Somebody had just killed this man, and I was going after whoever did it. Helena knew I had no choice. Helena would have come with me if she could cover ground as fast.

I touched her gently on the cheek and felt her fingers brush my wrist. Then without a second thought I started down the path.

Eight

This path was much less steep than the one we had come up by. It seemed to be heading into the city, a much longer way down. Sudden wicked turns forced me to watch my footing above astounding aerial vistas that would have made me quake if there had been time to look at them properly.

I was trying to be quiet as I hurried. Though I had no reason to think the fleeing man knew pursuit was hot on his tail, murderers rarely hang about studying the view.

I was passing through another valley gorge cut by watercourses like the one that had brought Helena and me to the summit. Flights of steps, inscriptions in the cliff face, sharp corners, and short stretches of narrow corridor led me downhill as far as a rock-carved lion. Five strides in length and pleasingly weathered, he served as a fountain; a straight channel brought fresh water down through a pipe and out of his mouth. Now I was certain the killer had come this way, for the sandstone ledge beneath the lion's head was damp, as if a man with wet clothing had sat there snatching a drink. I splashed water hastily over my own forehead, thanked the lion for his information, and rushed on again.

The water that had flowed through the lion now trickled downhill in a waist-high runnel cut into the cliff face, keeping me company. I stumbled down a steeply winding flight of steps then found myself in a secluded stretch of the wadi. Overhung by oleanders and tulips, its peaceful stillness nearly made me abandon my quest. But I hate murder. I strode on. The path came to a pleasant temple: two free-standing columns in a pilastered frame, with a shrine behind, darkly dug out of the mountain like a cavern. The portico was approached by wide steps, a parched garden in their base. There I saw an elderly Nabataean priest and a younger man, also a priest. I had the impression they had just come out from the temple sanctum. Both were gazing downhill.

My arrival made both of them gape at me instead. In Latin first, automatically, then in careful Greek I asked the elder man if anyone had just passed that way in a hurry. He merely stared at me. There was no way I could attempt the local Arabic tongue. Then the younger man suddenly spoke to him as if translating. I explained briskly that somebody had died at the High Place, apparently not by accident. This too was relayed, without much result. Impatient, I started walking on again. The elder priest spoke. The younger one came straight out from the garden, and loped downhill alongside me. He said nothing, but I accepted his company. Glancing back I saw that the other had turned to go to the place of sacrifice and investigate.

My new ally had a dark desert-dweller's skin and intense eyes. He was wearing a long white tunic that flapped around his

ankles, but he managed to shift along pretty fast. Although he
never spoke I felt we had shared motives. So, feeling slightly better than strangers, we hurried downhill together and eventually
reached the city wall, far over in western precincts, where the
main habitation lay.

We had passed no one. Once we entered by the city gate there
were people everywhere, and no way of discerning the man we
sought. His clothes must be dry by now, as mine almost were.
There seemed nothing else I could do. But the young man with
me still strode ahead, so I found myself drawn along with him.

We had emerged close to the public monuments. Passing
through an area of impressive homes built from well-dressed
sandstone blocks, we reached the craftsmen's quarter on the
main thoroughfare. The graveled street cried out for decent
paving and colonnades, but possessed its own exotic grandeur.
Here, the great covered markets lay to our left, with an area of
casual stalls and tethering posts between them. The main watercourse ran alongside this street, about ten feet below. Poky stair-
ways ran down to that lower level, while handsome bridges
spanned the gulley to reach important buildings on the far
side—the royal palace, and one of the monumental temples that
dominated this part of the city. These lay on wide terraces and
were approached by spectacular flights of steps.

We were heading purposefully past them to the large terminal
gate. This, I knew, was the heart of the city. Impressive temples
stood back from the street on either side, though the greatest
temple lay ahead of us within the sanctuary area. We reached
and crossed a small piazza, then went through the tall gateway,
which had massive doors folded back. Immediately inside were
administrative buildings. My young priest stopped there and
spoke to someone in a doorway but then pressed on, waving me
to accompany him. We had entered a long open space, enclosed
by a high wall on the watercourse side—a typically Eastern temple sanctuary. Stone benches ran around the perimeter. At the far

end on a raised platform was an open-air altar. This lay in front of Petra's main temple, dedicated to Dushara, the mountain god.

It was a colossal structure. We clambered up to an immense, marble-clad platform approached by wide marble steps. Four plain but massive pillars formed a portico, deep in welcome shade, below a rather static frieze of rosettes and triglyphs. The Greeks had been to Petra, possibly by invitation. They had left their mark in the carved work, yet it was a fleeting influence, quite unlike the domination they exerted on Roman art.

Within, we came to a vast entrance chamber where high windows lit elaborately molded plasterwork and wall frescoes of architectural patterns. A character who was evidently a very senior priest had noticed us. My companion marched forward in his dogged way. I would have had about two seconds to turn around and make a run for it. I had done nothing wrong, so I stood my ground. Sweat trickled down my back. Hot and exhausted, it was difficult to assume my normal air of confidence. I felt far from home, in a land where mere innocence might be no defense.

Our news was relayed. There came a sudden upsurge of chatter, as there normally is when an unnatural death has been announced unexpectedly in a public place. The sacrilege had caused a shock. The senior functionary jumped, as if it were the most alarming event of the last six months. He gabbled away in the local dialect, then appeared to reach a decision; he exclaimed some formal pronouncement, and made a couple of urgent gestures.

My young companion turned and finally spoke: "You must tell this!"

"Certainly," I answered, in my role as an honest traveler. "Whom shall I tell?"

"He will come." To sensitive ears it had an ominous ring.

I recognized my predicament. A person of extreme consequence was about to interest himself in my story. I had been hoping to remain unobtrusive in Petra. As a Roman who was not a valid trader my presence here would be awkward to explain. Something told me that drawing attention to myself might be a very bad idea. Still, it was too late now.

We had to wait.

In the desert, extremes of climate and distance encourage a leisurely attitude. Quick settlement of crises would be bad manners. People like to savor news.

I was led back outside: Dushara's temple was no place for a curious foreigner. I regretted this, for I would have liked to appreciate the fantastic interior with its striking ornamentation; to explore beyond the high arch leading to the dim inner sanctum, and climb up to the intriguing upper-story balconies. But after one swift glimpse of a tall dark god with clenched fists gazing out towards his mountains, I was hustled away.

From the first I realized that hanging about for the anonymous great one was going to be a trial. I wondered where Helena was. I gave up on the idea of sending her a message. Our address would be difficult to describe and I had nothing to write on. I wished I had brought the corpse's note tablet; he had no use for it now.

The young priest had been designated my official minder. That failed to make him communicative. He and I sat on one of the benches around the sanctuary, where he was approached by various acquaintances, but I was studiously ignored. I was growing restless. I had a strong sensation of sinking into a situation I would very much regret. I resigned myself to a lost day, with trouble at the end of it. Besides that, it was clear I would miss lunch—the kind of habit I deplore.

To overcome my depression, I insisted on making conversation with the priest. "Did you see the fugitive? What did he look like?" I asked firmly in Greek.

Addressed so directly it was hard for him to refuse me. "A man."

"Old? Young? My age?"

"I did not see."

"You couldn't see his face? Or only his back disappearing? Did he have all his hair? Could you see its coloring?"

"I did not see."

"You're not much help," I told him frankly.

Annoyed and frustrated, I fell silent. In the slow, aggravating way of the desert, just when I had given up on him, my companion explained: "I was within the temple. I heard footsteps, running. I went out and glimpsed a man far away, as he passed out of sight."

"So you didn't notice anything about him? Was he slight or tall? Light or heavy?"

The young priest considered. "I could not tell."

"This fellow will be easy to spot!"

After a second the priest smiled, unexpectedly seeing the joke. He still felt disinclined to communicate, but he was getting the hang of the game now. Softening up, he volunteered brightly: "I could not see his hair—he wore a hat."

A hat was unexpected. Most people around here wrapped their heads in their robes. "What sort of hat?" He gestured a widish brim, looking slightly disapproving. This was a definite rarity. Since Helena and I landed at Gaza we had seen lolling Phrygian caps, tight little skullcaps, and flat-topped felt circles, but a brimmed hat was a Western extravagance.

Confirming my own thoughts, he then said, "A foreigner, alone and in a great hurry near the High Place, is unusual."

"You could tell he was a foreigner? How?" The man shrugged.

I knew one reason: the hat. But people can always tell if they get a proper look at someone. Build, coloring, a way of walking, a style of beard or haircut all give a clue. Even a glimpse for a fraction of a second might do it. Or not a glimpse, but a sound: "He came down whistling," said the priest suddenly.

"Really? Know the tune?"

"No."

"Any other colorful details?" He shook his head, losing interest.

That seemed to be as far as I could take it. I had a tantalizing impression, from which nobody would be able to identify the fugitive.

We resumed our boring wait. I started to feel depressed again. The hot golden light, bouncing back from the stonework, was giving me a headache.

People came and went; some sat on the benches chewing or humming to themselves. Many ignored the seats but squatted in the shade, giving me a sharp feeling of being among nomads who despised furniture. I told myself not to feel complacent. These leathery men in dusty cloaks looked only one step up from beggars and one stride short of the grave; yet they belonged to the richest nation in the world. They handled frankincense and myrrh as casually as my own relatives inspected three radishes and a cabbage. Each wrinkled old prune probably had more gold in the saddlebags of his camel train than Rome possessed in the whole Temple of Saturn Treasury.

Thinking ahead, I tried to plan an escape. I realized I stood no chance of sliding out of trouble with the traditional diplomacy; the meager funds at my disposal would make an insulting bribe.

We were under obvious scrutiny, though it was polite. If you sat on the steps of the Forum Basilica for such a length of time you would fall prey to rude comments and be openly accosted by pickpockets, poets and prostitutes, sellers of lukewarm rissoles, and forty bores trying to tell you the story of their lives. Here they just waited to see what I would do; they liked their tedium bland.

The first hint of action: a small camel was led in through the arch of the great gate, carrying over its back the man I had found drowned. A quiet but curious crowd came following.

Simultaneously someone strode out from a great doorway cut through the enclosure wall. I never found out what lay behind it, whether the area beyond that impressive-looking portal housed the quarters of the priestly college, or was this high official's own stately residence. Somehow I knew he was important even before I looked at him directly. He carried the aura of power.

He was walking straight towards us. He was alone, but every man in the place was aware of him. Apart from a jeweled belt and a neat, high headdress with a Parthian look to it, little marked him out. My priestly companion hardly moved or changed expression, yet I sensed a frantic upsurge of tension in him.

"Who is it?" I managed to mutter.

For reasons I could guess, the young man could barely croak out his answer. "The Brother," he said. And now I could tell that he was terrified.

Nine

I stood up.

Like most Nabataeans the Petran Chief Minister was shorter than me, and slighter. He wore the usual full-length, long-sleeved tunic with other robes in fine material folded back over his upper arms. That was how I could see the glittering belt. There was a dagger thrust through it, with a ruby set in the hilt that barely left room for the handle's ornate metalwork. He had a high forehead, his hair well receded under the headdress, and his manner was energetic. The wide mouth gave an impression of smiling pleasantly, though I did not fall into the trap of believing it. He looked like a friendly banker—one with his heart set on diddling you on your interest rate.

"Welcome to Petra!" He had a deep, resonant voice. He had spoken in Greek.

"Thank you." I tried to make my accent as Athenian as possible—not easy when you've been taught your Greek under a ripped awning on a dusty street corner near the neighborhood middenheap.

"Shall we see what you have found for us?" It was like an invitation to open a basket of presents from an uncle in the country.

His eyes gave the game away. The lids were so deeply pouched and crinkled that no expression was visible in those dark, faraway glints. I hate men who hide what they think. This one had the difficult manner I normally associate with a vicious fornicating fraud who has kicked his mother to death.

We walked to the camel, which thrust its head towards us unnervingly. Someone grabbed the bridle, hissing at its disrespect for my companion. Two men lifted down the body, fairly gently. The Brother inspected the corpse just as I had done previously. It appeared an intelligent scrutiny. People stood back, watching him earnestly. Among the crowd I recognized the elder priest from the temple with the garden, though he made no move to contact his young colleague, who was now standing behind me. I tried to believe the youngster was there in case I needed support, but help seemed unlikely. I was on my own with this.

"What do we know of this person?" The Brother asked, addressing me. I gathered that I was expected to take responsibility for explaining the stranger.

I indicated the writing block at the dead man's waist. "A scholar or clerk maybe." Then I pointed to the grazes on the broad, slightly puffy face. "He had clearly suffered violence, though not an extreme beating. I found empty drinking vessels at the scene."

"This occurred at the High Place?" The Brother's tone was not particularly angry, but the careful posing of the question spoke volumes.

"Apparently. Seems to be some drunk who fell out with his friend."

"You saw them?"

"No. I had heard voices, though. They sounded amiable. I had no reason to rush up after them and investigate."

"What was your own purpose in visiting the Place of Sacrifice?"

"Reverent curiosity," I stated. It sounded unconvincing and crass, of course. "I had been told it is not forbidden?"

"It is not forbidden," agreed The Brother, as if he thought that in a just world it should have been. Legislation seemed likely to emanate from his office later that afternoon.

I took a stand. "I believe that is all the help I can give you." My remark was ignored. If a foreign visitor foolishly came across a drowned man in the Basin of Fundanus in Rome, he would be thanked for his sense of civic duty, given a public reward of modest proportions, and led quietly out of town—or so I told myself. Maybe I was wrong. Maybe he would be flung into the worst jail available, to teach him not to malign the Golden Citadel with sordid discoveries.

The Brother stood back from crouching over the corpse. "And what is your name?" he enquired, fixing me with those pleasant dark eyes. From deep in their wrinkled pouches of weariness those eyes had already noted the cut of my tunic and style of my sandals. I knew he knew that I was Roman.

"Didius Falco," I answered, with a more or less clear conscience. "A traveler from Italy—"

"*Ah yes!*" he said.

My heart sank. My name was already known here. Somebody had warned the King's Chief Minister to expect me. I could guess who it was. I had told everyone at home that I was going to Decapolis on a seek-and-retrieve for Thalia's water organist.

Apart from Helena Justina, only one person knew I was coming here: Anacrites.

And if Anacrites had written ahead to the Nabataeans, then as sure as honey makes your teeth rot, he wasn't asking The Brother to extend me any diplomatic courtesies.

Ten

I would have liked to punch The Brother in the solar plexus and make a run for it. If, as I guessed, he was hated and feared in Petra, then the crowd might let me through. If he was hated and feared even more than I suspected, however, it might be to their advantage to avert his wrath by stopping me.

We Romans are a civilized nation. I kept my fists at my sides and faced him out. "Sir, I am a man of humble origins. I am surprised you know of me." He made no attempt to explain. It was vital that I found out his source of information, and quickly. There was no point trying to bluff. "Can I guess that you heard about me from a functionary called Anacrites? And did he ask you to put me top of the list for sacrifice in Dushara's High Place?"

"Dushara requires immolation only from the pure!" commented The Brother. He had a gentle line in sarcasm—the most dangerous kind. I was in a tricky situation here, and he liked the fact that I was aware of it.

I noticed him make a surreptitious gesture to tell the surrounding crowd to stand off somewhat. A space promptly cleared. I was to be interrogated with a modicum of privacy.

Ignoring the disturbance, I answered him lightly: "No doubt Petra has other quick and easy systems of disposal?"

"Oh yes. You can be laid out on an offering block for the birds and the sun." He sounded as if he would enjoy giving the order. Just what I always wanted: to die by being frizzled like offal, then picked clean by a clan of vultures.

"I look forward to the privilege! And what have you been told about me?"

"Naturally that you are a spy." He appeared to be making a polite joke of it. Somehow I felt no urge to grin at the pleasantry. That was information on which he would certainly act.

"Ah, the usual diplomatic nicety! Do you believe it, though?"

"Should I?" he asked, still giving me the dubious courtesy of appearing open and frank. A clever man. Neither vain nor corrupt: nothing to bite back against.

"Oh I think so," I replied, employing similar tactics. "Rome has a new emperor, an efficient one for once. Vespasian is taking stock; that includes surveying all the territory which borders on his own. You must have been expecting visitors."

We both glanced down at the body. He deserved more personal consideration. Instead, some tawdry domestic quarrel had made him an opportunity for this unexpected high-flown discussion of world events. Whoever he was, he had wound himself into my mission. His fate was welded to mine.

"What is Vespasian's interest in Petra?" The Brother asked. His eyes were sly, deceptive slits in that passionless face. A man so astute must know exactly what Rome's interest would be in a rich nation that controlled important trade routes just outside our own boundaries.

I can argue politics as fiercely as the next man who is standing around the Forum with two hours to fill before dinner, but I did not relish putting the Empire's point of view in a foreign city. Not when nobody at the Palace had bothered to instruct me what the Empire's foreign policy was supposed to be. (Nor when the Emperor, being pedantic about such trifles, was likely to hear about my answer sooner or later.) I tried to escape. "I can't answer you, sir. I'm just a humble information-gatherer."

"Not so humble, I think!" It sounded elegant in Greek, but was not a compliment. He could sneer without the slightest change of expression.

The Brother folded his arms, still staring down at the dead man lying at our feet. Water from the sodden body and its clothing had seeped into the paving. Every fiber within the cadaver must be growing cold; soon flies would be coming to look for egg-laying sites. "What is your quality? Do you have many possessions?"

"My house is poor," I answered. Then I remembered Helena reading out to me a passage from a historian who said the Nabataeans particularly prized the acquisition of possessions. I managed to make my remark sound like polite modesty by adding, "Though it has seen feasting with the son of the Emperor." The Nabataeans were supposed to enjoy a good feast, and most cultures are impressed by men who dine freely with their own rulers.

My information left The Brother looking thoughtful. Well it might. My relationship with Titus Caesar had its puzzling aspects, plus one that was perfectly clear: we both hankered for the same girl. Unsure of the Nabataean attitude to women, I kept quiet on this subject.

I thought about it aplenty. Every time I went somewhere dangerous abroad, I wondered if Titus was hoping that I never came back. Maybe Anacrites was not merely plotting to get rid of me for his own reasons; perhaps he had sent me here on prompting from Titus. For all I knew, the Chief Spy's letter to The Brother had suggested that Titus Caesar, the heir to the Empire, would deem it a personal favor if I stayed in Petra for a very long time: forever, for instance.

"My visit has no sinister implications," I assured Petra's minister, trying not to look depressed. "Rome's knowledge of your famous city is somewhat thin and out of date. We rely on a few very old writings that are said to be based on eyewitness reports, chief among them an account by Strabo. This Strabo had his facts from Athenodorus, who was tutor to the Emperor Augustus. *His* value as an eyewitness may be tempered by the fact that he was blind. Our sharp new Emperor distrusts such stuff."

"So Vespasian's curiosity is scholarly?" queried The Brother.

"He is a cultured man." That was to say he was on record as once quoting a rude line from a play by Menander concerning a chap with an enormous phallus, which by the standards of previous emperors made Vespasian a highly educated wit.

But it was Vespasian the crusty old general who must preoccupy foreign politicians. "True," The Brother pointed out. "But he is also a strategist."

I decided to stop feinting. "And a pragmatic one. He has plenty to occupy his energies within his own borders. If he believes the Nabataeans are interested only in pursuing their own affairs peacefully, you can rely on it that he will elect, like his predecessors, to make gestures of friendship to Petra."

"And were you sent to say that?" queried The Brother, rather haughtily. For once I saw him tighten his mouth. So the Petrans *were* afraid of Rome—which meant there were terms we might negotiate.

I lowered my voice. "If and when Rome chooses to assimilate Nabataea within its Empire, then Nabataea will come to us. This is a fact. It is no treachery towards you, and perhaps not even an unkindness, to state it." I was taking a lot upon myself here, even by my risky standards. "I am a simple man, but it seems to me that time is not yet here. Even so, Nabataea might do well to plan ahead. You lie in an enclave between Judaea and Egypt, so the questions are not *will* you join the Empire, but when and on what terms. At present these are within your own control. A partnership could be achieved both peacefully and at a time that suited you."

"This is what your Emperor says to me?" queried The Brother. Since I had been told by Anacrites to avoid official contact, I had of course been given no instructions about speaking for Vespasian.

"You will realize," I confessed frankly, "I am a fairly low-grade messenger." The hooded eyes darkened angrily. One lean hand played with the jeweled dagger at his belt. "Don't be insulted," I urged him quietly. "The advantage to you is that a higher-powered embassy would necessitate action. Important men sent on delicate missions expect results; they have careers to found. The day you find a Roman senator measuring your civic monuments, you'll know he's trying to find a space for a statue of himself in a laurel wreath, looking like a conqueror. But any report *I* make can be filed away in a casket if Vespasian wants to preserve the status quo."

"Assuming you make a report!" The Brother rejoined, going back to the fun of threatening me.

I was blunt. "Best that I do. Pegging me out on top of one of your crow-step altars could rebound on you. The peremptory death of a Roman citizen—which I am, despite shabby appearance—might be a neat excuse for sending in a Roman army and annexing Nabataea immediately."

The Brother smiled faintly at this idea. The death of an informer, traveling without official documents, was unlikely to justify world-scale political initiatives. Besides, Anacrites had told him I was coming. Apart from his personal hatred of me, in diplomatic terms that was probably meant as a warning to the Nabataeans: *Here's one observer you know about; there may be others you fail to detect. Rome feels so confident, she's even spying on you openly.*

My own fate was not a diplomatic issue. Anyone who took a dislike to my face could safely cast my corpse on their local rubbish tip. Accepting it, I smiled back peacefully.

At our feet the man who really was dead still waited for attention.

"Falco, what does this unknown body have to do with you?"

"Nothing. I found him. It was coincidence."

"He brought you to me."

Coincidence has a habit of landing me in tight situations. "Neither the victim nor his killer knew me. I have merely reported the incident."

"Why did you do that?" enquired The Brother sedately.

"I believe his killer should be traced and brought to justice."

"There are laws in the desert!" he rebuked me, his deep voice soft.

"I was not suggesting otherwise. For that reason I alerted you."

"You may have wished to remain silent!" He was still niggling about my role in Petra.

Reluctantly I conceded: "It might have been more convenient! I'm sorry if you have been informed I'm a spy. To get this in perspective, let me tell you that your helpful informant is also the man who paid me to come here."

The Brother smiled. More than ever he looked like somebody you wouldn't trust to hold your purse while you were undressing at the baths. "Didius Falco, you have dangerous friends."

"He and I were never friends."

We had stood talking in the open outdoor area for much longer than could be customary. At first it must have appeared to the onlookers that we were speculating about the dead man. Now people in the crowd were growing restless as they sensed more going on.

This corpse had become a useful cover for The Brother. It could well be that at some future date the sensible Nabataeans would hand themselves over to Rome on negotiated terms—but there would be ample preparation. No disturbing rumor would be permitted to ruffle commerce prematurely. At this stage The Brother needed to hide from his people the fact that he had been talking with an official from Rome.

Suddenly my interview reached its end. The Brother told me that he would see me again tomorrow. He stared at the young priest for a moment, said something in Arabic, then instructed him in Greek to conduct me to my lodging. I understood that all too well: I had been released on parole. I was being watched. I would not be permitted to inspect places they wished to keep secret. I would not be allowed free talk with the populace. Meanwhile, a decision on whether or not to let me leave Petra would be taken without my knowledge and without leave to appeal.

From now on, the Chief Minister would always know where I was. All my movements, and even my continued existence, were at his whim. In fact, it struck me he was the sort of unreliable potentate who could well send me off now with a smile and a promise of mint tea and sesame cakes tomorrow—then dispatch his executioner after me in half an hour's time.

I was escorted from the sanctuary. I had no idea what was intended for the corpse. I never did find out what happened to it.

But that would not be my last connection with the man I had found on the High Place of Sacrifice.

Eleven

Helena was waiting in our room. Expecting trouble, she had dressed her hair neatly in a decorated net, though she covered it demurely with a white stole when we entered. Discreet strands of beads were evenly hung on her fine bosom; hints of gold glinted at the tips of her ears. She was sitting very upright. Her hands were folded; her ankles crossed. She looked severe and expectant. There was a stillness about her that spoke of quality.

"This is Helena Justina," I informed the young priest, as if he ought to treat her respectfully. "I am Didius Falco, as you know. And you are?"

This time he could not ignore it. "My name is Musa."

"We have been adopted as personal guests of The Brother," I stated, for Helena's benefit. Maybe I could impose duties of hospitality on the priest. (Maybe not.) "Musa, at The Brother's request, is to look after us while we are in Petra."

I could see that Helena understood.

Now we all knew everyone. All we had to do was communicate.

"How are we off for languages?" I asked, making it a matter of politeness. I was wondering how to shake Musa loose and drag Helena safely out of here. "Helena is fluent in Greek; she used to kidnap her brothers' tutor. Musa speaks Greek, Arabic and I presume Aramaic. My Latin's low class but I can insult an Athenian, read the price list in a Gallic inn or ask what's for breakfast of a Celt. . . . Let's stick to Greek," I offered gallantly, then switched to Latin, using an impenetrable street dialect. "What's the news, beautiful?" I asked Helena, as if I were accosting her in an Aventine fish market. Even if Musa understood more Latin than he was letting on, this ought to fool him. The only problem was, a respectable young noblewoman born in a Capena Gate mansion might not understand me either.

I helped Helena unpack some olives we had bought earlier that day; it seemed like weeks ago.

Helena busied herself dividing salad into bowls. She replied to me offhandedly as if discussing dressed beans and chickpeas: "When I came down from the High Place, I reported what had happened to a man who looked in authority who was standing outside the theater—" She peered at some strangely white cheeses.

"Ewe's milk," I said cheerfully, in Greek. "Or camel's!" I was not sure that was possible.

"People nearby must have been listening in," Helena continued. "I overheard speculation from a company of actors that the drowned man might belong to them, but I was so exhausted I just said they could contact you if they wanted more information. They seemed an odd lot; I don't know if we'll hear from them. The official collected his favorite cronies and went up to see about the body."

"I saw it later," I confirmed.

"Well, I left them to it and slipped away."

We sat on rugs and cushions. Our Nabataean guardian seemed shy of small talk. Helena and I had a lot to think about; the apparent murder at the High Place had upset both of us, and we knew we were in a sticky predicament as a result. I stared into my supper bowl.

"Didius Falco, you have three radishes, seven olives, two lettuce leaves and a piece of cheese!" listed Helena, as if I was checking the equality of our rations. "I divided it fairly, so there would be no quarreling . . ."

She had spoken Greek herself this time as a courtesy to our silent guest. I switched back to Latin, like the man of the house being stubborn. "Well, that's probably the last we'll hear of the drowned man, but you will gather you and I are now the subject of a tense political incident."

"Can we shed this overseer?" she queried in our own tongue, smiling graciously at Musa and serving him the burned segment of our flat Petran loaf.

"Afraid he sticks," I spooned him some mashed chickpeas.

Musa politely accepted our offerings, though with a worried air. He took what he was given—then did not eat. He probably knew he was the subject under discussion, and given the brevity of his instructions from The Brother he may have been feeling anxious about being alone with two dangerous criminals.

We tucked in. I wasn't his foster mother. If Musa chose to be picky, as far as I was concerned he could starve. But I wanted my strength.

Knocking summoned us to the door. We found a gang of Nabataeans who did not look like passing lamp-oil salesmen; they were armed and determined. They started jabbering excitedly. Musa had followed us to the threshold; I could tell he disliked what he heard.

"You have to go," he told me. His startled tone seemed genuine.

"Leave Petra?" It was amazing these people managed to conduct so much lucrative commerce if everyone who came to their city got sent away so promptly. Still, it could have been worse. I had been expecting The Brother to decide we should stay—probably in custody. In fact I had been pondering ways I could sneak us down the Siq to collect our oxcart from the caravanserai in secret, then dash for freedom. "We'll pack!" I volunteered eagerly. Helena had jumped up and was already doing it. "So this is good-bye, Musa!"

"Oh no," replied the priest, with an earnest expression. "I was told to stay with you. If you leave Petra, I shall have to come."

I patted his shoulder. We had no time to waste in argument. "If we're being asked to leave, no doubt somebody forgot to countermand your orders." He was unimpressed with this reasoning. I didn't believe it myself. If my corns had been in The Brother's boots, I too would have made sure an underling followed us to the Nabataean borders and put us firmly onboard ship. "Well, it's your decision."

Helena was used to me acquiring eccentric travel companions, but looked as if this one had stretched her tolerance. Grinning unconvincingly, I tried to reassure her: "He won't come with us far; he'll miss his mountains."

Helena smiled wearily. "Don't worry. I'm quite used to handling men I could do without!"

With as much dignity as we could muster we allowed ourselves to be marched out of Petra. From shadows among the rocks, dark figures watched us leave. The odd camel did us the honor of spitting after us disparagingly.

Once we stopped. Musa spoke almost crossly to the armed escort. They didn't like waiting, but he darted into a house and came back with a small baggage roll. Equipped with Nabataean underwear and toothpicks, presumably, we were hurried on.

By then night had fallen, so our journey took place by the light of flares. Their pallid flames flickered eerily on the lower carvings of the rock tombs, sending long shadows up the sandstone. Columns and pediments were glimpsed, then quickly lost. Square-topped doorways assumed a menacing air, their openings like mysterious black cave mouths. We were on foot. We let the Nabataeans carry our baggage across the city, but when we reached the narrow gorge through the mountains it was clear we were being sent on alone—almost. Musa definitely intended to stick all the way. To reach the outside world, I had to grapple with our baggage while Helena lit our way with a flaming brand. As she strode ahead of us in high annoyance, she looked like some devastating sibyl leading the way down a cleft into Hades.

"Lucky I hadn't spent my inheritance on a lifetime's supply of bales of silk and incense jars!" muttered Helena, loud enough for Musa to hear. I knew she had been looking forward to what ought to have been an unrivaled chance to make luxury purchases. If her mother was as efficient as mine, she had come with a three-scroll shopping list.

"I'll buy you a pair of Indian pearl earrings," I tried offering to her stately back.

"Oh thanks! That should overcome my disappointment . . ." Helena knew the pearls would probably never materialize.

We stumbled down the rocky path between cliffs that now craned together in complete blackness overhead. If we stopped, occasional tumbling stones were all that broke the silence of the Siq. We kept going.

I was now feeling mild despair. I always like to accomplish my tasks for the Emperor with dispatch, but even by my economical standards spending barely one day in Petra was not a good basis for briefing His Caesarship on the usual dire subjects (topography, fortifications, economics, social mores, political stability, and mental state of the populace). I could just about manage to tell him the market price of radishes—information Vespasian probably knew from other sources, and not much use for helping a war council decide whether to invade.

Without hard information to offer, my chances of screwing a fee from the Palace must be slim. Besides, if Anacrites had sent me here in the hope that it would be a terminal journey, I could assume he had never budgeted for a large outlay. Probably nobody expected to see my happy grin at the accounts kiosk again. It meant that not for the first time I was nose to nose with bankruptcy.

Helena, who discovered her sense of discretion while she was trying to handle a wildly flaring torch, found little to say about our situation. She had money. She would, if I allowed it, subsidize our journey home. I would let her do it eventually, if that was the only way to spare Helena herself discomfort. Biting back my pride would make me pretty short-tempered, so for both our sakes she refrained from asking pointedly what plans I had now. Maybe I could extricate us myself. More likely not.

Most likely, as Helena knew from experience, I had no plans at all.

This was not the worst disaster of our lives, nor my worst failure. But I was dangerously angry about it. So when a small group of camels and oxcarts came rattling down the gorge behind us, my first reaction was to stay in the middle of the gravel track, forcing them to slow and stick behind us. Then, when a voice called out offering a lift on a cart, irrational frivolity took over. I turned round, dumping my load. The first cart stopped, leaving me gazing into the dolorous eyes of an edgy-looking ox.

"Your offer's welcome, stranger! How far can you take us?"

The man grinned back, responding to the challenge. "Bostra, perhaps?" He was not Nabataean. We were talking in Greek.

"Bostra's not on my itinerary. How about dropping us at the caravanserai here, where I can pick up my own transport?"

"Done," he said, with an easygoing smile. His intonation had the same overlay as mine; I was now sure of it.

"You from Italy?" I asked.

"Yes."

I accepted the lift.

Only when we were ensconced on the wagon did I notice what a raggle-taggle company had picked us up. There were about ten of them, split between three carts and a couple of moth-eaten camels. Most of the people looked white-faced and anxious. Our driver caught the question in my eyes. "I'm Chremes, an actor-manager. My company has been ordered to depart from Petra. We saw them lift the curfew to let you out, so we're doing a quick flit before anybody changes their mind about us."

"Might somebody insist you stay?" I asked, though I had already guessed.

"We lost a friend." He nodded to Helena, whom he must have recognized. "You are the couple who found him, I believe. Heliodorus, who had the unfortunate accident up on the mountaintop."

That was the first time I heard our drowned man's name.

Immediately afterwards I heard something else: "Bostra might be an interesting town to visit, Marcus," suggested Helena Justina in a speculative voice.

That young lady could never resist a mystery.

Twelve

Of course we did go to Bostra. Helena knew she was doing me a favor by suggesting it. Having discovered the drowned man, I too was fascinated to have met up with his companions. I wanted to know much more about them—and him. Being nosy was my livelihood.

That first evening, Chremes took us to recover our own stabled ox, the sad beast I had taken on at Gaza, together with the shaky contraption that passed for our hired vehicle. The night was really too dark now to travel on further, but both our parties were keen to put distance between ourselves and Petra. For added security and confidence we drove on in convoy, sharing our torches. We all seemed to feel that in the desert chance encounters are important.

After we set up camp I approached the actor-manager curiously: "Are you certain the man Helena and I discovered was your friend?"

"Everything fits from your description—same build, same coloring. Same drinking habits!" he added bitterly.

"Then why didn't you come forward and claim the body?" I sprang at him.

"We were already in enough trouble!" twinkled Chremes like a conspirator.

I could understand that. But the situation intrigued me all the same.

We had all made our tents by hanging black goat-hair covers on rough wooden frames and were sitting outside these shelters by firelight. Most of the theatricals were huddled together, subdued by Heliodorus' death. Chremes came to join Helena and me, while Musa sat slightly apart in a world of his own. Hugging my knees I took my first good look at the leader of the theater troupe.

He was, like the dead man, broadly built and full of face. More striking, however, with a strong chin and a dramatic nose that would have looked good on a republican general. Even in normal conversation he had a powerful voice with a resonance that seemed almost overdone. He delivered his sentences crisply. I did not doubt there were reasons why he had come to talk this evening. He wanted to judge Helena and me; maybe he wanted more than that from us.

"Where are you from?" Helena inquired. She could draw out information as smoothly as a pickpocket slitting a purse-thong.

"Most of the group hail from southern Italy. I'm a Tusculum man."

"You're a long way from home!"

"I've been a long way from Tusculum for twenty years."

I chortled. "What's that—the old 'one wife too many and I was cut out of my inheritance' excuse?"

"There was nothing there for me. Tusculum's a dead-and-alive, ungrateful, uncivilized backwater." The world is full of people slandering their birthplaces, as if they really believe that small-town life is different elsewhere.

Helena seemed to be enjoying herself; I let her carry on. "So how did you end up here, Chremes?"

"After half a lifetime performing on rocky stages in thunderstorms to provincial thickheads who only want to talk among themselves about that day's market, it's like a drug. I do have a wife—one I hate, who hates me back—and I've no more sense than to carry on forever dragging a gang of tattered strutters into any city we find on our road . . ."

Chremes talked almost too readily. I wondered how much was a pose. "When did you actually leave Italy?" Helena asked.

"The first time, twenty years ago. Five years back we came east again with Nero's traveling sideshow, his famous Greek Tour. When he tired of receiving laurel chaplets from bribed judges and packed up for home, we kept on drifting until we floated into Antiochia. The real Greeks didn't want to see what the Romans have done to their stage heritage, but so-called Hellenic cities here, which haven't been Greek since Alexander, think we're presenting them with masterpiece theater. We found we could scrape a living in Syria. They are drama-mad. Then I wondered what Nabataea was like. Worked our way south—and now thanks to The Brother we're working north again."

"I'm not with you."

"Our offer of culture was about as welcome in Petra as a performance of *The Trojan Women* to a family of baboons."

"So you were already departing even before Heliodorus was drowned?"

"Seen off by The Brother. Happens often in our profession. Sometimes we get driven out of town for no reason. At least at Petra they produced a passable exuse."

"What was that?"

"We were planning a performance in their theater—though

the gods know the place was primitive. Aeschylus would have taken one glance and gone on strike. But we were going to give them *The Pot of Gold*—seemed appropriate, given that everyone there has plenty. Congrio, our poster-writer, had chalked up details all around the city. Then we were solemnly informed that the theater is only used ceremonially, for funeral rites. The implication was that if we desecrated their stage, the funeral rites might be our own . . . A strange people," Chremes stated.

This sort of comment normally produces a silence. Adverse remarks about foreigners make people remember their own folk—temporarily convincing themselves that those they have left at home are sensible and sane. Nostalgia seeped into our circle gloomily.

"If you were all about to leave Petra," Helena asked thoughtfully, "why had Heliodorus gone for a walk?"

"Why? Because he was a constant menace!" Chremes exclaimed. "Trust him to lose himself when we were set to leave."

"I still think you should have identified him formally," I told him.

"Oh it will be him," Chremes insisted airily. "He was the type to inflict himself on an accident, and at the worst possible moment. Just like him to die somewhere sacrilegious and get us all locked in an underground dungeon. Having dozy officials argue for years about who caused his death would have struck Heliodorus as a fine joke!"

"A comedian?"

"He thought so." Chremes caught Helena smiling, so added instructively, "Someone else had to write the jokes for him."

"Not creative?"

"If I told you exactly what *I* thought of Heliodorus it would sound unkind. So let's confine it to: He was a shabby, shambling dissolute with no sense of language, tact, or timing."

"You're a measured critic!" she answered solemnly.

"I try to be fair!"

"So he won't be missed?" I inquired quietly.

"Oh, he'll be missed! He was employed to do a certain job, which nobody else can undertake—"

"Ah, you mean no one else wants it?" I was speaking from experience in my own career.

"What was it?" Helena asked, with the light, careless inflection of a girl whose close companion needs to earn a crust.

"He was our jobbing playwright."

Even Helena sounded surprised by that. "The man we found drowned had written plays?"

"Certainly not!" Chremes was shocked. "We are a respectable troupe with a fine reputation; we only perform the established repertoire! Heliodorus *adapted* plays."

"What did that entail?" Helena Justina always asked the direct question. "Translations from Greek to Latin?"

"Anything and everything. Not full translations, but pepping up turgid ones so we could bear to speak the lines. Modifying the story if the cast did not suit our company. Adding better characters to liven up proceedings. He was *supposed* to add jokes, though as I told you, Heliodorus wouldn't recognize a funny line if it jumped up and poked him in the eye. We mainly put on New Comedy. It has two painful disadvantages: it's no longer new, and quite frankly, it's not comic.

Helena Justina was a shrewd, educated girl, and sensitive to atmosphere. She certainly knew what she was risking when she asked, "What will you do about replacing Heliodorus now?"

At once Chremes grinned at me. "Want a job?" He had an evil streak.

"What are the qualifications needed?"

"Able to read and write."

I smiled diffidently, like a man who is too polite to say no to a friend. People never take the hint.

"Marcus can do that," Helena put in. "He does need a job."

Some girls would be happy just to sit under the stars in the desert with the love of their heart, without trying to hire him out to any passing entrepreneur.

"What's your trade?" Chremes asked, perhaps warily.

"In Rome I am an informer." It was best to be frank, but I knew better than to mention my imperial sponsorship.

"Oh! What are the qualifications for *that*?"

"Able to duck and dive."

"Why Petra?"

"I came east to look for a missing person. Just a musician. For some unaccountable reason The Brother decided I must be a spy."

"Oh don't worry about that!" Chremes reassured me heartily. "In our profession it happens all the time." Probably when it suited them, it could be true. Actors went everywhere. According to their reputation in Rome, they were not fussy who they spoke to when they got there and they often sold much more than tasteful Athenian hexameters. "So, young Marcus, being whipped out of the mountain sanctuary leaves you a quadrans short of a denarius?"

"It does, but don't put me on the payroll before I've even heard your offer and its terms!"

"Marcus can do it," Helena interrupted. I like my girlfriends to have faith in me—though not that much faith. "He writes poetry in his spare time," she revealed, without bothering to ask whether I wanted my private hobbies publicly exposed.

"The very man!"

I stood my ground, temporarily. "Sorry, I'm just a scribbler of lousy satires and elegies. Besides, I hate Greek plays."

"Don't we all? There's nothing to it," Chremes assured me.

"You'll love it!" gurgled Helena.

The actor-manager patted my arm. "Listen, Marcus, if Heliodorus could do this job, anybody can!" Just the sort of career proposal I look for. It was too late for resistance, however.

Chremes raised a fist in greeting and cried, "Welcome to the company!"

I made one last attempt to extricate myself from this lunatic jape. "I still have to look for my missing person. I doubt if you're going where I need to be—"

"We are going," pronounced Chremes elaborately, "where the desert-dwelling populace barely recognize their sophisticated Greek heritage and are overdue for some permanent theater-building, but where the founders of their paltry Hellenic cities have at least provided them with *some* auditoria that purveyors of the dramatic arts are allowed to use. We are going, my fine young informer—"

I knew it already. I broke in on the long-windedness: "You are going to the Decapolis!"

Leaning against my knee and gazing up at the mysterious desert sky, Helena smiled contentedly. "That's convenient, Chremes. Marcus and I already had plans to travel to the same area!"

Thirteen

We were going to Bostra first, however, for we had to pick up the rest of the theater group. That meant we were traveling right past the region where I wanted to search for Sophrona, well east of the Decapolis towns. But I was used to making journeys backwards. I never expected a logical life.

Trekking to Bostra gave me a clear idea of what I would say to Vespasian about this region if I ever reached home safely and had the chance. This was still Nabataea—still, therefore, outside the Empire, if Helena and I really wanted to frighten ourselves by thinking about how remote our location was. In fact, even on the well-maintained Nabataean roads, which had once belonged to the great Persian Empire, the trip turned out to be a dreary haul and took a good ten days. Northern Nabataea ran up in a long finger beside the Decapolis, making geographical neatness yet another reason for Rome to consider taking over this territory. A straight frontier down from Syria would look much better organized on a map.

We were heading into a highly fertile region; a potential grain basket for the Empire. Given that Rome was keen to gain control of the incense trade, I reckoned it would make good sense to shift the trade routes eastwards to this northern capital, ignoring the Petrans' insistence that all caravans turn aside and stop there. Running the country from Bostra instead would provide a more pleasant center of government, one with a kinder climate and closer links with civilization. The people of Bostra would be amenable to such a change since it would enhance their current back-row status. And the uppity Petrans would be put in their place.

This wonderful theory of mine had nothing to do with the fact that the Petrans had bounced me out of town. I happen to believe that when you take over any new business, your first task should be to change the personnel so you can run things your own way, and with loyal staff.

The theory might never be implemented in my lifetime, but devising it gave me something to think about when I wanted to stop reading comedies.

Leaving behind us the harsh mountain barrier that enclosed Petra, we had first climbed through the sparse local settlements, then reached more level ground. The desert rolled easily to the horizon on all sides. Everyone told us it was not real desert, compared to the wilderness of Arabia Felix—ironically named— or the terrible wastes beyond the River Euphrates, but it seemed barren and lonely enough for me. We felt we were crossing an old, old land. A land over which varied peoples had rolled like tides for centuries, and would continue to do so in war or peaceful settlement as long as time lasted. A land in which our present journeying was insignificant. It was impossible to tell whether the little crooked cairns of stones beside the road that marked the graves of nomads had been set up last week or several thousand years ago.

Gradually the rocky features diminished; boulders gave way to stones; the stones, which had spread the landscape like acres of roughly chopped nuts on a cooking board, turned into scatters, then were lost together in rich, dark, arable soil supporting wheat fields, vineyards, and orchards. The Nabataeans conserved their meager rainfall with a system of shallow terracing on each side of the wadis: wide shelves of ground were held back by low walls some forty or fifty feet apart, over which any surplus water ran off to the terrace below. It seemed successful. They grew wheat as well as barley. They had olives and grapes for oil and wine. Their eating fruit consisted of a lush mixture of figs, dates and pomegranates, while their most popular nuts—among a handsome variety—were almonds.

The whole atmosphere was different now. Instead of long nomad tents, humpbacked as caterpillars, we saw increasingly pretty houses, each set within its garden and smallholding. Instead of free-ranging ibex and rock-rabbits, there were tethered donkeys and goats.

Once we hit Bostra we were supposed to be meeting up with the remainder of Chremes' company. The group Helena and I had met in Petra were the chief members of the troupe, mainly actors. Various hangers-on, with most of their stage equipment, had been left behind in the north, which did seem friendly, in case the rest found a hostile welcome in the mountains. As far as the murder was concerned, I could virtually ignore them. It was on the first group that I needed to concentrate.

Quite early in the trip I had asked Chremes, "Why did Heliodorus really go for that walk?" The scenario was still bothering me.

"It was like him to wander off. They all do it—minds of their own."

"Was it because he wanted a drink, quietly, on his own?"

"Doubt it." Chremes shrugged. He showed a distinct lack of interest in this death.

"Someone went with him anyway. Who was it?" A long shot, since I was asking the name of the killer.

"Nobody knows."

"Everyone accounted for?" Needless to say, he nodded. I would check that later for myself. "Someone else must have fancied a tipple, though?" I pressed.

"They'd be out of luck then. Heliodorus never reckoned to share his jar."

"Might the companion have had his own jar—or goatskin—that Heliodorus had his eye on?"

"Oh yes! That makes sense."

Maybe the playwright had had an acquaintance nobody else knew about. "Would Heliodorus have made friends with anybody in Petra, anybody outside your group?"

"I doubt that." Chremes seemed fairly definite. "The locals were reserved, and we don't mix much with merchants—or anyone else. We're a close-knit family; we find enough squabbles among ourselves without looking outside for more trouble. Besides, we hadn't been in the city long enough to make contacts."

"I heard him going up the mountain. I felt he knew the person he was with." Chremes obviously realized where my questions were heading. "That's right: what you say means he was killed by somebody from our group."

That was when Chremes asked me directly to keep my eyes and ears open. He did not exactly commission me; that, with a fee at the end of it, would have been too much to hope for. But despite his initial reluctance to involve himself, if he was harboring a killer he wanted to know who it was. People like to feel free to insult their companions or let them pay all of the wine bill without having to worry that it could annoy the kind of man who shoves his traveling companions face down in cold water until they stop breathing.

"Tell me about Heliodorus, Chremes. Did anyone in particular dislike him?" It had seemed a simple question.

"Hah! *Everyone* did!" scoffed Chremes.

That was a good start. The force with which he said it convinced me that every one of the group from Petra must be a suspect for killing the playwright. On the journey to Bostra, therefore, Helena and I had to think about all of them.

Fourteen

Bostra was a black basalt city built in this blackly ploughed land. It flourished. It had commerce, but it generated much of its own prosperity. There was a fine town gate in distinctly Nabataean architecture, and the King owned a second palace here. To Romans it was alien in flavor— yet it was the kind of city we understood. Irascible donkey drovers cursed us as we tried to decide where we were going. Shopkeepers looked out from ordinary lockups with calculating eyes, shouting at us to come in and see their merchandise. When we arrived, near evening, we were greeted by the familiar scent of woodsmoke from baths and ovens. The tempting odors from hot-food stalls were spicier, but the reek of the leather tannery was as disgusting as any at home, and the stuttering lamp oil in the slums smelled just as rancid as it does all over the Aventine.

At first we were unable to find the rest of the company. They were not at the caravanserai where they had been left. Chremes seemed reluctant to make inquiries openly, from which Helena and I gathered it was likely there had been trouble in his absence. Various members of our group set off to look for their colleagues in the city while we guarded the wagons and luggage. We set up our tent with Musa's silent help. We ate supper, then sat down to wait for the return of the others. It was our first chance to talk over our findings so far.

During the journey we had managed to survey individual members of the group by judiciously offering lifts on our wagon. Then, when Helena grew weary of my efforts at controlling our temperamental ox, she hopped off and invited herself into other transport. We had now made contact with most of them, though whether we had also made friends was less certain.

We were considering everyone for possible motives—females too.

"A man did it," I had explained cautiously to Helena. "We heard him on the mountain. But you don't have to be cynical to know that a woman may have provided his reason."

"Or brought the drink and devised the plan," Helena agreed, as if she herself regularly did such things. "What sort of motive do you think we are looking for?"

"I don't believe it can be money. No one here has enough of it. That leaves us with the old excuses—envy or sexual jealousy."

"So we have to ask people what they thought of the playwright? Marcus, won't they wonder why we keep inquiring?"

"You're a woman; you can be plain nosy. I shall tell them the killer must be one of our party and I'm worried about protecting you."

"Load of mule dung!" scoffed my elegant lady with one of the pungent phrases she had picked up from me.

*   *   *

I had already seen what the theater troupe was like. We were dealing with a fickle, feckless crowd here. We would never pin down any of them unless we set about it logically.

It had taken most of the trip just to work out who everyone was. Now we sat on a rug outside our tent. Musa was with us, though as usual he squatted slightly apart, not saying a word but calmly listening. There was no reason to hide our discussion from him so we talked in Greek.

"Right, let's survey the tattered cast list. They all look like stock characters, but I'm betting that not one of them is what they seem . . ."

The list had to be headed by Chremes. Encouraging us to investigate might exonerate him as a suspect—or it might mean he was cunning. I ran through what we knew about him: "Chremes runs the company. He recruits members, chooses the repertoire, negotiates fees, keeps the cash box under his bed when there's anything in it worth guarding. His sole interest is in seeing that things run smoothly. It would take a really serious grievance to make him jeopardize the company's future. He realized that a corpse in Petra could land them all in jail, and his priority was to get them away. But we know he despised Heliodorus. Do we know why?"

"Heliodorus was no good," Helena answered, impatiently.

"So why didn't Chremes simply pay him off?"

"Playwrights are difficult to find." She kept her head down while she said it. I growled. I was not enjoying reading through the dead man's box of New Comedy. New Comedy had turned out to be as dire as Chremes had predicted. I was already tired of separated twins, wastrels jumping into blanket chests, silly old men falling out with their selfish heirs, and roguish slaves making pitiful jokes.

I changed the subject. "Chremes hates his wife and she hates him. Do we know why? Maybe she had a lover—Heliodorus, say—so Chremes put his rival out of the way."

"You would think that," Helena sneered. "I've talked to her. She yearns to star in serious Greek tragedy. She feels dragged down by having to play prostitutes and long-lost heiresses for this ragged troupe."

"Why? They get to wear the best dresses, and even the prostitutes are always reformed in the last scene." I was showing off my research.

"I gather she gives her all powerfully while longing for better things—a woman's lot in most situations!" Helena told me drily. "People tell me her speech when she gives up brothelkeeping and becomes a temple priestess is thrilling."

"I can't wait to hear it!" In fact I'd be shooting out of the theater to buy a cinnamon cake at a stall outside. "She's called Phrygia, isn't she?" The players had all taken names from drama. This was understandable. Acting was such a despised profession, any performer would assume a pseudonym. I was trying to think up one myself.

Phrygia was the company's somewhat elderly female lead. She was tall, gaunt, and flamboyantly bitter about life. She looked over fifty but we were assured by everybody that when she stepped on stage she could easily persuade an audience she was a beautiful girl of sixteen. They made much of the fact that Phrygia could really act—which made me nervous about the talents of the rest.

"Why does Chremes hate her?" I wondered. "If she's good onstage she ought to be an asset to his company."

Helena looked dour. "He's a man, and she is good. Naturally he resents it. Anyway, I gather he's always lusting after more glamorous bits."

"Well that would have explained it if *he* had been found in the pool, and we had heard *Phrygia* luring him uphill." It seemed irrelevant to Heliodorus. But something about Chremes had always bothered me. I thought about him more. "Chremes himself plays the parts of tiresome old fellows—"

"Pimps, fathers, and ghosts," Helena confirmed. It didn't help.

I gave up and tried considering the other actors. "The juvenile lead is called Philocrates. Though he's not so juvenile if you look closely; in fact he creaks a bit. He takes on prisoners of war, lads about town, and one of the main set of twins in every farce which has that gruesome identity mixup joke."

Helena's summary was swift: "A dilettante handsome jerk!"

"He isn't my chosen dinner companion either," I admitted. We had exchanged words on one occasion when Philocrates had watched me trying to corner my ox to harness it. The words were cool in the circumstances—which were that I asked his assistance, and he snootily declined. I had gathered it was nothing personal; Philocrates thought himself above chores that might earn him a kicked shin or a dirty cloak. He was high on our list to investigate further when we could brace up to an hour of insufferable arrogance. "I don't know who he hates, but he's in love with himself. I'll have to find out how he got on with Heliodorus. Then there's Davos."

"The opposite type," Helena said. "A gruff, tough professional. I tried to chat with him, but he's taciturn, suspicious of strangers, and I guess he rebuffs women. He plays the second male lead—boasting soldiers and such. I reckon he's good—he can swagger stylishly. And if Heliodorus was a liability as a writer, Davos wouldn't think much of it."

"I'll watch my step then! But would he kill the man? Davos might have despised his work, but who gets shoved in a pool for bad writing?" Helena laughed at me suggestively.

"I rather took to Davos," she grumbled, annoyed with herself for being illogical. Somehow I agreed with her and wanted Davos to be innocent. From what I knew of Fate, that probably put poor Davos at the top of the suspects list.

"Next we have the clowns, Tranio and Grumio."

"Marcus, I find it hard to tell the difference between those two."

"You're not meant to. In plays that have a pair of young masters who are twins, these two play their cheeky servants—also identical."

We both fell silent. It was dangerous to view them as a pair. They were not twins; they were not even brothers. Yet of all the company they seemed most inclined to carry over their stage roles into normal life. We had seen them larking about on camels together, both playing tricks on the others. (Easy to do on a camel, for a camel will cause trouble for you without being asked.)

They went around in tandem. They were the same slim build—underweight and light-footed. Not quite the same height. The slightly taller one, Tranio, seemed to play the flashy character, the know-all city wit; his apparent crony, Grumio, had to make do with being the country clown, the butt of sophisticated jokes from the rest of the cast. Even without knowing them closely I could see that Grumio might grow tired of this. If so, however, surely he was more likely to put the boot into Tranio than strangle or drown the playwright?

"Is the clever one bright enough to get away with murder? Is he even as bright as he likes to think, in fact? And can the dopey one possibly be as dumb as he appears?"

Helena ignored my rhetoric. I put it down to the fact that only senators' sons have rhetoric tutors; daughters need only know how to twist around their fingers the senators they will marry and the bathhouse masseurs who will probably father those senators' sons.

I was feeling sour. An intellectual diet of *The Girl from Andros,* followed by *The Girl from Samos,* then *The Girl from Perinthos,* had not produced a sunny temperament. This turgid stuff might appeal to the kind of bachelor whose pickup line is asking a girl where she comes from, but I had moved on from that two years ago when a certain girl from Rome decided to pick me up.

Helena smiled gently. She always knew what I was thinking. "Well, that's the men. There's no particularly striking motive there. So maybe the killer we heard was acting for somebody else. Shall we consider the women?"

"I'll always consider women!"

"Be serious."

"Oh, I was. . . . Well, we've thought about Phrygia." I stretched luxuriantly. "That leaves the eavesdropping maid."

"Trust you to spot the beauty at the bar counter!" Helena retorted. It was hardly my fault. Even for a bachelor who had had to stop asking strange women where they hailed from, this beauty was unmissable.

Her name was Byrria. Byrria was genuinely young. She had looks that would withstand the closest inspection, a perfect skin, a figure worth grabbing, a gentle nature, huge, glorious eyes . . .

"Perhaps Byrria wanted Heliodorus to give her some better lines?" wondered Helena far from rhapsodically.

"If Byrria needs anyone murdered, it's obviously Phrygia. That would secure her the good parts."

I knew from my reading that in plays which could barely support one good female role, Byrria must be lucky to find herself a speaking part. Such meat as there was would be snaffled by Phrygia, while the young beauty could only watch yearningly. Phrygia was the stage manager's wife so the chief parts were hers by right, but we all knew who *should* be the female lead. There was no justice.

"In view of the way all you men are staring," said my beloved icily, "I shouldn't wonder if *Phrygia* would like *Byrria* removed!"

I was still searching for a motive for the playwright's death— though had I known just how long it would take me to find it I should have given up on the spot.

"Byrria didn't kill Heliodorus, but good looks like hers could well have stirred up strong feelings among the men, and then who knows?"

"I daresay you will be investigating Byrria closely," said Helena.

I ignored the gibe. "Do you think Byrria could have been after the scribe?"

"Unlikely!" scoffed Helena. "Not if Heliodorus was as disgusting as everyone says. Anyway, your wondrous Byrria could take her pick of the pomegranates without fingering him. But why don't you ask her?"

"I'll do that."

"I'm sure you will!"

I was not in the mood for a squabble. We had taken the discussion as far as we could, so I decided to abandon sleuthing and settled down on my back for a snooze.

Helena, who had polite manners, remembered our Nabataean priest. He had been sitting with us contributing total silence—his usual routine. Perhaps restraint was part of his religion; it would have been a tough discipline for me. "Musa, you saw the murderer come down the mountain. Is there anybody in this group of travelers whom you recognize?"

She did not know I had already asked him, though she ought to have guessed. Musa answered her courteously anyway. "He wore a hat, lady."

"We shall have to look out for it," replied Helena with some gravity.

I grinned at him, struck by a wicked possibility. "If we can't solve this puzzle, we could set a trap. We could let it be known that Musa saw the murderer, hint that Musa was planning to identify him formally, then you and I could sit behind a rock, Helena, and we could see who comes—hatted or hatless—to shut Musa up."

Musa received the suggestion as calmly as ever, with neither fear nor enthusiasm.

A few minutes later somebody did come, but it was only the company bill-poster.

Fifteen

Helena and I exchanged a surreptitious glance. We had forgotten this one. He had been in Petra and ought to have been included in our list of suspects. Something told us that being forgotten was his permanent role. Being constantly overlooked could give him a motive for anything. But maybe he accepted it. So often it is the people who *have* who think they deserve more. Those who *lack* expect nothing from life.

Such was our visitor—a miserable specimen. He had appeared around a corner of our tent very quietly. He could have been lurking about for ages. I wondered how much he had overheard.

"Hello there! Come and join us. Didn't Chremes mention to me that your name is Congrio?"

Congrio had a light skin covered with freckles, thin straight hair, and a fearful look. He had never been tall to begin with, and his slight, weedy body stooped under burdens of inadequacy. Everything about him spoke of leading a poor life. If he was not a slave now he probably had been at some stage, and whatever existence he snatched for himself these days could not be much better. Being a menial among people who have no regular income is worse than captivity on a rich landowner's farm. No one here cared whether Congrio ate or starved; he was nobody's asset, so nobody's loss if he suffered.

He shuffled near, the kind of mournful maggot who makes you feel crass if you ignore him or patronizing if you try to be sociable.

"You chalk up the advertisements, don't you? I'm Falco, the new jobbing playwright. I'm looking out for people who can read and write in case I need help with my adaptations."

"I can't write," Congrio told me abruptly. "Chremes gives me a wax tablet; I just copy it."

"Do you act in the plays?"

"No. But I can dream!" he added defiantly, apparently not without a sense of self-mockery.

Helena smiled at him. "What can we do for you?"

"Grumio and Tranio have come back from the city with a wineskin. They told me to ask whether you wanted to join them." He was addressing me.

I was ready for bed, but put on my interested face. "Sounds as if a sociable evening could be had here?"

"Only if you want to keep the caravanserai awake all night and feel like death tomorrow," Congrio advised frankly.

Helena shot me a look that said she wondered how the town-and-country twins could tell so easily who was the degenerate in our party. But I did not need her permission—or at least not when this offered a good excuse to ask questions about Heliodorus—so off I went to disgrace myself. Musa stayed with

Helena. I had never bothered to ask him, but I deduced that our Nabataean shadow was no drinking man.

Congrio seemed to be heading the same way as me, but then turned off on his own. "Don't you want a drink?" I called after him.

"Not with that pair!" he responded, vanishing behind a wagon.

On the surface he spoke like a man who had better taste in friends, but I noticed a violent undertone. The easy explanation was that they pushed him around. But there could be more to it. I would have to scrutinize this bill-poster.

Feeling thoughtful, I made my own way to the Twins' tent.

Sixteen

Grumio and Tranio had put up the uncomplicated bivouac that was standard in our ramshackle camp. They had slung a cover over poles, leaving one whole long side open so they could see who was passing (and in their case commentate rudely). I noticed that they had bothered to hang a curtain down the middle of their shelter, dividing it precisely into private halves. These were equally untidy, so it couldn't have been because they fell out over the housekeeping; it hinted instead at aloofness in their relationship.

Surveyed quietly at leisure they were not in the least alike. Grumio, the "country" twin who played runaway slaves and idiots, had a pleasant nature, a chubby face, and straight hair that fell evenly from the crown. Tranio, the taller "townee," had his hair cut short up the back and swept forwards on top. He was sharp-featured and sounded as though he could be a sarcastic enemy. They both had dark, knowing eyes with which they watched the world critically.

"Thanks for the invitation! Congrio refused to come," I said at once, as if I assumed the poster-writer would have been asked too.

Tranio, the one who played the boasting soldier's flashy servant, poured me a full winecup with an exaggerated flourish. "That's Congrio! He likes to sulk—we all do. From which you can immediately deduce that beneath the false bonhomie, our joyous company is seething with angry emotions."

"I gathered that." I took the drink and joined them, relaxing on sacks of costumes alongside the walkway that ran through our encampment. "Almost the first thing Helena and I were told was that Chremes hates his wife and she hates him."

"He must have admitted that himself," Tranio said knowingly. "They do make a big thing of it."

"Isn't it true? Phrygia openly laments that he has deprived her of stardom. And Helena reckons that Chremes frequently wanders from the hearth. So the wife is after a laurel wreath, while the husband wants to stuff a lyre-player. . . ."

Tranio grinned. "Who knows what they're up to? They've been at each other's throats for twenty years. Somehow he never quiet manages to run off with a dancer, and she never remembers to poison his soup."

"Sounds like any normal married couple." I grimaced.

Tranio was topping up my beaker almost before I had tried it. "Like you and Helena?"

"We're not married." I never explained our relationship. People would either not believe me, or not understand. It was no one else's business anyway. "Do I gather that inviting me tonight is a shameless attempt to find out what she and I are doing here?" I taunted, probing in return.

"We see you as a Hired Trickster," grinned Grumio, the supposedly dopey one, unabashed as he named one of the stock characters in New Comedy. It was the first time he had spoken. He sounded brighter than I had expected.

I shrugged. "I'm trying my hand with a stylus. Finding your playwright's soused body got me pitched out of Petra. It also happened at about the time I ran out of traveling funds. I needed work. Your job was the soft option: offering to scribble for Chremes looked easier work than straining my back lifting barrels of myrrh, or catching fleas driving camel trains." Both twins had their noses deep in their winecups. I was not sure I had deflected their curiosity about my interest in the playwright's death. "I've agreed to replace Heliodorus provided I'm not asked to play a tambourine in the orchestra and Helena Justina never acts on a public stage."

"Why not?" queried Grumio. "Does she come from a respectable family?" He ought to be able to see that. Maybe pretending to have a few brains was just a pose.

"No, I rescued her from slavery, in return for two bags of apples and a nanny goat. . . ."

"You're a takeoff merchant!" giggled Grumio. He turned to his friend, who was wielding the wineskin again. "We're onto a scandal."

Ineffectively shielding my cup from Tranio, I rebuked the other quietly: "The only scandal Helena was ever involved in was when she chose to live with me."

"Interesting partnership!" Grumio commented.

"Interesting girl," I said.

"And now she's helping you spy on us?" Tranio prodded.

It was a challenge, one I should have been waiting for. They had brought me here to find out what I was doing, and they would not be deterred. "We don't spy. But Helena and I found the body. Naturally we'd like to know who killed the man."

Tranio drained his winecup in one gulp. "Is it true you actually saw who did it?"

"Who told you that?" Not to be outdone, I quaffed my drink too, wondering whether Tranio was just nosy—or had a deadly earnest reason for wanting to know.

"Well, everyone's keen to know what you're doing with us now—assuming you were just a tourist in Petra," Tranio insinuated.

As I had started to expect, my refill came immediately. I knew when I was being set up. After years as an informer, I also had a clear idea of my limit for drink. I set down my overflowing cup as if I was carried away by strong feelings. "A tourist who made the journey of a lifetime only to get thrown out—" My rant as a disappointed traveler was received fairly coolly.

"So where does your sinister Arab fit in?" Tranio demanded bluntly.

"Musa?" I acted surprised. "He's our interpreter."

"Oh of course."

"Why," I asked with a light, incredulous laugh, "are people suggesting Musa saw the killer or something?"

Tranio smiled, answering in the same apparently friendly tone that I had used: "Did he?"

"No," I said. For all useful purposes it was the truth.

As Grumio prodded the fire I too picked up a twisted branch and played with it among the sparks. "So are either of you going to tell me why Heliodorus was so stinkingly unpopular?"

It was still Tranio, the exponent of mercurial wit, who enjoyed himself making up answers: "We were all in his power." He twirled his wrist elegantly, pretending to philosophize. "Weak parts and dull speeches could finish us. That crude bastard knew it; he toyed with us. The choice was either to flatter him, which was unspeakable, or to bribe him, which was often impossible, or just to wait for somebody else to grab him by the balls and squeeze till he dropped. Before Petra no one had done it—but it was only a matter of time. I should have taken bets on who would get to him first."

"That seems extreme," I commented.

"People whose livelihood depends on a writer exist under stress." As their new writer, I tried not to take it to heart. "To find his killer," Tranio advised me, "look for the despairing actor who had suffered one bad role too many."

"You, for instance?"

His eyes dropped, but if I had worried him he rallied. "Not me. I don't need a set text. If he wrote me out, I improvised. He knew I would do it, so being spiteful lost its fun. Grumio was the same, of course." I glanced at Grumio, who might have been patronized by the afterthought, but his cheerful face remained neutral.

I grunted, sipping wine again. "And I thought the man had just borrowed somebody's best silvered belt once too often!"

"He was a pig," Grumio muttered, breaking his silence.

"Well that's simple! Tell me why."

"A bully. He beat the lower orders. People he dared not attack physically he terrorized in more subtle ways."

"Was he a womanizer?"

"Better ask the women." Grumio was still the speaker—with what could have been a jealous glint. "There are one or two I'll help you interrogate!"

While I was at it, I checked every possibility: "Or did he chase young men?" They both shrugged offhandedly. In fact nobody in this company was young enough to appeal to the usual ogler of boys in bathhouses. If more mature relationships existed, I might as well look first for evidence here with the Twins; they lived closely enough. But Grumio seemed to have straightforward female interests; and Tranio had also grinned at his interrogation joke.

As before it was Tranio who wanted to elaborate: "Heliodorus could spot a hangover, or a pimple on a sensitive adolescent, or a disappointed lover at twenty paces. He knew what each of us wanted from life. He also knew how to make people feel that their weaknesses were enormous flaws, and their hopes beyond reach."

I wondered what Tranio thought his own weakness was—and what hopes he had. Or might once have had.

"A tyrant! But people here seem pretty strong-willed." Both Twins laughed easily. "So why," I asked, "did you all put up with him?"

"Chremes had known him a long time," suggested Grumio wearily.

"We needed him. Only an idiot would do the job," said Tranio, insulting me with what I thought was unnecessary glee.

They were an odd pair. At first glance they had seemed closely bonded, but I decided they hung together only in the way of craftsmen who work together, which gave them some basic loyalty, though they might not meet socially from choice. Yet in this traveling company Tranio and Grumio had to live under one goat hair roof with everyone presuming they formed one unit. Perhaps sustaining the fraud set up hidden strains.

I was fascinated. Some friendships are sounder for having one easygoing partner with one who seems more intense. I felt that this ought to have been the case here; that the stolid Grumio ought to have been grateful for the opportunity to pal up with Tranio, to whom I frankly warmed more. Apart from the fact that he kept refilling my winecup, he was a cynic and a satirist; exactly my kind of fellow.

I wondered if professional jealousy had come between them, though I saw no signs. There was scope onstage for both of them, as I knew from my reading. All the same, in Grumio, the quieter of the clowns, I sensed deliberate restraint. He looked pleasant and harmless. But to an informer that could easily mean he was hiding something dangerous.

The wineskin was empty. I watched Tranio shake out the very last drop, then he squashed the skin flat, clapping it under his elbow.

"So, Falco!" He seemed to be changing the subject. "You're new to playwriting. How are you finding it?"

I told him my thoughts on New Comedy, dwelling with morose despair on its dreariest features.

"Oh you're reading the stuff? So you've been given the company play box?" I nodded. Chremes had handed over a mighty trunk stuffed with an untidy mass of scrolls. Putting them together in sets to make whole plays had taken most of our journey to Bostra, even with help from Helena, who enjoyed that kind of puzzle. Tranio went on idly. "I might come and have a quick look sometime. Heliodorus borrowed something that wasn't left among his personal things. . . ."

"Anytime," I offered, curious, though not in my present condition wanting to pay too much attention to some lost stylus knife or bath oil flask. I swayed to my feet, suddenly anxious to stop torturing my liver and brain. I had been away from Helena for longer than I liked. I wanted my bed.

The sharp clown grinned, noticing how the wine had affected me. I was not alone, however. Grumio was lying on his back near the fire, eyes closed, mouth open, dead to the world. "I'll come back to your tent now," laughed my new friend. "I'll do it while I think of it."

Since I could use an arm to steady me home, I made no protest but let him bring a light and come with me.

Seventeen

Helena appeared to be sound asleep, though I noticed a smell of snuffed lamp wick. She made a show of waking drowsily: "Do I hear the morning cockerel, or is that my stupefied darling rolling back to his tent before he drops?"

"Me, stupefied . . ." I never lied to Helena. She was too sharp to delude. I added quickly, "I've brought a friend—" I thought she stifled a groan.

The light of Tranio's flare wavered crazily up the back wall of our shelter. I gestured him to the trunk of plays while I folded up on a baggage roll as neatly as possible and let him get on with it. Helena glared at the clown, though I tried to persuade myself she looked more indulgently on me.

"Something Heliodorus pinched," Tranio explained, diving

into the depths of the scroll box unabashed. "I just want to dip into the box. . . ." After midnight, in the close domestic privacy of our bivouac, this explanation fell short of convincing. Theatricals seemed a tactless lot.

"I know," I soothed Helena. "Little did you think when you found me in a black bog in Britannia and fell for my soft manners and sweet-natured charm that you'd end up having your sleep disturbed by a gang of drunkards in a desert khan—"

"You're rambling, Falco," she snapped. "But how right. Little did I think!"

I smiled at her fondly. Helena closed her eyes. I told myself that was the only way she could resist either the smile or the frank affection in it.

Tranio was thorough in his search. He delved right to the bottom of the trunk, then replaced every scroll, taking the opportunity to look at each a second time.

"If you tell me what you're looking for—" I offered blearily, longing to get rid of him.

"Oh, it's nothing. It's not here, anyway." He was still searching, however.

"What is it? Your diary of five years as a sex slave in the temple of some Eastern goddess with an ecstatic cult? A rich widow's will, leaving you a Lusitanian gold mine and a troupe of performing apes? Your birth certificate?"

"Oh much worse!" he laughed.

"Looking for a scroll?"

"No, no. Nothing like that."

Helena watched him in a silence that may have passed for politeness to a stranger. I liked more alluring entertainment. I watched her. Tranio finally banged down the lid and sat on the chest kicking his heels against its studded sides. The friendly fellow looked as if he intended to stay chatting until dawn.

"No luck?" I asked.

"No, damn it!"

Helena yawned blatantly. Tranio gave a flourishing gesture of acquiescence, took the hint, and left.

My tired eyes met Helena's for a moment. In the weak light of the flare Tranio had left us, hers looked darker than ever—and not devoid of challenge.

"Sorry, fruit."

"Well, you have to do your work, Marcus."

"I'm still sorry."

"Find anything out?"

"Early days."

Helena knew what that meant: I had found nothing. As I washed my face in cold water she told me, "Chremes dropped in to tell you he has found the rest of his people, and we're performing here tomorrow." She could have announced this while we were waiting for Tranio to go, but Helena and I liked to exchange news more discreetly. Discussing things together in private meant a lot to us. "He wants you to write out the moneylender's part Heliodorus used to play. You have to make sure that omitting the character doesn't lose any vital lines. If so—"

"I reallocate them to someone else. I can do that!"

"All right."

"I could always go onstage as the moneylender myself."

"You have not been asked."

"Don't see why not. I know what they're like. Jove knows I've dealt with enough of the bastards."

"Don't be ridiculous," Helena scoffed. "You're a freeborn Aventine citizen; you're much too proud to sink so low!"

"Unlike you?"

"Oh I could do it. I'm a senator's offspring; disgracing myself is my heritage! Every family my mother gossips with has a disgruntled son no one talks about who ran off to scandalize his grandfather by acting in public. My parents will be disappointed if I *don't*."

"Then they will have to be disappointed, so long as I'm in charge of you." Supervising Helena Justina was a rash claim; she laughed at me. "I promised your father I'd keep you respectable," I finished lamely.

"You promised him nothing." True. He had more sense than to ask me to take on that impossible labor.

"Feel free to carry on reading," I offered, fumbling with my boots.

Helena removed from under her pillow the scroll I guessed she had been peacefully perusing before I turned up like trouble. "How could you tell?" she demanded.

"Smut on your nose from the lamp." In any case, after living with her for a year I had deduced that if I left her anywhere near forty papyrus scrolls she would scoot through the lot in a week like a starved library beetle.

"This is pretty grubby too," she remarked, gesturing to her bedtime read.

"What is it?"

"A very rude collection of anecdotes and funny tales. Too saucy for you, with your pure mind."

"I'm not in the mood for pornography." I took several chances in succession, aiming myself at the bed, inserting my body under the light cover, and winding myself around my lass. She allowed it. Perhaps she knew better than to argue with a hopeless drunk. Perhaps she liked being enveloped.

"Could this be what Tranio was looking for?" she asked. Sick of Tranio, I pointed out that he had said quite decisively his lost item was not a scroll.

"People do sometimes tell lies!" Helena reminded me pedantically.

We too, like the Twins, had our tent divided up for privacy. Behind the makeshift curtain I could hear Musa snoring. The rest of the camp lay silent. It was one of our few moments of solitude, and I was not interested in a risqué Greek novel, if that was what Helena had been studying. I managed to extract the scroll from her and tossed it aside. I let it be known what mood I was in.

"You're not capable," she grumbled. Not without reason, and perhaps not without regret.

With an effort that may have surprised her I wrenched myself sideways and upended the flare in a pitcher of water. Then, as it hissed into darkness, I turned back to Helena intent on proving her wrong.

Once she accepted that I was serious, and likely to stay awake long enough, she sighed. "Preparations, Marcus . . ."

"Incomparable woman!" I let her go, apart from annoying her with delaying caresses as she struggled over me on her way out of bed.

Helena and I were one, a lasting partnership. But due to her fears of childbirth and my fears of poverty, we had taken the decision not to add to our family yet. We shared the burden of defying the Fates. We had rejected wearing a hairy spider amulet, as practiced by some of my sisters, mainly because its success seemed doubtful; my sisters had huge families. Anyway, Helena reckoned I was not sufficiently frightened of spiders to be driven off her by a mere amulet. Instead, I faced the deep embarrassment of bribing an apothecary to forget that controlling birth contravened the Augustan family laws; then she endured the humiliating, sticky procedure with the costly alum in wax. We both had to live with the fear of failing. We both knew if that happened we could never allow a child of ours to be killed in the womb by an abortionist, so our lives would take a serious turn. That had never stopped us giggling over the remedy.

Without a light, I heard Helena cursing and laughing as she rummaged for her soapstone box of thick cerate ointment that was supposed to keep us childless. After some muttering she hopped back to bed. "Quick, before it melts—"

Sometimes I thought the alum worked on the principle of making performance impossible. Instructed to be quick, as every man knows, the will to proceed is liable to collapse. Following too many winecups this seemed even more likely, though the wax at least helped provide a steady aim, after which maintaining a position, as my gymnasium trainer Glaucus would call it, did become more difficult.

Applying care to these problems, I made love to Helena as skillfully as a woman can expect from a man who has been made drunk by a couple of crass clowns in a tent. And since I always ignore instructions, I made sure that I did it very slowly, and for the longest possible time.

Hours later I thought I heard Helena murmur, "A Greek and a Roman and an elephant went into a brothel together; when they came out, only the elephant was smiling. Why?"

I must have been asleep. I must have dreamed it. It sounded like the sort of joke my tentmate Petronius Longus used to wake me up to howl over when we were wicked lads in the legions ten years before.

Senators' nicely brought-up daughters are not even supposed to know that jokes like that exist.

Eighteen

Bostra was our first performance. Certain aspects stick in the memory. Like an acrid sauce repeating after a cut-price dinner party given by a patron you had never liked.

The play was called *The Pirate Brothers*. Despite Chremes' claim that his notable company only tackled the standard repertoire, this drama was the product of no known author. It appeared to have developed spontaneously over many years from any bits of business the actors had enjoyed in other plays, expounded in whatever lines from the classics they could remember on the night. Davos had whispered to me that it went best when they were down to their last few coppers and seriously hungry. It required tight ensemble playing, with despair to give it an edge. There were no pirates; that was a ploy to attract an audience. And even though I had read what purported to be the script, I had failed to identify the brothers of the title.

We offered up this dismal vehicle to a small crowd in a dark theater. The audience on the creaking wooden seats was swelled by spare members of our company, well drilled in creating a vibrant mood with enthusiastic cheers. Any one of them could have earned a good living in the Roman Basilica egging on prosecuting barristers, but they were having a hard time breaking the morose Nabataean atmosphere.

At least we had an increased complement to give us confidence. Helena had nosed about the camp to see who the additions to our company were.

"Cooks, slaves, and flute girls," I informed her before she could tell me.

"You've certainly done your reading!" she replied, with admiring sarcasm. She was always annoyed at being forestalled.

"How many are there?"

"Quite a tribe! They're musicians as well as extras. They all double up making costumes and scenery. Some take the money if the performance is ticketed."

We had both learned already that the ideal ruse was to persuade a gullible local magistrate to subsidize our play, hoping to trade on the crowd's goodwill next election time. He would pay us a lump sum for the night, after which we needn't care if nobody bothered to come. Chremes had managed to swing this at towns in Syria, but in Nabataea they had not heard of the civilized Roman custom of politicians bribing the electorate. For us, playing to an empty arena would mean eating from empty bowls. So Congrio was sent out early to chalk up enticing notices for *The Pirate Brothers* on local houses, whole we hoped he didn't choose to annoy any householders who were keen theatergoers.

In fact, "keen" was not an epithet that seemed to apply in Bostra. Since our play was ticketed, we knew in advance that there must be some rival attraction in town: a snail race with heavy side bets, or two old men playing a very tense game of draughts.

It was drizzling. This is not supposed to happen in the wilderness, but as Bostra was a grain basket we knew they must get rain for their corn sometimes. Sometimes was tonight.

"I gather the company will perform even if the theater is being struck by lightning," Helena told me, scowling.

"Oh stalwart chaps!"

We clung together under a cloak among a thin crowd trying to make out the action through the miserable mist.

I was expecting to be hailed as a hero after the play. I had taken a great deal of trouble with my adaptation and had spent all morning perfecting new lines, or tinkering with tired old ones as much as time allowed. I had proudly presented the revisions to Chremes at lunch, though he brushed aside my eager offer to attend the afternoon rehearsal and point out significant changes. They called it a rehearsal, but when I stationed myself in a back row at the theater, trying to overhear how things were going, I was dismayed. Everyone spent most of their time discussing a flute girl's pregnancy and whether Chremes' costume would last in one piece another night.

The actual performance bore out my disquiet. My laborious redraft had been tossed aside. All the actors ignored it. As the action evolved they repeatedly referred to the missing moneylender, even though he would never appear, then in the last act they improvised a few haphazard speeches to get around the problem. The plot, which I had so wittily resurrected, dwindled into ludicrous tosh. For me, the most bitter insult was that the audience swallowed the gibberish. The somber Nabataeans actually applauded. They stood up politely, clapping their hands above their heads. Somebody even threw what looked like a flower, though it may have been an unpaid laundry bill.

"You're upset!" Helena observed, as we fought our way to the exit. We barged past Philocrates, who was hanging around the gateway, showing off his profile to admiring women. I steered Helena through a smaller group of men with entranced expressions who were waiting for the beauteous Byrria; she had taken herself off promptly, however, so they were looking over anything else in a long skirt. Having my nobly reared girlfriend mistaken for a flute girl was now my worst nightmare. "Oh, don't let it worry you, Marcus my love . . ." She was still talking about the play.

I explained to Helena succinctly that I didn't give a damn what a group of illogical, illiterate, impossible thespians did onstage or off it, and that I would see her in a while. Then I strode off to find somewhere I could kick rocks in a decent solitude.

Nineteen

It came on to rain more heavily. When you're down, Fortune loves stamping on your head.

Tearing off ahead of everyone else, I reached the center of our encampment. That was where the heavier wagons were drawn up in the hope that our encircling tents would deter sneak thieves. Hopping over the nearest tailboard I took shelter under the ragged leather roof that protected our stage properties from the weather. It was my first chance to inspect this battered treasure trove. After I had finished swearing about the performance, I devised a ferocious speech of resignation that ought to leave Chremes whimpering. Then I fetched out my tinderbox, wasted half an hour with it, but eventually lit the large lantern that was carried onstage in scenes of nighttime conspiracy.

As the pale flame wandered around dangerously in its ironwork container, I found myself crouching up against a small shrine (large enough to hide behind for overhearing secrets). Stacked opposite were several painted doorways, meant to distinguish the neighboring houses that featured in so much of the New Comedy. These had not been used in tonight's *Pirate Brothers* in order to save them from the wet. Instead the scene, which was originally "A Street in Samothrace," had been redesignated "A Rocky Coast" and "The Road to Miletus"; Chremes had simply played Chorus and announced these arbitrary locations to his hapless audience.

I struggled to settle more comfortably. Under my elbows was an old wooden log with a graying shawl nailed to it (the "baby"). Sticking out above my head was a gigantic sword of curved design. I assumed it was blunt—then cut my finger on the edge while testing out my assumption. So much for scientific experiment. Wicker baskets mostly overflowed with costumes, shoes, and masks. One basket had toppled over, showing itself nearly empty apart from a long set of rattly chains, a large ring with a big red glass stone (for recognition of long-lost offspring), some parcels of shopping, and a brown jar containing a few pistachio shells (the everpresent Pot of Gold). Behind it were a stuffed sheep (for sacrifice) and a wooden pig on wheels that could be towed across the stage by Tranio in his role as a merrily wittering Clever Cook who cracked thousand-year-old jokes about preparations for the Wedding Feast.

Once I had finished gloomily surveying the torn and faded panoply with which I was sharing this wagon, my thoughts naturally turned again to issues like Life, Fate, and however did I come to end up in this tip being paid zero for an unappealing job? Like most philosophy it was a waste of time. I noticed a woodlouse and began timing his progress, taking bets with myself about which direction he would wander in. I had grown cold enough to think I would now return to my own bivouac and allow Helena Justina to bolster my esteem, when I heard footsteps outside. Somebody stamped up to the wagon, the end flap was beaten aside, there came a flurry of irritated movement, and then Phrygia hauled herself inside. Presumably she too was seeking privacy, though she did not appear bothered by finding me.

Phrygia was as long as a leek; she could overtop most men. She increased her advantage of height by wearing her hair in a coronet of frizzled curls, and by teetering about on frightful plat-form shoes. Like a statue that had been purposely designed to stand in a niche, her front view was perfectly finished, but her back had been left in the rough. She was a model of immaculate face paint, with a whole breastplate of gilt jewelry that crackled in layers upon the meticulous pleats of the stole across her bosom. Seen from behind, however, every bone pin pegging down her hairstyle was visible, the frontispiece jewelry all hung from a single tarnished chain that had worn a red furrow in her scrawny neck, the stole was rumpled, the shoes were backless, and her gown was hoicked together and pinned in clumps in order to provide the more elegant drape on her frontal plane. I had seen her walk down a street with a sideways glide that pre-served her public image almost intact. Since her stage presence was strong enough to entrance an audience, she did not care if the louts behind the back wall sneered.

"I thought it might be you skulking here." She threw herself against one of the costume baskets, flapping her sleeves to shake off drops of rain. Some fell on me. It was like being joined on a small couch by a thin but energetic dog.

"I'd better be off," I muttered. "I was just sheltering—"

"I see! Don't want that girl of yours to hear you've been clos-eted in a wagon with the manager's wife?" I settled back weakly. I like to be polite. She looked fifteen years older than me, and might be more. Phrygia favored me with her bitter laugh. "Con-soling the ranks is my privilege, Falco. I'm the Mother of the Company!"

I joined in the laughter, as one does. I felt threatened, wondering briefly if accepting consolation from Phrygia was an obligation for men in the troupe. "Don't worry about me. I'm a big boy—"

"Really?" At her tone, I shrank mentally. "So how was your first night?" she challenged.

"Let's say I can now see how Heliodorus might have turned his back on society!"

"You'll learn," she consoled me. "Don't make it so literary. And don't waste time sticking in political allusions. You're not bloody Aristophanes, and the people who are paying for tickets are not educated Athenians. We're acting for turnips who only come to talk to their cousins and fart. We have to give them a lot of action and low-level jokes, but you can leave all that to us onstage. We know what's required. Your job is to hone the basic framework and remember the simple motto: short speeches, short lines, short words."

"Oh, and I foolishly thought I would be handling major themes of social disillusionment, humanity, and justice!"

"Skip the themes. You're handling old envy and young love." Like most of my career as an informer, in fact.

"Silly me!"

"As for Heliodorus," Phrygia went on, with a change of tone, "he was just nasty to begin with."

"So what was his problem?"

"Juno only knows."

"Did he make enemies with anyone in particular?"

"No. He was fair; he hated everyone."

"And everyone was evenhanded with their loathing in return? What about you, Phrygia? How did you get on with him? Surely an actress of your status was beyond reach of his spite?"

"My status!" she murmured drily. I sat quiet. "I've had my turn. I was offered the chance to play Medea at Epidaurus once. . . ." It must have been years ago, but I did not disbelieve

it. Tonight she had given a crisp cameo performance as a priestess that had let us glimpse what might have been.

"I'd like to have seen that. I can visualize you raving at Jason
and bashing the children. . . . What happened?"

"Married Chremes." And never forgave him. Still, it was premature for me to feel sorry for him when I had no idea what
other crises had distorted their relationship. My work had long
ago taught me never to judge marriages.

"Heliodorus knew about you missing this Medea?"

"Of course." She spoke quietly. I had no need to probe for details. I could imagine the use he must have made of the knowledge; a world of torment lay in her very restraint.

She was a great actress. And maybe she was acting now.
Maybe she and Heliodorus had really been passionate lovers—or
maybe she had wanted him, but he rebuffed her, so she arranged
his swimming accident. . . . Luckily Helena was not present to
pour scorn on these wild theories.

"Why did Chremes keep him on?" Even though she and her
husband were not speaking to each other generally, I had a feeling they could always discuss the company. Probably it was the
sole factor that kept them together.

"Chremes is too softhearted to boot anyone out." She grinned
at me. "Plenty of people rely on that to keep their position with
us!"

I felt my jaw set. "If that's a gibe at me, I don't need charity. I
had a job of my own before I met up with you people."

"He tells me you're an investigator?"

I let her probe. "I'm trying to find a young musician called
Sophrona."

"Oh! We thought you must be political."

I pretended to be amazed by that idea. Sticking with
Sophrona, I went on, "It's worth a parcel if I track her down. All
I know is she can play the water organ as if she had lessons di-

rect from Apollo, and she'll be with a man from the Decapolis, probably called Habib."

"The name should help."

"Yes, I'm relying on it. The Decapolis region sounds ill defined, too large for wandering about clueless like a prophet in the wilderness."

"Who wants you to find the girl?"

"Who do you think? The manager who paid the fee for training her."

Phrygia nodded; she knew that a trained musician was a valuable commodity. "What happens if you don't?"

"I go home poor."

"We can help you look."

"That seems a fair bargain. It's why I took this job. You help me when we get to the Decapolis, and even if my scribing is crude, in return I'll do my best to identify your murderer."

The actress shivered. It was probably real. "Someone here . . . Someone we know . . ."

"Yes, Phrygia. Someone you eat with; a man somebody probably sleeps with. Someone who may be late for rehearsals yet turns in a good performance. Someone who has done you kindnesses, made you laugh, sometimes irritated you to Hades for no reason in particular. Someone, in short, just like all the rest in the company."

"It's horrible!" Phrygia cried.

"It's murder," I said.

"We have to find him!" It sounded as if she would help if she could. (In my long experience that meant I should be prepared for the woman to try to jeopardize my search at every turn.)

"So who hated him, Phrygia? I'm looking for a motive. Just knowing who he had dealings with would be a start."

"Dealings? He used to try out his luck with Byrria, but she kept away from him. He hung around the musicians sometimes—though most of them would tell him where to put his little implement—but he was too wound up in his own black personality to have been involved in any special affairs."

"A man who bore grudges?"

"Yes. He was bitter against Byrria. But you know she didn't go up the mountain. Chremes told me you heard the killer talking, and it was a man."

"Could have been a man defending Byrria." When I see an attractive woman, I'm seeing motives for all kinds of stupid behavior. "Who else hankers after her?"

"All of them!" said Phrygia, at her most dry. She pursed her lips thoughtfully. "Byrria has no followers, I'll say that for her."

"There were plenty of oglers waiting here for her tonight."

"And was she visible?"

"No," I conceded.

"That surprised you! You thought Byrria was young enough to listen to them and only I was old enough to see through their flattery!"

"I think you have plenty of admirers—but you're right about the girl. So what's with Byrria if she turned down Heliodorus and she can live without cheap popularity?"

"She's ambitious. She doesn't want one short night of passion in return for the long disillusionment; she wants to work." I was reaching the conclusion that Phrygia hated the beauty less than we had supposed. Clearly she approved of intense dramatic ambition; perhaps she wished the younger woman well. It could be for that classic reason: Byrria reminded Phrygia of her younger self.

"So she studies her art, and keeps to herself." That could easily drive men mad. "Is anyone particularly soft on her? Who loves the dedicated Byrria from afar?"

"I told you: all of the bastards!" Phrygia said.

I sighed gently. "Well, tell me if you decide there was somebody who might have been prepared to kick Heliodorus out of her path."

"I'll tell you," she agreed calmly. "On the whole, Falco, taking action—especially for a woman—is alien to men."

Since she still seemed prepared to talk to me, although I was one of those feeble specimens, I went through the list of suspects in a businesslike way: "It has to be someone who came with you to Petra. Apart from your husband—" No flicker of emotion crossed her face. "That leaves the two clowns, the wonderfully handsome Philocrates, Congrio the bill-poster, and Davos. Davos looks an interesting case—"

"Not him!" Phrygia was crisp. "Davos wouldn't do anything stupid. He's an old friend. I won't have you insulting Davos. He's too sensible—and he's much too quiet." People always believe their personal cronies should be above suspicion; in fact the chances are high that anyone in the Empire who dies unnaturally has been set on by their oldest friend.

"Did he get on with the playwright?"

"He thought he was mule dung. But he thinks that about most playwrights," she informed me conversationally.

"I'll bear it in mind when I talk to him."

"Don't strain yourself. Davos will tell you quite freely himself."

"I can't wait."

By now I had heard one putdown too many about the creative craft. It was late, I had had a miserable day, Helena would be fretting and the thought of soothing her anxieties grew more appealing every minute.

I said I thought the rain had stopped. Then I bade the Mother of the Company a gruffly filial good night.

Hardly had I entered my tent when I knew that I should have been somewhere else tonight.

Twenty

Something had happened to our Nabataean priest.

Davos was holding Musa up as if he was going to collapse. They were in our section of the tent, with Helena in attendance. Musa was soaking wet and shuddering, either with cold or terror. He was deathly pale and looked in shock.

I glanced at Helena and could tell she had only just started extracting the story. She turned aside discreetly, attending to the fire while Davos and I stripped the priest of his wet clothes and wrapped him in a blanket. He was less sturdily built than either of us, but his physique was strong enough; years of climbing the high mountains of his native city had toughened him. He kept his eyes downcast.

"Not much to say for himself!" muttered Davos. With Musa, that was hardly unusual.

"What happened?" I demanded. "It's peeing down outside like customers in a cold bathhouse privy, but he shouldn't be this wet."

"Fell in a reservoir."

"Do me a favor, Davos!"

"No, it's right!" he explained, with an endearingly sheepish air. "After the play a group of us went looking for some wineshop that the clowns thought they knew about—"

"I don't believe it! In a storm like this?"

"Performers need to unwind. They persuaded your man to come along."

"I don't believe that either. I've never seen him drink."

"He seemed interested," Davos insisted stolidly. Musa himself remained clammed up, shivering in Helena's blanket and looking even more strained than usual. I knew I couldn't trust Musa, since he was representing The Brother; I scrutinized the actor, wondering whether I trusted him.

Davos had a square face with quiet, regretful eyes. Short, no-nonsense black hair topped his head. He was built like a cairn of Celtic rocks, basic, long-lasting, dependable, broadly based; not much would topple him. His view of life was dry. He looked as if he had seen the whole spectacle—and wouldn't waste his money on a second entrance fee. For my purposes, he seemed too bitter to waste effort on pretense. Though if he did want to delude me, I knew he was a good enough actor to do it.

Yet I could not see Davos as a killer.

"So what exactly happened?" I asked.

Davos continued his story. In his voice, which was a magnificent baritone, it seemed like a public performance. That's the trouble with actors; everything they say sounds completely believable. "The Twins' fabulous entertainment spot was supposed to be outside the rampart wall, on the eastern side of the city—"

"Spare me the tourists' itinerary." I was kicking myself for not having stayed close. If I had gone on this crazy tour myself I might at least have seen what had happened—maybe have prevented it. And I might even have got a drink out of the trip. "Where does a reservoir come into this?"

"There are a couple of great water cisterns to conserve rain." They must be full enough this evening. Fortune was now dumping a whole year's rainfall on Bostra. "We had to go around one. It's built within a huge embankment. There was a narrow elevated path, people were larking about a bit, and somehow Musa slipped into the water."

It would have been beneath him to trail off; Davos paused portentously. I gave him a long stare. Its meaning would have been obvious, onstage or off. "Who exactly was larking? And how did Musa come to 'slip'?"

The priest lifted his head for the first time. He still said nothing, but he watched Davos answer me. "Who do you think was larking? The Twins for two, and several of the stagehands. They were pretending to push one another about on the edge of the walkway. But I don't know how he slipped." Musa made no attempt to inform us. For the moment I left him alone.

Helena brought a warm drink for Musa. She fussed over him protectively, giving me a chance to talk to the actor apart. "You are sure you didn't see who pushed our friend?"

Like me, Davos had lowered his voice. "I wasn't aware I needed to look. I was watching my step. It was pitch dark and slippery enough without fools playing up."

"Was the accident on the way to the wineshop, or on the way back?"

"The way there." So no one had been drunk. Davos understood what I was thinking. If somebody had tripped up the Nabataean, whoever it was had fully intended him to fall.

"What's your opinion of Tranio and Grumio?" I asked thoughtfully.

"A mad pair. But that's traditional. Being witty all night on-stage makes clowns unpredictable. Who can blame them when you listen to the standard of playwrights' jokes?" Shrugging, I accepted the professional insult, as I was supposed to. "Most clowns have fallen off a ladder once too often anyway." A stage trick, presumably. I must have looked bemused; Davos interpreted: "Dented heads; not all there."

"Our two seem bright enough," I grunted.

"Bright enough to cause trouble," he agreed.

"Would they go as far as killing?"

"You're the investigator, Falco. You tell me."

"Who said I was an investigator?"

"Phrygia mentioned it."

"Well do me a favor, don't pass on the news any further! Blabbing isn't going to help my task." There was no chance of making discreet inquiries in this company. No one had any idea of how to hold their tongue and let you get on with it. "Are you and Phrygia close?"

"I've known the gorgeous old stick for twenty years, if that's what you mean."

Beyond the fire I could sense that Helena Justina was watching him curiously. Later, after observing him here, the intuitive girl would tell me whether Davos had been Phrygia's lover in the past, or was now, or merely wished to be. He had spoken with the assurance of an old acquaintance, a troupe member who had earned himself the right to be consulted about a newcomer.

"She told me about being asked to play Medea at Epidaurus."

"Ah that!" he commented quietly, with a soft smile.

"Did you know her then?" In reply to my question he nodded. It was a reply of sorts—the kind of simple answer that leads down a dead end. I tackled him directly: "And what about Heliodorus, Davos? How long had you known him?"

"Too long!" I waited, so he added more temperately: "Five or six seasons. Chremes picked him up in southern Italy. He knew

an alphabet or two; seemed ideal for the job." This time I ignored the arrow.

"You didn't get on?"

"Is that right?" He was not truculent, merely secretive. Trucu-
lence, being based on simple motives such as guilt or fear, is easier
to fathom. Secrecy could have any number of explanations—
including the straightforward one that Davos had a polite personality. However, I did not ascribe his reserved manner to mere tact.

"Was he just an awful writer, or was it personal?"

"He was a bloody awful writer—and I bloody loathed the
creep."

"Any reason?"

"Plenty!" Suddenly Davos lost patience. He stood up, leaving
us. But the habit of making an exit speech overtook him: "Somebody will no doubt whisper to you, if they haven't yet: I had just
told Chremes the man was a troublemaker and that he ought to
be dropped from the company." Davos carried weight; it would
matter. There was more, however. "At Petra I gave Chremes an
ultimatum: either he dumped Heliodorus, or he lost me."

Surprised, I managed to fetch out, "And what was his decision?"

"He hadn't made any decision." The contempt in his tone revealed that if Davos had hated the playwright, his opinion of the
manager was nearly as low. "The only time in his life Chremes
ever made a choice was when he married Phrygia, and she organized that herself, due to pressing circumstances."

Afraid I would ask, Helena kicked me. She was a tall girl, with
an impressive length of leg. A glimpse of her fine ankle gave me
a *frisson* I could not enjoy properly at that moment. The warning
was unnecessary. I had been an informer long enough; I recognized the allusion, but I asked the question anyway: "That, I
take it, is a dark reference to an unwelcome pregnancy?
Chremes and Phrygia have no children with them now, so I assume the baby died?" Davos screwed up his mouth in silence, as

if reluctantly acknowledging the story. "Leaving Phrygia shackled to Chremes, apparently pointlessly? Did Heliodorus know this?"

"He knew." Full of his own anger, Davos had recognized mine. He kept his answer short and left me to deduce for myself the unpleasant follow-on.

"I suppose he used it to taunt the people involved in his normal friendly manner?"

"Yes. He stuck the knife in both of them at every opportunity."

I didn't need to elaborate, but tried it to put pressure on Davos: "He ragged Chremes about the marriage he regrets—"

"Chremes knows it was the best thing he ever did."

"And tormented Phrygia over the bad marriage, her lost chance at Epidaurus, and, probably, over her lost child."

"Over all those things," Davos answered, perhaps more guardedly.

"He sounds vicious. No wonder you wanted Chremes to get rid of him."

As soon as I said it I realized that this could be taken as a suggestion that *Chremes* had drowned the playwright. Davos picked up the implication, but merely smiled grimly. I had a feeling that if Chremes was ever accused, Davos would cheerfully stand by and see him convicted—whether or not the charge was a just one.

Helena, ever quick to smooth over sensitivities, broke in. "Davos, if Heliodorus was always wounding people so painfully, surely the company manager had a good excuse—and a personal motive—to dismiss him when you asked for it?"

"Chremes is incapable of decisions, even when it's easy. This," Davos told Helena heavily, "was difficult."

Before we could ask why, he had left the tent.

Twenty-one

I was beginning to see the picture: Chremes, Phrygia, and where Davos himself fitted in as the old friend who had mourned for their mistakes and his own lost opportunities. When Helena caught my eye, I checked with her: "What do you think?"

"He's not involved," she answered slowly. "I think he may have meant more to Phrygia in the past than he does now, but it was probably a long time ago. After knowing her and Chremes for twenty years, now he's just a critical but loyal friend."

Helena had been warming some honey for me. She rose and fetched it from the fire. I took the beaker, settling down more comfortably and giving Musa a reassuring smile. For a while none of us spoke. We sat in a close group, considering events.

I was aware of a change in atmosphere. As soon as Davos left the tent, Musa had relaxed. His manner became more open. Instead of huddling under his blanket he ran his hands through his hair, which had started to dry and curl up at the ends ridiculously. It made him look young. His dark eyes had a thoughtful expression; the mere fact that I could judge his expression marked a change in him.

I realized what was up. I had seen Helena looking after him as if he belonged to us, while he accepted her anxious attentions with little trace of his old wariness. The truth was clear. We had been together for a couple of weeks. The worst had happened: the damned Nabataean hanger-on had joined the family.

"Falco," he said. I could not remember him addressing me by name before. I gave him a nod. It was not unfriendly. He had not yet attained the position of loathing I reserved for my natural relatives.

"Tell us what happened," Helena murmured. The conversation was taking place in low voices, as if we were afraid there might be lurking figures outside the tent. That seemed unlikely; it was still a filthy night.

"It was a ridiculous expedition, ill conceived and ill planned." It sounded as if Musa had viewed his jolly night on the town as some military maneuver. "People had not taken enough torches, and those we had were waning in the damp."

"Who asked you to go on this drinking spree?" I broke in.

Musa recollected. "Tranio, I think."

"I guessed it might have been!" Tranio was not my chief suspect—or at least not yet, because I had no evidence—but he was first choice as a general stirrer-up of trouble.

"Why did you agree to go?" Helena queried.

He flashed her an astonishing grin; it split his face apart. "I thought you and Falco were going to be quarreling about the play." It was Musa's first joke: one aimed at me.

"We never quarrel!" I growled.

"Then I beg your pardon!" He said it with the polite insincerity of a man who shared our tent and knew the truth.

"Tell us about the accident!" Helena urged him, smiling.

The priest smiled too, more wickedly than we were used to, but immediately grew intense as he told his story. "Walking was difficult. We were stumbling, our heads low. People were grumbling, but nobody wanted to suggest turning back. When we were on the cistern's raised embankment, I felt somebody push me, like this—" He suddenly aimed a hard blow with the flat of his palm against the lower middle of my back. I braced my calves to avoid falling into the fire; he had quite a shove. "I fell down over the wall—"

"Jupiter! And of course you can't swim!"

Unable to swim myself, I viewed his predicament with horror. However, Musa's dark eyes looked amused. "Why do you say that?"

"It seemed a reasonable deduction, given that you live in a desert citadel—"

He raised a disapproving eyebrow, as if I had said something stupid. "We have water cisterns in Petra. Small boys always play in them. I can swim."

"Ah!" It had saved his life. But somebody else must have made the same mistake as me.

"It was very dark, however," Musa went on in his light, conversational way. "I was startled. The cold water made me gasp and lose my breath. I could not see any place to climb out. I was afraid." His admission was frank and straightforward, like everything he said or did. "I could tell that the water below me was deep. It felt many times deeper than a man. As soon as I could breathe, I shouted out very loudly."

Helena frowned angrily. "It's terrifying! Did anyone help you?"

"Davos quickly found a way down to the water's edge. He was roaring instructions, to me and to the other people. He was, I think . . ." Musa searched for the word in Greek. "Competent.

Then everyone came—the clowns, the stagehands, Congrio. Hands pulled me out. I do not know whose hands." That meant nothing. As soon as it became obvious he hadn't sunk and would be rescued, whoever tipped Musa into the water would help him out again to cover his own tracks.

"It's the hand that shoved you in that matters." I was thinking about our suspects list and trying to envisage who had been doing what on that embankment in the dark. "You haven't mentioned Chremes or Philocrates. Were they with you?"

"No."

"It sounds as if we can eliminate Davos as perpetrator, but we'll keep an open mind on all the rest. Do you know who had been walking closest to you beforehand?"

"I am not sure. I thought it was the Twins. A while before I had been talking to the bill-poster, Congrio. But he had fallen behind. Because of the height of the walkway and the wind, everyone had slowed up and strung out more. You could see figures, though not tell who they were."

"Were you in single file?"

"No. I was alone, others were in groups. The walkway was wide enough; it only seemed dangerous because it was high, and in darkness, and made slippery by the rain." When he did talk, Musa was extremely precise, an intelligent man talking in a language not his own. A man full of caution too. Not many people who have narrowly escaped death remain so calm.

There was a small silence. As usual it was Helena who faced up to asking the trickiest question: "Musa was pushed into the reservoir deliberately. So why," she inquired gently, "has he become a target?"

Musa's reply to that was a precise one too: "People think I saw the man who murdered the previous playwright." I felt a slight jar. His phrasing made it sound as if merely being a playwright was dangerous.

I considered the suggestion slowly. "We have never told any-body that. I always call you an interpreter."

"The bill-poster may have overheard us talking about it yes-terday," said Musa. I liked the way his mind worked. He had noticed Congrio lurking too close, just as I had, and had already marked him as suspicious.

"Or he may have told somebody else what he overheard." I swore quietly. "If my lighthearted suggestion that we made you a decoy brought this accident upon you, I apologize, Musa."

"People had been suspicious of us anyway," Helena rebutted. "I know there are all sorts of rumors about all three of us."

"One thing is sure," I said. "It looks as if we have made the playwright's murderer extremely jumpy merely by joining the group."

"He was there," Musa confirmed in a somber tone. "I knew he was there on the embankment above me."

"How was that?"

"When I first fell into the water, no one seemed to hear the splash. I sank fast, then rose to the surface. I was trying to catch my breath; at first I could not shout. For a moment I felt entirely alone. The other people sounded far off. I could hear their voices growing fainter as they walked away." He paused, staring into the fire. Helena had reached for my hand; like me she was sharing Musa's dreadful moment of solitude as he struggled to survive down in the black waters of the reservoir while most of his companions carried on oblivious.

Musa's face stayed expressionless. His whole body was still. He did not rant or make wild threats about his future actions. Only his tone clearly told us that the playwright's killer should be wary of meeting him again. "He is here," Musa said. "Among the voices that were going into the darkness, one man had started whistling."

Exactly like the man he had heard whistling as he came down from the High Place.

"I'm sorry, Musa." Apologizing again I was terse. "I should have foreseen this. I should have protected you."

"I am unharmed. It is well."

"Do you own a dagger?" He was vulnerable; I was ready to give him mine.

"Yes." Davos and I had not found it when we stripped him.

"Then wear it."

"Yes, Falco."

"Next time you'll use it," I commented.

"Oh yes." Again that commonplace tone, belying the compelling words. He was a priest of Dushara; I reckoned that Musa would know where to strike. There could be a swift, sticky fate awaiting the man who had whistled in the dark. "You and I will find this hill bandit, Falco." Musa stood up, keeping the blanket around him modestly. "Now I think we should all sleep."

"Quite right." I threw his own joke back at him: "Helena and I still have a lot of *quarreling* to do."

There was a teasing glint in Musa's eye. "Hah! Then until you have finished I must go back to the reservoir."

Helena scowled. "Go to bed, Musa!"

Next day we were setting off for the Decapolis. I made a vow to keep a watchful eye out for the safety of all of us.

Act Two
The Decapolis

The next few weeks. The settings are various rocky roads and hillside cities with unwelcoming aspects. A number of camels are walking about watching the action curiously.

SYNOPSIS: *Falco,* a jobbing playwright, and *Helena,* his accomplice, together with *Musa,* a priest who has left his temple for rather vague reasons, are traveling through the Decapolis in a search for Truth. Suspected of being imposters, they soon find themselves in danger from an anonymous *Plotter* who must be concealing himself among their newfound friends. Somebody needs to devise a sharp plan to penetrate his disguise. . . .

Twenty-two

Philadelphia: A pretty Greek name for a pretty Greek town, rather knocked about at present. It had been pillaged a few years earlier by the rebelling Jews. The inward-looking fanatics of Judaea had always hated the Hellenistic settlements across the Jordan in the Decapolis, places where good citizenship—which could be learned by anybody at a decent Greek city school—counted for more than inheriting a stern religion in the blood. The marauders from Judaea had made it plain with vicious damage to property what they thought of such airy tolerance. Then a Roman army under Vespasian had made it plain to the Judaeans what *we* thought about damage to property by heavily damaging theirs. Judaea was pretty quiet these days, and the Decapolis was enjoying a new period of stability.

Philadelphia was enclosed by steep-sided hills, seven in number, though far more parched than the founding hills of Rome. There was a well-placed precipitous citadel, with the town spilling outwards and downwards onto a broad valley floor where a stream wandered attractively, doing away with any obvious need for cisterns, I was glad to see. We made camp, and sat down in our tents for what I gathered was likely to be a long wait while Chremes tried to negotiate terms for performing a play.

We had now entered Roman Syria. On our original journey between Petra and Bostra I had been working through the company play box, but on the way here to the Decapolis I had been able to give more attention to our surroundings. The road from Bostra to Philadelphia was supposed to be a good one. That meant a lot of people used it: not the same thing.

To be a traveling theater group was not easy in these parts. The country people hated us because they identified us with the Greekified towns where we played, yet the townsfolk all thought we were uncivilized nomads because we traveled about. In the villages were the weekly markets, where we had nothing to offer that people valued; the cities were administrative centers where we paid neither poll tax nor property tax and had no voting rights, so we were outsiders there too.

If the cities despised us, there was a certain amount of prejudice on our side as well. We Romans viewed these Greek-founded towns as hotbeds of licentiousness. Philadelphia offered little promise of that, however. (Believe me, I looked hard for it.) The city was thriving in a pleasant way, although to a Roman the place was a backwater.

I sensed that this was typical. Had it not been for the great trade routes, the East would never have been more to Rome than a buffer against the might of Parthia. Even the trade routes could not alter the impression that the Ten Towns were mostly *small* towns, often in the middle of nowhere. Some had gained status when Alexander noticed them on his progress to world domination, but they had all achieved a position in history when Pompey first liberated them from the recurrent Jewish plunderers and established Roman Syria. Syria was important because it was our frontier with Parthia. But the Parthians were smoldering on the other side of the River Euphrates, and the Euphrates lay many miles from the Decapolis.

At least in the cities they all spoke Greek, so we could haggle and pick up the news.

"Are you going to send your 'interpreter' home now?" quipped Grumio rather pointedly when we arrived.

"What, to spare him another ducking?" With Musa scarcely dry from his near-fatal dip I was angry.

Helena answered him more quietly: "Musa is our traveling companion, and our friend."

Musa said nothing as usual until the three of us were in our tent. Then his eyebrows shifted upwards again in teasing wonder as he commented, "I am your friend!"

It carried a world of gentle amusement. Musa had the sweet-natured charm of many people in this region—and he was wielding it to notable effect. He had grasped that belonging to the Didius family conferred the perpetual right to play the fool.

To liven up Philadelphia, Chremes was planning to give them *The Rope* by Plautus. In the plot rope hardly features; the important item of interest is a disputed traveling trunk (more of a satchel in the Greek original; we Roman playwrights know how to think big when we adapt). There is, however, a protracted tug-of-war for possession of the trunk, to be performed in our staging by Tranio and Grumio. I had seen them rehearsing the scene already. Their hilarious performance had a lot to teach a budding playwright: mainly, that his script is irrelevant. It's the "business" that brings the crowd to its feet, and however sharp your stylus is, you can't write "business" down.

I wasted some effort in Philadelphia asking about Thalia's

missing person, without luck. Nor did anybody recognize the other name I was touting: Habib, the mysterious Syrian businessman who had visited Rome and expressed a questionable interest in circus entertainment. I wondered if his wife knew that while he was acting the world traveler he liked to make friends with bosomy snakedancers. (*Oh don't worry about it,* Helena assured me. *She knows all right!*)

On my return to camp I saw Grumio practicing dramatic stunts. I asked him to teach me how to fall off a ladder, a trick for which I could see plenty of uses in daily life. It was stupid to try; I had soon landed badly on a leg I had broken two years previously. It left me bruised and limping, worried that I might have shattered the bone a second time. While Grumio shook his head over the incident, I hopped off to recover in my tent.

As I lay complaining on my bed, Helena sat outside with something to read.

"Whose fault was this?" she had demanded. "You being stupid, or somebody putting you out of action?"

Reluctantly I admitted I had asked for the lesson myself. After a sketchy murmur of sympathy, she rolled down the tentflap and left me in semidarkness, as I had been concussed. I thought her attitude was a little satirical, but a nap seemed called for anyway.

The weather had grown hot. We were taking things extremely gently, knowing we would be baked far hotter later on; you have to beware of exhaustion when you are unused to desert conditions. I was all ready for a long snooze, but as I drowsed on the verge of it, I heard Helena call out "Hello there!" to a passerby.

I might have taken no notice, had not the masculine voice that answered her been laden with self-satisfaction. It was a handsome rich-toned tenor with seductive modulations, and I knew to whom it belonged: Philocrates, who thought himself the idol of all the girls.

Twenty-three

"Well, hello!" he responded, evidently overjoyed to find he had attracted the attention of my highly superior bloom. Men didn't need an exploratory chat with her banker before they found Helena Justina worth talking to.

I stayed put. But I had sat up.

From my dim hiding place I heard him tramp closer, the smart leather boots that always showed off his manly calves crunching on the stony ground. Footwear was his one extravagance, though he wore the rest of his threadbare outfit as if he were in regal robes. (Actually, Philocrates wore all his clothes like a man who was just about to shrug them off for indecent purposes.) From a theater seat he was extravagantly good-looking; stupid to pretend otherwise. But he turned into a ripe damson if you peered into the punnet closely: too soft, and browning under the skin. Also, though his physique was all in proportion, he was extremely small. I could look right over his neatly combed locks, and most of his scenes with Phrygia had to be played with her sitting down.

I imagined him striking a pose in front of Helena—and tried *not* to imagine Helena being impressed by the haughty good looks.

"May I join you?" He didn't mess about.

"Of course." I was all set to thunder out and defend her, though Helena seemed to be making a brave effort to cope. I could hear from her voice that she was smiling, a sleepy, happy smile. Then I heard Philocrates stretching out at her feet, where instead of looking like a smug dwarf he would simply look well honed.

"What's a beautiful woman like you doing here all on her own?" Dear gods, his chat line was so old it was positively rancid. Next thing he would be flaring his nostrils and asking her if she would like to see his war wounds.

"I'm enjoying this lovely day," replied Helena, with more serenity than she had ever shown with me when I first tried getting to know her. She used to swat me like a hornet on a honey jar.

"What are you reading, Helena?"

"Plato." It put a quick stop to the intellectual discussion.

"Well, well!" said Philocrates. This seemed to be his pause-filler.

"Well, well," echoed Helena placidly. She could be very unhelpful to men who were trying to impress her.

"That's a beautiful dress." She was in white. White had never suited Helena; I repeatedly told her so.

"Thank you," she answered modestly.

"I'll bet you look even better with it off. . . ." Mars blast his balls! Wide awake now, I was expecting my young lady to call out to me for protection.

"It's a paradox of science," stated Helena Justina calmly, "but when the weather gets as hot as this, people are more comfortable covered up."

"Fascinating!" Philocrates knew how to sound as if he meant it, though somehow I thought science was not his strong point. "I've been noticing you. You're an interesting woman." Helena was more interesting than this facile bastard knew, but if he started to investigate her finer qualities he would be sent on his way with my boot. "What's your star sign?" he mused, one of those pea-brained types who thought astrology was the straight route to a quick seduction. "A Leo, I should say . . ."

Jupiter! I hadn't used "What's your horoscope?" since I was eleven. He ought to have guessed Virgo; that would always get them giggling, after which you could cruise home.

"Virgo," stated Helena herself crisply, which should put a blight on astrology.

"You surprise me!" She surprised me too. I had been thinking Helena's birthday was in October, and was mentally making up jokes about Librans weighing up trouble. Trouble was what *I* would be in if I didn't learn the correct date.

"Oh I doubt if I could surprise you much, Philocrates!" she answered. The annoying wench must think I was asleep. She was playing up to him as if I didn't exist at all, let alone lying behind a tent wall growing furious, barely a stride away.

Philocrates had missed her irony. He laughed gaily. "*Really*? In my experience, girls who appear terribly serious and seem like vestal virgins can be a lot of fun!"

"Have you had fun with a lot of girls, Philocrates?" asked Helena innocently.

"Let's say, a lot of girls have had fun with me!"

"That must be very gratifying for you," Helena murmured.

Anyone who knew her well could hear her thinking, *Probably not so much fun for them!*

"I've learned a few tricks with the pleasure pipe." Two more words, and I would spring from the tent and tie up his pleasure pipe in a very tight Hercules knot.

"If that's an offer, I'm flattered, naturally." Helena was smiling, I could tell. "Apart from the fact that I couldn't possibly live up to your sophisticated standards, I'm afraid I have other commitments."

"Are you married?" he shot in.

Helena loathed that question. Her voice acquired bite. "Would that be a bonus? Deceiving husbands must be so amusing. . . . I was married once."

"Is your husband dead?"

"I divorced him." He *was* dead now in fact, but Helena Justina never referred to it.

"Hard-hearted girl! What was the fellow's crime?"

Helena's worst insults were always delivered in cool tone. "Oh he was just a normal arrogant male—deficient in morals, incapable of devotion, insensitive to a wife who had the good manners to be honest."

Philocrates passed it over as a reasonable comment. "And now you're available?"

"Now I live with someone else."

"Well, well . . ." I heard him shifting his ground again. "So where is the happy scribbler?"

"Probably up a date palm writing a play. He takes his work very seriously." Helena knew I had never done that, whatever job I was pretending to hold down. However, I did have an idea for a completely new play of my own. I had not discussed it with Helena; she must have noticed me thinking and guessed.

Philocrates sneered. "Pity his skill doesn't match his dedication!" What a bastard. I made a note to write him out of at least three scenes in my next adaptation. "I'm intrigued. What can this Falco have to offer a smart and intelligent girl like you?"

"Marcus Didius has wonderful qualities."

"An amateur author who looks as if he's been dragged through a thicket by a wild mule? The man's haircut should be an indictable offense!"

"Some girls like raffish charm, Philocrates. . . . He's entertaining and affectionate," Helena rebuked him. "He tells the truth. He doesn't make promises unless he can keep them, though sometimes he keeps promises he never even made. What I like most," she added, "is his loyalty."

"Is that right? He looks as if he knows his way around. How can you be certain he's faithful?"

"How can anyone ever be certain? The point is," Helena said gently, "that I believe it."

"Because he tells you?"

"No. Because he never feels he needs to."

"I suppose you're in love with him."

"I suppose I am." She said it unrepentantly.

"He's a lucky man!" exclaimed Philocrates insincerely. His mockery was evident. "And have *you* ever betrayed *him?*" His voice held a hopeful note.

"No." Hers was cool.

"And you're not going to try it now?" At last he was catching on.

"Probably not—though how can anyone ever be certain?" responded Helena graciously.

"Well, when you decide to try sipping from a different bowl— and you will, Helena, believe me—I'm available."

"You'll be the first candidate," she promised in a light tone. Ten minutes beforehand I would have burst from the tent and wrapped a guy rope around the actor's neck; instead I sat tight. Helena's voice hardly changed tone, though because I knew her I was ready for her new tack. She had finished with whimsy; she was taking charge. "Now may I ask you something very personal, Philocrates?"

His big chance to talk about himself. "Of course!"

"Would you mind telling me what your relations with the drowned playwright used to be?"

There was a brief pause. Then Philocrates complained spitefully, "So this is the price for being permitted to converse with your ladyship?"

Helena Justina did not balk. "It's simply the price for knowing someone who has been murdered," she corrected him. "And probably knowing his killer too. You can refuse to answer the question."

"From which you will draw your own conclusions?"

"That would seem reasonable. What have you to say?"

"I didn't get on with him. In fact we damn nearly came to blows," Philocrates confessed shortly.

"Why was that?" She hardly waited before adding, "Was it a quarrel over a girl?"

"Correct." He hated saying it. "We both received a put-down from the same woman. I did less badly then him, though." He was probably boasting to console himself. Helena, who understood arrogance, did not bother pursuing it.

"I'm sure you did," she flattered him sympathetically. "I won't ask who it was."

"Byrria, if you must know," he told her before he could stop himself. The poor rabbit was helpless; Helena had moved effortlessly from an object of seduction to his most confidential friend.

"I'm sorry. I doubt if it was personal, Philocrates. I've heard she is extremely ambitious and declines all approaches from men. I'm sure you rose above the rejection, but what about Heliodorus?"

"No sense of discretion."

"He kept on pestering her? That would make her all the more obdurate, of course."

"I hope so!" he growled. "There was better sport on offer, after all."

"There certainly was! If *you* had done her the honor . . . So you and the playwright had an ongoing rivalry. Did you hate him enough to kill him, though?"

"Great gods, no! It was only a tiff over a girl."

"Oh quite! Was that his attitude too?"

"He probably let it rankle. That was his kind of stupidity."

"And did you ever tackle Heliodorus about him bothering Byrria?"

"Why should I do that?" Philocrates' surprise sounded genuine. "She turned me down. What she did or did not do after that was no concern of mine."

"Did other people notice that he was being a nuisance?"

"Must have done. She never complained about it; that would have made him worse. But we all knew he kept putting pressure on her."

"So the man had no finesse?"

"No pride, anyway."

"And Byrria was constantly avoiding him. Did he write her bad parts?"

"Stinkers."

"Do you know of any other admirers Byrria might have?"

"I wouldn't notice."

"No," Helena agreed thoughtfully. "I don't expect you would. . . . Where were you when Heliodorus took his fatal walk to the High Place?"

"The last afternoon? I'd packed my bags for leaving Petra and was making good use of some spare time before we left."

"What were you doing?"

Helena had walked straight into it. He turned triumphantly vindictive: "I was up in one of the rock tombs with a frankincense merchant's pretty wife—and I was giving her the screwing of her life!"

"Silly of me to ask!" my lass managed to rally, though I guessed she was blushing. "I wish I'd known you then. I would have asked you to ask her the proper rate for buying incense gum."

Either her courage or simply her sense of humor finally broke through to him. I heard Philocrates laugh shortly, then there was a sudden movement and his voice came from a different level; he must have swung himself to his feet. His tone had changed. For once the admiration was unfeigned and unselfish: "You're incredible. When that bastard Falco ditches you, don't weep too long; make sure you come and console yourself with me."

Helena made no answer, and his small feet in their expensive boots scrunched away across the pebbly road.

I waited a suitable time, then emerged from the tent, stretching.

"Ah here's the mellifluous bard awakening!" teased the love of my life. Her quiet eyes surveyed me from the deep shadow of a sloppily brimmed sunhat.

"You're asking for a very rude pentameter."

Helena was reclining in a folding chair with her feet on a bale. We had learned the essential desert trick of pitching tent in the shade of a tree wherever possible; Helena had taken all the remaining patch of coolness. Philocrates must have been charcoal grilled like a mullet as he lay out in full sun while he talked to her. I was pleased to see it.

"You look nicely settled. Had a good afternoon?"

"Very quiet," said Helena.

"Anyone bother you?"

"No one I couldn't deal with . . ." Her voice dropped gently. "Hello, Marcus." She had a way of greeting me that was almost unbearably intimate.

"Hello, beautiful." I was tough. I could cope with having my wrath undermined by female trickery. Then she smiled at me softly so I felt my resolve going limp.

It was later now. The burning sun was dropping towards the horizon and losing its power. When I took the actor's place lying at her feet the situation would be virtually pleasant, even though the ground was stony and the stones still hot.

She knew I had been listening in. I pretended to look her over. Despite an effort to appear nonchalant I could feel a tendon going rigid in my neck at the thought of Philocrates eyeing her, then making suggestive remarks. "I hate that dress. White makes you look washed out."

Helena wriggled her toes in her sandals and answered peacefully, "When I want to attract someone in particular, I'll change it." A certain glint in her eye held a private message for me.

I grinned. Any man of taste liked Helena wearing blue or red. I was a man of taste who liked to be frank. "Don't bother. Just take the white one off." I assumed my station on the ground like a loyal dog. She leaned down and rumpled my indictable curls, while I looked up at her thoughtfully. I said, in a lower voice, "He was perfectly happy cruising the colonnades looking for a frolic with a flute girl. You didn't have to do that to him."

Helena raised an eyebrow. Watching her, I thought she colored up slightly. "Are you objecting to me flirting, Marcus?" We both knew I was in no position to do that. Hypocrisy had never been my style.

"Flirt with whom you like, if you can handle the results. I meant, you didn't have to make that poor peristyle prowler fall in love with you."

Helena didn't realize, or wouldn't acknowledge her influence. Five years of marriage to a disinterested prig in a senatorial toga had crushed most of her confidence. Two years of being adored by me had so far failed to revive it. She shook her head. "Don't be romantic, Marcus."

"No?" I was on his side, partly. "I just happen to know what it feels like to realize abruptly that the girl you are mentally undressing is staring back at you with eyes that can see your soul naked." Hers were the eyes I meant. Rather than look into them at that moment I changed the subject flippantly: "That's certainly not a scroll of Plato in your lap."

"No. It's the collection of ribald stories I found among your box of plays."

"What is this thing—some notes by Heliodorus?"

"I shouldn't think so, Marcus. There seem to be several hand-writings, but none look like his awful scrawl." I had been complaining about the dead man's revisions on the play scrolls, most of which were illegible. Helena went on, "In places the ink has faded; it looks quite old. Besides, everyone says Heliodorus had no feeling for jokes, and these are very funny. If you like," she suggested seductively, "I'll read some of the rude ones out to you . . ."

The actor was right. Serious girls who look like vestal virgins can be a lot of fun—provided you can persuade them it's you they want to have fun with.

Twenty-four

The Rope went well. We put it on for a second night, and nobody came. We left town.

Our next destination was Gerasa. It lay forty miles to the north—two days with decent transport, but probably twice that with our group of cheap camels and heavily laden wagons. Cursing Philadelphia for an uncultured dump and damning Plautus as an unfunny hack, we turned out backs on the town, flung the play to the bottom of the heap, and creaked on our way. At least Gerasa had a prosperous reputation; people with money might be looking for something to spend it on. (More likely, news that our production of *The Rope* was as stiff as cheese would run ahead of us.)

One way and another the pointers were strong for an urgent interview with Byrria. The dead playwright had been nursing his lust for her, and most of our male suspects seemed to be tangled in the same set. Besides, if Helena could flirt with the masculine star, I could allow myself a chat with his delicious female counterpart.

It was easy to arrange. A few nosy passersby had spotted my darling's dalliance with Philocrates; already everyone knew about it. Pretending to quarrel with her about her diminutive admirer, I hopped off our cart and sat on a rock with my chin in my hands, looking glum. I had left Helena with Musa; protection for both of them. I was unwilling to leave either for long without cover.

Slowly the tired parade of our company went past me, all bare legs on backboards, bursting baskets, and bad jokes. Those who had camels mostly led them on foot; if you've ever been up on a camel you'll know why. Those in the wagons were scarcely more comfortable. Some of the stagehands had given up having their ribs jolted and had chosen to walk. People carried cudgels or long knives in their belts in case we were attacked by desert raiders; some of the orchestra piped or banged on their instruments—an even more successful deterrent to nomadic thieves.

Byrria drove her own cart. That summed her up. She shared herself with no one, and relied on no one. As she drew level I stood up and hailed her. She didn't want to give me a lift, but she was almost at the end of the caravan and had to accept that if she didn't I might be left behind. Nobody thought they needed a writer, but people like keeping a target to mock.

"Cheer up!" I cried, as I sprang aboard with a lithe twist of the torso and a charming grin. "It won't happen!"

She continued to scowl bleakly. "Drop the antique routine, Falco."

"Sorry. The old lines are the best—"

"Diana of the Ephesians! Put a lid on it, poser."

I was about to think, *This never happens to Philocrates,* when I remembered that it had.

She was twenty, perhaps less. She had probably been on the stage for eight or nine years; it's one of those professions where girls with looks start young. In a different social circle she would have been old enough to become a vestal. There can't be much difference between being a priestess and an actress, except for public status. They both involve fooling an audience with a ritual performance in order to make the public believe in the unbelievable.

I did my best to be professional, but Byrria's looks were impossible to ignore. She had a triangular face with green eyes like an Egyptian cat's set wide above high cheekbones and a thin, perfect nose. Her mouth had a strange lopsided quirk that gave her an ironic, world-weary air. Her figure was as watchable as her face, small and curvaceous, and hinting of unrevealed possibilities. To finish the business, she had a dramatic knack of looping up her warm brown hair with a couple of bronze hairpins, so it not only looked unusual but stayed in place, showing off a tantalizing neck.

Her voice seemed too low for such a neat person; it had a huskiness that was completely distracting when combined with her experienced manner. Byrria gave the impression she was holding all the competition at arm's length while she waited for the right person to move in on her. Even though he knew it was a false impression, any man she met would have to try.

"Why the hatred of men, flower?"

"I've known some, that's why."

"Anyone in particular?"

"Men are never particular."

"I meant, anyone special?"

"Special? I thought we were talking about men!"

I can recognize an impasse. Folding my arms, I sat in silence.

In those days the road to Gerasa was a poor one, begging for a military highway to be thrust through to Damascus. It would be done. Rome had spent a great deal of money on this region during the Judaean troubles, so inevitably in peacetime we would be spending even more. Once the region settled down the Decapolis would be dragged up to decent Roman standards. In the meantime we were suffering on an old Nabataean caravan route that nobody maintained. It was a lonely landscape. Later we reached a level plain and crossed a tributary of the Jordan through more fertile pasture into thick pine forest. But this early stage of our trip involved a rocky track among scrubby hills with only occasional glimpses of low nomad tents, few of them with visible occupants. Driving was not easy; Byrria had to concentrate.

As I expected, after a short time the lady felt obliged to fire more arrows at me. "I have a question, Falco. When do you intend to stop slandering me?"

"Goodness, I thought you were about to ask for the address of my cloak-maker or my recipe for tarragon marinade! I know nothing about any slander."

"You're making out to everyone that Heliodorus died because of me."

"I never said that." It was only one possibility. So far it seemed the most likely explanation for the playwright's drowning, but until I had proof I kept an open mind.

"I had nothing to do with it, Falco."

"I do know you didn't push him into the cistern and hold his head under. A man did that."

"Then why keep hinting I was involved?"

"I wasn't aware that I had. But face facts: like it or not, you're a popular girl. Everyone keeps telling me Heliodorus was after you but you weren't having it. Maybe one of your friends tackled him. Maybe it was a secret admirer. It's always possible someone knew you would be pleased if the bastard was out of the way, and tried to help."

"That's a horrible suggestion!" She was frowning bitterly. On Byrria a frown looked good.

I was starting to feel protective. I *wanted* to prove the murder was nothing to do with her. I wanted to find a different motive. Those wonderful eyes were working impossible magic. I told myself I was too professional to let a dainty little actress with a pretty set of wide-spaced peepers overcome me—then I told myself not to be such a fool. I was stuck, just as anyone would be. We all hate murderers to be beautiful. Before long if I did unearth evidence implicating Byrria as an accomplice I would find myself considering whether to bury it in an old hay sack at the bottom of a drainage ditch. . . .

"All right, just tell me about Heliodorus." My voice was rasping; I cleared my throat. "I know he was obsessed with you."

"Wrong." She spoke very quietly. "He was just obsessed with getting what he wanted."

"Ah! Too pushy?"

"That's a man's way of putting it!" Now she sounded bitter, her voice rising. " '*A bit too pushy*' almost makes it sound as though it was my fault he went away disappointed."

She was staring ahead, even though the road was easier to travel at this point. Away to our right a teenaged girl watched over a small flock of lean brown goats. In another direction vultures wheeled gracefully. We had started out early on purpose; now the heat was beginning to reflect off the stony track with dazzling force.

Byrria was not intending to help me. I pressed for more details: "Heliodorus tried it on, and you rebuffed him?"

"Correct."

"Then what?"

"What do you think?" Her voice remained dangerously level. "He assumed that saying 'No' meant 'Yes, please—with force.' "

"He *raped* you?"

She was a person who showed anger by very carefully keeping her temper. For a moment, while I reeled at this new angle, she also stayed silent. Then she attacked me contemptuously: "I suppose you're going to tell me that there is always provocation, that women always want it, that rape never happens."

"It happens."

We were raging at one another. I suppose I knew why. Understanding it did not help.

"It happens," I repeated. "And I don't just mean men attacking women, be it strangers or acquaintances. I mean husbands misusing their wives. Fathers having 'special secrets' with their children. Masters treating their slaves like so much bought meat. Guards torturing their prisoners. Soldiers bullying new recruits. High officials blackmailing—"

"Oh be quiet!" There was no mollifying her. Her green eyes flashed and she tossed her head so the ringlets danced, but there was nothing charming in the gesture. Undoubtedly enjoying the fact that she had misled me, she exclaimed, "It did not happen to me, in fact. He had me on the ground, he had my wrists pinioned above my head and my skirts up, and the bruises he made forcing his knee between my thighs were still showing a month later, but somebody came looking for him and rescued me."

"I'm glad." I meant it, even though something in the way she had forced me to hear the details was subtly disturbing. "Who was the useful friend?"

"Mind your own business."

"Maybe it matters." I wanted to force her to say it. Instinct told me I ought to identify her rescuer. She knew something I wanted to hear, and I could easily have become as much of a bully as Heliodorus.

"What matters to me," Byrria flared angrily, "is that I *thought* Heliodorus was going to rape me. Afterwards I was living with the knowledge that if he ever caught me on my own he was bound to try again—but all you need to know is that I never, ever went near him. I tried to know where he was always, because I made certain that I kept as far away from him as possible."

"You can help me then," I said, ignoring her hysterical edge. "Did you know he was going up the mountain that last day at Petra? Did you see who went with him?"

"You mean, do I know who killed him?" The girl was effortlessly bright—and deliberately made me feel like an idiot. "No. I just noticed the playwright was missing when the rest of us gathered at the theater ready to leave."

"All right." Refusing to be put off, I tackled it another way. "Who *was* there—and when did they arrive at the meeting point?"

"It won't help you," Byrria assured me. "When we noticed your girlfriend telling an official a body had been found, we had already missed Heliodorus and were complaining about him. Allowing time for you to have found the body and Helena to have come back down the hill—" I hate witnesses who have done my thinking for me "—then he must have been dead before any of us gathered at the theater. Actually I was one of the last to get there. I turned up at the same time as Tranio and Grumio, who were looking the worse for wear, as usual."

"Why were you late?" I grinned cheekily, in the vain hope of reasserting myself. "Saying a fond farewell to a manly paramour?"

Up ahead people were stopping so we could rest during the simmering heat of midday. Byrria reined in, then literally pushed me out of her cart.

I sauntered back to my own wagon.

"Falco!" Musa had his headdress wrapped across his lower face in the Eastern manner; he looked lean, cool, and much wiser than I felt in my short Roman tunic, with my bare arms and legs burning and sweat rivuleting down my back beneath the hot cloth. Byrria must have worked her spell on him too; for once he seemed actively curious. "Did you learn anything from the beautiful one?"

I burrowed in our lunch basket. "Not much."

"So how did you get on?" asked Helena innocently.

"The woman's incorrigible. I had to fend off her advances in case the donkey bolted."

"That's the problem with being so witty and good-looking," retorted Helena. Musa burst into a rare fit of giggling. Helena, having denounced me in her normal offhand manner, merely carried on with the more important work of cleaning dust from her right sandal.

Ignoring them both, I sat spitting out date stones like a man who had something extremely intriguing to think about.

Twenty-five

Gerasa: otherwise known as "Antioch on the Chrysorhoas."

Antiochia itself had a reputation for soft living. My brother Festus, who could be relied on as a scandalmonger, had told me that as a legionary posting it was notorious for the routine debauchery of its happy garrison. Life there was continual festivity; the city resounded to minstrels playing harps and drums. . . . I was hoping to visit Antiochia. But it lay a long way north, so for now I had to be content with its namesake. Chrysorhoan Antiochia had plenty to offer, though I personally was never offered much debauchery, with or without minstrels.

Gerasa had grown from a small walled town on a knoll into a larger suburban center through which ran the River Chrysorhoas, the Golden River, a bit of a stream that, compared to the noble

Tiber, could barely support three minnow-fishers and a few
women slapping dirty shirts on stones. Pillaged by Jews in the
Rebellion, and then plundered again by Romans because one of
the main leaders of the Jewish Revolt was a Gerasene, the town
had been fitted up recently with new city walls that sprouted a
coronet of watchtowers. Two of these defended the Watergate
through which the Golden River rushed out via a sluice that di-
rected its water under some pressure over a ten-foot waterfall. As
we waited to enter the city we could see and hear the cascade to
our right.

"This looks like a fine place for accidents!" I warned anyone
who would listen. Only Musa took notice; he nodded, with his
usual seriousness. He had the air of a fanatic who for the sake of
Truth might volunteer to stand beside the sluice waiting for our
murderer to tip him into the racing stream.

We were held up at the Southern Gate, waiting for customs
clearance. Gerasa lay conveniently at the junction of two major
trade routes. Its income from caravan tributes was such that
twice it had smoothly survived being plundered. There must
have been plenty of raiders to pillage, then afterwards, in the Pax
Romana, there remained ample cash for restoration work. According to a site plan we later saw pegged up in the cleared area
that was to become the main piazza, Gerasa was in the grip of a
spectacular building program that had started twenty years earlier and was projected to continue for several decades. Children
were growing up here who had only ever seen a street that was
half roped off by stonemasons. A bunch of shrines on the acropolis were being given cosmetic attention; waiting at the town
gate we could hear hammers clanging frenziedly in the sanctuary
of Zeus; suburban villas were being knocked out by smiling con-
tractors like beans from a pod; and surveyors' poles impeded
progress everywhere, marking out a new street grid and an ambitious elliptical forum.

In any other city in any corner of the Empire, I would have

said the grandiose plan would never happen. But Gerasa undoubtedly possessed the wherewithal to drape itself in colonnades. Our own interrogation gave an indication of what kind of tribute (a polite word for bribe) the citizens expected to extract from the thousand or so caravans that plodded up each year from Nabataea.

"Total camels?" barked the tariff master, a man in a hurry.

"Twelve."

His lip curled. He was used to dealing in scores and hundreds. Even so, his scroll was at the ready. "Donkeys?"

"None with salable merchandise. Only private goods."

"Detail the camels. Number of loads of myrrh in alabaster vessels?"

"None."

"Frankincense? Other aromatics? Balsam, bdellium, ladanum gum, galbanum, any of the four types of cardamom?"

"No."

"Number of loads of olive oil? A load equals four goatskins," he qualified helpfully.

"None."

"Gemstones, ivory, tortoiseshell, or pearls? Select woods?" To save time we simply shook our heads. He was getting the picture. He ran through the straightforward spices almost without looking up from his list: "Peppers, ginger, allspice, turmeric, sweet flag, mace, cinnamon, saffron? No . . . Dried goods?" he tried hopefully.

"None."

"Individual number of slaves? Other than for personal use," he added, with a sneer that said he could see none of us had been manicured or massaged by a sloe-eyed, sleek-skinned bondsman in the recent past.

"None."

"What exactly," he asked us, with an expression that veered between suspicion and horror, "*are* you dealing in?"

"Entertainment."

Unable to decide whether we were daft or dangerous, he waved us angrily to a holding post while he consulted with a colleague.

"Is this delay serious?" whispered Helena.

"Probably."

One of the girls from our scratch orchestra laughed. "Don't worry. If he wants to cause trouble we'll set Afrania onto him!"

Afrania, who was a creature of wondrous and self-assured beauty, played the flute for us and danced a bit. Those who were not accompanied by fastidious girlfriends found other uses for her. As we waited she was flirting lazily with Philocrates but heard her name and glanced over. She made a gesture whose grossness belied her superbly placid features. "He's all yours, Ione! Salting officials calls for an expert. I couldn't compete!"

Her friend Ione turned away dismissively. Attaching herself to us, she gave us a grin (minus two front teeth), then hoicked half a loaf from somewhere among her crumpled skirts, ripped it into portions, and handed them around.

Ione was a tambourinist, and a startling character. Helena and I tried not to stare, though Musa gazed at her openly. Ione's compact form was swathed in at least two stoles, wound crossways over her bosom. She wore a snake bracelet covering half her left arm and various glass-stoned finger-rings. Triangular earrings, so long they brushed her shoulders, clattered with red and green beads, loops of wire, and metallic spacers. She went in for whippy belts, thongy sandals, swoony scarves, and clownish face makeup. Her wild crinkly hair flared back from her head in all directions like a radiate diadem; odd sections of the mass of untamed locks were braided into long thin plaits, tied up with wisps of wool. In color the hair was mainly a tarnished bronze, with matted reddish streaks that were almost like dried blood after a messy fight. There was a positive air to her; I reckoned Ione would win all her fights.

Somewhere beneath these flash trappings lay a small-featured young woman with a sharp wit and a big heart. She was brighter than she pretended. I can handle it, but for most men that's a dangerous girl.

She had noticed Musa gaping. Her grin widened in a way that did finally make him look uncomfortable. "Hey you!" Her shout was raucous and brisk. "Better not stand too close to the Golden River—and don't go near the double pool! You don't want to end up as a soggy sacrifice in the Festival of Maiuma!"

Whether or not the Petran mountain god Dushara demands that his priests be chaste, Ione's boldness was too much for ours. Musa rose to his feet (he had been squatting on his heels like a nomad while we were held up by the customs officer). He turned away, looking haughty. I could have told him; it never works.

"Oh bull's balls, I've offended him!" laughed the tambourinist easily.

"He's a shy lad." It was safe for me to smile at her; I had protection. Helena was lolling against me, probably to annoy Philocrates. I tickled her neck, hoping he would spot the proprietary gesture. "What's Maiuma, Ione?"

"Gods, don't you know? I thought it was famous."

"It's an antique nautical festival," Helena recited. She always did the heavy reading-up when we were planning foreign trips. "Of resonant notoriety," she added, as if she knew that would catch my interest. "Believed to derive from Phoenicia, it involves, among other shameless public practices, the ritual immersion of naked women in sacred pools."

"Good idea! While we're here, let's try to take in an evening of sacred pond-watching. I like to collect a salacious rite or two to liven up my memoirs—"

"Shut up, Falco!" I deduced that my senator's daughter was

not planning a plunge at the pleasure ground. She enjoyed herself being superior. "I imagine there is a great deal of shrieking, plenty of overpriced sour red wine on sale, and everyone goes home afterwards with sand down their tunics and foot fungus."

"Falco?" Whether it was Helena's use of my name that roused her, Ione suddenly bolted down the last of her bread. She squinted at me sideways, still with crumbs on her face. "You're the new boy, aren't you? Hah!" she exclaimed derisively. "Written any good plays lately?"

"Enough to learn that my job is to provide creative ideas, neat plots, good jokes, provocative thoughts, and subtle dialogue, all so that cliché-ridden producers can convert them into trash. Played any good tunes lately?"

"All I have to do is bash in time for the boys!" I might have known she was a girl who liked innuendo. "What sort of plays do you like then, Falco?" It sounded a straight question. She was one of those girls who seem to threaten abuse, then disarm you by taking a sensible interest in your hobbies.

Helena joked: "Falco's idea of a good day at the theater is watching all three Oedipus tragedies, without a break for lunch."

"Oh, very Greek!" Ione must have been born under the Pons Sublicius; she had the authentic twang of the Tiber. She was a Roman; "Greek" was the worst insult she could hand out.

"Ignore the silly patter from the tall piece in the blue skirt," I said. "Her family all sell lupins on the Esquiline; she only knows how to tell lies."

"That so?" Ione gazed at Helena admiringly.

I heard myself admitting, "I had a good idea for a play I want to write myself." We were obviously going to be stuck in customs for a long time. Bored and weary after the forty miles from Philadelphia, I fell into the trap of betraying my dreams: "It starts off with a young wastrel meeting the ghost of his father—"

Helena and Ione looked at each other, then chorused frankly: "Give up, Falco! It will never sell tickets."

"That's not all you do, is it?" young Ione demanded narrowly. After my long career as an informer, I recognized the subtle air of self-importance before she spoke. Some evidence was about to emerge. "They say you're sniffing out what happened up on the magic mountain in Petra. I could tell you a few things!"

"About Heliodorus? I found him dead, you know." She presumably did know, but openness is inoffensive and fills in time while you gather your wits. "I'd like to know who held him under," I said.

"Maybe you should ask why they did it?" Ione was like a young girl teasing me on a treasure hunt, openly excited. Not a good idea if she really did know something. Not when most of my suspects were all close by and probably listening.

"So are you able to tell me that?" I pretended to grin in return, keeping it light.

"You're not so dumb; you'll get there in the end. I bet I could give you some clues, though."

I wanted to press for details, but the customs post was far too public. I had to shut her up, for her own sake as much as for my own chances of finding the killer.

"Are you willing to talk to me sometime, but maybe not here?"

In response to my question she glanced downwards, until her eyes were virtually closed. Painted spikes lengthened the appearance of her eyelashes; her lids were brushed with something that looked like gold dust. Some of the expensive prostitutes who serviced senators at Roman dinner parties would pay thousands for an introduction to Ione's cosmetics mixer. Long practiced in buying information, I wondered how many amethystine marbled boxes and little pink glass scent vials I would have to offer to acquire whatever she was touting.

Unable to resist the mystery, I tried suggestion: "I'm working on the theory it was a man who hated him for reasons connected with women—"

"Ha!" Ione barked with laughter. "Wrong direction, Falco! Completely wrong! Believe me, the scribe's ducking was purely professional."

It was too late to ask her more. Tranio and Grumio, who were always hanging about near the orchestra girls, came mooching up like spare waiters at an orgy wanting to offer limp garlands in return for a large tip.

"Another time," Ione promised me, winking. She made it sound like an offer of sexual favors. "Somewhere quiet when we're on our own, eh Falco?"

I grinned bravely, while Helena Justina assumed the expression of the jealous lover in a one-sided partnership.

Tranio, the taller, wittier clown, gave me a long dumb stare.

Twenty-six

The customs officer suddenly turned on us as if he could not imagine why we were loitering in his precious space, and shooed us off. Without giving him a chance to change his mind, we shot in through the town gate.

We had come about fifteen years too early. It was not much in the scheme of town planning, but too long for hungry performers who were gnawing on their last pomegranate. The site diagram of the future Gerasa showed an ambitious design with not one but two theaters of extravagant proportions, plus another, smaller auditorium outside the city at the site of the notorious water festival where Helena had forbidden me to go and leer. They needed all these stages—now. Most were still only architectural drawings. We soon discovered that the situation for performers was desperate. At present we were stuck with one very basic arena in the older part of town, over which all comers had to haggle—and there was plenty of competition.

It was turmoil. In this town we were just one small act in a mad circus. Gerasa had such a reputation for riches that it drew buskers from all the parched corners of the East. To be offering a simple play with flute, drum, and tambourine accompaniment was nothing. In Gerasa they had every gaggle of scruffy acrobats with torn tunics and only one left boot between them, every bad-tempered fire-eater, every troupe of sardine-dish spinners and turnip jugglers, every one-armed harpist or arthritic stilt-walker. We could pay half a denarius to see the Tallest Man in Alexandria (who must have shrunk in the Nile, for he was barely a foot longer than I was), or a mere copper for a backward-facing goat. In fact for a quadrans or two extra I could have actually *bought* the goat, whose owner told me he was sick of the heat and the slowness of trade and was going home to plant beans.

I had a long conversation with this man, in the course of which I nearly did acquire his goat. So long as he kept me talking, taking on an unconvincing sideshow freak seemed quite a decent business proposition. Gerasa was that kind of town.

Entering by the South Gate had placed us near the existing theater, but it had the disadvantage of marking us out for hordes of grubby children who mobbed us, trying to sell cheap ribbons and badly made whistles. Looking serious and cute, they offered their wares in silence, but otherwise the noise from the packed streets was unbearable.

"This is hopeless!" shouted Chremes, as we huddled together to discuss what to do. His disgust with *The Rope* after its failed second outing at Philadelphia had faded so quickly that he was now planning for us to repeat it while the Twins were in practice for their tug-of-war. However, the indecisiveness Davos had complained about soon reappeared. Almost before we dug the props out, new doubts set in. "I'd like you to brush up *The Arbitration,* Falco." I had read it; I complained wittily that *The Rope* had much more pulling power. Chremes ignored me. Quibbling about the play was only half his problem. "We can either travel on straightaway, or I'll do what I can to obtain an appearance. If we stay, the bribe to the booker will wipe out most of the ticket money, but if we go on we've lost a week without earning—"

Clearly irritated, Davos weighed in. "I vote to see what you can get. Mind you, with all this cheap competition it's going to be like doing The Play We Never Mention on a wet Thursday in Olynthus. . . ."

"What's the unmentionable play?" asked Helena.

Davos gave her a shifty look, pointed out that by definition he wasn't allowed to mention it, and shrugged off her meek apology.

I tried another ploy for avoiding the manager's turgid idea of a repertoire: "Chremes, we need a good draw. I've a brand-new idea you may like to try. A lad about town meets the ghost of his newly dead father, who tells him—"

"You say the father's dead?" He was already confused and I hadn't even reached the complicated bit.

"Murdered. That's the point. You see, his ghost catches the hero by the tunic sleeve and reveals who snuffed out his pa—"

"Impossible! In New Comedy ghosts never speak." So much for my big idea. Chremes could be firm enough when crushing a genius; having rejected my masterpiece he went wittering on as usual. I lost interest and sat chewing a straw.

Eventually, when even he was tired of havering, Chremes stumped off to see the theater manager; we sent Davos along to stiffen him. The rest of us moped around looking sick. We were too hot and depressed to do anything until we knew what was happening.

Grumio, who had a provocative streak, spoke up: "The play we don't mention is *The Mother-in-Law* by Terence."

"You just mentioned it!" Stung by Davos, Helena had become a literalist.

"I'm not superstitious."

"What's wrong with it?"

"Apart from the off-putting title? Nothing. It's his best play."

"Why the dirty reputation then?" I demanded.

"It was a legendary failure, due to the rival attractions of boxers, tightrope walkers, and gladiators." I knew how Terence must have felt.

We all looked gloomy. Our own situation seemed horribly similar. Our struggling little dramas were unlikely to draw crowds at Gerasa, where the populace had devised their own sophisticatedly ribald festival, the Phoenician Maiuma, to fill any quiet evening. Besides we had already glimpsed the street performers, and knew Gerasa could call on other entertainment that was twice as unusual and three times as noisy as ours, at half the cost.

Rather than think about our predicament, people started wandering off.

Grumio was still sitting nearby. I got talking to him. As usual when you look as if you're having a rich literary conversation, our companions left us severely alone. I asked him more about The Play We Never Mention, and quickly discovered he had a deep knowledge of theatrical history. In fact he turned out to be quite an interesting character.

It was easy to dismiss Grumio. His round face could be taken for a sign of simplicity. Playing the dullard of the two clowns, he had been forced into a secondary role offstage as well as on. In fact he was highly intelligent, not to mention professional. Getting him on his own, without the noisy brilliance of Tranio to overshadow him, I learned that he saw himself as an exponent of an ancient and honorable craft.

"So how did you get into this line, Grumio?"

"Partly heredity. I'm following my father and grandfather.

Poverty comes into it. We never owned land; we never knew any other trade. All we had—a precious gift that most folk lack— was natural wit."

"And you can survive by this?"

"Not easily anymore. That's why I'm in a stage company. My ancestors never had to suffer like this. In the old days laughter-men were independent. They traveled around earning their meals with their varied skills—sleight of hand and tumbling, recitation, dancing—but most of all with a crackling repertoire of jokes. I was trained to the physical jerks by my father, and of course I inherited sixty years of family wisecracks. For me, it's a letdown to be stuck in Chremes' gang like this and tied to a script."

"You're good at it though," I told him.

"Yes, but it's dull. It lacks the edge of living on your wits; de-vising your patter on your feet; improvising the apt rejoinder; snapping out the perfect quip."

I was fascinated by this new side to the country clown. He was a much more thoughtful student of his art than I had given him credit for, though it was my own fault for assuming that playing the fool meant he was one. Now I saw that Grumio had a devotee's respect for the practice of humor; even for our dread-ful comedies he would polish his performance, though all the time he was hankering for better things. For him the old jokes really were the best—especially if he turned them out in a new guise.

This dedication meant he had a deep, private personality. There was far more to him than the sleepy character who yearned for girls and drink and let Tranio take the lead as much in their off-duty lives as in some tiresome plot. Under that fairly lightly worn mask, Grumio was his own man. Communicating wit is a lonely art. It demands an independent soul.

Being an informal stand-up comic at formal reclining dinners seemed a nerve-racking way of life to me. But if someone could do it, I would have thought there was a market for a satirist. I asked why Grumio had had to turn to lesser things.

"No call. In my father or grandfather's day all I would have needed in life were my cloak and shoes, my flask and strigil, a cup and knife to take to dinner, and a small wallet for my earnings. Everyone who could find the wherewithal would eagerly ask a wandering jokesmith in."

"Sounds just like being a vagrant philosopher!"

"A cynic," he agreed readily. "Exactly. Most cynics are witty and all clowns are cynical. Meet us on the road, and who could tell the difference?"

"Me, I hope! I'm a good Roman. I'd take a five-mile detour to avoid a philosopher."

He disabused me. "You won't be tested. No clown can do that any longer. I'd be run out of town like a warty beggar by the idlers who hang around the water tower inventing slander. Now everyone wants to be the funny man himself; all people like me can do is flatter them silly and feed them material. It's not for me; I won't be a yes-man. I get sick of pandering to other people's stupidity." Grumio's voice had a raw note. He had a real hatred for the amateur rivals he was deriding, a real lament for the deterioration of his trade. (I also noticed a strident belief in his own brilliance; clowns are an arrogant lot.) "Besides," he complained, "There are no morals. The new 'humor,' if you can call it that, is pure malicious gossip. Instead of making a genuine point, it's now good enough to repeat any ribald story without a thought for whether it's even true. In fact, making up a spiteful lie has become respectable. Today's 'jesters' are outright public nuisances."

A similar charge is often laid against informers. We too are supposed to be amoral vendors of overheard dirt, gutter know-alls who fabricate freely if we cannot produce hard facts; deliberate mixers, self-seekers, and stirrers. It's even regarded as a suitable insult for people to call us comedians. . . .

Abruptly Grumio lurched to his feet. There was a restlessness about him I had overlooked before; perhaps I had caused it by discussing his work. That does depress most people.

For a moment I felt I had annoyed or upset him. But then he waved a hand amiably enough, and sauntered off.

"What was all that about?" asked Helena curiously, coming up as usual just when I had been assuming she had her head down in business of her own.

"Just a history lesson about clowns."

She smiled. Helena Justina could make a thoughtful smile raise more questions than a dead mouse in a pail of milk. "Oh, men's talk!" she commented.

I leaned on my chin and gazed at her. She had probably been listening, then being Helena she had done some thinking too. We both had an instinct for certain things. I found myself being niggled by a sensation she must have shared: somewhere an issue that might be important had been raised.

Twenty-seven

To the great surprise of all of us, within the hour Chremes came rushing back to announce he had secured the theater; moreover it was for the very next night. Obviously the Gerasenes had no notion of fair turns. Chremes and Davos had happened to be demanding attention from the booking manager just when that grafter received a cancellation, so for the proverbial small fee we were allowed to snap up the vacancy, never mind who else had been waiting around town.

"They like an easy life here," Chremes told us. "All the booker wanted to be sure of was that we'd pay his sweetener." He told us how much the bribe had been, and some of us were of the opinion it would be more profitable to leave Gerasa now and play *The Arbitration* to a nomad's herd of sheep.

"Is this why the other troupe packed their traps?"

Chremes looked huffed that we were complaining after he had pulled off a triumph. "Not according to my information. They were a sleazy circus act. Apparently they could cope when their chief trapezist had a fall that left him paralyzed, yet when their performing bear caught a cold—"

"They lost their nerve," Tranio broke in snappily. "As we may do when all the groups who arrived here ahead of us find out how we jumped the queue and come looking for us!"

"We'll show the town something worth watching, then do a quick flit," Chremes answered with a casual air that said just how many times the company had fled places in a hurry.

"Tell that to the Chersonesus Taurica weightlifting team!" muttered Tranio.

Still, when you think you are about to make some money, nobody likes to be too ethical.

We all had an evening to ourselves. Revived by the prospect of work tomorrow we pooled our food and ate as a group, then went our separate ways. Those with cash could spend it on seeing a classic Greek tragedy performed by an extremely somber group from Cilicia. Helena and I were not in the mood. She sauntered off to talk to the girls from the orchestra while I had a few swift stabs at improving the scenes in *The Arbitration* that I decided the great Menander had left slightly rough.

There were things to be done during our visit and this seemed the night for it. I wanted an urgent talk with the tambourinist Ione, but I could see her among the group Helena had just joined. I then realized Helena was probably trying to arrange a discreet meeting. I approved. If Helena persuaded the girl to talk, it could work out cheaper than if Ione spilled the tale to me. Girls don't bribe one another for gossip, I assured myself cheerfully.

Instead I turned my attention to Thalia's missing artiste. Chremes had already told me he had managed to ascertain that the theater manager knew nothing of any water organist. That reasonably put an end to my search in this city. A water organ is not something you miss if one ever comes to town; apart from the fact they are as big as a small room, you cannot possibly avoid the noise. I felt clear to forget Sophrona, though I was prepared to make a show of double-checking by taking a turn around the forum and asking whether anybody knew a businessman called Habib who had been to Rome.

Musa said he would come with me. There was a Nabataean temple we wanted to visit. After his enforced swim at Bostra I was not prepared to let him out on his own, so we joined forces.

As we were setting off we noticed Grumio standing on a barrel at a street corner.

"What's this, Grumio—found some old jokes to sell?"

He had just started his patter but a crowd had already gathered, looking quite respectful too. He grinned. "Thought I'd try and earn back the bribe Chremes had to pay to get the theater!"

He was good. Musa and I watched for a while, laughing along with his audience. He was juggling quoits and handballs, then performing wonderful sleight-of-hand tricks. Even in a city full of tumblers and magicians his talent was outstanding. We wished him good luck eventually, but were sorry to leave. By then even other performers had left their pitches to join his fascinated audience.

It was a superb night. Gerasa's mild climate is its chief luxury. Musa and I were happy to stroll about seeing the sights before we tackled our real business. We were men on the loose, not looking for lechery, nor even for trouble, but enjoying a sense of release. We had a quiet drink. I bought a few presents to take home. We stared at the markets, the women, and the foodstalls. We slapped donkeys, tested fountains, saved children from being crushed under cartwheels, were polite to old ladies, invented directions for lost people who thought we must be locals, and generally made ourselves at home.

North of the old town, in what was planned as the center of the expanding new metropolis, we found a group of temples dominated by a dramatic shrine to Artemis, the ancestral goddess of this place. There was scaffolding around some of the twelve dramatic Corinthian columns—nothing new for Gerasa. Alongside lay a temple to Dionysus. Within that, since a synthesis could apparently be forced between Dionysus and Dushara, Nabataean priests had an enclave. We made their acquaintance, then I buzzed off to make extra inquiries about Thalia's girl, telling Musa not to leave the sanctuary without me.

The inquiries were unfruitful. Nobody had heard of Sophrona or Habib; most people claimed to be strangers there themselves. When my feet had had enough I went back to the temple. Musa was still chattering, so I waved at him and sank down for a rest in the pleasant Ionic portico. Given the abruptness of his departure with us from Petra, there could be fairly urgent messages Musa wanted to send home: to his family, his fellow priests at the Garden Temple on the mountainside, and perhaps to The Brother too. I myself felt a nagging guilt that it was time to let my mother know I was alive; Musa might be in the same trouble. He may have looked for a messenger while we were at Bostra, but if so I never saw him doing it. This was probably his first chance. So I let him talk.

When acolytes came to light the temple lamps, we both realized we had lost all sense of time. Musa dragged himself away from his fellow Nabataeans. He came and squatted beside me. I reckoned there was something on his mind.

"Everything all right?" I kept my voice neutral.

"Oh yes." He liked his touch of mystery.

Musa drew his headcloth across his face and folded his hands together. We both stared out at the temple precincts. Like any other sanctuary, this temenos was full of devout old women who ought to be at home with a stiff toddy, swindlers selling religious statuettes, and men looking out for tourists who might pay for a night with their sisters. A peaceful scene.

I had been sitting on the temple steps. I adjusted my position so I could look at Musa more directly. With him formally wrapped, all I could see were his eyes, but they seemed honest and intelligent. A woman might find their dark, inscrutable gaze romantic. I judged him on his behavior. I saw someone lean and tough, straightforward in his way, though when Musa started looking abstracted, I remembered that he had come with us because he thought it was what had been ordered by The Brother.

"Are you married?" Because of the way he had joined us, as The Brother's parole officer, we had never asked the normal questions. Now, although we had traveled together, I knew nothing of him socially.

"No," he answered.

"Any plans?"

"One day perhaps. It is allowed!" A smile had anticipated my curiosity about sexual stipulations for Dushara's priests.

"Glad to hear it!" I grinned back. "Family?"

"My sister. When I am not at the High Palace of Sacrifice, I live in her house. I sent her news of my travels." He sounded almost apologetic. Maybe he thought I found his behavior suspicious.

"Good!"

"And I sent a message to Shullay."

Again, an odd note in his voice caught my attention, though I could not decide why. "Who's Shullay?"

"The elder at my temple."

"The old priest I saw you with when I was chasing after the killer?"

He nodded. I must have been mistaken about the nuance in his voice. This was just a subordinate worried about explaining to a skeptical superior why he had dodged off from his duties.

"Also there was a message for me here," he brought out.

"Want to tell me?"

"It is from The Brother." My heart took a lurch. The Decapolis had come under Roman authority, but the cities preserved their independent status. I was unsure what would happen if Nabataea tried to extradite Helena and me. You had to be realistic: Gerasa relied on Petra for its prosperity. If Petra wanted us, Gerasa would comply.

"The Brother knows you are here, Musa?"

"He sent the message in case I should come. The message is," Musa revealed with some difficulty, "I do not have to remain with you."

"Ah!" I said.

So he was leaving. I felt quite upset. I had grown used to him as a traveling companion. Helena and I were outsiders among the theater group; Musa was another, which had made him one of us. He pulled his weight and had an endearing personality. To lose him halfway through our trip seemed too great a loss.

He was watching me, without wanting me to see it. "Is it possible I may ask you something, Falco?" I noticed his Greek was wandering more than normal.

"Ask away. We are friends!" I reminded him.

"Ah yes! If it were convenient, I would like to help you find this murderer."

I was delighted. "You want to stay with us?" I noticed he still looked uncertain. "I see no problem."

I had never known Musa so diffident. "But before, I was under orders from The Brother. You did not have to take me in your tent, though you did so—"

I burst out laughing. "Come along, Helena will be worrying about us both!" I leaped up, holding out my hand to him. "You are our guest, Musa. So long as you help me drive the bloody oxcart and pitch the tent, you're welcome. Just don't let anybody drown you while the rules of hospitality make me responsible for you!"

Back at the camp it turned out we need not have hurried home. There were three or four people talking quietly in a close-knit group outside Chremes' tent, looking as if they had spent the evening together. All the girls had gone off somewhere; that included Helena. I expected a consoling message, but no such luck.

Musa and I strolled out, intending to look for her. We assured ourselves we were not anxious, since she was in company, but I wanted to know what was going on. It might be something we would like to join in. (Wild hopes that the party Helena had dis-appeared to might involve an exotic dancer in some smoky den where they served toasted almonds in dainty bowls and the wine was free—or at least extremely cheap . . .) Anyway, we ourselves had been out in the city for several hours. I was a good boy sometimes; I was probably missing her.

At the same street corner as before, standing on the same bar-rel, we found Grumio. What looked like the same enthusiastic crowd was still clustering around. We joined them again.

By now Grumio had developed a close relationship with his audience. From time to time he pulled somebody out to assist with his conjuring; in between he tossed insults at individuals, all part of running jokes he must have set up before we arrived. This teasing had enough bite to tingle the atmosphere, but no-body was complaining. He was developing a theme; insulting the other towns of the Decapolis.

"Anyone here from Scythopolis? No? That's lucky! I won't say Scythopolitans are stupid . . ." We sensed an expectant ripple. "But if you ever see two Scythopolitans digging a huge hole in the road outside a house, just ask them—go on, ask them what they're doing. I bet they tell you they've forgotten the doorkey again! Pella! Anybody from Pella? Listen, Pella and Scythopolis

have this ancient feud—oh forget it! What's the point of insulting the Pellans if they're not here? Probably couldn't find their
way! Couldn't ask. No one can understand their accent. . . .
Anyone from Abila?" Amazingly a hand was raised. "That's your
misfortune, sir! I won't say Abilans are daft, but who else would
own up? Your moment of fame . . . Excuse me, is that your
camel looking over your shoulder, or is your wife extremely
ugly?" This was low stuff, but he was pitching it right for the
street trade.

It was time for a mood change; he switched the monologue
into a more reflective tone. "A man from Gadara had a smallholding, nothing immodest, built it up slowly. First a pig . . ."
Grumio did a farmyard impression, each animal in turn, slowly
to begin with, then he changed to little dialogues between them,
and finally a furious intercutting that sounded just like the
whole group honking and mooing at once. He topped it off by
introducing the farmer—represented by an elaborately disgusting human fart.

"What a swine . . . Hey, Marcus!" Musa grabbed my arm, but
it was too late. Grumio must have spotted us earlier but he was
ready now to turn me into embarrassing material. "This is my
friend Marcus. Come up here, Marcus! Give him a hand here." A
routine had been set for nervous volunteers; people reached for
me as soon as I was identified and I was manhandled into the
performance area without a chance. "Hello, Marcus." Jumping
off his barrel to greet me, his voice dropped but his eyes twinkled wickedly. I felt like a herring about to be filleted. "Marcus is
going to help me with my next trick. Just stand there. Try not to
look as if you've wet yourself." He squared me up to the audience. Obediently I looked as dumb as possible. "Ladies and gen-
tlemen, pay attention to this boy. He looks nothing, but his
girlfriend's a senator's daughter. So stiff that when they want to
you-know-what, he just kicks her ankles and she falls straight
on her back—"

Such disrespect for Helena from anyone else and I would have broken his neck. But I was trapped. I stood there enduring it while the crowd could feel the tension. They must have seen me color up, and my teeth had set gratingly. Next time Grumio wanted a discussion of humorous history, I would be teaching him some very serious new words.

I had to get out of this first.

We started with illusions. I was the stooge, of course. I held scarves from which wooden eggs vanished, then had eggs discovered tucked into parts of my person that caused fits of giggles in the audience: an unsophisticated lot. I had feathers produced from behind one ear and colored knucklebones from up my sleeve. Finally a set of balls appeared in a manner I still blush to remember, and we were ready for some juggling.

It was very good. I was given an improvised lesson, then every now and then Grumio made me take part. If I dropped the ball, it raised a laugh because I looked ridiculous. If I caught it, people roared at my surprise. Actually I caught quite a few. I was meant to; that was Grumio's throwing skill.

Finally the handballs were exchanged one by one for an assortment: a knucklebone, a quoit, one ball, a flywhisk, and a cup. This was much more difficult, and I supposed I was now out of it. But suddenly Grumio bent low; in a flash he had extracted my own dagger, which I kept hidden down by my boot. Jove only knew how he had spotted it there. He must be damned observant.

A gasp ran through the crowd. By some terrible luck the knife had come into his hand unsheathed.

"Grumio!" He would not stop. Everyone could see the danger; they thought it was intentional. It was bad enough to see the blade flash as he spun it in the air. Then he started whizzing items at me again. The crowd, which had chuckled at my astonishment when the knife was produced, now leaned forward in silence. I was gripped by terror that Grumio would cut off his hand; the crowd all hoped he would hurl the naked blade at me.

I managed to catch and return the quoit and the cup. I was expecting the knucklebone or the flywhisk, then thought Grumio would finish the whole scene gracefully. The bastard was drawing out the final moment. Sweat poured off me as I tried to concentrate.

Something beyond the audience caught my eye.

Not a movement: she was absolutely still on the edge of the crowd. A tall, straight-backed girl in blue with softly looped dark hair: Helena. She looked angry and terrified.

When I saw her my nerve went. I did not want her to watch me near danger. I tried to warn Grumio. His eyes met mine. Their expression was totally mischievous, completely amoral. The whisk flickered; the ball spooled up.

Then Grumio threw the knife.

Twenty-eight

I caught it. By the handle, of course.

Twenty-nine

Why the surprise?

Anyone who had spent five years in the legions, banged up in a freezing estuary fortress in western Britain, had tried knife-throwing. There was not much else to do. There were no women, or if there were they just wanted to marry centurions. Draughts palled after a hundred nights of the same strategy. We would bathe, eat, drink, some would fornicate, we would shout insults into the mist in case any British homunculi were listening, then, naturally, being young lads a thousand miles from our mothers, we tried to kill ourselves playing Dare.

I can catch knives. In Britain, catching a knife thrown after I had turned away was my specialty. When I was twenty I could do it blind drunk. Better drunk than sober, in fact, or if not drunk, then thinking about a girl.

My thoughts were on a girl now.

I put my knife back down my boot—in its sheath. The crowd was whistling ecstatically. I could still see Helena, still not stirring. Nearby, Musa was making frantic efforts to break through the crush to her.

Grumio was flapping: "Sorry, Falco. I meant to throw the knucklebone. You caught me off guard when you moved. . . ." *My fault, eh!* He was an idiot. I forced my attention back to him. Grumio had been bowing low in response to the crowd's applause. When he looked up, his eyes were veiled. He was breathless, like a man who had had a nasty shock. "Dear gods, you know I wasn't trying to kill you!"

"No harm done." I sounded calm. Possibly I was.

"Are you going to take the hat around for me?" He was holding out his collection cap, one of those woollen Phrygian efforts that flop over on top like wearing a long sock on your head.

"Something else to do—" I hopped into the crowd leaving the clown to make the best of it.

As I barged through the press he was continuing the patter: "Well, that was exciting. Thanks Marcus! What a character . . . Now then, anyone here from Capitolias?"

Musa and I reached Helena simultaneously. "Olympus! What's wrong?" I stopped in my tracks.

Musa heard my urgency and drew back slightly.

There was a deep stillness about her. Knowing her best I interpreted it first, but our friend soon saw her agitation too. It had nothing to do with Grumio's act. Helena had come here to find me. For a moment she could not tell me why. The worst conclusions flashed into my mind.

Musa and I were both assuming she had been attacked. Gently but quickly I drew her to a quiet corner. My heart was pounding. She knew that. Before we moved far she stopped me. "I'm all right."

"My darling!" I clutched her, for once grateful to the Fates. I must have looked ghastly. She bowed her head on my shoulder briefly. Musa stumbled, thinking he ought to leave us alone. I shook my head. There was still some problem. I might yet need help.

Helena looked up. Her face was set, though she was in control again. "Marcus, you must come with me."

"What's happened?"

She was full of grief. But she managed to say, "I was supposed to meet Ione at the pools of Maiuma. When I got there I found her in the water. She seems to have drowned."

Thirty

I remember the frogs.

We had come to a place whose calm beauty should bemuse the soul. In daytime the sacred site must be flooded with sunlight and birdsong. As darkness descended the birds fell silent, while all around those still-warm, sensuous waters, scores of frogs started a chorus mad enough to delight Aristophanes. They were croaking their heads off frenziedly, insensitive to human crisis.

The three of us had ridden here on hastily collected donkeys. We had had to cross the whole city northwards, cursing as we were held up twice where the main street, the Decumanus, hit major crossroads; needless to say, both junctions had been undergoing road maintenance, as well as being packed with the usual aimless crush of beggars and sightseers. Emerging through the North Gate, we followed a much less frantic processional road along a fertile valley, coming through prosperous suburban villas that nestled peacefully among the trees on rolling hill slopes. It was cool and quiet. We passed a temple lying deserted for the night.

By now it was growing too dark to see our way easily. But when we emerged through an archway at the sacred pools we found lamps hung like glowworms in the trees and bitumen torches screwed into the earth. Somebody must attend the site, though nobody was visible.

Helena and I had ridden one donkey, so I could hold her close. She had told me more about what happened, while I tried not to rage at her for taking risks.

"Marcus, you know we needed to speak to Ione about her hints regarding Heliodorus."

"I'm not arguing with that."

"I managed to have a word with her, and arranged to talk privately at the pools."

"What was this for—a promiscuous skinny-dip?"

"Don't be silly. Several of us were coming, just to see the site. We heard that people bathe here normally outside the festival."

"I bet!"

"Marcus, just listen! The arrangements were fairly flexible, because we all had other things to do first. I wanted to tidy our tent—"

"That's good. Nice girls always do their housework before they slip off to a rude festival. Decent mothers tell their daughters, don't be dunked until you've done the floors!"

"Please stop ranting."

"Don't alarm me then!"

I have to admit I was disturbed by the thought of my girl going near a lewd cult. No one would ever suborn Helena easily, but any informer of standing has been asked by distraught relations to try rescuing supposedly sensible acolytes from the clutches of peculiar religions. I knew too much about the blank-eyed smiles of brainwashed little rich girls. I was determined that my lass would never be sucked into any dirty festival. In Syria, where the cults involved women ecstatically castrating men, then hurling the bits around, I felt uneasiest of all about exotic shrines.

I found myself gripping Helena's arm so tightly I must be bruising her; angrily I released my hold and buffed up her skin. "You should have told me."

"I would have done!" she exclaimed hotly. "You were nowhere around to be told."

"Sorry." I bit my lip, annoyed with myself for staying out so long with Musa.

A girl was dead; our feelings were unimportant. Brushing off the quarrel, Helena continued her story. "To be honest, it seemed best not to rush. Ione gave the impression she had an assignation."

"With a man?"

"So I presumed. She only said, 'I'll go ahead. I've some fun fixed up . . .' The plan was for me to meet her at the pools ahead of the others, but I didn't hurry because I was nervous about interrupting her fun. I hate myself now; it made me too late to help her."

"Who else was going?"

"Byrria. Afrania had shown interest, but I was not sure she meant to turn up."

"All women?"

Helena looked cool. "That's right."

"Why did you have to go at night?"

"Oh, don't be silly! It wasn't dark then."

I tried to stay calm. "When you got to the pools Ione was in the water?"

"I noticed her clothes beside the pool. As soon as I saw her lying still, I knew."

"Oh love! I should have been with you. What did you do?"

"No one else was about. There are steps at the edge for drawing water. She was there in the shallow water on the ledges. That was how I saw her. It helped me drag her out by myself; I don't think I could have managed otherwise. It was hard even so, but I was very angry. I remembered how you tried to revive Heliodorus. I don't know if I did it properly, but it didn't work—"

I hushed her soothingly. "You didn't fail her. You tried. Probably she was already dead. Tell me the rest."

"I looked nearby for evidence, then suddenly I became frightened in case whoever killed Ione was still there. There are fir trees all around the site. I seemed to feel someone watching me—I ran for help. On the way back to the city I met Byrria coming to join us."

I was surprised. "Where is she now?"

"She went to the pools. She said she was not afraid of any murderer. She said Ione should have a friend guarding her."

"Let's hurry then . . ."

Not long after that we were among the same fir trees that had made Helena feel threatened. We rode under the arch and reached the pools, dimly lit and resonant with the frenzied croaking of the frogs.

There was a large rectangular reservoir, so large it must be used to supply the city. It was divided into two by a retaining wall that formed a sluice. On the long side steps led down into the water, which looked deep.

At the far end we could hear people cavorting, not all of them women. Like the frogs, they were ignoring the tragic tableau, too lost in their private riot even to be curious. Ione's body lay at the edge of the water. A kneeling figure kept guard alongside: Byrria, with a face that said she was blaming a man for this. She rose at our approach, then she and Helena embraced in tears.

Musa and I walked quietly to the dead girl. Beneath a white covering, which I recognized as Helena's stole, Ione lay on her back. Apart from a heavy necklace, she was naked. Musa gasped. He drew back, shamed by the blatant bare flesh. I fetched a lamp for a close look.

She had been beautiful. As beautiful as a woman could wish to be, or a man yearn to possess.

"Oh cover her!" Musa's voice was rough.

I was angry too, but losing my temper would be no help to anyone. "I mean the woman no disrespect."

I made my decisions, then covered her again and stood.

The priest turned away. I stared at the water. I had forgotten he was not my friend Petronius Longus, the Roman watch captain with whom I had surveyed so many corpses destroyed by violence. Male or female made no difference. Stripped, clad, or merely rumpled, what you saw was the pointlessness of it. That, and if you were lucky, clues to the criminal.

Still appalled but controlling it, Musa faced me again. "So what did you find, Falco?"

"Some things I *don't* find, Musa." I talked quietly while I thought. "Heliodorus had been beaten to overpower him; Ione shows no similar marks." I glanced quickly around the spot where we stood. "Nothing here implies the taking of drink, either."

Accepting my motives, he had calmed down. "It means?"

"If it was the same man, he is from our company and she knew him. So did Heliodorus. But unlike him, Ione was quite off her guard. Her killer had no need to surprise or subdue her. He was a friend of hers—or more than a friend."

"If her killer was the person she had been prepared to name to you, it was rash to arrange to meet him just before she spoke of it to Helena."

"Yes. But an element of danger appeals to some—"

"Marcus!"

Helena herself suddenly said my name in a low voice. A reveler with a conscience may after all have reported a disturbance. We were being joined by one of the sanctuary servants. My heart sank, expecting inconvenience.

He was an elderly attendant in a long striped shirt and several days' growth of whiskers. In one dirty claw he carried an oil flagon so he could pretend to replenish lamps. He had arrived silently in thonged slippers, and I knew straightaway his chief pleasure in life was creeping about among the fir trees, spying on women frolicking.

When he shuffled into our circle both Musa and I squared up defensively. He whipped aside the stole and had a good look at Ione anyway. "Another accident!" he commented in Greek that would have sounded low class even on the Piraeus waterfront. Musa said something curt in Arabic. The curator's home language would be Aramaic, but he would have understood Musa's contemptuous tone.

"Do you suffer many deaths in this place?" My own voice sounded haughty, even to me. I could have been some stiff-necked tribune on foreign service letting the locals know how much he despised them.

"Too much excitement!" cackled the lecherous old water flea. It was obvious he thought there had been dangerous fornication, and he assumed Musa and I, Helena and Byrria, were all part of it. I ceased to regret sounding arrogant. Wherever they are in the world, some types cry out to be despised.

"And what is the procedure?" I asked, as patiently as I could manage.

"Procedure?"

"What do we do with the body?"

He sounded surprised: "If the girl is a friend of yours, take her away and bury her."

I should have realized. Finding a girl's naked corpse at the site of a promiscuous festival at the end of the Empire is not like finding a corpse in the well-policed city sectors of Rome.

For a second I was on the verge of demanding an official inquiry. I was so angry, I actually wanted the watch, the local magistrate, an advertisement scrawled in the forum asking witnesses to come forward, our own party to be detained pending the investigation, and a full case in court in half a year's time . . . Sense prevailed.

I drew the greasy curator to one side, palming across as much small change as I could bear.

"We'll take her," I promised. "Just tell me, did you see what happened?"

"Oh no!" He was lying. There was absolutely no doubt about it. And I knew that with all the barriers of language and culture between Rome and this grubby pleasure ground, I would never be able to nail his lies. For a moment I felt overwhelmed. I ought to go home to my own streets. Here, I was no use to anyone.

Musa appeared at my shoulder. He spoke out in his deepest, most sonorous voice. There was no threat, simply a clean-cut authority: Dushara, the grim mountain god, had entered this place.

They exchanged a few sentences in Aramaic, then the man with the oil flagon slithered away into the trees. He was heading for the noises at the far end of the reservoir. The merrymakers' lamps looked bright enough, but he had his own unsavory business there.

Musa and I stood. The night's darkness seemed to be growing and as it did the sanctuary felt colder and ever more sordid. The frogs' chorus sounded harsher. At my feet were the ceaseless, restlessly lapping waters of the reservoir. Midges swarmed in my face.

"Thanks, friend! Did you get the tale?"

Musa reported grimly: "He sweeps up leaves and fir cones,

and is supposed to keep order. He says Ione came alone, then a man joined her. This fool could not describe the man. He was watching the girl."

"How did you get him to talk?"

"I said you were angry and would cause trouble, then he would be blamed for the accident."

"Musa! Where did you learn to bully a witness?"

"Watching you." It was gently said. Even in a situation like this, Musa sustained his teasing streak.

"Lay off! My methods are ethical. So what else did you screw out of the poolside peeper?"

"Ione and the man were acting as lovers, in the water. During their passion the girl seemed to be in trouble, struggling towards the step; then she stopped moving. The man climbed out, looked around quickly, and vanished into the trees. The unpleasant one thought he had run for help."

"The unpleasant one did not offer such help?"

"No." Musa's voice was equally dry. "Then Helena arrived and discovered the accident."

"So it was this gruesome brushman whom Helena sensed was watching her . . . Musa, Ione's death was no accident."

"Proven, Falco?"

"If you are willing to look."

I knelt beside the dead girl one final time, drawing back the cover just as far as necessary. The girl's face was darkly discolored. I showed Musa where the beaded chains of her necklace seemed to have dragged at her throat, leaving indented marks. Some pairs of the heavy stone beads were still trapping tiny folds of skin. Trickles of kohl and whatever other paint she used disfigured her face. Beneath the necklace burns and charcoal smears, numerous small red flecks showed on her flesh. "This is why I examined her so closely earlier. The necklace *may* simply have dragged at her throat as she thrashed in the water, but I think it shows pressure from a man's hands. The tiny red clusters are what appear on the corpse of somebody who has died in particular circumstances."

"Drowning?"

"No. Her face would be pale. Ione was strangled," I said.

Thirty-one

The rest of that night, and the following day, passed in various struggles that left us exhausted. We wrapped the corpse as best we could. Helena and Byrria then rode together on one animal. Musa and I had to walk, on either side of the donkey that was carrying Ione. Keeping the poor soul decent, and firmly across the donkey's back, was tricky. In the hot climate her corpse was already stiffening fast. On my own, I would have strapped her methodically and disguised her as a bale of straw. In company I was expected to behave with reverence.

We stole lamps from the sanctuary to light our way but even before the end of the processional road we knew it would be impossible to recross the entire city with our burden. I have done flamboyant things in my time, but I could not take a dead girl, her hennaed hair still dripping and her bare arms outflung to the dust, down a packed main street while merchants and local inhabitants were all out strolling and looking for somebody else in an interesting predicament to gawp at. The crowds here were the type to form a jostling procession and follow us.

We were saved by the temple outside the city gate which we had passed earlier. Priests had turned up for night duty. Musa appealed to them as a fellow professional with colleagues at the Temple of Dionysus-Dushara, and they agreed to let the body rest in their care until the next day.

Ironically, the place where we left Ione was the Temple of Nemesis.

Unencumbered, we were able to travel more quickly. I was now riding with Helena sidesaddle in front of me again. Byrria had consented to go with Musa. They both looked embarrassed about it as he sat extremely upright on his shaggy beast while she perched behind him, barely willing to hold on to his belt.

Squeezing back through the town was an experience I would have paid a lot to miss. We reached our camp in darkness, though the streets were still busy. Merchants play hard and late. Grumio was still standing on his barrel. With nightfall the humor had grown more obscene and he was slightly hoarse but gamely calling out endless cries of "Anyone here from Damascus or Dium?"

We signaled to him. He sent around his collection cap one last time, then knotted the top on the money and joined us; we told him the news. Visibly shocked, he wandered off to tell the rest. In an ideal world I ought to have gone with him to observe their reactions, but in an ideal world heroes never get tired or depressed; what's more, heroes are paid more than me—in nectar and ambrosia, willing virgins, golden apples, golden fleeces, and fame.

I was worried about Byrria. She had hardly spoken since we

found her at the sacred pools. Despite her original bravery, she now looked chilled, horrified, and deeply shocked. Musa said he would escort her safely to her tent; I advised him to try and find one of the other women to stay with her that night.

Not being entirely hopeless, I did have something urgent to attend to. Once I had seen Helena back to our own quarters, I forayed among the orchestra girls to try and learn who Ione's fatal lover was. It was a hopeless quest. Afrania and a couple of other dancers were easy to find from the noise. They were expressing their relief that it was Ione who had ended in trouble and not themselves. Their hysterical wailing only varied as they opted to shriek with feigned terror when I, a man, who might be slightly dangerous, tried to talk to them. I mentioned the well-known medical cure for hysteria, saying that it would be smacks all round if they didn't stop screaming, so then one of the pan-pipe-players jumped up and offered to ram me in the guts with a cart axle.

It seemed best to retire.

Back at my tent, another crisis: Musa had failed to reappear. I had a look round, but apart from the distant rumpus from the orchestra (and even the girls were tiring), the whole camp now lay quiet. A light shone dimly in Byrria's tent, but the side flaps were rolled firmly down. Neither Helena nor I could imagine that Musa had managed close relations with Byrria, but neither of us wanted to look stupid by interrupting if he had. Both Helena and I lay awake worrying about him most of the night.

"He's a grown man," I muttered.

"That's what I'm worried about!" she said.

He didn't come back until morning. Even then he looked perfectly normal and made no attempt to explain himself.

"Well!" I scoffed when Helena went outside to tend the fire and we were free to indulge in men's talk. "Couldn't find a woman to sit up with her?"

"No, Falco."

"Sat up with her yourself then?" This time he made no answer to my dig. He was definitely not going to tell me the story. Well that made him fair game for ribbing. "Jupiter! This doesn't look like a fellow who spent all last night consoling a beautiful young woman."

"What should such a man look like?" he challenged quietly.

"Exhausted, sunshine! No, I'm teasing. I assume if you had asked her, the famously chaste Byrria would have pitched you out into the night."

"Very probably," said Musa. "Best not to ask." You could take that two ways. A woman who was used to being asked might find reticence strangely alluring.

"Do I gather Byrria was so impressed, that *she asked you?* Sounds a good plan!"

"Oh yes," agreed Musa, smiling at last like a normal male. "It's a good *plan,* Falco!" Only in theory, apparently.

"Excuse me, Musa, but you seem to lead your life in the wrong order. Most men would seduce the beauty and *then* get shoved off an embankment by a jealous rival. *You* get the painful part over with first!"

"Of course, you're the expert on women, Marcus Didius!" Helena had popped back without us noticing. "Don't underestimate our guest."

I thought a faint smile crossed the Nabataean's face.

Helena, who always knew when to change the subject, then soothed Musa adroitly. "Your host carries out intrusive work; he forgets to stop when he comes home. There are plenty of other aspects to investigate. Marcus spent some time last night trying to ask Ione's friends about her life."

Musa ducked his head rather, but said, "I have found some information."

He sounded shy about his source, so I demanded cheerfully,

"Was this while you were sitting up all night comforting Byrria?" Helena threw a cushion at me.

"The girl who played the tambourine," said Musa patiently, as reluctant to name the corpse he had seen naked as he was to specify his informant, "had probably been connected with Chremes the manager and with Philocrates the handsome one."

"I expected it," I commented. "Chremes exacted a routine dalliance, probably as the price of her job. Philocrates just thought it was his duty as a seducer to go through the orchestra the way a hot knife skims a dripping pan."

"Even Davos probably liked her, I am told."

"She was a likable girl," Helena said. There was a trace of rebuke in her tone.

"True," Musa answered gravely. He knew how to handle disapproval. Somebody somewhere had taught him when to look submissive. I wondered if by chance the sister he lived with in Petra was like any of mine. "It is suggested that Ione was most friendly on a regular basis with the Twins."

Helena glanced at me. We both knew that it must be Byrria who had made these suggestions. I reckoned we could rely on her information. Byrria struck me as observant. She might not like men herself, but she could still watch the behavior of other girls curiously. The others may even have talked freely to her about their relationships, though they were more likely to avoid a woman with Byrria's reputation, thinking her stuck-up and sanctimonious.

"It would fit," I answered thoughtfully. "The Twins were both at Petra. Both of them are already on our suspects list for killing Heliodorus. And it looks as if we can straightaway narrow the focus to one, because *Grumio* was making the Gerasenes crack up with laughter by insulting their neighbors all night."

"Oh no!" Helena sounded regretful. "So it seems to be Tranio!" Like me, she had always found Tranio's wit appealing.

"Looks like it," I conceded. Somehow I never trust solutions that appear so readily.

Instead of breakfast, which I could not fancy, I went out for an early prod at the personnel. First I cleared the ground by eliminating those who were least likely to be involved. I soon established that Chremes and Phrygia had been dining together; Phrygia had invited their old friend Davos, and for most of the evening they had also been joined by Philocrates. (It was unclear whether Chremes had deliberately brought in the arrogant actor, or whether Philocrates had invited himself.) I remembered seeing this group sitting quietly outside the manager's tent the night before, which confirmed their alibis.

Philocrates had had a later appointment too, one he readily mentioned. He was proud to tell me he had been chalking up a success with a female cheese-seller.

"What's her name?"

"No idea."

"Know where to find her?"

"Ask a sheep."

However, he did produce a couple of ewe's milk cheeses—one half-eaten—which I accepted at least temporarily as proof.

I was ready to tackle Tranio. I found him emerging from the flute girl Afrania's tent. He seemed to expect my questions, and struck a truculent attitude. His story was that he had spent the evening drinking and doing other pleasant things with Afrania. He called her out from her tent, and of course she backed him up.

The girl looked as if she were lying, but I was unable to shake her. Tranio had an odd appearance too—but a strange expression won't convict. If he was guilty, he knew how to cover himself. When a winsome flutist declares that a man with all his faculties has been bedding her, any jury tends to believe it's true.

I looked Tranio straight in the face, knowing these defiantly flashing dark eyes might be the eyes of a man who had killed twice, and who had attempted to drown Musa too. An odd sensation. He stared straight back tauntingly. He dared me to accuse him. But I was not ready to do that.

When I left them I was certain that Tranio and Afrania were turning back to each other as if to argue about what they had told me. If it had been the truth, of course, there should have been nothing to argue about.

I felt my morning's investigations were unsatisfactory. More pressing business loomed. We had to give Ione a funeral, and I was needed to arrange it. All I could add to my inquiries was a rapid chat with Grumio.

I found Grumio alone in the clowns' tent. He was exhausted and had the grandfather of hangovers. I decided to put the situation to him directly: "Ione was killed by a man she was close to. I'll be straight. I hear that you and Tranio were her most frequent contacts."

"Probably correct." Gloomily, he made no attempt to dodge the issue. "Tranio and I are on free-and-easy terms with the musicians."

"Any intense relationships?"

"Frankly," he admitted, "no!"

"I'm plotting everyone's movements yesterday evening. You're easy to rule out, of course. I know you were delighting the crowds. That was all night?" The question was routine. He nodded. Having witnessed him on his barrel myself on two or three occasions last evening, that ended it. "Tranio tells me he was with Afrania. But did he have a similar friendship with Ione too?"

"That's right."

"Special?"

"No. He just slept with her." Helena would say that was special. Wrong; I was being romantic about my beloved. Helena had been married, so she knew the facts of life.

"When he wasn't sleeping with Afrania?" I said dourly.

"Or when Ione wasn't sleeping with someone else!" Grumio seemed troubled about his partner. I could see he had a personal interest. He had to share Tranio's tent. Before he next passed out after a few drinks, he needed to know whether Tranio might stick his head in a water pail. "Is Tranio cleared? What does Afrania say?"

"Oh, she supports Tranio."

"So where does that leave you, Falco?"

"Up a palm tree, Grumio!"

We spent the rest of that day, with the help of Musa's Nabataean colleagues, organizing a short-notice funeral. Unlike Heliodorus at Petra, Ione was at least claimed, honored, and sent to the gods by her friends. The affair was more sumptuous than might have been expected. She had a popular send-off. Even strangers made donations for a monument. People in the entertainment community had heard of her death, though not the true manner of it. Only Musa and I and the murderer knew that. People thought she had drowned; most thought she had drowned *in flagrante,* but I doubt if Ione would have minded that.

Naturally *The Arbitration* went ahead that night as planned. Chremes dragged out the old lie about *"She would have wanted us to continue . . ."* I hardly knew the girl but I believed all Ione would have wanted was to be alive. However, Chremes could be certain we would pack the arena. The poolside voyeur in the filthy shirt was bound to have spread our company's notoriety.

Chremes proved to be right. A sudden death was perfect for trade—a fact I personally found bad for my morale.

We traveled on next day. We crossed the city before dawn. At first repeating our journey toward the sacred pools, we left by the North Gate. At the Temple of Nemesis once more we thanked the priests who had given Ione her last resting place, and paid them to oversee setting up her monument alongside the road. We had commissioned a stone plaque, in the Roman manner, so other musicians passing through Gerasa would pause and remember her.

I know that, with the priests' permission, Helena and Byrria covered their heads and went together into the temple. When they prayed to the dark goddess of retribution, I can assume what they asked.

Then, still before dawn, we took the great trade road that ran west into the Jordan Valley and on to the coast. This was the road to Pella.

As we journeyed there was one notable difference. In the early hours of morning, we were all hunched and silent. Yet I knew that an extra sense of doom had befallen us. Where the company had once seemed to carry lightly its loss of Heliodorus, Ione's death left everybody stricken. For one thing, he had been highly unpopular; she had had friends everywhere. Also, until now people may have been able to pretend to themselves that Heliodorus could have been murdered in Petra by a stranger. Now there was no doubt: they were harboring a killer. All of them wondered where he might strike next.

Our one hope was that this fear would drive the truth into the light.

Thirty-two

Pella: founded by Seleucus, Alexander's general. It possessed an ancient and highly respectable history, and a modern, booming air. Like everywhere else it had been pillaged in the Rebellion, but had bounced back cheerfully. A little honey pot, aware of its own importance.

We had moved north and west to much more viable country that produced textiles, meat, grain, wood, pottery, leather, and dyes. The export trade up the River Jordan valley may have reduced during the Judaean troubles, but it was reviving now. Old Seleucus knew how to pick a site. Pella straddled a long spur of the lush foothills, with a fabulous view across the valley. Below the steep-sided domed acropolis of the Hellenic foundation, Romanized suburbia was spreading rapidly through a valley that contained a crisply splashing spring and stream. They had water, pasture, and merchants to prey on: all a Decapolis city needed.

We had been warned about a bitter feud between the Pellans and their rivals across the valley in Scythopolis. Hoping for fights in the streets, we were disappointed, needless to say. On the whole, Pella was a dull, well-behaved little city. There was, however, a large new colony of Christians there, people who had fled when Titus conquered and destroyed Jerusalem. The native Pellans now seemed to spend their energy picking on them instead.

With their wealth, which was quite enviable, the Pellans had built themselves smart villas nuzzling the warm city walls, temples for every occasion, and all the usual public buildings that show a city thinks itself civilized. These included a small theater, right down beside the water.

The Pellans obviously liked culture. Instead we gave them our company favorite, *The Pirate Brothers,* an undemanding vehicle for our shocked actors to walk through.

"No one wants to perform. This is crass!" I grumbled, as we dragged out costumes that evening.

"This is the East," answered Tranio.

"What's that supposed to mean?"

"Expect a full house tonight. News flashes around here. They will have heard we had a death at our last venue. We're well set up."

As he spoke of Ione I gave him a sharp look, but there was nothing exceptional in his behavior. No guilt. No relief, if he was feeling he had silenced an unwelcome revelation from the girl. No sign any longer of the defiance I had thought he exhibited when I questioned him at Gerasa. Nor, if he noticed me staring, did he show any awareness of my interest.

Helena was sitting on a bale sewing braid back onto a gown for Phrygia (who in turn was holding nails for a stagehand mending a piece of broken scenery). My lass bit through her thread, with little thought for the safety of her teeth. "Why do you think Easterners have lurid tastes, Tranio?"

"Fact," he said. "Heard of the Battle of Carrhae?" It was one of Rome's famous disasters. Several legions under Crassus had been massacred by the legendary Parthians, our foreign policy lay in ruins for decades afterwards, the Senate was outraged, then more plebian soldiers' lives had been chucked away in expeditions to recapture lost military standards: the usual stuff. "On the night after their triumph at Carrhae," Tranio told us, "the Parthians and Armenians all sat down to watch *The Bacchae* of Euripides."

"Strong stuff, but a night at a play seems a respectable way to celebrate a victory," said Helena.

"What," Tranio demanded bitterly, "with the severed head of Crassus kicked around the stage?"

"Juno!" Helena blanched.

"The only thing we could do to please people better," Tranio continued, "would be *Laureolus* with a robber king actually crucified live in the last act."

"Been done," I told him. Presumably he knew that. Like Grumio, he was putting himself forward as a student of drama history. I was about to enter into a discussion, but he was keeping himself aloof from me now and swiftly made off.

Helena and I exchanged a thoughtful look. Was Tranio's delight in these lurid theatrical details a reflection of his own involvement in violence? Or was he an innocent party, merely depressed by the deaths in the company?

Unable to fathom his attitude, I filled in time before the play by asking in the town about Thalia's musician, without luck, as usual.

However, this did provide me with an unexpected chance to do some checking up on the wilfully elusive Tranio. As I sauntered back to camp, I happened to come across his girlfriend

Afrania, the tibia-player. She was having trouble shaking off a group of Pellan youths who were following her. I didn't blame them, for she was a luscious armful with the dangerous habit of looking at anything masculine as if she wanted to be followed home. They had never seen anything like her; I had not seen *much* like it myself.

I told the lads to get lost, in a friendly fashion, then when this had no effect I resorted to old-fashioned diplomacy: hurling rocks at them while Afranis screamed insults. They took the hint; we congratulated ourselves on our style; then we walked together, just in case the hooligans found reinforcements and came after us again.

Once she regained her breath, Afrania suddenly stared at me. "It was true, you know."

I guessed what she meant, but played the innocent. "What's that?"

"Me and Tranio. He really was with me that night."

"If you say so," I said.

Having chosen to talk to me, she seemed annoyed that I didn't believe her. "Oh, don't be po-faced, Falco!"

"All right. When I asked you, I just gained the impression," I told her frankly, "there was something funny going on." With girls like Afrania I always liked to play the man of the world. I wanted her to understand I had sensed the touchy atmosphere when I questioned the pair of them.

"It's not me," she assured me self-righteously, tossing back her rampant black curls with a gesture that had a bouncing effect on her thinly clad bosom as well.

"If you say so."

"No, really. It's that idiot Tranio." I made no comment. We were nearing our camp. I knew there was unlikely to be another opportunity to persuade Afrania to confide in me; there was unlikely to be another occasion when she needed rescuing from men. Normally Afrania accepted all comers.

"Whatever you say," I repeated in a skeptical tone. "If he was with you, then he's cleared of murdering Ione. I assume you wouldn't lie about that. After all, she was supposed to be your friend."

Afrania made no comment on that. I knew there had been a degree of rivalry between them, in fact. What she did say amazed me. "Tranio was with me all right. He asked me to deny it though."

"Jupiter! Whatever for?"

She had the grace to look embarrassed. "He said it was one of his practical jokes, to get you confused."

I laughed bitterly. "It takes less than that to get me confused," I confessed. "I don't get it. Why should Tranio put himself on the spot for a killing? And why should you be a party to it?"

"Tranio never killed Ione," Afrania said self-righteously. "But don't ask me what the silly bastard thought he was up to. I never knew."

The practical joke idea seemed so far-fetched I reckoned it was just a line Tranio had come up with for Afrania. But I was hard pressed to think of another reason why he would want her to lie. The only slim possibility might be drawing the heat away from someone else. But Tranio would need to owe someone a truly enormous debt if he would risk being accused of a murder he had not committed.

"Has anyone done Tranio any big favors recently?"

"Only me!" quipped the girl. "Going to bed with him, I mean."

I grinned appreciatively, then quickly changed tack: "Do you know who Ione might have been meeting at the pools?"

Afrania shook her head. "No. That's the reason she and I had a few words sometimes. The person I used to reckon she had her eye on was Tranio."

Very convenient. Here was Tranio being fingered as a possible associate of the dead girl just when he was also being given a firm alibi. "Yet it couldn't be him," I concluded, with a certain dryness, "because wonderful Tranio was doing acrobatic tricks with you all night."

"He was!" retorted Afrania. "So where does that leave you, Falco? Ione must have been up to it with the whole company!"

Not much help to the sleuth trying to fix who had murdered her.

As our wagons came in sight, Afrania rapidly lost interest in talking to me. I let her go, wondering whether to have another talk with Tranio, or whether to pretend to forget him. I decided to leave him unchallenged, but to observe him secretly.

Helena always reckoned that was the informer's lazy way out. However, she would not be hearing about this. Unless it was essential, I never told Helena when I had gathered information from a very pretty girl.

If the Pellans were baying for blood they held their vile tastes well in check. In fact they behaved with quiet manners during our performance of *The Pirate Brothers,* sat in neat rows eating honeyed dates, and applauded us gravely afterwards. Pellan women mobbed Philocrates in sufficient numbers to keep him insufferable; Pellan men mooned after Byrria but were satisified with the orchestra girls; Chremes and Phrygia were invited to a decent dinner by a local magistrate. And the rest of us were paid for once.

In other circumstances we might have stayed longer at Pella, but Ione's death had made the whole company restless. Luckily the next town lay very close, just across the Jordan Valley. So we moved on immediately, making the short journey to Scythopolis.

Thirty-three

Scythopolis, previously known as Nysa after its founder, had been renamed to cause confusion and pronunciation difficulties, but otherwise lacked eccentricity. It held a commanding position on the main road up the west bank of the Jordan, drawing income from that. Its features were those we had come to expect: a high citadel where the Greeks had originally planted their temples, with more modern buildings spreading fast down the slopes. Surrounded by hills, it was set back from the River Jordan, facing Pella across the valley. Once again, signs of the famous feud between the two towns were disappointingly absent.

By now the places we visited were starting to lose their individuality. This one called itself the chief city of the Decapolis, hardly a distinguishing feature since half of them assumed that title; like most Greek towns, they were a shameless lot. Scythopolis was as large as any of them, which meant not particularly large to anybody who had seen Rome.

For me, however, Scythopolis was different. There was one aspect of this particular city that made me both anxious to come here, and yet full of dread. During the Judaean Revolt, it had been the winter quarters of Vespasian's Fifteenth Legion. That legion had now left the province, reassigned to Pannonia once its commander had made himself Emperor and hiked back to Rome to fulfill a more famous destiny. Even now, however, Scythopolis seemed to have a more Roman atmosphere than the rest of the Decapolis. Its roads were superb. There was a cracking good bathhouse built for the troops. As well as their own minted coins, shops and stalls readily accepted denarii. We heard more Latin than anywhere else in the East. Children with a suspiciously familiar cast of feature tumbled in the dust.

This atmosphere upset me more than I admitted. There was a reason. I had a close interest in the town's military past. My brother Festus had served in the Fifteenth Apollinaris, his final posting before he became one of the fatalities of Judaea. That last season before he died, Festus must have been here.

So Scythopolis does stay in my memory. I spent a lot of time there walking about on my own, thinking private thoughts.

Thirty-four

I was drunk.

I was so drunk even I could hardly pretend I had not noticed. Helena, Musa, and their visitor, all sitting demurely around the fire outside our tent waiting for me to come home, must have summed up the situation at once. As I carefully placed my feet in order to approach my welcome bivouac, I realized there was no chance of reaching it unobserved. They had seen me coming; best to brazen it out. They were watching every step. I had to stop thinking about them so I could concentrate on remaining upright. The flickering blur that must be the fire warned me that on arrival I would probably pitch face first into the burning sticks.

Thanks to a ten-year career of debauched living, I made it to the tent at what I convinced myself was a nonchalant stroll.

Probably about as nonchalant as a fledgling falling off a roof finial. No one commented.

I heard, rather than saw, Helena rising to her feet, then my arm found its way around her shoulders. She helped me tiptoe in past our guests and tumble onto the bed. Naturally I expected a lecture. Without a word she made me sit up enough to take a long quaff of water.

Three years had taught Helena Justina a thing or two. Three years ago she was a primly scowling fury who would have spurned a man in my condition; now she made him take precautions against a hangover. Three years ago, she wasn't mine and I was lost . . .

"I love you!"

"I know you do." She had spoken quietly. She was pulling off my boots for me. I had been lying on my back; she rolled me partly on my side. It made no difference to me as I could not tell which way up I was, but she was happy to have given me protection in case I choked. She was wonderful. What a perfect companion.

"Who's that outside?"

"Congrio." I lost interest. "He brought a message for you from Chremes about the play we are to put on here." I had lost interest in plays too. Helena continued talking calmly, as if I were still rational. "I remembered we had never asked him about the night Ione died, so I invited him to sit with Musa and me until you came home."

"Congrio . . ." In the way of the drunk I was several sentences behind. "I forgot Congrio."

"That seems to be Congrio's destiny," murmured Helena. She was unbuckling my belt, always an erotic moment; blearily I enjoyed the situation, though I was helpless to react with my usual eagerness. She tugged the belt; I arched my back, allowing it to slither under me. Pleasantly I recalled other occasions of such unbuckling when I had not been so incapable.

In a crisis Helena made no comment about the emergency. Her eyes met mine. I gave her the smile of a helpless man in the hands of a very beautiful nurse.

Suddenly she bent and kissed me, though it cannot have been congenial. "Go to sleep. I'll take care of everything," she whispered against my cheek.

As she moved away I gripped her fast. "Sorry, fruit. Something I had to do . . ."

"I know." Understanding about my brother, there were tears in her eyes. I made to stroke her soft hair; my arm seemed impossibly heavy and nearly caught her a clout on the side of the brow. Seeing it coming, Helena held my wrist. Once I stopped flailing she laid my arm back tidily alongside me. "Go to sleep." She was right; that was safest. Sensing my silent appeal, she came back at the last minute, then kissed me again, briskly on the head. "I love you too." Thanks, sweetheart.

What a mess. Why does solitary, deeply significant thought lead so inevitably to an amphora?

I lay still, while the darkened tent zoomed to and fro around me and my ears sang. Now that I had collapsed, the sleep I had been heavily craving refused to come. So I lay in my woozy cocoon of misery, listening to the events at my own fireside that I could not join.

Thirty-five

"Marcus Didius has things on his mind."

It was the briefest excuse, as Helena sank back in her place gracefully. Neither Musa nor the bill-poster answered; they knew when to keep their heads down.

From my position the three figures looked dark against the flames. Musa was leaning forwards, rebuilding the fire. As sparks suddenly crackled up, I caught a glimpse of his young, earnest face and the scent of smoke, slightly resinous. I wondered how many nights my brother Festus had spent like this, watching the same brushwood smoke lose itself in the darkness of the desert sky.

I had things on my mind all right. Death, mostly. It was making me intolerant.

Loss of life has incalculable repercussions. Politicians and generals, like murderers, must ignore that. To lose one soldier in battle—or to drown an unlovable playwright and strangle an unwanted witness—inevitably affects others. Heliodorus and Ione both had homes somewhere. Slowly the messages would be winding back, taking their domestic devastation: the endless search for a rational explanation; the permanent damage to unknown numbers of other lives.

At the same time as I was pledging a violent vow to right these wrongs, Helena Justina said lightly to Congrio, "If you give me the message from Chremes to Falco, I will pass it on tomorrow."

"Will he be able to do the work?" Congrio must be the kind of messenger who liked returning to the source with a pessimistic announcement of "It can't be done." He would have made a good cartwheel-mender in a backstreet lockup workshop.

"The work will be completed," replied Helena, a firm girl. Optimistic too. I would probably not be able to see a scroll tomorrow, let alone write on it.

"Well, it's to be *The Birds,*" said Congrio. I heard this impassively, unable to remember if it was a play, whether I had ever read it, and what I thought if I had done so.

"Aristophanes?"

"If you say so. I just write up the playbills. I like the ones with short names; takes less chalk. If that's the scribe's name who wrote it, I'll leave him off."

"This is a Greek play."

"That's right. Full of birds. Chremes says it will cheer everyone up. They all get a chance to dress in feathers, then hop about squawking."

"Will anyone notice the difference from normal?" Helena quipped. I found this incredibly funny. I heard Musa chuckle, though sensibly he was keeping out of the rest of it.

Congrio accepted her wit as a straight comment. "Doubt it.

Could I draw birds on the posters? Vultures, that's what I'd like to have a go at."

Avoiding comment, Helena asked, "What does Chremes want from us? Not a full translation into Latin, I hope?"

"Got you worried!" Congrio chortled, though in fact Helena was perfectly calm (apart from a slight quiver as she heard his plans for artwork). "Chremes says we'll do it in Greek. You've got a set of scrolls in the box, he says. He wants it gone through and brought up to date if the jokes are too Athenian."

"Yes, I've seen the play in the box. That will be all right."

"So you reckon your man in there is up to it?"

"My man in there is up to anything." Like most girls with a strongly ethical upbringing, Helena lied well. Her loyalty was impressive too, though perhaps rather dry in tone. "What will happen about these elaborate beak-and-feather costumes, Congrio?"

"Same as usual. People have to hire them off Chremes."

"Does he already possess a set of bird costumes?"

"Oh yes. We did this one a few years ago. People who can sew," he menaced cheerfully, "had better get used to the idea of stitching feathers on!"

"Thanks for warning me! Unfortunately, I've just developed a terrible whitlow on my needle finger," said Helena, making up the excuse smoothly. "I shall have to back out."

"You're a character!"

"Thanks again."

I could tell from her voice Helena had now decided that she had sufficient details of my writing commission. The signs were slight, but I knew the way she bent to toss a piece of kindling on the fire, then sat back tidying her hair under one of its combs. For her, the actions marked a pause. She was probably unaware of it.

Musa understood the change of atmosphere. I noticed him

silently shrink deeper into his headcloth, leaving Helena to interrogate the suspect.

"How long have you been with Chremes and the company, Congrio?"

"I dunno . . . a few seasons. Since they were in Italy."

"Have you always done the same job?"

Congrio, who could sometimes appear taciturn, now seemed blissfully keen to talk. "I always do the posters."

"That requires some skill?"

"Right! It's important too. If I don't do it, nobody comes to see the stuff, and none of us earns. The whole lot depends on me."

"That's wonderful! What do you have to do?"

"Fool the opposition. I know how to get through the streets without anybody spotting me. You have to get around and write the notices real quick—before the locals see you and start complaining about you ruining their white walls. All they want is space to advertise their pet gladiators and draw rude signs for brothels. You have to dodge in secretly. I know the methods." He knew how to boast like an expert too. Carried away by Helena's interest, he then confided, "I have done acting once. I was in this play *The Birds,* as it happens."

"That's how you remember it?"

"I'll say! That was an experience. I was an owl."

"Goodness! What did that entail?"

"In this play, *The Birds,*" Congrio expounded gravely, "there are some scenes—probably the most important ones—where all the birds from the heavens come on the stage. So I was the owl." In case Helena had missed the full picture, he added, "I hooted."

I buried my face in my pillow. Helena managed to stifle the laughter that must be threatening to bubble up. "The bird of wisdom! That was quite a part!"

"I was going to be one of the other birds, but Chremes took me off it because of the whistling."

"Why was that?"

"Can't do it. Never could. Wrong teeth or something."

He could have been lying, to give himself an alibi, but we had told nobody Musa had heard the playwright's killer whistling near the High Place at Petra.

"How did you get on with hooting?" Helena asked politely.

"I could hoot really well. It sounds like nothing difficult, but you have to have timing, and put feeling into it." Congrio sounded full of himself. This had to be the truth. He had ruled himself right out of killing Heliodorus.

"Did you enjoy your part?"

"I'll say!"

In that short speech Congrio had revealed his heart. "Would you like to become one of the actors, someday?" Helena asked him with gentle sympathy.

He was bursting to tell her: "I could do it!"

"I'm sure you could," Helena declared. "When people really want something, they can usually manage it."

Congrio sat up straighter, hopefully. It was the kind of remark that seemed to be addressed to all of us.

Once again I saw Helena push up the side comb above her right ear. The soft hair that grew back from her temples had a habit of slithering out of control and drooping, so it bothered her. But this time it was Musa who punctuated the scene by finding sticks to twiddle in the embers. A rogue spark flew out and he stamped on it with his bony sandaled foot.

Even though he was not talking, Musa had a way of staying silent that still kept him in the conversation. He pretended being foreign made him unable to take part, but I noticed how he listened. At such times my old doubts about him working for The Brother tended to sneak up again. There still could be more to Musa than we thought.

"All this trouble in the company is very sad," Helena mused. "Heliodorus, and now Ione . . ." I heard Congrio groan in agreement. Helena continued innocently, "Heliodorus does seem to have asked for what happened to him. Everyone tells us he was a very unpleasant character. How did you get on with him, Congrio?"

The answer came out freely: "I hated him. He knocked me about. And when he knew I wanted to be an actor he plagued me with it. I didn't kill him, though!" Congrio inserted quickly.

"Of course not," said Helena, her voice matter-of-fact. "We know something about the person who killed him that eliminates you, Congrio."

"What's that then?" came the sharp question, but Helena avoided telling him about the whistling fugitive. This brazen habit was still the only thing definite we knew about the killer.

"How did Heliodorus plague you about acting, Congrio?"

"Oh, he was always trumpeting on about me not being able to read. That's nothing; half the actors do their parts by guesswork anyway."

"Have you ever tried to learn reading?" I saw Congrio shake his head: a big mistake. If I knew Helena Justina she was now planning to teach him, whether or not he wanted it. "Someone might give you lessons one day. . . ."

To my surprise, Musa suddenly leaned forward. "Do you remember the night at Bostra when I fell into the reservoir?"

"Lost your footing?" chuckled Congrio.

Musa stayed cool. "Somebody helped me dive in."

"Not me!" Congrio shouted hotly.

"We had been talking together," Musa reminded him.

"You can't accuse me of anything. I was miles away from you when Davos heard you splashing and called out!"

"Did you see anyone else near me just before I fell?"

"I wasn't looking."

As Musa fell silent, Helena took up the same incident. "Congrio, do you remember hearing Marcus and me teasing Musa that we would tell people he had seen the murderer at Petra? I wonder if you told anyone about that?"

Once again Congrio appeared to answer frankly—and once again he was useless: "Oh I reckon I told everyone!"

Evidently the kind of feeble weevil who liked to make himself big in the community by passing on scandal.

Helena betrayed none of the irritation she probably felt. "Just to complete the picture," she went on, "on the night when Ione was killed in Gerasa, do you happen to have anyone who can vouch for where you were?"

Congrio thought about it. Then he chuckled. "I should say so! Everyone who came to the theater the next day."

"How's that?"

"Easy. When you girls went off to the sacred pools for a splash, I was putting up the playbills for *The Arbitration*. Gerasa was a big place; it took all night. If I hadn't done my job like that, nobody would have come."

"Ah, but you could have done the bills the next morning," Helena challenged.

Congrio laughed again. "Oh I did that, lady! Ask Chremes. He can vouch for it. I wrote up bills everywhere in Gerasa the night Ione died. Chremes saw them first thing next morning and I had to go around to every one of them again. He knows how many I did and how long it must have taken. He came around with me the second time and stood over the job. Ask me why? Don't bother. The first time I did it, I spelled the word wrong."

"The title? *Arbitration?*"

"Right. So Chremes insisted that I had to sponge off every single one next day and do it again."

Not long after that Helena stopped asking questions so, bored with no longer being the center of attention, Congrio stood up and left.

For a while Musa and Helena sat in silence. Eventually Musa asked, "Will Falco do the new play?"

"Is that a tactful way of asking what is up with him?" queried

Helena. Musa shrugged. Helena answered the literal question first. "I think Falco had better do it, Musa. We need to insist *The Birds* is performed, so you and I—and Falco if he ever returns to the conscious world—can sit beside the stage and listen out for who *can* whistle! Congrio seems to be ruled out as a suspect, but it leaves plenty of others. This slim clue is all we have."

"I have sent word of our problem to Shullay," Musa said abruptly. This meant nothing to Helena, though I recognized the name. Musa explained to her, "Shullay is a priest at my temple."

"So?"

"When the killer ran down the mountain ahead of Falco, I had been within the temple and only caught a fleeting sight of him. I cannot describe this man. But Shullay," Musa revealed quietly, "had been tending the garden outside."

Helena's excitement overcame any anger that this was the first Musa had told us of it. "You mean, Shullay had a proper view of him?"

"He may have done. I never had a chance to ask. Now it is difficult to receive a message from him, since he cannot know where I am," Musa said. "But every time we reach a new city I ask at their temple in case there is news. If I learn anything, I will tell Falco."

"Yes, Musa. Do that!" Helena commented, still restraining herself commendably.

They fell silent for a while. After some time, Musa reminded Helena, "You did not say what is troubling our scribe? Am I permitted to know this?"

"Ah well!" I heard Helena sigh gently. "Since you are our friend I daresay I can answer."

Then she told Musa in a few sentences about brotherly affection and rivalry, just why she supposed I had got drunk in Scythopolis. I reckon she got it more or less right.

Not long after that, Musa rose and went to his own part of the tent.

*   *   *

Helena Justina sat on alone in the dying firelight. I thought of calling out to her. The intention was still at the thought stage when she came inside anyway. She curled up, tucking herself into the curve of my body. Somehow I dragged one sluggish arm over her, then stroked her hair, properly this time. We were good enough friends to be perfectly peaceful together even on a night like this.

I felt Helena's head growing heavier against my chest; then almost immediately she fell asleep. When I was sure she had stopped worrying about the world in general and me in particular, I did some more worrying for her, then fell asleep myself.

Thirty-six

When I awoke the next day, I could hear the furious scratching of a stylus. I had a good idea why: Helena was reworking the play Chremes wanted from me.

I rolled off the bed. Stifling a groan, I scooped a beaker of water from a pail, put my boots on, drank the water, felt sick, managed to keep everything in place, and emerged from the tent. Light exploded in my head. After a pause for readjustment, I opened my eyes again. My oil flask and strigil had been placed on a towel, together with a laundered tunic—a succinct hint.

Helena Justina sat cross-legged on a cushion in the shade, looking neat and efficient. She was wearing a red dress that I liked, with bare feet and no jewelry. Always a fast worker, she had already amended two scrolls, and was whipping through the third. She had a double inkstand, one belonging to Heliodorus that we had found in the play box. It had one black and one red compartment; she was using the red ink to mark up her corrections to the text. Her handwriting was clear and fluent. Her face looked flushed with enjoyment. I knew she was loving the work.

She glanced up. Her expression was friendly. I gave her a nod, then without speaking went to the baths.

When I returned, still moving slowly but now refreshed, shaved, and cleanly clad, the play must have been finished. Helena had dressed up more with agate earrings and two arm bracelets, in order to greet the master of her household with the formal respect that was appropriate in a well-run Roman home (unusual meekness, which proved she was aware she had better look out after pinching my job). She kissed my cheek, with the formality I mentioned, then went back to melting honey in a pan to make us a hot drink. There were fresh bread rolls, olives, and chickpea paste on a platter.

For a moment I stood watching her. She pretended not to notice. I loved to make her shy. "One day, lady, you shall have a villa crammed with Egyptian carpets and fine Athenian vases, where marble fountains soothe your precious ears, and a hundred slaves are hanging about just waiting to do the dirty work when your disreputable lover staggers home."

"I'll be bored. Eat something, Falco."

"Done *The Birds?*"

Helena shrieked like a herring gull, confirming it.

Exercising caution I sat, ate a small quantity, and with the experience of an ex-soldier and hardened man about town, waited to see what would happen. "Where's Musa?" I asked, to fill in time while my disturbed guts wondered what unpleasant tricks to throw at me.

"Gone to visit a temple."

"Oh why's that?" I queried innocently.

"He's a priest," said Helena.

I hid a smile, allowing them their secret over Shullay. "Oh, it's religion? I thought he might be pursuing Byrria."

After their night of whatever it was (or wasn't), Helena and I had surreptitiously watched for signs of romantic involvement. When the pair next met in public all they exchanged were somber nods. Either the girl was an ungrateful hag, or our Musa was exceedingly slow.

Helena recognized what I was thinking, and smiled. Compared with this, our own relationship was as old and solid as Mount Olympus. Behind the two of us were a couple of years of furious squabbling, taking care of each other in crazy situations, and falling into bed whenever possible. She could recognize my step from three streets away; I could tell from a room's atmosphere if Helena had entered it for only half a minute several hours before. We knew each other so closely we hardly needed to communicate.

Musa and Byrria were a long way from this. They needed some fast action. They would never be more than polite strangers unless they got stuck into some serious insults, a few complaints about table manners, and a bit of light flirting. Musa had come back to sleeping in our tent; that would never achieve much for him.

Actually, neither he nor Byrria seemed the type to want the kind of mutual dependency Helena and I had. That did not stop us from speculating avidly.

"Nothing can come of it," Helena decided.

"People say that about us."

"People know nothing then." While I toyed with my breakfast, she tucked into her lunch. "You and I will have to try to look after them, Marcus."

"You speak as if falling for someone were a penalty."

She flashed me a smile of joyous sweetness. "Oh, that depends who you fall for!" Something in the pit of my stomach took a familiar lurch; this time it had nothing to do with last night's drink. I grabbed more bread and adopted a tough stance. Helena smiled. "Oh, Marcus, I know you're a hopeless romantic, but be practical. They come from different worlds."

"One of them could change cultures."

"Who? They both have work they are closely tied to. Musa is taking an extended holiday with us, but it can't last. His life is in Petra."

"You've been talking to him?"

"Yes. What do you make of him, Marcus?"

"Nothing particular. I like him. I like his personality." That was all, however. I regarded him as a normal, fairly unexciting foreign priest.

"I get the impression that in Petra he is thought of as a boy with promise."

"Is that what he says? It won't be for long," I chortled. "Not if he returns to the mountain fastness with a vibrant Roman actress on his elbow." No priest who did that would stand a chance of acceptance, even in Rome. Temples are havens of sordid behavior, but they do have some standards.

Helena grimaced. "What makes you think Byrria would abandon her career to hang on *any* man's elbow?"

I reached out and tucked in a loose strand of hair—a good opportunity to tickle her neck. "If Musa really is interested—and that's a debatable issue in itself—he probably only wants one night in her bed."

"I was assuming," Helena asserted pompously, "that was all Byrria would be offering! She's just lonely and desperate, and he's intriguingly different from the other men who try to nobble her."

"Hmm. Is that what you thought when you nobbled me?" I was remembering the night we had first managed to recognize we wanted each other. "I've no objection to being thought intriguing, but I did hope that falling into bed with me was more than a desperate act!"

"Afraid not." Helena knew how to aggravate me if I pushed my luck. "I told myself, *Once, just to know what passion feels like.* . . . The trouble was, *once* led straight to *once again!*"

"So long as you never start feeling it's been *once too often* . . ." I held out my arms to her. "I haven't kissed you this morning."

"No you haven't!" exclaimed Helena in a changed tone, as if being kissed by me was an interesting proposition. I made sure I kissed her in a way that would reinforce that view.

After a while she interrupted me: "You can look through what I've done to *The Birds* if you like, and see if you approve." Helena was a tactful scribe.

"Your revising is good enough for me." I preferred to embark on extra kissing.

"Well, my work may be wasted. There's a big question mark hanging over whether it can be performed."

"Why's that?"

Helena sighed. "Our orchestra has gone on strike."

Thirty-seven

"Hey, hey! Things must be bad if they have to send the scribbler to sort us!"

My arrival amid the orchestra and stagehands caused a surge of mocking applause. They lived in an enclave at one end of our camp. Fifteen or twenty musicians, scene-shifters, and their hangers-on were sitting about looking militant while they waited for people in the main company to notice their complaint. Babies toddled about with sticky faces. A couple of dogs scratched their fleas. The angry atmosphere was making my own skin prickle uneasily.

"What's up?" I tried playing the simple, friendly type.

"Whatever you've been told."

"I've been told nothing. I've been drunk in my tent. Even Helena has stopped talking to me."

Still pretending not to notice the ominous tension, I squatted in the circle and grinned at them like a harmless sightseer. They glared back while I surveyed who was here.

Our orchestra consisted of Afrania the flutist, whose instrument was the single-piped tibia; another girl who played pan-pipes; a gnarled, hook-nosed old chap whom I had seen clashing a pair of small hand cymbals with an incongruous delicacy; and a pale young man who plucked the lyre when he felt like it. They were led by a tall, thin, balding character who sometimes boomed away on a big double wind instrument that had one pipe turned up at the end, while he beat time for the others on a foot clacker. This was a large group, compared with some theater company ensembles, but allowed for the fact that the paticipants also danced, sold trays of limp sweetmeats, and offered entertainment afterwards to members of the audience.

Attached to them were the hard-labor boys, a set of small, bandy-legged stagehands whose wives were all hefty boot-faced wenches you wouldn't push in front of a baker's queue. In contrast to the musicians, whose origins were varied and whose quarters had an artistic abandon, the scenery-movers were a closely related group, like bargees or tinkers. They lived in spotless tidiness; they had all been born to the roving life. Whenever we arrived at a new venue, they were the first to organize themselves. Their tents were lined up in straight rows with elaborate sanitary arrangements at one end, and they shared a huge iron broth cauldron that was stirred by a strict rota of cooks. I could see the cauldron now, breathing out coils of gravy steam that reminded me of my stomach's queasiness.

"Do I detect an atmosphere?"

"Where've you been, Falco?" The hook-nosed cymbalist sounded weary as he threw a stone at a dog. I felt lucky he chose the dog.

"I told you: drunk in bed."

"Oh, you took to the life of a playwright easily!"

"If you wrote for this company you'd be drunk too."

"Or dead in a cistern!" scoffed a voice from the back.

"Or dead," I agreed quietly. "I do worry about that sometimes. Maybe whoever had it in for Heliodorus dislikes all playwrights, and I'm next." I was carefully not mentioning Ione yet, though she must matter more here than the drowned scribe.

"Don't worry," sneered the girl who played the panpipes. "You're not that good!"

"Hah! How would you know? Even the actors never read the script, so I'm damned sure you musicians don't! But surely you're not saying Heliodorus was a decent writer?"

"He was trash!" exclaimed Afrania. "Plancina's just trying to annoy you."

"Oh, for a moment I thought I was hearing that Heliodorus was better than everyone tells me—though aren't we all?" I tried to look like a wounded writer. This was not easy since naturally I knew my own work was of fine quality—if anyone with any true critical sense ever did read it.

"Not you, Falco!" laughed the panpipe girl, the brash piece in a brief saffron tunic whom Afrania had called Plancina.

"Well, thanks. I needed reassurance. . . . So what's the black mood in this part of the camp all about?"

"Get lost. We're not talking to management."

"I'm not one of them. I'm not even a performer. I'm just a freelance scribe who happened upon this group by accident; one who's starting to wish he'd given Chremes a wide berth." The murmur of discontent that ran around warned me I had best take care or else instead of persuading the group back to work I would end up leading their walkout. That would be just my style: from peacemaker to chief rebel in about five minutes. Smart work, Falco.

"It's no secret," said one of the stagehands, a particular misery. "We had a big row with Chremes last night, and we're not backing down."

"Well, you don't have to tell me. I didn't mean to pry into your business."

Even with a hangover that made my head feel like the spot on a fortress gate that's just been hit by a thirty-foot battering ram, my professional grit had stayed intact: as soon as I said they need not spill the tale, they all wanted to tell me everything.

I had guessed right: Ione's death was at the heart of their discontent. They had finally noticed there was a maniac in our midst. He could murder dramatic writers with impunity, but now that he had turned his attention to the musicians they were wondering which of them would be picked off next.

"It's reasonable to feel alarmed," I sympathized. "But what was last night's row with Chremes about?"

"We are not staying on," said the cymbalist. "We want to be given our money for the season—"

"Hang on, the rest of us were paid our share of the takings last night. Are your contract terms very different?"

"Too damn right! Chremes knows actors and scribes are pushed to find employment. You won't leave him until you're given a firm shove. But musicians and lifters can always find work so he gives us a fraction, then keeps us waiting for the rest until the tour packs up."

"And now he won't release your residue?"

"Fast, Falco! Not if we leave early. It's in the trunk under his bed, and he says it's staying there. So now we're saying to him, he can stick *The Birds* in his aviary and tweet all the way from here to Antiochia. If we've got to stay around, he won't be able to take on replacements because we'll warn them off. But we're not going to work. He'll have no music and no scenery. These Greek towns will laugh him off the stage."

"*The Birds!* That was about the final straw," grumbled the youthful lyre-player, Ribes. He was no Apollo. He could neither play well nor strike awe with his majestic beauty. In fact he looked as appetizing as yesterday's ground-millet polenta. "Wanting us to chirp like bloody sparrows."

"I can see that would be a liberty to a professional who can tell his Lydian modes from his Dorians!"

"One more crack from you, Falco, and you'll be picked with a plectrum in a place you won't like!"

I grinned at him. "Sorry. I'm employed to write jokes."

"About time you started doing it, then," someone chuckled; I didn't see who.

Afrania broke in, softening slightly. "So, Falco, what made you venture here among the troublemaking low-life?"

"Thought I might be able to help."

"Like how?" jeered a stagehand's wife.

"Who knows? I'm a man of ideas—"

"He means filthy thoughts," suggested another broad-beamed female whose thoughts were undoubtedly much grimier than mine.

"I came to consult you all," I carried on bravely. "You may be able to help me work out who caused the two deaths. And I be-lieve I can assure you that none of you is at risk."   ·

"How can you do that?" demanded the leader of the orchestra.

"Well, let's take this slowly. I'll not make rash promises about any man who can take life in such a cruelly casual way. I still don't have any real idea why he killed Heliodorus. But in Ione's case, the reason is much clearer."

"Clear as mud on a bootstrap!" Plancina declared. There was still much hostility, though most of the group were now listening intently.

"Ione thought she knew who killed the playwright," I told them. "She had promised to reveal the man's name to me; she must have been killed to stop her giving him away."

"So we are safe so long as we all go around saying 'I've ab-solutely no idea who killed them!' in loud voices?" The orchestra leader was dry, though not unbearably sarcastic.

Ignoring him, I announced: "If I knew whom Ione was meeting on the night she died, I would know everything. She was
your friend. One of you must have an idea. She will have said
something about her movements that evening, or at some other
time she may have mentioned a man she was friendly with—"
Before the jeers could break out I added hastily, "I do know she
was very popular. There must be some of you here she had
banged her tambourine for on occasions, am I right?"

One or two present owned up to it freely. Of the rest, some
declared they were married, which was supposed to imply they
were innocent; at any rate, in the presence of their wives it gave
them immunity from questioning. Those men who had not tangled with Ione had certainly thought about it; this was accepted
by everyone.

"Well, that illustrates my problem." I sighed. "It could be any
of you—or any of the actors."

"Or you!" suggested Afrania. She looked sullen, and developed a nasty streak whenever this subject was discussed.

"Falco never knew Heliodorus," someone else pointed out
fairly.

"Maybe I did," I conceded. "I *said* I found him as a stranger,
but maybe I *had* known him, took against him, then attached
myself to the company afterwards for some perverted reason—"

"Such as you wanted his job?" cried Ribes the lyre-player with
a wit that was rare for him. The rest dissolved into roars of
laughter, and I was deemed innocent.

No one could offer any useful information. That did not mean
no one had any. I might yet hear a furtive whisper outside my
tent as someone became braver and came to pass on some vital
clue.

"I cannot advise you about staying with the company," I declared. "But look at it this way. If you withdraw your labor, the
tour will fold. Chremes and Phrygia cannot put on comedy

without music or scenery. Both are traditional and the audience expects them."

"A Plautian monologue without enhancing flute music is a loaf made with dead yeast," pronounced the orchestra leader somberly.

"Oh, quite!" I tried to look respectful. "Without you, bookings would become harder and eventually the troupe would disperse. Remember, if we break up, the killer gets away with it." I stood up. That meant I could see all of them and address each conscience. I wondered how often they had received appeals to the heart from a gray-faced, nauseous inebriate who had nothing substantial to offer them: quite often if they worked for actor-managers. "It's up to you. Do you want Ione's death to be avenged, or don't you care?"

"It's too dangerous!" wailed one of the women, who happened to be holding a small child on her hip.

"I'm not so crass that I don't know what I'm asking. Each of you must make the choice."

"What's your interest, Falco?" It was Afranio who asked. "You said you're a freelance. Why don't you just cut and run?"

"I am involved. I cannot avoid it. I discovered Heliodorus. My girlfriend found Ione. We have to know who did that—and make sure he pays."

"He's right," argued the cymbalist reasonably. "The only way to catch this man is to stick together as a group and keep the killer among us. But how long will it take, Falco?"

"If I knew how long, I would know who he was."

"He knows you're looking for him," warned Afrania.

"And I know he must be watching me." I gave her a hard stare, remembering her odd claims about the alibi she had given Tranio. I still felt certain that she had lied.

"If he thinks you are close, he may come after you," suggested the cymbalist.

"He probably will."

"Aren't you afraid?" Plancina asked, as if waiting to see me struck down was the next best thing to a gory chariot race.

"Coming after me will be his mistake." I sounded confident.

"If you need a drink of water during the next few weeks," the orchestra leader advised me in his usual pessimistic tone, "I should make sure you only use a very small cup!"

"I'm not intending to drown."

I folded my arms, planting my feet astride like a man who could be trusted in a tight spot. They knew about decent acting and were unconvinced by this. "I can't make your decisions. But I can make one promise. There is more to me than some jobbing scribe Chremes picked up in the desert. My background's tough. I've worked for the best—don't ask me names. I've been involved in jobs I'm not allowed to discuss, and I'm trained in skills you'd rather I didn't describe. I've tracked down plenty of felons, and if you haven't heard about it that just proves how discreet I am. If you agree to stay on, I'll stay too. Then you will at least know that you have me looking after your interests. . . ."

I must have been mad. I had had more sense and sanity when I was totally befuddled by last night's drink. Guarding them was not the problem. What I hated was the thought of explaining to Helena that I had offered my personal protection to wild women like Plancina and Afrania.

Thirty-eight

The musicians and stagehands stayed with us and continued to work. We gave Scythopolis *The Birds*. Scythopolis gave us—an ovation.

For Greeks, they were surprisingly tolerant.

They had an interesting theater, with a semicircular orchestra that could only be reached by steps. In a Roman play we would not have used it, but of course we were doing a Greek one, with a very large chorus, and Chremes wanted a flock of birds to spill down towards the audience. The steps made life difficult for anyone foolish enough to be acting while dressed in a large padded costume, with gigantic claws on their shoes, and a heavy beaked mask.

While we were there some cheapskate salesman was trying to

persuade the magistrates to spend thousands on an acoustic system (some bronze devices to be hung on the theater wall). The theater architect was happily pointing out that he had already provided seven splendid oval niches that would take the complex equipment; he was obviously in on the deal with the salesman, and stood to receive a cut.

We tested the samples of the salesman's toys to the limit with tweeting, twittering, and booming, and frankly they made no difference. Given the perfect acoustics of most Greek theaters, this was no surprise. The taxpayers of Scythopolis settled back in their seats and looked as if they were quite content to place wreaths in the seven niches. The architect looked sick.

Even though Congrio had told us it had happened before, I never really understood why Chremes had suddenly abandoned his normal repertoire. With Aristophanes we had leaped back in time about four hundred years, from New Roman Comedy to Old Greek ditto. I liked it. They say the old jokes are the best. They are certainly better than none at all. I want a play to have bite. By that, speaking as a republican, I mean some political point. Old Comedy had that, which made a sophisticated change. For me New Comedy was dire. I hate watching meaningless plots about tiresome characters in grisly situations on a provincial street. If I wanted that, I could go home and listen to my neighbors through their apartment walls.

The Birds was famous. At rehearsal Tranio, always ready with an anecdote, told us, "Not bad considering it only won second prize at the festival it was written for."

"What a showoff! Which archive did you drag that one out of, Tranio?" I scoffed.

"And what play actually won then?" Helena demanded.

"Some trifle called *The Revelers,* now unknown to man."

"Sounds fun. One of the people in my tent has been reveling too much lately, though," Helena commented.

"This play is not half as obscene as some Aristophanes,"

grumbled Tranio. "I saw *Peace* once—not often performed, as we're always at war, of course. It has two female roles for wicked girls with nice arses. One of them has her clothes taken off on-stage, then she's handed down to the man in the center of the front row. She sits on his lap for starters, then spends the rest of the play going up and down, 'comforting' other members of the audience."

"Filth!" I cried, feigning shock.

Tranio scowled. "It hardly compares with showing Hercules as a glutton, giving out cookery tips."

"No, but recipes won't get us run out of town," said Helena. She was always practical. Offered a prospect of wicked women with nice arses "comforting" the ticket holders, her practical nature became even more brisk than usual.

Helena knew *The Birds*. She had been well educated, partly by her brothers' tutors when her brothers slipped off to the race-course, and partly through grabbing any written scrolls that she could lay her hands on in private libraries owned by her wealthy family (plus the few tattered fifth-hand items I kept under my own bed). Since she had never been one for the senators' wives' circuit of orgies and admiring gladiators, she had always spent time at home reading. So she told me, anyway.

She had done a good job on the script; Chremes had accepted it without change, remarking that at last I seemed to be getting on top of the job."

"Fast work," I congratulated her.

"It's nothing."

"Don't let having your adaptations accepted first time go to your head. I'd hate to think you're becoming an intellectual."

"Sorry, I forgot. You don't like cultured women."

"Suits me." I grinned at her. "I'm no snob. I'm prepared to put up with brains in an exceptional case."

"Thank you very much!"

"Don't mention it. Mind you, I never expected to end up in

bed with some learned scroll-beetle who's studied Greek and knows that *The Birds* is a famous play. I suppose it sticks in the mind because of the feathers. Like when you think about the Greek philosophers and can only remember that the first premise of Pythagoras was that nobody should eat beans."

"Philosophy's a new side to you." She smiled.

"Oh, I can run off philosophers as well as any dinner-party bore. My favorite is Bias, who invented the informers' motto—"

"All Men are Bad!" Helena had read the philosophers as well as the dramatists. "Everyone has to play a bird in the chorus, Marcus. Which has Chremes given you?"

"Listen, fruit, when I make my acting debut, it will be a moment to memorize for our grandchildren. I will be a Tragic Hero, striding on through the central doorway in a coronet, not hopping from the wings as a bloody bird."

Helena chortled. "Oh, I think you're wrong! This play was written for a very prosperous festival. There is a full chorus of twenty-four named cheepers, and we all have to participate."

I shook my head. "Not me."

Helena Justina was a bright girl. Besides, as the adapter she was the only person in our group who had read the entire play. Most people just skimmed through to find their own parts. Helena soon worked out what Chremes must have me down for, and thought it hilarious.

Musa, who had been silent as usual, looked bemused—though not half as bemused as when Helena explained that *he* would be appearing as the reed warbler.

So what was I playing? They had found me the dross, needless to say.

In our performance the two humans who run away from Athens in disgust at the litigation, the strife, and the hefty fines were played by handsome Philocrates and tough Davos. Naturally Philocrates had grabbed the major part, with all the speeches, while Davos took the stooge who puts in the obscene one-line rejoinders. His part was shorter, though more pungent.

Tranio was playing Hercules. In fact he and Grumio were to be a long succession of unwelcome visitors who call at cloud-cuckoo-land in order to be chased off ignominiously. Phrygia had a hilarious cameo as an elderly Iris whose lightning bolts refused to fulminate, while Byrria appeared as the hoopoe's beautiful wife and as Sovereignty (a symbolic part, made more interesting by a scanty costume). Chremes was chorus leader for the famous twenty-four named birds. These included Congrio hooting, Musa warbling, and Helena disguised as the cutest dabchick who ever hopped onto a stage. I was unsure how I would confess to her noble father and disapproving mother that their elegant daughter with the centuries-old pedigree had now been witnessed by a crowd of raw Scythopolitans acting as a dabchick. . . .

At least from now on I would always be able to call up material to blackmail Helena.

My role was tiresome. I played the informer. In this otherwise witty satire, my character creeps in after the ghastly poet, the twisting fortune-teller, the rebellious youth, and the cranky philosopher. Once they have come to cloud-cuckoo-land and all been seen off by the Athenians, an informer tries his luck. Like mine, his luck is in short supply, to the delight of the audience. He is stirring up court cases on the basis of questionable evidence and wants some wings to help him fly about the Greek islands quicker as he hands out subpoenas. If anyone had been prepared to listen, I could have told them an informer's life is so boring it's positively respectable, while the chances of a lucrative court case are about equal with discovering an emerald in a goose's gizzard. But the company were used to abusing my profession (which is much mocked in drama) so they loved this chance to heap insults on a live victim. I offered to play the sacrificial pig instead, but was overruled. Needless to say, in the play, the informer fails to get his wings.

Chremes deemed me fit to act my role without coaching, even though it was a speaking part. He claimed I could talk well enough without assistance. By the end of rehearsals I was tired of people crying "Oh just be yourself, Falco!" ever so wittily. And the moment when Philocrates was called upon to whip me off-stage was maddening. He really enjoyed handing out a thrashing. I was now plotting a black revenge.

Everyone else hugely enjoyed putting on this stuff. I decided that perhaps Chremes did know what he was doing. Even though we had always complained about his judgment, the mood lightened. Scythopolis kept us for several performances. The company was calmer, as well as richer, by the time we moved on up the Jordan Valley to Gadara.

Thirty-nine

Gadara called itself the Athens
of the East. From this Eastern outpost had come the cynic
satirist Menippos, the philosopher and poet Philodemos, who
had had Virgil as his pupil in Italy, and the elegiac epigrammatist
Meleager. Helena had read Meleager's poetic anthology *The Gar-
land,* so before we arrived she enlightened me.

"His themes are love and death—"

"Very nice."

"And he compares each poet he includes to a different flower."

I said what I thought, and she smiled gently. Love and death
are gritty subjects. Their appropriate handling by poets does not
require myrtle petals and violets.

The city commanded a promontory above a rich and vital
landscape, with stunning views to both Palestine and Syria,

westwards over Lake Tiberias and north to the far snow-capped mountain peak of Mount Hermon. Nearby, thriving villages studded the surrounding slopes, which were lush with pasture-land. Instead of the bare tawny hills we had seen endlessly rolling elsewhere, this area was clothed with green fields and woodlands. Instead of lone nomadic goatherds, we saw chattering groups watching over fatter, fleecier flocks. Even the sunlight seemed brighter, enlivened by the nearby twinkling presence of the great lake. No doubt all the shepherds and swineherds in the desirable pastures were busy composing sunlit, elegantly elegiac odes. If they were kept awake at night struggling with metric imperfections in their verse, they could always put themselves off to sleep by counting their obols and drachmas; people here had no financial worries that I could see.

As always in our company, argument about what play to put on was raging; eventually, with matters still unresolved, Chremes and Philocrates, supported by Grumio, strolled off to see the local magistrate. Helena and I took a walk around town. We made inquiries about Thalia's lost musical maiden, fruitlessly as usual. We didn't much care; we were enjoying this short time alone together. We found ourselves following a throng of people who were ambling down from the acropolis to the river valley below.

Apparently the routine here was for the citizens to flock out in the evening, go to the river, bathe in its reputedly therapeutic waters, then flog back uphill (complaining) for their nightly dose of public entertainment. Even if bathing in the river had cured their aches, walking back afterwards up the precipitous slope to their lofty town was likely to set their joints again, and half of them probably caught a chill when they reached the cooler air. Still, if one or two had to take to their beds, all the more room on the comfortable theater seats for folk who had come direct from the shop or the office without risking their health in water therapy.

We joined the crowds of people in their striped robes and twisted headgear on the banks of the river, where Helena cautiously dipped a toe while I stood aloof, looking Roman and superior. The late evening sunlight had a pleasantly soothing effect. I could happily have forgotten both my searches and relaxed into the theatrical life for good.

Further along the bank I suddenly noticed Philocrates; he had not spotted us. He had been drinking—wine, presumably—from a goatskin. As he finished he stood up, demonstrating his physique for any watching women, then blew up the skin, tied its neck, and tossed it to some children who were playing in the water. As they fell on it, squealing with delight, Philocrates stripped off his tunic ready to dive into the river.

"You'd need a lot of *those* to fill a punnet!" giggled Helena, noticing that the naked actor was not well endowed.

"Size isn't everything," I assured her.

"Just as well!"

She was grinning, while I wondered whether I ought to play the heavy-handed patriarch and censor whatever it was she had been reading to acquire such a low taste in jokes.

"There's a very odd smell, Marcus. Why do spa waters always stink?"

"To fool you into thinking they are doing you good. Who told you the punnet joke?"

"Aha! Did you see what Philocrates did with his wineskin?"

"I did. He can't possibly have killed Heliodorus if he's kind to children," I remarked sarcastically.

Helena and I started the steep climb up from the elegant waterfront to the town high on its ridge. It was hard going, reminding us both of our wearying assault on the High Place at Petra.

Partly to gain a breathing space, but interested anyway, I stopped to have a look at the town's water system. They had an aqueduct that brought drinking water over ten miles from a

spring to the east of the city; it then ran through an amazing underground system. One of the caps to a flue had been removed
by some workmen for cleaning; I was leaning over the hole and
staring down into the depths when a voice behind made me
jump violently.

"That's a long drop, Falco!"

It was Grumio.

Helena had grabbed my arm, though her intervention was
probably unnecessary. Grumio laughed cheerfully. "Steady!" he
warned, before clattering downhill the way we had just come.

Helena and I exchanged a wry glance. The thought crossed
my mind that if someone fell down into those tunnels and the
exit was recovered, even if he survived the tumble no one would
ever hear him call for help. His body would not be found until it
had decayed so much that townsfolk started feeling poorly. . . .

If Grumio had been a suspect who could not account for his
movements, I might have found myself shivering.

Helena and I made our way back to camp slowly, amorously
intertwined.

Not for the first time with this company, we had walked into a
panic. Chremes and the others had been gone too long; Davos
had sent Congrio to wander around town in his most unobtrusive manner, trying to find out where they were. As we reached
the camp Congrio came scampering back, shrieking: "They're all
locked up!"

"Calm down." I made a grab at him, and held him still.
"Locked up? What for?"

"It's Grumio's fault. When they got in to see the magistrate, it
turned out he had been at Gerasa when we were there; he'd
heard Grumio doing his comic turn. Part of it was insulting
Gadarenes. . . ." As I recalled Grumio's stand-up act, *most* of it
had involved being rude about the Decapolis towns. Thinking of
Helena's recent joke, we were only lucky he hadn't mentioned

punnets in connection with the private parts of their pompous magistrates. Maybe he had never read whatever scroll Helena had found for herself. "Now our lot are all thrown into prison for slander," Congrio wailed.

I wanted my dinner. My chief reaction was annoyance. "If Grumio said the Gadarenes were impetuous and touchy and have no sense of humor, where's the slander? It's obviously true! Anyway, that's nothing to what I heard him say about Abila and Dium."

"I'm just telling you what I heard, Falco."

"And I'm just deciding what we can do."

"Cause a fuss," suggested Davos. "Tell them we intend to warn our Emperor about their unkind welcome for innocent visitors, then beat the local jailer over the head with a cudgel. After that, run like mad."

Davos was the kind of man I could work with. He had a good grasp of a situation and a down-to-earth attitude to handling it.

He and I went into town together, dressed up to look like respectable entrepreneurs. We wore newly polished boots and togas from the costume box. Davos was carrying a laurel wreath for an even more refined effect, though I did think that was overdoing it.

We presented ourselves at the magistrate's house, looking surprised there could be a problem. The nob was out: at the theater. We then presented ourselves at one end of the orchestra stalls and hung around for a break in what turned out to be a *very* poor satyr play. Davos muttered, "At least they could tune their damned panpipes! Their masks stink. And their nymphs are rubbish."

While we fretted on the sidelines, I managed to ask, "Davos, have you ever seen Philocrates blow up an empty wineskin and throw it into water, the way children like to do? Is making floats a habit of his?"

"Not that I've noticed. I've seen the clowns do it."

As usual, what had looked like a pinpointing clue caused more confusion than it solved.

Luckily, satyr plays are short. A few disguises, a couple of mock rapes, and they gallop offstage in their goatskin trousers.

At last there was a pause to let the sweetmeat trays go round. Seizing our moment we leaped across the pit to beard the elected nincompoop who had incarcerated our gang. He was an overbearing bastard. Sometimes I lose faith in democracy. Usually, in fact.

There was not much time to argue; we could hear tambourines rattling as a fleet of overweight female dancers prepared to come onstage next and titillate with some choric frivolity in see-through skirts. After three minutes of fast talking we had achieved nothing with the official, and he signaled the theater guards to shift us.

Davos and I left of our own accord. We went straight to the jail, where we bribed the keeper with half our proceeds from performing *The Birds* at Scythopolis. Anticipating trouble, we had already left instructions for the wagons and camels to be loaded up by my friends the scene-shifters. Once we had organized our jailbreak, we spent a few moments in the forum loudly discussing our next move eastwards to Capitolias, then we met the rest of our group on the road and galloped off in the northerly direction of Hippos.

We traveled fast, cursing the Gadarenes for the indelicate swine they had shown themselves to be.

So much for the Athens of the East!

Forty

Hippos: a jumpy town. Not as jumpy as some of its visitors were, however.

It was located halfway along the eastern shore of Lake Tiberias on a hilltop site—fine vistas, but inconvenient. The site set it back from the lake a considerable distance, with no nearby river, so water for domestic consumption was scarce. Across the lake lay Tiberias, a city that had been much more conveniently placed at shore level. The people of Hippos hated the people of Tiberias with passionate hostility—much more real than the vaunted feud between Pella and Scythopolis, which we had been hard put to spot.

Hippos had its water shortage and feud to contend with, which ought to have left little time for parting traders from their money or spending that money on grandiose building schemes, yet with the tenacity of this region its people were managing both. From the gate where we entered (on foot, for we camped out of town in case we needed to flee again) ran an established main street, a long black basalt thoroughfare whose gracious colonnades traveled the length of the ridge on which the town stood, giving fine views of Lake Tiberias.

Perhaps due to our own nervous situation, we found the populace edgy. The streets were full of swarthy faces peering from hoods with an air that told you not to ask directions to the marketplace. The women had the guarded expressions of those who spend many hours every day jostling to fill pitchers with water; thin, harassed little pieces with the sinewy arms of those who then had to carry the full pitchers home. The men's role was to stand about looking sinister; they all carried knives, visible or hidden, ready to stab anyone they could accuse of having a Tiberias accent. Hippos was a dark, introverted huddle of suspicion. To my mind this was the sort of place poets and philosophers ought to come from, to give them the right tone of cynical distrust; of course none did.

In a town like Hippos, even the most hardened informer starts to feel nervous about asking questions. Nevertheless, there was no point coming here unless I carried out my commission. I had to try to find the missing organist. I braced myself and tackled various leathery characters. Some of them spat; not many directly at me, unless their aim was truly bad. Most gazed into the middle distance with blank faces, which appeared to be the Hippos dialect for "No, I'm terribly sorry, young Roman sir, I've never seen your delightful maiden nor heard of the raffish Syrian businessman who snaffled her. . . ." Nobody actually stuck a knife into me.

I crossed off one more possible destination for Sophrona and Habib (assuming he was the person she did the flit with), then took the long haul out of town to our camp. All the way back I kept looking over my shoulder to see if the people of Hippos were tailing me. I was growing as nervy as they were.

Luckily my mind was taken off my unease when halfway along the trail I caught up with Ribes the lyre-player.

Ribes was a pasty youth who believed his role as a musician was to sit around in a lopsided haircut describing plans for making vast sums of money with popular songs he had yet to compose. So far there was no sign of him being mobbed by Egyptian accountants keen to rob him of huge agency fees. He wore the sort of belt that said he was tough, with a facial expression that belonged on a moonstruck vole. I tried to avoid him, but he had seen me.

"How's the music?" I asked politely.

"Coming along . . ." He did not ask how the playwriting was.

We strolled along together for a short time while I tried to twist my ankle so I could fall behind.

"Have you been looking for clues?" he asked earnestly.

"Just looking for a girl." Perhaps because he knew Helena, this appeared to worry him. It was not a concept that had ever worried me.

"I've been thinking about what you said to us," Ribes offered after a few more strides. "About what happened to Ione . . ." He tailed off. I forced myself to look interested, though talking to Ribes thrilled me about as much as trying to pick my teeth at a banquet without a toothpick and without the host's wife noticing.

"Thought of anything to help me?" I encouraged gloomily.

"I don't know."

"Nobody else has either," I said.

Ribes looked more cheerful. "Well, I might know something." Fortunately, six years as an informer had taught me how to wait patiently. "Ione and I were friendly, actually. I don't mean— Well, I mean we never— But she used to talk to me."

This was the best news I had had for days. Men who had slept with the tambourinist would be useless; they had certainly proved slow to come forward. I welcomed this feeble reed with the bent stalk, in whom the girl could well have confided since he had so little else to offer.

"And what did she say, Ribes, that now strikes you as possibly significant?"

"Well, did you know that at one time she had dealings with Heliodorus?" This could be the link I was needing to find. Ione had implied to me that she knew more about the playwright than most people. "He used to boast to her about what he'd got on other people—stories that would upset them, you know. He never told her much, just hints, and I don't remember much that she passed on." Ribes was not exactly bursting with curiosity about the rest of the human race.

"Tell me what you can," I said.

"Well . . ." Ribes ticked off some tantalizing references: "He reckoned he had Chremes in his power; he used to laugh about how Congrio hated his guts; he was supposed to be pals with Tranio, but there was something going on there—"

"Anything about Byrria?"

"No."

"Davos?"

"No."

"Grumio?"

"No. The only thing I really remember is that Ione said Heliodorus had been horrible to Phrygia. He found out she had once had a baby; she'd had to leave it behind somewhere and she was desperate to find out what had happened to it since. Heliodorus told her he knew somebody who had seen the child, but he wouldn't tell her who it was, or where. Ione said Phrygia had had to pretend that she didn't believe him. It was the only way to stop him tormenting her with it."

I was thinking hard. "This is interesting, Ribes, but I'd be surprised if it relates to why Heliodorus died. Ione told me very definitely that he was killed for 'purely professional' reasons. Can you say anything about that?"

Ribes shook his head. We spent the rest of the walk with him trying to tell me about a dirge he had composed in Ione's memory, and me doing my best to avoid letting him sing it.

Contrary to our expectations, Hippos offered a warm welcome to theatrical performers. We easily obtained a booking at the auditorium, although we could not attract a local sponsor, so had to play on a directly ticketed basis; however, we did sell tickets. It was hard to say who was buying them, and we went into the opening night with some trepidation. Every good Roman has heard stories of riots in provincial theaters. Sooner or later our turn might arrive to become part of disreputable folklore. Hippos seemed the place.

Our performance must have had a calming influence, however. We put on *The Pirate Brothers*. The townsfolk seemed to be genuinely informed critics. Villains were booed with gusto (no doubt on the assumption that they might come from Tiberias) and love scenes enthusiastically cheered.

We gave them two more performances. *The Rope* was rather quietly received, up to the scene with the tug-of-war, which went down superbly. This brought increased crowds the following day for *The Birds*. After much silly debate of the kind he loved and we all hated, Chremes had risked this as a gamble, since piquant satire was not obvious fare for an audience who spent their time seething with pent-up suspicions and fingering their daggers. However, the costumes swayed them. Hippos took to *The Birds* so well that at the end we were mobbed by members of the audience. After a moment of panic as they came swarming onto the stage, we realized they all wanted to join in. Then ensued the fascinating spectacle of somber men in long flowing robes all losing their inhibitions with joyous glee and hopping about for half an hour, flapping their elbows as imitation wings, like chickens who had eaten fermented grain. We, meanwhile, stood about rather stiffly, unsure what to make of it.

Exhausted, we crept away that night, before Hippos could demand even more excitement from our repertoire.

Forty-one

Approaching Dium we were told there was a plague. We retreated very fast.

Forty-two

Abila was not officially one of the fabled ten in the region of the Ten Towns. Like other places, this one claimed to belong in order to acquire prestige and the sense of mutual protection against raiders that was enjoyed among the true federation. If raiders turned up and asked to see their certificate of membership, presumably the claim failed and they had to submit to pillage meekly.

It did have all the qualifying features of the best of the Decapolis: a beautiful location, a rippling stream, good defensive walls, a Greek acropolis plus a more Romanized settlement, a huge temple complex honoring deities to suit every palate, and a theater. The local architecture was a rich mixture of marble, basalt, and gray granite. Abila was set on a high rolling plateau where a restless wind eerily seethed. There was something remote and lonely about it. The people looked at us thoughtfully; they were not directly hostile but we found the atmosphere unsettling.

Our thwarted trip to Dium, leading to an unexpectedly lengthened journey, had caused us to arrive at an awkward time of day. Normally we traveled through the night to avoid the worst heat, and tried to enter cities in the morning. Then Chremes could investigate the possibilities for a booking at an early stage while we others rested and complained about him among ourselves.

Having come on a poor track, we reached Abila well after noon. No one was happy. One of the wagons had had a broken axle, which held us up on a road that had seemed likely to be patrolled by brigands, and we were all shaken to bits by the roughness of the ground. On arrival we threw up tents, then straightaway retired into them without wanting to make plans.

Outside our tent, Musa doggedly lit a fire. However tired we were, he always did this, and also always fetched water, before he would relax. I forced myself to cooperate and fed the ox, having my foot stepped on by the ridiculous beast in return for my act of duty. Helena found food for us, though no one was hungry.

It was too hot, and we were too ill tempered to sleep. Instead we all sat cross-legged and talked restlessly.

"I feel depressed," Helena exclaimed. "We're running out of cities but not solving anything. What are the places we have left to visit? Just Capitolias, Canatha, and Damascus." She was in a brisk mood again, answering her own questions as if she expected Musa and me to stare into space lethargically. We did that for a while, not deliberately intending to annoy her but because it seemed natural.

"Damascus is big," I offered eventually. "There seems a good hope of finding Sophrona."

"But what if she was at Dium?"

"Then she's probably caught the plague. Thalia wouldn't want her back."

"Meanwhile, we go on searching for her, though, Marcus." Helena hated wasted effort. I was an informer; I was used to it.

"We have to do something, fruit. We're trapped at the ends of the Empire, and we need to earn our keep. Look, we'll go to the last three cities with the company and if Sophrona doesn't turn up then we'll know we should have tried Dium. If it happens, we can decide what we think about this plague."

It was one of those moments that hit travelers, a moment when I reckoned our decision would be to take a fast ship home. I didn't say it, because we were both so frustrated and gloomy that even mentioning a retreat would have had us packing our bags that minute. These moods pass. If they don't, *then* you can suggest going home.

"Maybe there was nothing really wrong at Dium," Helena fretted. "We only have the word of a caravan we met. The men who told us may have been lying for some reason. Or it could be no more than one child with spots. People panic too easily."

I tried myself not to sound panicky. "Risking our own lives would be stupid—and I'm not going to be responsible for extracting a runaway musician from Dium if taking her to Rome might bring an epidemic there. It's too high a price for a water-organ fugue, however brilliant a player she is."

"All right." After a moment Helena added, "I hate you when you're sensible."

"The caravanners looked pretty grim when they waved us away," I insisted.

"I said, all right!"

I saw Musa smile faintly. As usual he was sitting there saying nothing. It was the kind of irritating day when I could easily have lost my temper with him for this silence, so I covered by taking charge: "Maybe we need to take stock." If I thought this would perk up my companions, I was disappointed. They both remained listless and glum. Still, I pressed on: "Looking for Sophrona may be pointless, I agree. I know the girl could be anywhere by now. We're not even certain she ever left Italy." This was verging on too much pessimism. "All we can do is to be as thorough as possible. Sometimes these jobs are impossible. Or you may run across a piece of luck and solve the case after all."

Helena and Musa looked as impressed as a desert vulture who had flown down to an intriguing carcass only to find it was a piece of old tunic blowing against a broken amphora. I try to stay cheerful. However, I gave up on the girl musician. We had been looking for her for too long. She had ceased to seem real. Our interest in the creature had waned, along with any chances we had ever had of finding her out here.

Suddenly Helena rallied. "So what about the murderer?"

Once again I tried to liven us up with a review of the facts. "Well, what do we know? He's a man, one who can whistle, who must be fairly strong, who wears a hat sometimes—"

"His nerve holds," contributed Musa. "He has been with us for weeks. He knows we are looking for him, yet he makes no mistake."

"Yes, he's confident—although he does jump sometimes. He panicked and tried to put you out of action, Musa, then he soon silenced Ione."

"He's ruthless," said Helena. "And also persuasive: he did make both Heliodorus and Ione agree to go somewhere alone with him. Ione even suspected he was a killer, though I presume that didn't apply in the playwright's case."

"Let's think about Petra again," I suggested. "The chief players went there and came back without the playwright. What have we found out about them? Who hated Heliodorus enough to turn his walk into a swim?"

"Most of them." Helena ticked them off on her fingers: "Chremes and Phrygia, because he plagued them about their unhappy marriage and Phrygia's lost baby. Philocrates because they

were unsuccessful rivals for Byrria. Byrria, too, because he tried
to rape her. Davos partly because of his loyalty to Phrygia, but
also because he thought the man was . . ." She hesitated.

"A shit," I supplied.

"Worse: a bad writer!" We all grinned briefly, then Helena carried on: "Congrio loathed Heliodorus because he was bullied,
but Congrio is let off because he can't whistle."

"We'd better check that," I said.

"I asked Chremes," she whipped back crisply. "As for the
Twins, they have told us they disliked Heliodorus. But do we
have a particular reason? A strong enough motive to kill him?"

I agreed: "If there was one, we haven't unearthed it yet. They
told me that Heliodorus couldn't succeed in doing them down
on the stage. If he tried to write poor parts, they could improvise. Well, we know that's true."

"So they were not in his power," Helena mused. "Yet they do
say they despised him."

"Right. And if we come forward in time, one at least—
Tranio—has an unsatisfactory alibi for the night Ione died.
Everyone else seems to be accounted for that night. Poor Con-
grio was running around Gerasa writing wrongly spelled play-
bills. Grumio was joking his heart out in the street. Chremes,
Davos, and Philocrates were all dining together—"

"Apart from when Philocrates says he left to bed his cheese-
maker," scowled Helena. She seemed to have developed an an-
tipathy for her admirer.

I grinned. "He showed me the cheese!"

Musa openly chortled too. "I think the handsome one is too
busy to find time for killing people."

"Eating cheese!" I laughed abusively.

Helena stayed serious: "He could have acquired the cheese at
any time—"

"So long as the shop had a low counter!"

"Oh shut up, Marcus!"

"Right." I pulled myself together. "Everyone has an alibi except Tranio. Tranio ducks out by claiming he was with Afrania; I don't believe him, though."

"So we really suspect Tranio?" said Helena, pushing for a decision.

I still felt uneasy. "There's a worrying lack of evidence. Musa, *could* Tranio be your whistling man?"

"Oh yes." He too was troubled, though. "But the night I was pushed off the embankment at Bostra—" If I ever forgot that incident, Musa never did. He thought about it again now, cautious as ever. "That night, I am sure Tranio was walking up ahead of me. Congrio, Grumio, Davos—they were all behind. It could have been any one of them, but not Tranio."

"You're quite certain?"

"Oh yes."

"When I asked you about it straight after the incident—"

"I have thought about it a lot more since. Tranio was in front."

I considered this. "Are we still sure what happened to you that night was deliberate? Nothing else has been done to you."

"I stay near you— I have perfect protection!" He said it deadpan, though I was trying to decide if there was a trace of irony. "I felt the hard push," he reminded me. "Whoever did that must have known we had collided. He made no call for help when I fell."

Helena weighed in thoughtfully. "Marcus, they all know that you are trying to find the killer. Perhaps he is being more careful. He has not attacked you." Nor had he attacked Helena herself, which at one time had been my unspoken fear.

"I wish he'd try," I murmured. "Then I'd have the creep!"

In my head I carried on thinking. This had a bad taste. Either we had missed something crucial, or it would be difficult ever to expose this villain. The vital proof was eluding us. The more time passed, the less chance we stood of solving the mystery.

"We have never seen anybody wearing the hat again," Helena pointed out. She must have been thinking hard, like me.

"And he has stopped whistling," Musa added.

He seemed to have stopped killing too. He must know I was utterly stumped. If he did nothing else he would be safe.

I would have to *make* him do something.

Refusing to give up, I nagged at the problem: "We have a situation where all the suspects are ruled out on at least one of the attacks. That cannot be right. I still feel one person is responsible for everything, even what happened to Musa."

"But there can be other possibilities?" asked Helena. "An accomplice?"

"Oh yes. Perhaps a general conspiracy, with people providing false alibis. Heliodorus was universally loathed, after all. It is possible more than one of them was actively involved."

"You don't believe that, though?" Musa tackled me.

"No. A man was killed, for a reason we don't know, but we'll assume it made sense at the time. Then a possible witness was attacked, and another who intended to name him was strangled. This is a logical progression. To me, it fits one killer acting alone, and then reacting alone as he tries to escape discovery."

"It's very confusing," Helena complained.

"No, it's simple." I corrected her, suddenly sure of myself. "There is a lie somewhere. There must be. It cannot be obvious, or one of us would have spotted a discrepancy."

"So what can we do?" Helena demanded. "How can we find out?"

Musa shared her despondency. "This man is too clever to change the lie just because we ask the same questions a second time."

"We'll test everything," I said. "Make no assumptions, recheck every story, but asking somebody different whenever we can. We may jog a memory. We may drag more information to the surface just by putting pressure on. Then, if that fails, we'll have to force the issue."

"How?"

"I'll think of something."

As usual it had a futile ring, yet the others did not question my claim. Maybe I would think of a way to break this man. The more I remembered what he had done, the more I was determined to better him.

Forty-three

For Abila, Chremes came up with another new play, an unfunny farce about Hercules sent down to earth on a mission from the other gods. It was deep Greek myth rendered as crass Roman satire. Davos played Hercules. The actors all seemed to know the work and there was nothing required of me beforehand. At rehearsal, while Davos, in a ridiculous rolling baritone, sailed confidently through his stuff needing no direction from Chremes, I took the opportunity to ask the manager for a private word sometime. He invited me to dinner that evening.

There was no performance; we were having to wait for the theater behind a local group who had the run of the stage for a week doing something proclamatory with drumbeats and harps. I could hear the throb of their music as I walked through the camp to attend my tryst. By then I was starving. Chremes and Phrygia dined late. At my own bivouac Helena and Musa, who were not included in my invitation, had made a point of tucking into a lavish spread while I hung about waiting to go. Outside the tents I passed on the way, happy people who had already eaten were tipsily waving beakers or spitting olive stones after me.

It must have been perfectly obvious where and why I was going, for I had my napkin in one hand and the good guest's gift of an amphora under the other arm. I wore my best tunic (the one with least moth holes) and had combed the desert grit out of my hair. I felt strangely conspicuous as I ran the gauntlet of the rows of long black tents that we had pitched in nomad fashion at right angles to the track. I noticed that Byrria's tent lay in near darkness. Both Twins were outside theirs, drinking with Plancina. No sign of Afrania tonight. As I passed, I thought one of the clowns stood up and silently stared after me.

When I arrived at the manager's tent, my heart sank. Chremes and Phrygia were deep in some unexplained wrangle and the dinner was not even ready yet. They were such an odd, ill-assorted couple. By firelight Phrygia's face appeared more gaunt and unhappy than ever as she swooped about like a very tall Fury who had some harsh torments lined up for sinners. As she made desultory motions towards eventually feeding me I tried to be affable, even though my reception was offhand. Slouching outside with a furious scowl, Chremes looked older too, his striking looks showing signs of early ruin, with deep hollows in his face and a wine gut flowing over his belt.

He and I opened my amphora furtively while Phrygia crashed platters inside the tent.

"So what's the mystery, young Marcus?"

"Nothing, really. I just wanted to consult you again over this search for your murderer."

"Might as well consult a camel driver's hitching post!" cried Phrygia from indoors.

"Consult away!" boomed the manager, as if he had not heard his jaded consort. Probably after twenty years of their angry marriage his ears were genuinely selective.

"Well, I've narrowed the field of suspects but I still need the vital fact that will pin this bastard down. When the tambourinist died I had hoped for extra clues, but Ione had so many men friends that sorting them out is hopeless."

Without appearing to watch him, I checked Chremes for a re-action. He seemed oblivious to my subtle suggestion that he might have been one of the girl's "friends." Phrygia knew better, and popped out of the tent again to supervise our conversation. She had transformed herself into a gracious hostess for the night with a few deft touches: a flowing scarf, probably silk, thrown over her shoulders dramatically; silver earrings the size of spoonbowls, daring swaths of facepaint. She had also switched on a more attentive manner as she produced our food with a lazy flourish.

Despite my fears, the meal was impressive: huge salvers of Eastern delicacies decorated with olives and dates; warmed bread; grains, legumes, and spiced meats; small bowls of sharp pastes for dipping; plenty of salt and pickled fish from Lake Tiberias. Phrygia served with an offhand manner, as if she was surprised by her own success in concocting the feast. Both hosts implied that food was incidental to their lives, though I noticed that all they ate was of the best.

Their traveling dinner set was one of bold ceramics, with heavy metal drinking cups and elegant bronze servingware. It was like dining with a family of sculptors, people who knew shape and quality; people who could afford style.

The domestic quarrel had gone into abeyance; probably not abandoned, but deferred.

"The girl knew what she was doing," Phrygia commented on Ione, neither bitter nor condemning.

I disagreed. "She can't have known she would be killed for it." Minding my manners, for the mood seemed more formal than I was used to, I scooped up as many tastings as I could fit in my feeding bowl without looking greedy. "She enjoyed life too much to give it up. But she didn't fight back. She wasn't expecting what happened at the pool."

"She was a fool to go there!" Chremes exclaimed. "I can't understand it. She thought the man she was meeting had killed Heliodorus, so why risk it?"

Phrygia tried to be helpful: "She was just a girl. She thought no one who loathed him could have the same reason for loathing her. She didn't understand that a killer is illogical and unpredictable. Marcus—" we were on first-name terms apparently "—enjoy yourself. Have plenty."

"So do you think," I asked, manipulating a honey dip on my flat bread, "that she wanted to let him know she had identified him?"

"I'm sure she did," Phrygia answered. I could tell she had been thinking this through for herself; perhaps she had wanted to feel certain her own husband could not be involved. "She was attracted by the danger. But the little idiot had no real idea this man would see her as a threat. She was not the type to blackmail him, though he would probably suspect it. Knowing Ione, she thought it was a good giggle."

"So the killer would have felt she was laughing at him. The worst thing she could have done," I groaned. "What about the playwright? Did she have no sense of regret that Heliodorus had been removed from society?"

"She didn't like him."

"Why? I heard he once made a play for her?"

"He made a play for anything that moved," said Chremes.

According to what I had heard, this was rich coming from him. "We were always having to rescue the girls from his clutches."

"Oh? Was it you who rescued Byrria?"

"No. I would have said she could take of herself."

"Oh would you!" Phrygia exclaimed, with a scornful note. Chremes set his jaw.

"Did you know about Heliodorus trying to rape Byrria?" I asked Phrygia.

"I may have heard something."

"There's no need to be secretive. She told me herself." I noticed that Chremes was stuffing his bowl with seconds, so I leaned forward too and gathered up more.

"Well, if Byrria told you . . . I knew about it because she came to me in great distress afterwards, wanting to leave the company. I persuaded her to stay on. She's a good little actress. Why should she let a bully destroy a promising career?"

"Did you say anything to him?"

"Naturally!" muttered Chremes through another mouthful of bread. "Trust Phrygia!"

Phrygia rounded on him. "I knew *you* would never do it!" He looked shifty. I felt shifty myself, without any reason. "He was impossible. He had to be dealt with. You should have kicked him out then and there."

"So you warned him?" I prompted, licking sauce off my fingers.

"It was more of a threat than a warning!" I could believe that. Phrygia was some force. But in view of what Ribes had told me, I wondered if she really would have kicked out the playwright while she thought he might know something about her missing child. She seemed definite, however. "I told him, one more wrong move and he could no longer rely on Chremes to be soft; he would march. He knew I meant it too."

I glanced at Chremes. "I was growing extremely dissatisfied with the man," he declared, as if it was all his idea. I hid a smile as he made the best of a losing situation. "I was certainly ready to take my wife's advice."

"But when you reached Petra he was still with the company?"

"On probation!" said Chremes.

"On notice!" snapped Phrygia.

I decided I could risk a more delicate subject. "Davos hinted you had good reason to take against him anyway, Phrygia?"

"Oh, Davos told you that story, did he?" Phrygia's tone was hard. I thought Chremes sat up fractionally. "Good old Davos!" she raved.

"He didn't pass on details. As a friend, he was angry about Heliodorus tormenting you. He only spoke to illustrate what a bastard the man had been," I muttered, trying to soften the atmosphere.

Phrygia was still in a huff. "He was a bastard all right."

"I'm sorry. Don't upset yourself—"

"I'm not upset. I saw exactly what he was. All talk—like most men."

I glanced at Chremes, as if appealing for help to understand what she was saying. He lowered his voice in a useless attempt at sensitivity. "According to him, he had some information about a relative Phrygia has been trying to trace. It was a trick, in my opinion—"

"Well, we'll never know now, will we?" Phrygia blazed angrily.

I knew when to retreat. I let the subject drop.

I savored some nuggets of meat in a hot marinade. Evidently the tattered appearance of the troupe as a whole belied how well its leading players lived. Phrygia must have invested lavishly in peppers while she traveled around, and even in Nabataea and Syria, where there were no middlemen to pay if you bought direct from the caravans, such spices were expensive. Now I could understand more fully the mutters of rebellion among the stagehands and musicians. Frankly, given the meager cut I was awarded as playwright, I could have gone on strike myself.

I was developing a fascinating picture of my predecessor's situation during those last days of his life. At Petra he had been a marked man. Davos had told me previously that *he* had given Chremes an ultimatum to dismiss the scribe. Now Phrygia said she had done the same, despite the hold Heliodorus had tried to apply using the whereabouts of her missing child.

Having taken over his job and gained some insight into his feelings, I almost felt sorry for Heliodorus. Not only was he badly paid and his work hated, but his career with the company was firmly under threat.

The atmosphere had relaxed enough for me to speak again. "So really, by the time you hit Petra, Heliodorus was on his way out?"

Phrygia confirmed it. Chremes was silent, but that meant nothing.

"Did everyone know that he was being given the heave-ho?"

Phrygia laughed. "What do you think?"

Everyone knew.

I found it interesting. If Heliodorus had been so visibly under threat, it was highly unusual that somebody had snapped. Normally, once a troublemaking colleague is known to have attracted attention from management, everyone else relaxes. When the thieving cook is about to be sent back to the slave market, or the dozy apprentice is to be packed off home to mother at last, the rest just like to sit back and watch. Yet even with Heliodorus on the hop, somebody still could not wait.

Who could hate him so much they wanted to risk all by killing him when he was leaving anyway? Or was it a case where his very leaving caused the problem? Did he possess something, or know something, that he was starting to use as a lever? *If I go, I take the money!* . . . *If I go, I tell all* . . . Or even, *If I go, I don't tell, and you'll never find your child?* The issue of the child was too sensitive to probe.

"Did anyone owe him a debt? One they would have to repay if he left?"

"He wouldn't lend a copper, even if he had one," Phrygia told me.

Chremes added in a morose tone, "The way he drank, if his purse ever contained anything, it all went on the wine." Thoughtfully, we both drained our goblets, with that air of extreme sense men acquire when discussing a fool who can't handle it.

"Did he owe anyone himself?"

Phrygia answered: "No one would lend to him, mainly because it was obvious they would never get it back." One of the simpler, and more reliable, laws of high finance.

Something niggled me. "Tranio lent him something, I believe?"

"Tranio?" Chremes laughed briefly. "I doubt it! Tranio's never had anything worth borrowing, and he's always broke!"

"Were the clowns on good terms with the playwright?"

Chremes discussed them happily enough. "They had an on-off friendship with him." Again I had a sense that he was hedging. "Last time I noticed they were all at loggerheads. Basically he was a loner."

"You're sure of that? And what about Tranio and Grumio? However they look on the surface, I suspect both of them are complex characters."

"They're good boys," Phrygia rebuked me. "Lots of talent."

Talent was her measure for everyone. For talent she would forgive a great deal. Maybe it made her judgment unreliable. Even though Phrygia shivered at the thought of harboring a murderer, maybe a usefully talented comedian with the ability to improvise would seem too valuable to hand over to justice if his only crime was eliminating an unpleasant hack who couldn't write.

I smiled pleasantly. "Do you know how the Twins were applying their talent when Heliodorus went up Dushara's mountain?"

"Oh stop it, Falco! They never did it." I had definitely offended against Phrygia's code of company behavior: good boys never did bad things. I loathed that kind of shortsightedness, though in the world of informing it was nothing new.

"They were packing their bags," Chremes told me, with an attitude that suggested he was being more impartial and reasonable than his wife. "Same as everyone else."

"Did you see them doing it?"

"Of course not. I was packing mine."

According to this weak theory the entire group would have alibis. I did not bother to ask where he thought Davos, Philocrates, and Congrio might have been. If I wanted to be bamboozled, I could ask the suspects individually in the hope that the murderer at least would be inventive in his lies. "Where were you staying?"

"The others were in an indifferent rooming house. Phrygia and I had found a slightly better place." It fitted. They always liked to pretend we were one big share-alike family; but they preferred to have their comforts. I wondered if Heliodorus had ragged them about this snobbery.

I remembered Grumio saying something. "According to Grumio, all a clown needs are a cloak, a strigil and oil flask, and a wallet for his takings. On that basis, a clown's trappings could be flung together pretty rapidly."

"Grumio's all fantasy," Chremes mourned, shaking his head. "It makes him a wonderful artiste, but you have to know it's just talk."

Phrygia was losing patience with me. "So where is all this getting you, Falco?"

"It's filling in the picture helpfully." I could take a hint. I had been munching their wonderful tidbits until I could hold no more. It was time to go home and make my tent companions jealous by happily belching and describing the goodies. "That was quite a feast! I'm grateful. . . ."

I made the usual offers of they must come over to us sometime (with the usual underlying suggestion that all they might get would be two winkles on a lettuce leaf); then I turned to leave.

"Oh, just tell me one more thing. What happened to the playwright's personal property after he died?" I knew Heliodorus must have owned more than Helena and I had acquired with the play box.

"There wasn't much," said Chremes. "We picked out anything of value—a ring and a couple of inkstands—then I gave his few rags to Congrio."

"What about his heirs?"

Phrygia laughed her dismissive laugh. "Falco, nobody in a traveling theater company has heirs!"

Forty-four

Davos stood behind the tree under which he had pitched his tent. He was doing what a man does when it's night, when he thinks there is nobody about, and he can't be bothered to walk further off into open countryside. The camp had fallen silent; so had the distant town. He must have heard my feet crunching up the stony track. After quaffing my share of my amphora, I was in dire need of relief myself, so I greeted him, walked up alongside, and helped water his tree.

"I'm very impressed with your Hercules."

"Wait until you see my bloody Zeus!"

"Not in the same play?"

"No, no. Once Chremes thinks of one 'Frolicking Gods' farce, we tend to get given a run of them."

A huge moon had risen over the uplands. The Syrian moon

seemed bigger, and the Syrian stars more numerous, than those we had back home in Italy. This, with the restless wind that always hummed around Abila, gave me a sudden, poignant feeling of being lost in a very remote place. To avoid it, I kept talking. "I've just been for a meal with our gregarious actor-manager and his loving spouse."

"They normally put on a good spread."

"Wonderful hospitality . . . Do they do this often?"

Davos chuckled. He was not a snob. "Only for the right strata of society!"

"Aha! I'd never been invited before. Have I come up in the world, or was I just lumbered originally with the backwash of disapproval for my scribbling predecessor?"

"Heliodorus? He was asked, once, I believe. He soon lost his status. Once Phrygia got the measure of him, that was the end of it."

"Would that be when he claimed to know where her offspring might be?"

Davos gave me a sharp look when I mentioned this. Then he commented, "She's stupid to look!"

I rather agreed with that. "The child's probably dead, or almost certainly won't want to know."

Davos, in his dour way, said nothing.

We finished the horticulture, tightened our belts in the time-honored manner, casually stuck our thumbs in them, and sauntered back to the track. A stagehand came by, saw us looking innocent, immediately guessed what we must have been doing, got the idea himself, and vanished sideways behind somebody else's tent looking for the next tree. We had started a craze.

Without comment, Davos and I waited to see what would happen, since the next tent was clearly occupied and a desperate pee tends to be audible. A muffled voice soon shouted in protest. The stagehand scuttled guiltily on his way. Silence fell again.

We stood on the path while the breeze bustled around us. A tent roof flapped. Somewhere in the town a dog howled mournfully. Both of us raised our faces to the wind, absorbing the night's atmosphere contemplatively. Davos was not normally one to chat, but we were two men with some mutual respect who had met at night, neither ready for sleep. We spoke together quietly, in a way that at other times might have been impossible. "I'm trying to fill in missing facts," I said. "Can you remember what you were doing in Petra when Heliodorus wandered up to the High Place?"

"I most certainly do remember: loading the bloody wagons. We had no stagehands with us, if you recall. Chremes had issued his orders like a lord, then taken himself off to fold up his underwear."

"Were you loading up alone?"

"Assisted in his pitiful manner by Congrio."

"He can't help being a flyweight."

Davos relented. "No, he did his best, for what it was worth. What really got up my nose was being supervised by Philocrates. Instead of shifting bales with us, he took the opportunity to lean against a pillar looking attractive to the women and passing the kind of remarks that make you want to spew."

"I can imagine. He drove me wild once by standing about like a demigod while I was trying to hitch my damned ox. . . . Was he there all the time?"

"Until he fixed himself a bit of spice and went up among the tombs with the skirt." The frankincense merchant's wife; he had mentioned her to Helena.

"So how long did the lading take you?"

"All bloody afternoon. I'm telling you, I was doing it as a one-man job. I still hadn't finished the stage effects—those two doorways are a trial to lift on your own—when your girl came down the hill and word whizzed round that somebody was dead. By then the rest of our party had assembled to watch me struggling.

We were supposed to be all ready for the off, and people were starting to wonder where Heliodorus was. Someone asked Helena what the corpse looked like, so then we guessed who it must be."

"Any idea where the Twins were while you were piling up the wagons?"

"No."

He made no attempt to offer possibilities. Whether they were under suspicion or in the clear, Davos left it up to me to judge them. But I did gather that if they were accused, he would not care. Another case of professional jealousy among the players, presumably.

Probably the Twins would give each other alibis. That would land me in the usual situation: none of the known suspects actually available to do the deed. I sighed gently.

"Davos, tell me again about the night Musa was shoved off the embankment at Bostra. You must have been walking behind him?"

"I was right at the back of the queue."

"Last in line?"

"Correct. To tell the truth, it was such a godawful night I was losing interest in drinking in some dive with the Twins, knowing we would have to walk back through that weather just when we had got dry and warm again. I was planning to peel off unnoticed and scamper back to my own tent. I had been dropping behind stealthily. Two minutes more and I would never have heard your Nabataean shout."

"Could you see who was near Musa when he was pushed?"

"No. If I'd seen it I'd have told you before this. I'd like to get the villain sorted," Davos chortled, "so I can avoid being plagued by questions from you!"

"Sorry." I wasn't, and I refused to give up. "So you won't want to tell me about the night Ione died?"

"Dear gods . . ." he muttered good-humoredly. "Oh all right, get on with it!"

"You were dining with Chremes and Phrygia, and Philocrates was there too."

"Until he bunked off as usual. That was quite late. If you're suggesting he drowned the girl, then judging by the time we all heard the news after you got back from the pools, he must have sped there on Mercury's wings. No, I reckon he was with his dame when it happened, and probably still hard at it while you were finding the corpse."

"If there ever was a dame."

"Ah, well. You'll have to check with him." Once again the disinterested way he threw it back to me seemed convincing. Killers looking to cover their own tracks like to speculate in detail about how others might be implicated. Davos always seemed too straight for such nonsense. He said what he knew; he left the rest to me.

I was getting nowhere. I tried the hard screw. "Somebody told me that *you* liked Ione."

"I liked her. That was all it amounted to."

"It wasn't you who met her at the pools?"

"It was not!" He was crisp in denying it. "You know damn well that was my night for dining with Chremes and Phrygia."

"Yes, we've been over that rather convenient tale. One thing I'm asking myself is whether your party at the manager's tent was a setup. Maybe the whole gang of you were in a conspiracy."

By the light of his campfire I could just make out Davos' face: skeptical, world-weary, utterly dependable. "Oh, stuff you, Falco. If you want to talk rot, go and do it somewhere else."

"It has to be thought about. Give me one good reason to discard the idea."

"I can't. You'll just have to take our word." Actually, Davos giving his word seemed fairly convincing to me. He was that kind of man.

Mind you, Brutus and Cassius probably seemed decent, dependable, and harmless until somebody offended them.

I clapped Davos on the shoulder and was off on my way when another point struck me. "One final thought. I've just had an odd conversation with Chremes. I'm sure he was holding back on me. Listen, could he have known anything significant about the playwright's finances?"

Davos said nothing. I knew I had got him. I turned back, square to him. "So that's it!"

"That's what, Falco?"

"Oh, come on, Davos, for a man whose timing is so tight on-stage, you're lousy off it! That silence was too long. There's something you don't want to tell me, and you're working out how to be uncooperative. Don't bother. It's too late now. Unless you tell me yourself, I'll only press the matter elsewhere until someone gives."

"Leave it, Falco."

"I will if you tell me."

"It's old history. . . ." He seemed to be making up his mind. "Was Phrygia there when you had this strange chat?" I nodded. "That explains it. Chremes on his own might have told you. The fact is, Heliodorus was subsidizing the company. Phrygia doesn't know."

I gaped. "I'm amazed. Explain this!"

Davos sounded reluctant. "You can fill in the rest, surely?"

"I've seen that Chremes and Phrygia like enjoying the good life."

"More than our proceeds really cover."

"So are they peeling off the takings?"

"Phrygia doesn't know," he repeated stubbornly.

"All right, Phrygia's a vestal virgin. What about her tiresome spouse?"

"Chremes spent what he owes to the stagehands and the

orchestra." That explained a lot. Davos continued glumly: "He isn't hopeless with money, but he's scared that Phrygia will finally leave him if their lifestyle gets too basic. That's what he's convinced himself, anyway. I doubt it myself. She's stayed so long she can't leave now; it would make all her past life pointless."

"So he put himself in hock to Heliodorus?"

"Yes. The man is an idiot."

"I'm starting to believe it. . . ." He was also a liar. Chremes had told me Heliodorus spent all his cash on drink. "I thought Heliodorus drank all his wages?"

"He liked to cadge other people's flagons."

"At the scene of his death I found a goatskin and a wicker flask."

"My guess would be the flask was his own, and he probably drained it himself too. The goatskin may have belonged to whoever was with him, in which case Heliodorus would not have objected to helping the other party drink what it contained."

"Going back to Chremes' debt, if it was a substantial sum, where did the money come from?"

"Heliodorus was a private hoarder. He had amassed a pile."

"And he let Chremes borrow it in order to gain the upper hand?"

"You're brighter than Chremes was about his reasoning! Chremes walked right into the blackmail: borrowed from Heliodorus, then had no way to pay him back. Everything could have been avoided if only he had come clean with Phrygia instead. She likes good things, but she's not stupidly extravagant. She wouldn't ruin the company for a few touches of luxury. Of course, they discuss everything—except what matters most."

"Like most couples."

Obviously hating to dump them in trouble, Davos blew out his cheeks, as if breathing had become difficult. "Oh gods, what a mess. . . . Chremes didn't kill him, Falco."

"Sure? He was in a tight spot. Both you and Phrygia were in-

sisting that the inkblot should be kicked out of the company.
Meanwhile, Heliodorus must have been laughing up his tunic
sleeve because he knew Chremes could not repay him. Incidentally, is this why he was kept on for so long in the first place?"

"Of course."

"That and Phrygia hoping to extract the location of her child?"

"Oh, she'd given up expecting him to tell her that, even if he
really knew."

"And how did you find out about the situation with
Chremes?"

"At Petra. When I marched in to say it was Heliodorus or me.
Chremes cracked and admitted why he couldn't give the playwright the boot."

"So what happened?"

"I'd had enough. I certainly wasn't going to hang around and
watch Heliodorus hold the troupe to ransom. I said I would
leave when we got back to Bostra. Chremes knew Phrygia would
hate that. We have been friends for a long time."

"She knows your value to the company."

"If you say so."

"Why not just tell Phrygia yourself?"

"No need to. She would certainly insist on knowing why I was
leaving—and she'd make sure she heard the right reason. If she
pressed him, Chremes would crumble and tell her. He and I
both knew that."

"So, I see what your plan was. You were really intending to
stick around until that happened."

"You get it." Davos seemed relieved now to be talking about
this. "Once Phrygia knew the situation, I reckoned Heliodorus
would have been sorted—paid off somehow, and then told to
leave."

"Was he owed a large amount?"

"Finding it would have hit us all very hard, but it was not un-
manageable. Worth it to get rid of him, anyway."

"You were confident the whole business could have been cleared up?" This was important.

"Oh yes!" Davos seemed surprised that I asked. He was one of life's fixers; the opposite of Chremes, who collapsed when trouble flared. Davos did know when to cut and run in a crisis (I had seen that when our people were in jail at Gadara), but if it were possible, he preferred to face a bully out.

"This is the crux then, Davos. Did *Chremes* believe that he could be rescued?"

Davos considered his answer carefully. He understood what I was asking: whether Chremes felt so hopeless he might have killed as his only escape. "Falco, he must have known that telling Phrygia would cause some harrowing rows, but after all these years, that's how they live. She wasn't in for any surprises. She knows the man. To save the company she—and I—would rally around. So, I suppose you are asking, ought he to have felt privately optimistic? In his heart, he must have."

This was the only time Davos actively sought to clear another person. All I had to decide now was whether he was lying (perhaps to protect his old friend Phrygia), or whether he was telling the truth.

Forty-five

We never did put on a show at Abila. Chremes learned that even when the local amateurs had finished impressing their cousins we would still be waiting in a queue behind some acrobats from Pamphilia.

"This is no good! We're not dawdling in line for a week only to have some damned handstand boys wobble on ahead of us—"

"They were already ahead," Phrygia put him straight, tight-lipped. "We happened to arrive in the middle of a civic festival, which has been planned for six months. Unfortunately, no one informed the town councilors that they needed to consult you! The good citizens of Abila are celebrating the formal entry into the Empire of Commagene—"

"Stuff Commagene!"

With this acid political commentary (a view most of us

shared, since only Helena Justina had any idea where Commagene was, or whether well-informed men should afford it significance), Chremes led us all off to Capitolias.

Capitolias had all the usual attributes of a Decapolis town. I'm not some damned itinerary writer—you can fill in the details for yourselves.

You can also guess the results of my search for Sophrona. As at Abila, and all the other towns before, there was no trace of Thalia's musical prodigy.

I admit, I was starting to feel bad tempered about all this. I was sick of looking for the girl. I was tired of one damned acropolis after another. I didn't care if I never saw another set of neat little city walls with a tasteful temple, shrouded in expensive scaffolding, peeping Ionically over them. Stuff Commagene? Never mind it. Commagene (a small, previously autonomous kingdom miles to the north of here) had one wonderful attribute: nobody had ever suggested M. Didius Falco ought to pack his bags and traipse around it. No, forget harmless pockets of quaintness that wanted to be Roman, and instead just stuff the whole pretentious, grasping, Hellenic Decapolis.

I had had enough. I was sick of stones in my shoes and the raw smell of camels' breath. I wanted glorious monuments and towering, teeming tenements. I wanted to be sold some dubious fish that tasted of Tibet grit, and to eat it gazing over the river from my own grubby nook on the Aventine while waiting for an old friend to knock on the door. I wanted to breathe garlic at an aedile. I wanted to stamp on a banker. I wanted to hear that solid roar that slams across the racecourse at the Circus Maximus. I wanted spectacular scandals and gigantic criminality. I wanted to be amazed by size and sordidness. I wanted to go home.

"Have you a toothache or something?" asked Helena. I proved that my teeth were all in working order by gnashing them.

For the company, things looked brighter. At Capitolias we acquired a two-night booking. We first put on the Hercules play, since that was newly rehearsed; then, as Davos had prophesied, Chremes became keen on this horrible species and handed us a further "Frolicking Gods" effort, so we did see Davos do his famous Zeus. Whether people liked it depended on whether they enjoyed farces full of ladders at women's windows, betrayed husbands helplessly banging on locked doors, divinity mocked relentlessly, and Byrria in a nightgown that revealed pretty well everything.

Musa, we gathered, either liked this very much indeed, or not at all. He went silent. In essence it was hard to tell any difference from normal, but the quality of his silence assumed a new mood. It was brooding; perhaps downright sinister. In a man whose professional life had been spent cutting throats for Dushara, I found this alarming.

Helena and I were uncertain whether Musa's new silence meant he was now in mental and physical agony over the strength of his attraction to the beauty, or whether her bawdy part in the Zeus play had completely disgusted him. Either way, Musa was finding it hard to handle his feelings. We were ready to offer sympathy, but he plainly wanted to work out his solutions for himself.

To give him something else to think about I drew him more closely into my investigations. I had wanted to proceed alone, but I hate to abandon a man to love. My verdict on Musa was twofold: he was mature, but inexperienced. This was the worst possible combination for tackling a hostile quarry like Byrria. The maturity would remove any chance of her feeling sorry for him; the lack of experience could lead to embarrassment and bungling if he ever made a move. A woman who had so ferociously set herself apart from men would need a practiced hand to win her over.

"I'll give you advice if you want it." I grinned. "But advice rarely works. The mistakes are waiting to be made—and you'll have to walk straight into them."

"Oh yes," he replied rather vacantly. As usual, his apparent affirmative sounded ambiguous. I never met a man who could discuss women so elusively. "What about our task, Falco?" If he wanted to lose himself in work, frankly that seemed the best idea. As a lad about town Musa was hard work to organize.

I explained to him that asking people questions about money would be as difficult as advising a friend on a love affair. He screwed out a smile, then we buckled down to checking on the story Davos had told me.

I wanted to avoid questioning Chremes about his debt directly. Tackling him would be useless while we had no evidence against him for actually causing either death. I had strong doubts whether we would find that evidence. As I told Musa, he remained a low priority on my suspects list: "He's strong enough to have held Heliodorus down but he was not on the embankment at Bostra when you were pushed in the water, and unless someone is lying, he was also out of the picture when Ione died. This is depressing—and typical of my work, Musa. Davos has just given me the best possible motive for killing Heliodorus, but in the long run it's likely to prove irrelevant."

"We have to check it, though?"

"Oh yes!"

I sent Musa to confirm with Phrygia that Chremes really had been packing his belongings when Heliodorus was killed. She vouched for it. If she still didn't entertain any notion that Chremes had been in debt to the playwright, then she had no reason to think we might be closing in on a suspect, and so no reason to lie.

"So, Falco, is this story of the debt one we can forget?" Musa pondered. He answered himself: "No, we cannot. We must now check up on Davos."

"Right. And the reason?"

"He is friendly with Chremes, and especially loyal to Phrygia. Maybe when he found out about the debt he himself killed Heliodorus—to protect his friends from the blackmailing creditor."

"Not only his friends, Musa. He would have been safeguarding the future of the theater group, and also his own job, which he had been saying he would leave. So yes, we'll check on him—but he looks in the clear. If he went up the mountain, then who packed the stage props at Petra? We know *somebody* did it. Philocrates would think himself above hard labor, and anyway, half the time he was off screwing a conquest. Let's ask the Twins and Congrio where they all were. We need to know that too."

I myself tackled Congrio.

"Yes, Falco. I helped Davos load the heavy stuff. It took all afternoon. Philocrates was watching us some of the time; then he went off somewhere. . . ."

The twins told Musa they had been together in the room they shared: packing their belongings: having a last drink, rather larger than they had anticipated, to save carrying an amphora to their camel; then sleeping it off. It fitted what we knew of their disorganized, slightly disreputable lifestyle. Other people agreed that when the company assembled to leave Petra the Twins had turned up last, looking dozy and crumpled and complaining of bad heads.

Wonderful. Every male suspect had somebody who could clear him. Everyone, except possibly Philocrates during the time he was philandering. "I'll have to put pressure on the rutting little bastard. I'll enjoy that!"

"Mind you, Falco, a big-brimmed hat would swamp him!" Musa qualified, equally vindictively.

This clarified one thing anyway: Philocrates spent several scenes in the Zeus play cuddling up to the lovely Byrria. Musa's anger appeared to clinch the question of *his* feelings for the girl.

Forty-six

A restless mood hit the company once we performed at Capitolias. One reason for it was that decisions now had to be taken. This was the last in the central group of Decapolis cities. Damascus lay a good sixty miles to the north—further than we had been accustomed to traveling between towns. The remaining place, Canatha, was awkwardly isolated from the group, far out to the east on the basalt plain north of Bostra. In fact, because of its remote position, the best way to get there was going back via Bostra, which added half as much again to the thirty- or forty-mile distance it would have been direct.

The thought of revisiting Bostra gave everyone a feeling that we were about to complete a circle, after which it might seem natural for ways to part.

It was now deep summer. The weather had grown almost unbearably hot. Working in such temperatures was difficult, though at the same time audiences seemed to welcome performances once their cities cooled slightly at night. By day people huddled in whatever shade they could find; shops and businesses were shuttered for long periods; and no one traveled unless they had a death in the family, or they were idiotic foreigners like us. At night, the locals all came out to meet one another and be entertained. For a group like ours, it posed a problem. We needed the money. We could not afford to stop working, however great a toll of our energy the heat took.

Chremes called everyone to a meeting. His vagabond collection squashed together on the ground in a ragged circle, all jeering and jostling. He stood up on a cart to give a public address. He looked assured, but we knew better than to hope for it.

"Well, we've completed a natural circuit. Now we have to decide where to go next." I believe somebody suggested Chremes might try Hades, though it was in a furtive undertone. "Wherever is chosen, none of you are bound to continue. If needs be, the group can break up and re-form." That was bad news for those of us who wanted to keep it together in order to identify the murderer. That blowfly would be early in the queue for terminating contracts and flitting away.

"What about our money?" called one of the stagehands. I wondered if they had sniffed out a rumor that Chremes might have spent their season's earnings. They had said nothing to me when we discussed their grievances, but it would explain some of their anger. I knew they had been suspicious that I might be reporting back to the management, so they might well have kept their fears on this subject to themselves.

I noticed Davos fold his arms and gaze at Chremes sardonically. Without a blush Chremes announced, "I'm going to settle up now for what you've earned." He was absurdly confident. Like Davos, I could smile over it. Chremes had diced with disaster, and been rescued in the nick of time by the maniac who killed his creditor. How many of us can hope for such luck? Now Chremes had the satisfied air of those who are constantly saved from peril by the Fates. It was a trait I had never been favored with. But I knew these men existed. I knew they never learned from their mistakes because they never had to suffer for them. A few moments of panic were the worst effects Chremes would ever know. He would float through life, behaving as badly as possible and risking everyone else's happiness, yet never having to face responsibility.

Of course he could produce the money his workforce was owed; Heliodorus had bailed him out. And although Chremes ought to have paid the playwright back, he blatantly had no intention of remembering the debt now. He would have diddled the man himself, if he could have got away with it, so he would certainly rob the dead. My question about heirs, and Phrygia's easy answer that Heliodorus was assumed to have had none, took on a dry significance. Not knowing about her husband's debt, even Phrygia could not understand the full irony.

This was the moment when I looked at the manager hardest. However, Chremes had been cleared as a suspect pretty convincingly. He had alibis for both murders, and had been somewhere else the night Musa was attacked. Chremes had a serious motive for killing Heliodorus, but for all I knew so did half the group. It had taken a long time for me to unearth this debt of Chremes'; maybe there were other lurking maggots if I turned over the right cowpat.

As if by chance, I had seated myself at our manager's feet, on the tail of the same cart. This put me staring out at the assembly. I could see most of their faces—among which had to be the one I was looking for. I wondered whether the killer was gazing back, aware of my complete bafflement. I tried to look at each one as if I was thinking about some vital fact he was unaware I knew: Davos, almost too reliable by half (could anyone be *quite* so straight as Davos always seemed?); Philocrates, chin up so his profile showed best (could anyone be so totally self-obsessed?); Congrio, undernourished and unappealing (what twisted ideas might that thin, pale wraith be harboring?); Tranio and Grumio, so clever, so sharp, each so secure in his mastery of their craft— a craft that relied on a devious mind, an attacking wit, and visual deceit.

The faces returning my gaze all looked more cheerful than I liked. If anyone had worries, they had not been posed by me.

"The options," stated Chremes importantly, "are, firstly, to go around the same circuit again, trading on our previous success." There were a few jeers. "I reject this," the manager agreed, "on the grounds that it poses no dramatic challenge—" This time some of us laughed outright. "Besides, one or two towns hold bad memories. . . ." He subsided. Public reference to death was not in his style of speechmaking. "The next alternative is to move further afield in Syria—"

"Are there good pickings?" I prompted in a not very quiet mutter.

"Thanks, Falco! Yes, I think Syria still holds out a welcome for a reputable theater group like ours. We still have a large repertoire which we have not properly explored—"

"Falco's ghost play!" suggested a satirist. I had not been aware that my idea for writing a play of my own was so widely known about.

"Jupiter forfend!" cried Chremes as raucous merriment erupted and I grinned gamely. My ghost play would be better than these bastards knew, but I was a professional writer now; I had learned to keep my smoldering genius quiet. "So where shall we take ourselves? The choices are various."

His options had turned into choices, but the dilemma remained.

"Do we want to complete the Decapolis towns? Or shall we

travel north more quickly and tackle the sophisticated cities there? We won't want to go into the desert, but beyond Damascus there is a good route in a fairly civilized area, through Emesa, Epiphania, Beroia, and across to Antiochia. On the way we can certainly cover Damascus."

"Any drawbacks?" I queried.

"Long distances, mainly."

"Longer than going to Canatha?" I pressed.

"Very much so. Canatha would mean a detour back through Bostra—"

"Though there would be a good road up to Damascus afterward?" I had already been looking at itineraries myself. I never rely on anyone else to research a route.

"Er, yes." Chremes was feeling hard pressed, a position he hated. "Do you particularly want us to go to Canatha, Falco?"

"Taking the company or not is up to you. Myself, I've no option. I'd be happy to stay with you as your playwright but I have my own business in the Decapolis, a commission I want to clear up—"

I was trying to give the impression my private search for Sophrona was taking precedence over finding the murderer. I wanted the villain to think I was losing interest. I hoped to make him relax.

"I dare say we can accommodate your wish to visit Canatha," Chremes offered graciously. "A city which is off the beaten track may be ripe for some of our high-class performances—"

"Oh, I reckon they are starved of culture!" I encouraged, not specifying whether I thought "culture" would be a product handed out by us.

"We'll go where Falco says," called one of the stagehands. "He's our lucky talisman." Some of the others gave me nods and winks that proclaimed in a far from subtle manner that they wanted to keep me close enough to protect them. Not that I had done much on their behalf so far.

"Show of hands, then," answered Chremes, as usual letting anybody other than himself decide. He loved the fine idea of democracy, like most men who couldn't organize an orgy with twenty bored gladiators in a women's bathhouse on a hot Tuesday night.

As the stagehands shuffled and glanced around them it seemed to me the killer must have detected the widespread conspiracy building up against him. But if he did, he uttered no protest. A further quick scan of our male suspects revealed nobody visibly cursing. No one seemed resentful that the chance to shed me, or to break up the troupe altogether, had just been deferred.

So to Canatha it was. The group would be staying together for two more Decapolis cities, Canatha, then Damascus. However, after Damascus—a major administrative center, with plenty of other work on offer—group members might start drifting off.

Which meant that if I was to expose the killer, time was now running out.

Forty-seven

The temperature was definitely bothering all of us now. Travel by day, previously inadvisable, had become quite impossible. Travel in the dark was twice as tiring since we had to go more slowly while drivers constantly peered at the road, needing to concentrate. Our animals were restless. Fear of ambush was increasing as we reentered Nabataea, and ahead of us lay expanses of desert where the nomads were by our standards lawless and their livelihood openly depended on a centuries-old tradition of robbing passersby. Only the fact that we were obviously not a caravan of rich merchants gave us any protection; it seemed to suffice, but we could never be off guard.

All the time the heat grew daily. It was relentless and inescapable—until night fell abruptly, bringing fierce cold as the warmth lifted like a curtain under open skies. Then, lit by a few flares, we had to set off on the road again, on journeys that seemed far longer, more uncomfortable, and more tiresome than they would have been in daylight.

The climate was draining and dehydrating. We saw little of the country, and met hardly anyone to talk to; Musa told us the local tribes all migrated towards the mountains in summer. At roadside stops, our people stood about stamping their feet to get the blood running, miserably taking refreshments and talking in hushed voices. Millions of stars watched us, probably all wondering just what we were doing there. Then, by day, we collapsed in our tents, through which the baking heat soon breathed with suffocating strength, killing the sleep we needed so desperately. So we tossed and turned, groaned and quarreled with each other, threatening to turn around, head for the coast, and go home.

On the road it was difficult for me to continue reinterviewing people. The conditions were so unpleasant everyone stuck with their own camels or wagons. The strongest and those with the best eyesight were always needed for driving. The quarrelsome were always bickering with their friends too angrily to listen to me. None of the women were interested in handing out personal favors, so none of them developed the kind of jealousies that normally bring them running to confide in a handy informer. None of the men wanted to stop threatening to divorce their wives long enough to answer rational questions, especially if they thought the questions might be about the generous Ione. Nobody wanted to share food or precious water, so hitching a lift on another wagon was discouraged. At stops on the road everyone was too busy feeding themselves and their animals or swatting flies.

I did manage one useful conversation, just as we were heading into Bostra. Philocrates lost the pin from one wheel of his wagon. Nothing was broken, luckily; it had just loosened and dropped out. Davos, in the cart behind, saw it happen and shouted a warning before the whole wheel fell off. Davos seemed to spend his life averting disasters. A cynic might have suspected it was some kind of bluff, but I was in no mood for that kind of subtlety.

Philocrates managed to halt his smart equipage gently. He made no attempt to ask for help; he must have known how unpopular this would be after all the times he had refused assistance to the rest of us. Without a word, he jumped down, inspected the problem, cursed, and started to unload the cart. Nobody else was prepared to help him out, so I volunteered. The rest drew up on the road ahead, and waited while I helped with the repair.

Philocrates had a light, zippy two-wheeler—a real fast chaser's vehicle—with flashy spokes and metal felloes welded onto the rims. But whoever sold him this hot property had passed on a salvage job: one wheel did have a decent hub that was probably original, but the other had been cobbled together with a museum-piece arrangement of a linchpin on the axle.

"Somebody saw you coming!" I commented. He made no reply.

I had expected Philocrates to be useless, but it turned out he could be a pretty handy technician if his alternative was to be abandoned on a lonely road in Nabataea. He was small but muscular, and certainly well exercised. We had to unhitch his mule, which had sensed trouble; then we improvised blocks to support the weight of the cart. Philocrates had to use some of his valuable water supply to cool down the axle-bush. Normally I would have peed on it, but not with a jeering audience.

I pushed against the good wheel while Philocrates straightened the loose one; then we hammered in the pin. The problem was to bang it in hard enough to stay there. One of the stagehands' children brought us a mallet just when we were pondering how to tackle it. The child handed the tool to me, probably under instructions, and waited to take it straight back to her father afterwards. I reckoned I would be the best hitter, but Philocrates grabbed the mallet from me and swung down on the pin himself. It was his cart, so I let him. He was the one who would be stuck with a broken axle and shattered wheel if the pin worked loose again. He did have a small tent-peg hammer of his own, though, so I took that and put in alternate blows.

"Phew! We're a good team," commented the actor when we stopped to take a breath and contemplate our work. I gave him a dirty look. "I reckon that should hold it. I can get a wheelwright to look at it at Bostra. Thanks," he forced out. It was perfunctory, but no less valid for that.

"I was brought up to pull my weight in the community!" If he knew this crack of mine was a hint, no flicker showed on his haughty, high-cheeked face.

We returned the mallet to the urchin. She scampered off, and I helped Philocrates reload his cart. He owned a lot of fancy stuff—presents from grateful women, no doubt. Next came the moment I had been waiting for all along: he had to rehitch the mule. This was exquisite. After having watched me chase my stupid ox that time, I felt he owed me the privilege of sitting at the roadside doing nothing while he stumbled around offering straw to his frisky beast. Like most mules, it applied all its high intelligence to leading the life of a bad character.

"I'm glad of a chat," I offered, as I squatted on a rock. It was not what Philocrates wanted to hear at that moment, but I was ready to have some fun. "It's only fair to warn you, you're chief suspect in the murder case."

"What?" Philocrates stopped stock still in outrage. His mule saw its moment, snatched the straw, and skipped away. "I never heard such rubbish—"

"You've lost him," I pointed out helpfully, nodding at his animal. "Obviously you ought to be given a chance to clear yourself."

Philocrates responded with a short phrase that referred to a part of his anatomy he overused. I pondered how easy it is to make a confident man flustered merely by saying something grossly unfair.

"Clear myself of what?" he demanded. He was definitely hot, and it had nothing to do with the climate or our recent laboring. Philocrates' life veered between two themes: acting and philandering. He was highly competent at both, but in other fields he was starting to look stupid. "Clear myself of nothing, Falco! I've done nothing, and nobody can suggest I have!"

"Oh, come on! This is pathetic. You must have had plenty of angry husbands and fathers accusing you. With all that practice behind you, I expected a better-rehearsed plea. Where's your famous stage sparkle? Especially," I mused thoughtfully, "when these charges are so serious. A few adulteries and the occasional bastard may litter your off-color past, but this is hard crime, Philocrates. Murder is called to account in the public arena—"

"You'll not send me to the bloody lions for something I had nothing to do with! There is some justice."

"In Nabataea? Are you sure of that?"

"I'll not answer the case in Nabataea!" I had threatened him with the barbarians; instant panic had set in.

"You will if I make the charges here. We're in Nabataea already. Bostra's just up the road. One murder took place in its sister city, and I have with me a Petran representative. Musa has come all this way, on command of the Nabataean Chief Minister, specifically to condemn the killer who committed the sacrilege at their High Place!" I loved this sort of high-flown oratory. Incantations may be complete rubbish, but they have a gorgeous effect.

"Musa?" Philocrates was suddenly more suspicious.

"Musa. He may look like a lovelorn adolescent, but he's The Brother's personal envoy, charged with arresting the killer—who looks like you."

"He's a junior priest, without authority." Maybe I should have known better than to trust oratory with an actor; he knew all about the power of words, especially empty ones.

"Ask Helena," I said. "She can give you the straight story. Musa has been singled out for high position. This embassy abroad is a training job. He urgently needs to take a criminal back to preserve his reputation. I'm sorry, but you're the best candidate."

Philocrates' mule had become disappointed by the lack of action. It strolled up and nudged its master on the shoulder, telling him to get on with the chase.

"How?" Philocrates spat at me; no use to a mule who was looking for entertainment. One ear up and one ear down, the fun-loving beast gazed across at me sadly, deploring its lot.

"Philocrates," I advised him like a brother, "you are the only suspect who has no alibi."

"What? *Why?*" He was well equipped with interrogatives.

"Facts, man. When Heliodorus was murdered you say you were bunked up in a rock tomb. When Ione died in the pools of Maiuma, you came up with exactly the same shabby story— bumping a so-called 'cheese-seller.' Sounds fine. Sounds in keeping. But do we ever have a name? An address? Anyone who ever saw you with either of these bits of flotsam? A furious father or fiancé trying to cut your throat for the insult? No. Face it, Philocrates. Everyone else provides proper witnesses. You only hand me feeble lies."

The fact that the "lies" were completely in character should offer him a good defense. The fact that I also knew he had not been on the embankment at Bostra when Musa was attacked clinched his innocence for me. But he was too dumb to argue.

"As a matter of fact—" I continued the pressure, as he kicked his natty boot against a stone in helpless outrage, "—I do think you were with a girl the night Ione died—I think it was Ione herself."

"Oh come on, Falco!"

"I think you were the lover Ione met at the Maiuma pools." I noticed that every time I said Ione's name he jumped guiltily. Real criminals are not so nervous.

"Falco, I'd had a fling with her—who hadn't?—but that was long past. I like to keep moving. So did she, for that matter. Anyway, life is much less complicated if you confine your attentions outside the company."

"Ione herself was never that scrupulous."

"No," he agreed.

"So do you know who her special lover in the company was?"

"I don't. One of the clowns could probably enlighten you."

"You mean either Tranio or Grumio was Ione's special friend?"

"That's not what I said!" Philocrates grew snappy. "I mean they were friendly enough with the silly girl to have heard from her what she was up to. She didn't take either of those two idiots seriously."

"So who did she take seriously, Philocrates? Was it you?"

"Should have been. Somebody worth it." Automatically, he swept one hand back across his sleek hair. His arrogance was intolerable.

"You reckon so?" I lost my temper. "One thing about you, Philocrates: your intellect is nowhere near as lively as your prick." I fear he took it as a compliment.

Even the mule had registered its master's uselessness. It came up behind Philocrates, gave a sudden shove with its long-nosed head, and knocked the furious actor face down.

A cheer went up from the rest of our group. I grinned and walked back to my own slow, solid-wheeled oxcart.

"What was going on there?" Helena demanded.

"I just told Philocrates he's lost his alibi. He'd already lost his cartwheel, his mule, his temper, and his dignity—"

"The poor man," murmured Musa, with little sign of sympathy. "A bad day!"

The actor had told me virtually nothing. But he had cheered me up completely. That can be as much use as any piece of evidence. I had met informers who implied that to succeed they needed not just sore feet, a hangover, a sorry love life, and some progressive disease, but a dour, depressing outlook too. I disagree. The work provides enough misery. Being happy gives a man a boost that can help solve cases. Confidence counts.

I rode into Bostra hot, tired, dusty, and dry. But all the same, every time I thought of Philocrates' mule flooring him, I felt ready to tackle anything.

Forty-eight

Bostra again.

It seemed an age since we had arrived here the last time and performed *The Pirate Brothers* in the rain. An age since my first effort as a playwright was ignored by everyone. Since then I had grown quite used to critical hammerings, though when I remembered my early disappointment I still did not like the place.

We were all glad to stop. Chremes staggered off to see about a booking. He was plainly exhausted; he had no sense of priorities and was bound to bungle it. He would come back with nothing for us; that was obvious.

Nabataean or not, Bostra was a capital city and boasted good amenities. Those of us who were willing to spend money on comfort had been looking forward to leaving our tents on the wagons and finding real rooms to stay in. Walls; ceilings; floors with spiders in the corners; doors with cold drafts flooding under them. Chremes' no-hope aura cast a blight. I clung to my optimism and still meant to find lodgings for Helena, Musa and myself, a basic roost that would not be too far from a bathhouse and not noticeably a brothel, where the landlord scratched his lice discreetly and the rent was small. Being unwilling to waste even a small deposit on rooms we might not enjoy for long, I waited for the manager's return before I booked a place.

Some of the group were camping as usual. Pretending it was just my day for helping out, I presented myself as if by chance at the wagon that was driven by Congrio. Our weedy bill-poster had little equipment of his own. On the road he took charge of one of the props carts; then, instead of putting up a tent, he just hung an awning off the side of it and huddled under that. I made a show of lending a hand to unload his few bits and bobs.

He was not stupid. "What's this for, Falco?" He knew nobody helps the bill-poster unless they want a favor.

I came clean. "Somebody told me you came in for the stuff Heliodorus left behind. I wondered if you'd be prepared to show me what his effects consisted of."

"If that's what you want. Just speak up another time!" he instructed grumpily. Almost at once he started pulling apart his baggage roll, tossing some things aside, but laying certain items in a neat line at my feet. The discards were plainly his own originals; the kit offered up for inspection was his heirloom from the drowned man.

What Phrygia had passed on to him would not have raised much excitement at an auctioneer's house clearance. My father, who was in that business, would have dumped the dead playwright's clothes with his glassware porter for use as packing rags. Among the awful duds were a couple of tunics, now pleated on the shoulders with large stitches where Congrio had taken them in to fit his skinnier frame; a pair of disgusting old sandals; a twisted belt; and a toga not even I would have plucked off a secondhand stall, since the wine stains on it looked twenty years old and indelible. Also a battered satchel (empty); a bundle of quills, some of them partly whittled into pens; a rather nice tinderbox; three drawstring purses (two empty, one with five dice and a bronze coin with one blank face, evidently a forgery); a broken lantern; and a wax tablet with one corner snapped off.

"Anything else?"

"This is the lot."

Something in his manner attracted my attention. "You've laid it out nice and correct."

"Practice!" sniffed Congrio. "What makes you think you're the first busybody wanting to do an inventory?" He was enjoying being difficult.

I lazily lifted one eyebrow. "Somehow I can't see a finance tribune trying to screw you for inheritance tax on this lot! So who was so intrigued? Is somebody jealous because you came in for the handout?"

"I just took the stuff when I was offered. If anybody wants to look at it, I let them see. You finished?" He started packing it all up again. Even though the items were horrible his packing was systematic and his folding neat. My question remained tantalizingly unanswered.

If Congrio was hedging, my interest grew. The clothes had a nasty, musky smell. It was impossible to tell whether this had derived from their previous owner or been imposed since they were taken over, but nobody with any taste or discretion would want them now. The other objects mostly made a sad collection too. It was hard to see in anything here either a motive or any other clue.

I shook two of the dice around in my hand then let them fall casually on a spread tunic. Both turned up six. "Hello! Looks like he left you a lucky set."

"You found the right two to test," said Congrio. I lifted the dice, weighing them in my hand. As I expected they were weighted. Congrio grinned. "The rest are normal. I don't think I've got the nerve to use those two, but don't tell anyone, in case I change my mind. Anyway, now we know why he was always winning."

"Was he?"

"Famous for it."

I whistled quietly. "I'd not heard. Was he a big player?"

"All the time. That was how he gathered his pile."

"A pile? That wasn't part of your handout, I take it?"

"Hah! No. Chremes said he would take care of any cash."

"A nice gesture!" We grinned wryly together. "Did Heliodorus play dice against the other members of the company?"

"Not normally. Chremes had told him it caused trouble. He liked to go off and fleece the locals the night we left a place. Chremes was always nagging him about that as well, afraid one day we'd be followed by an angry mob and set upon."

"Did Chremes know why Heliodorus had such permanent good luck?" I asked, shaking the dice tellingly.

"Oh no! He never looked like a bent player." He must have been a subtle one. From what I had already heard about his ability to judge people, cleverly finding their weak points, it made sense that he could also pull the old weighted-dice trick without being detected. A clever, highly unlikable man.

"So Heliodorus knew better than to upset the party by cheating his own? Yet if Chremes issued a warning, does that mean it happened once?"

"There were a few rows," offered Congrio, his pale face crinkling up slyly.

"Going to tell me who else was involved?"

"Gambling debts are private," he replied. He had a cheek. I was not prepared to give him a bribe.

"Fair enough." Now I had a clue to work with, I would simply ask someone else. "Davos told me Heliodorus went through a phase of being friendly with the Twins."

"Oh, you know, then?" It had been a lucky connection on my part; the bill-poster looked irritated by my guessing correctly.

"About them all drinking together at one time? Yes. Did they dice too? May as well tell it, Congrio. I can always ask Davos. So was there gambling going on among those three?"

"I reckon so," Congrio agreed. "Nobody tells me things, but I got the idea Heliodorus won too much off them, and that was when they stopped drinking with him."

"Was this once? Was it a long time ago?"

"Oh no," sneered Congrio. "It was always happening. They'd pal up for a few weeks, then next thing they weren't speaking. After a bit they'd forget they had quarreled, and start over again. I used to notice because the times they were friendly with Heliodorus was when the Twins caught his nasty habits. He always shoved me around, and while they were in league with him, I copped for it from them too."

"What phase of this happy cycle were they all in when you went to Petra?"

"Ignoring each other. Had been for months, I was happy to know."

I applied my innocent face. "So who apart from me," I inquired suddenly, "has been wanting a perusal of your wonderful inheritance?"

"Oh just those clowns again," scoffed Congrio.

"You don't like them?" I commented quietly.

"Too clever." Cleverness was not an offense in Roman law, though I had often shared Congrio's view that it ought to be. "Every time I see them, I get knotted up and start feeling annoyed."

"Why's that?"

He kicked at his baggage roll impatiently. "They look down on you. There's nothing so special about telling a few jokes. They don't make them up, you know. All they do is say what some other old clown thought up and wrote down a hundred years ago. I could do it if I had a script."

"If you could read it."

"Helena's teaching me." I might have known. He continued boasting recklessly: "All I need is a joke collection and I'll be a clown myself."

It seemed to me it would take him a long time to put together enough funny stories to be a stand-up comic of Grumio's caliber. Besides, I couldn't see him managing the right timing and tone. "Where are you going to get the collection, Congrio?" I tried not to sound patronizing—without much success.

For some reason it didn't bother him. "Oh, they do exist, Falco!"

I changed the subject to avoid an argument. "Tell me, did the clowns come together to look at your property?" The bill-poster nodded. "Any idea what they were looking for?"

"No."

"Something particular?"

"They never said so."

"Trying to get back some IOUs maybe?"

"No, Falco."

"Did they want these dice? After all, the Twins do magic tricks—"

"They saw the dice were here. They never asked for them." Presumably they did not realize the dice were crooked. "Look, they just strolled up, laughing, and asking what I had got. I thought they were going to pinch my stuff, or ruin it. You know what they're like when they're feeling mischievous."

"The Twins? I know they can be a menace, but not outright delinquents, surely?"

"No," Congrio admitted, though rather reluctantly. "Just a pair of nosy bastards then."

Somehow I wondered about that.

Forty-nine

He was right. The two clowns *were* clever. It would take more than a bland expression and a quick change of subject to trip them up. I was aware before I started that the minute they had any idea I was trying to squeeze particular information from them, fending me off would become a joyous game. They were seditious. I would need to watch for exactly the right opportunity to tackle them. And when I did, I would need all my skill.

Wondering how I could choose the moment, I came back to my own tent.

Helena was alone. She told me that as I had predicted, Chremes had bungled acquiring a booking here.

"When he was waiting to see the town councilor who runs the

theater, he overheard the fellow scoff to a servant, *"Oh, not the ghastly tribe who did that terrible piece about the pirates?"* When Chremes finally got in to see the big man, relations failed to improve. So we're moving off straightaway—"

"Today?" I was horrified.

"Tonight. We get a day's rest, then go." It was good-bye to booking rooms then. No landlord was going to screw me for a night's rent when I only had a few daylight hours for sleeping. Helena sounded bitter too. "Chremes, with his nose put out of joint by a rude critic, does not dally for more insults. Canatha, here we come! Everyone is furious—"

"That includes me! And where's Musa?"

"Gone to find a temple and send a message to his sister. He seems rather low. He never gives much away, but I'm sure he was looking forward to spending some time here, back in his own country. Let's just hope the message Musa is sending his sister doesn't say, *'Put out my slippers. I'm coming home. . . .'*"

"So he's a homesick boy? This is bad news. He was miserable enough with mooning over Byrria."

"Well, I'm trying to help out there. I've invited Byrria to dine with us the first time we stop properly. We've been doing so much traveling she must be lonely driving all by herself."

"If she is lonely, it's her own fault." Charity was not on my agenda at the moment. "She could have had a lusty young Nabataean to crack the whip for her!" Come to that, she could have had pretty well any man in the company, except those of us with strict companions. "Does Musa know you're brokering romance for him? I'll take him for a decent haircut and shave!"

Helena sighed. "Better not be too obvious."

"Really?" I grinned, grabbing hold of her suddenly. "Being obvious always worked for me." I pulled Helena close enough for my own obvious feelings to be unmissable.

"Not this time." Helena, who had had a great deal of practice, wriggled free. "If we're moving on, we need to sleep. What did you find out from Congrio?"

"That Heliodorus was a hardened gambling cheat, and his victims may just have included Tranio and Grumio."

"Together or separately?"

"This is unclear."

"Lot of money involved?"

"Another unknown quantity." But my guess was, probably.

"Do you plan to question them next?"

"I plan to know just what I'm asking before I attempt anything. Those two are a tricky pair." In fact, I was surprised that even a seasoned cheat had managed to mug them. But if they were accustomed to feeling sure of themselves, being fleeced might have come as a nasty surprise. Congrio was right; they had a streak of arrogance. They were so used to sneering at others that if they found they had been set up, I hated to speculate how they would react.

"Do you think they are hiding something?" Helena asked. "Something significant?"

"More and more it looks that way. What do you think, fruit?"

"I think," Helena prophesied, "anything with those two in it will be even more complicated than it looks."

On the way to Canatha I asked Davos about the gambling. He had known it went on. He also remembered Heliodorus and the Twins arguing on occasions, though nothing too spectacular. He had guessed the playwright used to swindle local townsfolk. He himself had nothing to do with it. Davos was a man who could smell trouble; when he did he walked away.

I was reluctant to speak to Chremes about financial smears on Heliodorus. It touched too closely on his own problems, which I was holding in reserve at present. I did ask Phrygia. She assumed gambling was something all men did, and that cheating came naturally into the process. Like most disgusting male habits she ignored it, she said.

Helena offered to make enquiries of Philocrates, but I decided we could manage without help from him.

If Byrria was in a receptive mood, we would ask her when she came to dine.

Fifty

Halfway to Canatha, on a high, flat, volcanic plain with distant views to the snow-capped peak of Mount Hermon, Helena and I tried our hands as matchmakers. For reasons we only found out later, we were wasting our time.

Entertaining two people who like to ignore each other's existence is quite a strain. As hosts we had supplied tasty wines, delectable fish, stuffed dates (stuffed by me, in my masquerade as an efficient cook), elegantly spiced side dishes, olives, nuts, and sticky sweets. We had tried to place the romantic pair together, but they gave us the slip and took up stations at opposite ends of the fire. We sat side by side between them. Helena found herself talking to Byrria, while I just glared at Musa. Musa himself found a ferocious appetite for eating, buried his head in a bowl, and made no attempt to show off. As a wooer he had a slack technique. Byrria paid no attention to him. As a victim of his wiles, she was a tough proposition. Anyone who managed to tear this daisy from the pasture would need to tug hard.

The quality of the dinner did compensate for the lack of action. I helped myself to much of the wine while passing among the company, pointlessly trying to animate them with a generous jug. In the end I simply lay back with my head pillowed in Helena's lap, relaxed completely (not hard, in the state I had reached), and exclaimed, "I give up! A man should know his limitations. Playing Eros is not my style. I must have the wrong kind of arrows in my bow."

"I'm sorry," murmured Byrria. "I didn't realize the invitation was conditional." Her reproach was lighthearted. The refills I had been plying her with had mellowed her somewhat. Either that or she was too practical to try flouncing off in a huff while she was tipsy.

"The only condition—" Helena smiled "—is that all present quietly tolerate the romantic nature of their host." Byrria tipped her winecup at me obligingly. There was no problem. We were all in a sleepy, well-filled, amenable mood.

"Maybe," I suggested to Helena, "Musa has perched so far from our lovely guest so he can gaze at her through the firelight." While we talked about her, Byrria merely sat looking beautiful. She did it well. I had no complaints.

Helena Justina tickled my chin as she chimed in with my dreamy speculations. "Admiring her in secret through the leaping sparks?"

"Unless he's just avoiding her because he hasn't washed."

"Unfair!"

Helena was right. He was always clean. Given the fact that he had joined us in Petra so unexpectedly, and with so little luggage, it was a puzzle how Musa remained presentable. Sharing a tent, Helena and I would soon have known if his habits were unpleasant. His worst feature at the moment was a sheepish expression as I tried to set him up as a sophisticated lover.

Tonight he was turned out the same as always in his long white robe. He only had one, and yet he seemed to keep it laundered. He looked washed and tidy; he had definitely shaved (something none of us bothered with much on the road). On close examination there were one or two gestures to smart presentation: a soapstone scarab amulet on his chest, which I remembered him buying when he was out with me at Gerasa, a rope girdle that looked so new he must have picked it up in Bostra, and he was bare-headed in the Roman way. That made him look too boyish; I would have warned against it, but he had not asked for my sartorial advice.

Byrria, too, had probably dressed up slightly in response to our formal invitation. She was in green, rather plain if anything, with a very long skirt and long sleeves against the flies, which tended to descend on us at twilight. It marked a change from her spangled and revealing stage costumes, and signified that tonight she was being herself. Being herself also involved long bronze earrings that rattled all the time. Had I been in a less forgiving mood, they would have severely annoyed me.

Helena was looking sophisticated in a brown dress I had not known she owned. I had favored a casual approach, trying out a long striped Eastern robe I had bought to fend off the heat. I felt like a goat farmer and was in need of a scratch; I hoped it was just due to the newness of the material.

While we teased him, Musa put on a patient face but stood up, breathing the cool night air and gazing somewhere away to the south.

"Be kind to him," Helena said to Byrria. "We think Musa is homesick." He turned back to her, as if she had accused him of being impolite, but stayed on his feet. At least it gave Byrria a better view of him. He was passable, though not much more.

"It's just a ploy," I informed the girl confidentially. "Somebody once told him women like men who have an air of mysterious sadness."

"I am not sad, Falco." Musa gave me the controlled look of a man who was just trying to ease his indigestion after eating too much.

"Maybe not. But ignoring the most beautiful woman in Syria is pretty mysterious."

"Oh, I am not ignoring her!"

Well that was better. His somber, deliberate manner of speech did make it sound vaguely admiring. Helena and I knew Musa always talked that way, but Byrria might read it as restrained ardor.

"There you are." I grinned at her, encouraging this. "You are quite right to be wary. Under the glacially aloof pose smolders a hot-blooded philanderer. Compared to this man, Adonis was a ruffianly buck with bad breath and dandruff. In a moment he'll be tossing you roses and reciting poetry."

Musa smiled politely. "Poetry I can do, Falco."

We were lacking the floristry, but he came to the fire, sitting opposite Helena and me, which at last brought him nearer to the girl he was supposed to be entrancing, though in fact he forgot to gaze at her. He dropped to a cushion (conveniently placed by Helena before the meal just where it would allow things to develop if our guests had wanted that). Then Musa started to recite. It was obviously going to be a very long poem, and it was in Nabataean Arabic.

Byrria listened with the faintest of smiles and her slanting green eyes well cast down. There was not much else the poor girl could do.

Helena sat still. Musa's posture for recitation was to stare straight ahead, which meant Helena was catching most of the performance. The soft pressure of her thumb on my windpipe warned me not to interrupt. Still lying in her lap I closed my eyes and forced myself to leave our idiotic tent guest to his fate.

Sooner than I had dared to hope, Musa stopped—or at least paused long enough for me to break in without upsetting him. Rolling over and smiling at Byrria, I said quietly, "I think a certain young lady has just been favorably compared to a soft-eyed gazelle, running free on the mountains—"

"Falco!" Musa was tutting, fortunately with a laugh in his tone. "Are you speaking more of my language than you pretend?"

"I'm a spare-time poet and I know how to guess."

"You're an acting playwright; you should be able to interpret well-spoken verse." There was a hard note in Byrria's voice. "And how are your other guesses, Falco?" Without appearing graceless, Byrria had turned the conversation. Her long earrings tinkled slightly, though whether with amusement or embarrassment I could not tell. She was a girl who hid her thoughts. "Are you any nearer identifying the person who killed Ione?"

Giving up on the priest now that I had seen his technique for seduction, I too welcomed the new subject. "I'm still looking for Ione's unknown lover, and I'd be grateful for suggestions. With regard to the playwright, motives have suddenly started turning up as thick as barnacles on a boat bottom. The newest concerns Tranio, Grumio, and the possibility of bad gambling debts. Know anything about this?"

Byrria shook her head. She seemed very relieved that the talk had changed pace. "No I don't, except that Heliodorus gambled in the same way he drank—hard, yet always staying in control." Recalling it, she shivered slightly. Her earrings trembled, soundlessly this time, reflecting the fire in tiny ripples of light. If she had been a girlfriend of mine, I would have reached to caress her earlobes—and deftly removed the jewelry. "No one bettered him."

"Custom-made dice!" I explained. She hissed angrily at the

news. "So how do you see Heliodorus relating to the Twins, Byrria?"

"I would have thought they were a match for him."

I could tell that she liked them. On an impulse I asked, "Are you going to tell me which of them pulled Heliodorus off, that time he jumped on you?"

"It was Grumio." She said it without drama.

At her side I thought Musa tensed. Byrria herself sat extremely quietly, no longer showing her anger over the bad experience. All evening, in fact, she had behaved with reserve. She seemed to be watching us, or some of us. I almost felt that she, not Musa, was the foreigner at our fireside, subjecting our strange manners to curious scrutiny.

"You refused to tell me that before," I reminded her. "Why now?"

"I refused to be interrogated like a criminal. But here I am with friends." From her, that was quite a compliment.

"So what happened?"

"Just at the right moment—for me—Grumio burst in. He had come to ask Heliodorus for something. I don't know what it was about really, but Grumio pulled the brute off me and started asking him about a scroll—a play I suppose. I managed to flee. Obviously," she said to me in a reasonable tone, "I am hoping you are not going to tell me Grumio is your main suspect."

"The Twins have alibis, at least for Ione's death. Grumio in particular. I saw him otherwise occupied myself. For what happened at Petra, they're vouching for each other. Of course they may be conspiring—"

Byrria looked surprised. "Oh, I don't think they like each other that much."

"What do you mean?" Helena picked it up at once. "They spend a lot of time together. Is there some rivalry?"

"Plenty!" Byrria replied quickly, as though it ought to be well known. Uneasily, she added, "Tranio really does have more flair as a comedian. But I know Grumio feels that's merely a reflection of Tranio having more showy parts in plays. Grumio is much better at standing up to improvise, entertaining a crowd, though he hasn't done it so much recently."

"Do they fight?" Musa put in. It was the kind of blunt question I like to ask myself.

"They have occasional squabbles." She smiled at him. Must have been an aberration. Musa found enough spirit to mock himself by basking in the favor; then Byrria seemed to blush, though she could have been overheated by the nearness of the fire. I must have been looking thoughtful. "Does that help, Falco?"

"Not sure. It may give me a way to approach them. Thanks, Byrria."

It was late. Tomorrow there would be more traveling as we pressed on to Canatha. Around us the rest of the camp had quieted. Many people were already asleep. Our group seemed the only active party. It was time to break up. Glancing at Helena, I abandoned the attempt to bring the reluctant pair together.

Helena yawned, making the hint refined. She began collecting dishes, Byrria helping her. Musa and I confined our efforts to manly procedures such as poking the fire and finishing the olives. When Byrria thanked us for the evening, Helena apologized. "I hope we didn't tease you too unbearably."

"In what way?" Byrria responded drily. Then she smiled again. She was an extraordinarily beautiful young woman; the fact that she was barely twenty suddenly became more evident. She had enjoyed herself tonight; we could satisfy ourselves with that. Tonight she was as near to contentment as she might ever be. It made her look vulnerable for once. Even Musa seemed more mature, and more her equal.

"Don't mind us." Helena spoke informally, licking sauce off her hand where she had picked up a sticky plate. "You have to make your life as you wish. The important thing is to find and to keep real friends." Reluctant to make too much of it, she went into the tent with the pile of dishes.

I was not prepared to let this go so easily. "Even so, that doesn't mean she ought to be afraid of men!"

"I fear no one!" Byrria shot back, with a burst of her hot temper. It was a passing moment; her voice dropped again. Staring at a tray she had picked up, she added. "Maybe I just fear the consequences."

"Very wise!" quipped Helena, reappearing in an instant. "Think of Phrygia, whose whole life has been embittered and ruined by having a baby and marrying wrongly. She lost the child, she lost her chance to develop fully as an actress, and I think maybe she also gave up the man she should really have been with all these years—"

"You give a bad example," Musa broke in. He was terse. "I could say, look at Falco and you!"

"Us?" I grinned. Somebody had to play the fool and lighten the conversation. "We're just two completely unsuitable people who knew we could have no future together but liked each other enough to go to bed for a night."

"How long ago was that?" demanded Byrria hotly. Not a girl who could take irony.

"Two years," I confessed.

"That's your one night?" laughed Byrria. "How carefree and cosmopolitan! And how long, Didius Falco, do you suppose this unsuitable relationship may last?"

"About a lifetime," I said cheerfully. "We're not unreasonable in our hopes."

"So what are you trying to prove to me? It seems contradictory."

"Life is contradictory sometimes, though most times it just stinks." I sighed. Never give advice. People catch you out and start fighting back. "On the whole, I agree with you. So, life stinks; ambitions disappoint; friends die; men destroy and women disintegrate. But if, my dear Byrria and Musa, you will listen to one kind word from a friend, I should say, if you do find true affection, never turn your back on it."

Helena, who was standing behind me, laughed lovingly. She ruffled my hair, then bent over me and kissed my forehead. "This poor soul needs his bed. Musa, will you see Byrria safely to her tent?"

We all said our good nights; then Helena and I watched the others go.

They walked uneasily together, space showing between them. They did stroll slowly, as if there might be things to be said, but we could not hear them talking as they left. They appeared to be strangers, and yet if I had given a professional judgment I would have said they knew more about each other than Helena and I supposed.

"Have we made a mistake?"

"I don't see what it can be, Marcus."

We had done, though it was to be some time before I understood the obvious.

Helena and I cleared the debris and did what packing we needed, ready to drive on before dawn. Helena was in bed when I heard Musa returning. I went out and found him crouched beside the remnants of the fire. He must have heard me, but he made no move to evade me, so I squatted alongside. His face was buried in his hands.

After a moment I thumped his shoulder consolingly. "Did something happen?"

He shook his head. "Nothing that matters."

"No. I thought you had the miserable air of a man with a clean conscience. The girl's a fool!"

"No, she was kind." He spoke offhandedly, as if they were friends.

"Talk about it if you want, Musa. I know it's serious."

"I never felt like this, Falco."

"I know." I let a moment pass before I spoke again. "Sometimes the feeling goes away."

He looked up. His face was drawn. Intense emotion racked him. I liked the poor idiot; his unhappiness was hard to contemplate. "And if not?" he squeezed out.

I smiled sadly. "If not, there are two alternatives. Most frequently—and you can guess this one—everything sorts itself out because the girl leaves the scene."

"Or?"

I knew how low the chances were. But with Helena Justina asleep a few feet away, I had to acknowledge the fatal possibility: "Or sometimes your feeling stays—and so does she."

"Ah!" Musa exclaimed softly, as if to himself. "In that case what am I to do?" I assumed he meant, *If I do win Byrria, what am I to do with her?*

"You'll get over this, Musa. Trust me. Tomorrow you could wake up and find yourself adoring some languid blonde who always wanted a flurry with a Nabataean priest."

I doubted it. But on the off chance that he might be needing his strength, I hauled Musa to his feet and made him go to bed.

Tomorrow, if a cold blast of sanity seemed less likely to damage him, I would explain my theory that it is better to show off your multifaceted personality in their own language than to bore them stiff reciting poetry they cannot understand. If that failed, I would just have to get him interested in drinking, rude songs, and fast chariots.

Fifty-one

Canatha.

It was an old, walled, isolated city huddled on the northern incline of the basalt plain. As the only habitation of any substance in this remote area, it had acquired a special reputation and a special atmosphere. Its territory was small. Its commercial activity was greater, for a major trade route up from Bostra came this way. Even with the fine Hellenic attributes we had come to expect—the high acropolis, civilized amenities, and heavy program of civic refurbishment—Canatha had strange touches. Hints of both Nabataean and Parthian architecture mingled exotically with its Greek and Roman features.

Though it lay too far out to be at risk of jealous Jewish incursions, there were other dangers lurking beyond the close clasp of its walls. Canatha was a lonely outpost in traditional bandit country. The mood here reminded me more of frontier fortresses in Germany and Britain than the pleasure-grasping, money-loving cities further west in the Decapolis. This was a self-reliant, self-involved community. Trouble had always lain not far outside the city gates.

We, of course, as a hapless band of vagabonds, were scrutinized keenly in case we were bringing trouble in with us. We played it straight, patiently letting them question and search us. Once in, we found the place friendly. Where craftsmen look long distances for influences, there is often a welcome for all comers. Canatha lacked prejudice. Canatha liked visitors. Canatha, being a town many people omitted from their itinerary, was so grateful to see traveling entertainers that its audiences even liked us.

The first play we gave them was *The Pirate Brothers*, which Chremes was determined to rehabilitate after the slurs cast upon it by the Bostra magistrate. It was well received, and we busily plundered our repertoire for *The Girl from Andros* and Plautus' *Amphitryon* (one of Chremes' beloved gods-go-a-fornicating japes). I was anticipating thunder from Musa over *Amphitryon* but luckily the play had only one substantial female part, the virtuous wife unknowingly seduced by Jupiter, and this role was snatched by Phrygia. Byrria only got to play a nurse; she had one scene, at the very end, and no hanky-panky. She did get a good speech, however, where she had to describe the infant Hercules dispatching a snake with his chubby little hands.

To liven things up, Helena constructed a strangled snake to appear in the play. She stuffed a tube made from an old tunic and sewed on eyes with fringed, flirty lashes to produce a python with a silly expression (closely based on Thalia's Jason). Musa made it a long forked tongue, utilizing a piece of broken belt. Byrria, who unexpectedly turned out to be a comedienne, ran onstage with this puppet dangling limply under her elbow, then made it waggle about as if it was recovering from strangulation, causing her to beat it into submission irritatedly. The unscripted effect was hilarious. It caused a joyous roar at Canatha, but earned some of us a reprimand from Chremes, who had not been forewarned.

So, with the company funds restored at least temporarily, and a new reputation for the ridiculous among my own party, we traveled from Canatha to Damascus.

We had to cross dangerous country, so we kept our wits about us. "This seems a road on which the unexpected could happen," I muttered to Musa.

"Bandits?"

His was a true prophecy. Suddenly we were surrounded by menacing nomads. We were more surprised than terrified. They could see we were not exactly laden down with panniers of frankincense.

We pushed up Musa, finally useful as an interpreter, to speak to them. Adopting a solemn, priestly manner (as he told me afterward), he greeted them in the name of Dushara and promised a free theatrical performance if they would let us go in peace. We could see the thieves thought this was the funniest offer they had had since the Great King of Persia tried to send them a tax demand, so they sat down in a half circle while we sped through a quick version of *Amphitryon,* complete with stuffed snake. Needless to say, the snake received the best hand, but then there was a tricky moment when the bandits made it plain they wanted to purchase Byrria. While she contemplated life being beaten and cursed as some nomad's foreign concubine, Musa strode forwards and exclaimed something dramatic. They cheered ironically. In the end we satisfied the group by making them a present of the python puppet and providing a short lesson in waggling him.

We rode on.

"Whatever did you say, Musa?"

"I told them Byrria is to be a sacrificial virgin on a High Place."

Byrria shot him a worse glance than she had given the nomads.

Our next excitement was being waylaid by a band of Christians. Tribesmen stealing our props was fair business, but cult adherents after freeborn Roman souls was an outrage. They were casually scattered across the road at a stopping place so that we had to go around them or submit to conversation. As soon as they smiled and said how pleasant it was to meet us, we knew they were bastards.

"Who are they?" whispered Musa, puzzled by their attitude.

"Wide-eyed lunatics who meet secretly for meals in upstairs rooms in honor of what they say is the One God."

"One? Is that not rather limiting?"

"Surely. They'd be harmless, but they have bad-mannered politics. They refuse to respect the Emperor."

"Do you respect the Emperor, Falco?"

"Of course not." Apart from the fact I worked for the old skinflint, I was a republican. "But I don't upset him by saying so publicly."

When the fanatical sales talk moved to offering us a guarantee of eternal life, we beat the Christians up soundly and left them whimpering.

With the rising heat and these annoying interruptions, it took three stages to reach Damascus. On the last leg of our journey I did finally achieve a private talk with Tranio.

Fifty-two

Due to these disturbances, we had regrouped somewhat. Tranio happened to come alongside my wagon, while I noticed that for once Grumio was some way behind. I myself was alone. Helena had gone to spend some time with Byrria, diplomatically taking Musa. This was too good a chance to miss.

"Who wants to live forever anyway?" Tranio joked, referring to the Christians we had just sorted out. He made the comment before he realized whose wagon he was riding next to.

"I could take that as a giveaway!" I shot back, seizing the chance to work on him.

"For what, Marcus Didius?" I hate people who try to unnerve me by unbidden familiarity.

"Guilt," I said.

"You see guilt everywhere, Falco." He switched smartly back to the formal mode of address.

"Tranio, everywhere I run up against guilty men."

I should like to pretend that my reputation as an informer was so grand that Tranio felt drawn to stay and challenge my skills. What really happened was that he tried hard to get away. He kicked his heels into his animal to spur it off, but being a camel it refused; a pain in the ribs was better than being obedient. This beast with the sly soul of a revolutionary was the usual dust-colored creature with unsavory bare patches on its ragged pelt, a morose manner, and a tormented cry. It could run fast, but only ever did so as an excuse to try and unseat its rider. Its prime ambition was to abandon a human to the vultures forty miles from an oasis. A nice pet—if you wanted to die slowly of a septic camel bite.

Now Tranio was surreptitiously attempting to remove himself, but the camel had decided to lollop along beside my ox in the hope of unsettling him.

"I think you're trapped." I grinned. "So tell me about comedy, Tranio."

"That's based on guilt mostly," he conceded with a wry smile.

"Oh? I thought it was meant to tap hidden fears?"

"You a theorist, Falco?"

"Why not? Just because Chremes keeps me on the routine hack work doesn't mean that I never dissect the lines I'm revising for him."

As he rode alongside me it was difficult to watch him too closely. If I turned my head I could see that he had been to a barber in Canatha; the cropped hair up the back of his head had been scraped off so close the skin showed red through the stubble. Even without twisting in my seat, I could catch a whiff of the rather overpowering balsam he had slopped on while shaving—a young man's mistaken purchase, which as a poor man he now had to use up. An occasional glance sideways gave me the impression of darkly hairy arms, a green signet ring with a gash in the stone, and whitened knuckles as he fought against the strong will of his camel. But he was riding in my blind spot. As I myself had to concentrate on calming our ox, which was upset by the bared teeth of Tranio's savage camel, it was impossible to look my subject directly in the eye.

"I'm doing a plodder's job," I continued, leaning back with my whole weight as the ox tried to surge. "I'm interested, did Heliodorus see it the way I do? Was it just piecework he flogged through? Did he reckon himself worthy of much better things?"

"He had a brain," Tranio admitted. "And the slimy creep knew it."

"He used it, I reckon."

"Not in his writing, Falco!"

"No. The scrolls I inherited in the play box prove that. His corrections are lousy and slapdash—when they are even legible."

"Why are you so intrigued by Heliodorus and his glorious lack of talent?"

"Fellow feeling!" I smiled, not giving away the true reason. I wanted to explore why Ione had told me that the cause of the previous playwright's death had been purely professional.

Tranio laughed, perhaps uneasily. "Oh, come! Surely you're not telling me that underneath everything, Heliodorus was secretly a star comedian! It wasn't true. His creative powers were enormous when it came to manipulating people, but fictionally he was a complete dud. He knew that too, believe me!"

"You told him, I gather?" I asked rather drily. People were always keen to tell me too if they hated my work.

"Every time Chremes gave him some dusty old Greek masterpiece and asked to have the jokes modernized, his dearth of intellectual equipment became pitifully evident. He couldn't raise a smile by tickling a baby. You've either got it or you haven't."

"Or else you buy yourself a joke collection." I was remembering something Congrio had said. "Somebody told me they're still obtainable."

Tranio spent a few moments swearing at his camel as it practiced a war dance. Part of this involved skidding sideways into my cart. I joined in the bad language; Tranio got his leg trapped painfully against a cartwheel; my ox lowed hoarsely in protest; and the people traveling behind us shouted abuse.

When peace was restored, Tranio's camel was more interested than ever in nuzzling my cart. The clown did his best to jerk the beast away while I said thoughtfully, "It would be nice to have access to some endless supply of good material. Something like Grumio talks about—an ancestral hoard of jests."

"Don't live in the past, Falco."

"What does that mean?"

"Grumio's obsessed—and he's wrong." I seemed to have tapped some old professional disagreement he had had with Grumio. "You can't bid at auction for humor. That's all gone. Oh, maybe once there *was* a golden age of comedy when material was sacrosanct and a clown could earn a fortune raffling off his great-great-grandfather's precious scroll of antique pornography and musty puns. But nowadays you need a new script every day. Satire has to be as fresh as a barrel of winkles. Yesterday's tired quips won't get you a titter on today's cosmopolitan stage."

"So if you inherited a collection of old jokes," I put to him, "you'd just toss it away?" Feeling I might be on to something, I struggled to remember details of my earlier conversation with Grumio. "Are you telling me I shouldn't believe all that wonderful rhetoric your tentmate exudes about the ancient hereditary trade of the jester? The professional laughter-man, valued according to his stock in trade? The old stories, which can be sold when in dire straits?"

"Crap!" Tranio cried.

"Not witty, but succinct."

"Falco, what good have his family connections done him?

Myself, I've had more success relying on a sharp brain and a five-year apprenticeship doing the warm-ups in Nero's Circus before gladiatorial shows."

"You think you're better than him?"

"I know it, Falco. He *could* be as good as he wants, but he'll need to stop whining about the decline in stage standards, accept what's really wanted, and forget that his father and grandfather could survive on a few poor stories, a farmyard impression, and some trick juggling. Dear gods, all those terrible lines about funny foreigners: Why do Roman roads run perfectly straight?" Tranio quipped harshly, mimicking every stand-up comedian who had ever made me wince. "To stop Thracian foodsellers setting up hot-and-cold foodstalls on the corners! And then the unsubtle innuendoes: What did the vestal virgin say to the eunuch?"

It sounded a good one, but he was cut short by the need to yank at his camel as it tried to dash off sideways across the road. I refrained from admitting my low taste by asking for the punch line.

Our route had been tilting slightly downhill, and now up ahead we could make out the abrupt break in the dry landscape that heralds Damascus, the oasis that hangs at the edge of the wilderness like a prosperous port on the rim of a vast infertile sea. On all sides we could see more traffic converging on this ancient honey pot. Any moment now either Grumio would trot up to join his supposed friend or Tranio would be leaving me.

It was time to apply blatant leverage. "Going back to Heliodorus. You thought he was an untalented stylus-pusher with less flair than an old pine log. So why were you and Grumio so thick with him that you let the bastard encumber you with horrific gambling debts?"

I had struck a nerve. The only problem was to deduce which nerve it was.

"Who told you that, Falco?" Tranio's face looked paler under

the lank fall of hair that tumbled forwards over his clever, dark
eyes. His voice was dark too, with a dangerous mood that was
hard to interpret.

"Common knowledge."

"Common lies!" From being pale he suddenly flushed a raw
color, like a man with desperate marsh fever. "We hardly ever
played with him for money. Dicing with Heliodorus was a fool's
game!" It almost sounded as if the clowns knew that he had
cheated. "We gambled for trifles, casual forfeits, that's all."

"Why are you losing your temper, then?" I asked quietly.

He was so furious that at last he overcame his camel's perver-
sity. Tearing at its mouth with a rough hand on the bridle, he
forced the animal to turn and galloped off to the back of the caravan.

Fifty-three

Damascus claimed to be the oldest inhabited city in the world. It would take somebody with a very long memory to disprove the claim. As Tranio said, who wants to live that long? Besides, the evidence was clear enough. Damascus had been working its wicked systems for centuries, and knew all the tricks. It money-changers were notorious. It possessed more liars, embezzlers, and thieves among the stone-framed market stalls that packed its colorful grid of streets than any city I had ever visited. It was outstandingly famous and prosperous. Its colorful citizens practiced an astonishing variety of villainy. As a Roman I felt quite at home.

This was the last city on our route through the Decapolis, and it had to be the jewel of the collection. Like Canatha, its position was remote from the rest, though here the isolation was simply a matter of long distance rather than atmosphere. This was no huddled bastion facing acres of wilderness—even though there were deserts in several directions. Damascus simply throbbed with power, commerce, and self-assurance.

It had the normal Decapolis features. Established in a flourishing oasis where the River Abana dashed out through a gorge in the long mountain range, the stout city walls and their protecting towers were themselves encircled for a wide area by water meadows. On the site of an ancient citadel within the city stood a modest Roman camp. An aqueduct brought water for both public baths and private homes. As the terminus of the old, jealously guarded Nabataean trade route from the Red Sea and also a major crossroads, it was well supplied with markets and caravanserai. As a Greek city it had town planning and democratic institutions. As a Roman acquisition it had a lavish civic building program, which centered on a grandiose plan to convert the local cult precinct into a huge sanctuary of Jupiter that would be set in a grotesquely oversized enclosure overloaded with colonnades, arches, and monumental gates.

We entered town from the east by the Gate of the Sun. Immediately the hubbub hit us. Coming out of the desert, the cries of rapacious street sellers and the racket of banter and barter were a shock. Of all the cities we had visited this bore the closest resemblance to the setting of a lively Greek play, a place where babies might be given away or treasure stolen, runaway slaves lurked behind every pillar, and prostitutes rarely survived to retirement age. Here, without doubt, sophisticated wives would berate their enfeebled husbands for not coming good in bed. Wayward sons bamboozled doddering fathers. Dutiful daughters were a rarity. Anyone passing for a priestess was likely to have had a first career preparing virgins for deflowerment by off-duty soldiers in a damp quayside brothel, and anyone who openly admitted to being a madam was best avoided hastily in case she turned out to be your long-lost grandmother.

From the Gate of the Sun to the Gate of Jupiter at the opposite end of town ran the Via Recta, a street some surveyor with a
sense of humor had once named "Straight." An embarrassing
thoroughfare. Not exactly the place to hire a quiet room for a
week of contemplative soul-searching. It ought to have been a
stately axis of the city, yet singularly lacked grandeur. In Roman
terms it was a Decumanus Maximus, though one that took several demeaning wiggles around hillocks and inconvenient old
buildings. It was a foundation line in what should have been a
classical Greek street grid. But Hippodamnus of Miletus, who
laid down the principles of gracious town planning, would have
chucked up his dinner in disgust if faced with this.

It was chaotic too, and characterized by a forest of columns
that held up cloth awnings. In the turgid heat that soon built up
beneath the heavy roofing as the sun climbed, official traders
worked from solidly constructed lockups. Numerous illegal
stalls were also crammed in, spilling in unsupervised rows across
most of the width of the street. A Roman aedile would have become apoplectic. Controlling the irreverent mayhem would be
impossible. Traffic ground to a standstill soon after dawn. People
stopped for long conversations, planting themselves immovably
in the road.

We clapped our hands on our purses, clung together, and
tried to forge our way through the impasse, wincing at the noise.
We were assailed by entrancing scents from huge piles of spices
and blinked at the glitter of tawdry trinkets hung in streamers
on the stalls. We ducked to avoid casually wielded bales of fine-
weave material. We gaped at the array of sponges and jewelry,
figs and whole honeycombs, household pots and tall candelabra,
five shades of henna powder, seven kinds of nuts. We were
bruised. We were crushed against walls by men with handcarts.
Members of our party panicked as they glimpsed an exotic bargain, some bauble in copper, with a twirl to its handle and an

Oriental spout; they only turned round for a second, then lost sight of the rest of us among the jostling crowds.

Needless to say, we had to traverse almost the whole of this chaotic street. The theater where Chremes had secured us a booking was at the far end, slightly south of the main thorough-fare, near the Jupiter Gate. It stood close to the secondhand clothes-sellers, in what people had honestly named the louse market.

Since we were to have the honor of performing at the monu-mental theater built by Herod the Great, we could live with a few lice.

We never did find out how Chremes pulled off this coup. With a slight sign of awareness that people despised his powers as an organizer, he clammed up proudly and refused to say.

How he did it ceased to matter once we ascertained the local rate for theater tickets and started selling them. At that point we cheered up tremendously. We had a smart venue (for once), and found no difficulty filling the auditorium. In this teeming hive of buyers and sellers people handed over good money regardless of repertoire. They all prided themselves on driving a hard bargain; once off the commodities in which they were experts, most of them became easy touches. Culture was merely a facet of retail-ing here. Plenty of brokers were looking to impress clients; they bought tickets to entertain their guests without bothering with what might be on. Commercial hospitality is a splendid invention.

For a couple of days we all thought Damascus was a wonder-ful place. Then, as people started to realize they had been rooked by the money-changers and as one or two purses were lifted in the narrow alleys off the main streets, our views cooled. Even I went out on my own one morning and bought as a pres-ent for my mother a large quantity of what I believed to be myrrh, only to have Musa sniff at it and sadly tell me it was bdellium, a much less pure aromatic gum that should sell at a much less aromatic price. I went back to challenge the stall-holder; he had disappeared.

Our booking was for three nights. Chremes settled on performing what he regarded as the gems of our repertoire: *The Pirate Brothers,* then a fornicating gods farce, and *The Girl from Mykonos.* The last sparkler had been cobbled together by Heliodorus some-time before he died: maybe he should have died of shame. It was "loosely based" on all the other *Girl from . . .* comedies, a teaser for lustful merchants who were on the razzle in a big city with-out their wives. It had what the Samos, Andros, and Perinthos plays all lacked: Grumio's falling-off-a-ladder trick, Byrria fully clothed but doing a revealing dance while pretending to be mad, and all the girls in the orchestra playing topless. (Plancina asked to be paid a bonus after trapping a nipple between her cas-tanets.)

Chremes' choice caused groans. He had no real sense of at-mosphere. We knew these were the wrong plays and after a morning of muttering, the rest of the company, led by me as their literary expert, gathered to put matters right. We allowed *The Girl from Mykonos,* which was obviously a runner in a bad city, but overruled the other two; they were altered by democratic vote to *The Rope,* with its ever-popular tug-of-war, and a play Davos liked that enabled him to show off in his Boasting Soldier role. Philocrates, so in love with himself and public adulation, would probably have argued as his own part in the latter was minimal, but he happened to be hiding in his tent after spotting a woman he had seduced on our visit to Pella in the company of a rather large male relative who looked as if he had something on his mind.

That was the trouble with Damascus. All roads led there.

"And lead away," Helena reminded me, "in three days' time. What are we going to do, Marcus?"

"I don't know. I agree we didn't come to the East to spend the rest of our lives with a cheap drama company. We're earning enough to live on—but not enough to stop and take a holiday, and certainly not enough to pay our fares home if Anacrites won't sign for it."

"Marcus, I could pay those."

"If I lost all self-respect."

"Don't exaggerate."

"All right, you can pay, but let me try to complete at least one commission first."

I led her into the streets. Uncomplainingly she took my arm. Most women of her status would have frizzled up in horror at the thought of stepping into the public hubbub of a loud, lewd foreign metropolis with neither a litter nor a bodyguard. Many citizens of Damascus eyed her with obvious suspicion for doing so. For a senator's daughter Helena had always had a strange sense of propriety. If I was there, that satisfied her. She was neither embarrassed nor afraid.

The size and liveliness of Damascus suddenly reminded me of the rules we had left behind in Rome, rules that Helena broke there, too, though at least it was home. In Rome scandalous behavior among senatorial females was just a feature of fashionable life. Causing trouble for their male relatives had become an excuse for anything. Mothers regarded it as a duty to educate daughters to be rebellious. Daughters reveled in it, throwing themselves at gladiators, joining queer sects, or becoming notorious intellectuals. By comparison, the vices open to boys seemed tame.

Even so, running off to live with an informer was an act more shocking than most. Helena Justina had good taste in men, but she was an unusual girl. Sometimes I forgot how unusual.

I stopped at a street corner, caught by an occasional need to check up on her. I had one arm tight around her to protect her from the bustle. She tipped her head to look at me questioningly; her stole fell back from her face, its trimming caught on her earring. She was listening, though trying to free the strands of fine gold wire, as I said, "You and I lead a strange life. Sometimes I feel that if I cared for you properly I would keep you somewhere more suitable."

Helena shrugged. She was always patient with my restless attempts to make her more conventional. She could take pomposity, if it came as a near relative to a cheeky grin. "I like my life. I'm with an interesting man."

"Thanks!" I found myself laughing. I should have expected her to disarm me, but she still caught me unawares. "Well, it won't last forever."

"No," she agreed solemnly. "One day you will be a prim middle-rank bureaucrat who wears a clean toga every day. You'll talk of economics over breakfast and only eat lettuce for lunch. And I'll have to sit at home with my face in an inch-thick flour pack, forever checking laundry bills."

I controlled a smile. "Well, that's a relief. I thought you were going to be difficult about my plans."

"I am never difficult, Marcus." I swallowed a chortle. Helena slipped in thoughtfully, "Are you homesick?"

I probably was, but she knew I would never admit to it. "I can't go home yet. I hate unfinished business."

"So how are you proposing to finish it?"

I liked her faith in me.

Luckily I had put arrangements in hand for resolving at least one commission. Pointing to a nearby house wall, I showed off my cunning device. Helena inspected it. "Congrio's script is getting more elaborate."

"He's being well taught," I said, letting her know I realized who had been improving him.

Congrio had drawn his usual poster advertising our performance of *The Rope* that evening. Alongside it he had chalked up another bill:

HABIB
(VISITOR TO ROME)
URGENT MESSAGE: ASK FOR FALCO
AT THEATER OF HEROD
IMMEDIATE CONTACT IS
TO YOUR DEFINITE ADVANTAGE

"Will he answer?" asked Helena, a cautious girl.

"Without a doubt."

"How can you be so sure?"

"Thalia said he was a businessman. He'll think it's a promise of money."

"Oh, well done!" said Helena.

Fifty-four

The specimens called Habib who asked for Falco at the theater were varied and sordid. This was common in my line of work. I was ready for them. I asked several questions they could answer by keen guesswork, then slipped in the customary clincher: "Did you visit the imperial menagerie on the Esquiline Hill?"

"Oh yes."

"Very interesting." The menagerie is outside the city by the Praetorian Camp. Even in Rome not many people know that. "Don't waste my time with cheating and lies. Get out of here!"

They did eventually catch on, and sent their friends to try "Oh no" as the answer to the trick question; one spectacularly blatant operator even attempted to delude me with the old "Maybe I did, maybe I didn't" line. Finally, when I was starting to think the ploy had failed, it worked.

On the third evening, a group of us who had suddenly become very interested in helping out with the costumes were stripping off the female musicians for their half-naked starring roles in *The Girl from Mykonos*. At the crucial moment I was called out to a visitor. Torn between pulchritude and work, I forced myself to go.

The runt who might be about to help me with Thalia's commission was clad in a long striped shirt. He had an immense rope girdle wrapped several times about his unimpressive frame. He had a lazy eye and dopey features, with tufts of fine hair scattered on his head like an old bedside rug that was fast losing its grip on reality. He was built like a boy, yet had a mature face, reddened either by life as a furnace stoker or some congenital fear of being found out in whatever his routine wrongdoing was.

"I suppose you're Habib?"

"No, sir." Well that was different.

"Did he send you?"

"No, sir."

"Are you happy speaking Greek?" I queried drily, since his conversation did seem limited.

"Yes, sir."

I would have told him he could drop the "sir," but that would have left us staring in silence like seven-year-olds on their first day at school.

"Cough it up, then. I'm needed onstage for prompting." I was anxious to see the panpipe girl's bosom, which appeared to be almost as alarmingly perfect as the bouncing attributes of a certain rope dancer I had dallied with in my bachelor days. For purely nostalgic reasons I wished to make a critical comparison. If possible, by taking measurements.

I wondered if my visitor had just come to cadge a free ticket. Obviously I would have obliged just to escape and return to the theater. But as a hustler he was sadly slow, so I spelled it out for him. "Look, if you want a seat, there are still one or two at the top of the auditorium. I'll arrange it, if you like."

"Oh!" He sounded surprised. "Yes, sir!"

I gave him a bone token from the pouch at my belt. The roars and whoops from the theater behind us told me the orchestra girls had made their entrance. He didn't move. "You're still hanging around," I commented.

"Yes."

"Well?"

"The message."

"What about it?"

"I've come to get it."

"But you're not Habib."

"He's gone."

"Gone where?"

"The desert." Dear gods. The whole damn country was desert. I was in no mood to start raking through the sands of Syria to find this elusive entrepreneur. In the rest of the world there were vintages to sample, rare works of art to accumulate, fine foods to cadge off rich buffoons. And not far from here there were women to ogle.

"When did he go?"

"Two days ago."

My mistake. We should have omitted Canatha.

No. If we had omitted Canatha, Canatha would have turned out to be where the bastard lived. Destiny was against me as usual. If the gods ever did decide to help me out, they would mislay their map and lose themselves on the road down from Mount Olympus.

"So!" I took a deep breath and started off again with the brief and unproductive dialogue. "What did he go for?"

"To fetch his son back. Khaleed."

"That's two answers to one question. I haven't asked you the second."

"What?"

"What's his son's name?"

"He's called Khaleed!" wailed the red-faced drip of rennet plaintively. I sighed.

"Is Khaleed young, handsome, rich, wayward, and utterly insensitive to the wishes and ambitions of his outraged parent?"

"Oh, you've met him!" I didn't need to. I had just spent several months adapting plays that were stuffed with tiresome versions of this character. Nightly I had watched Philocrates shed ten years, put on a red wig, and stuff a few scarves down his loincloth in order to play this lusty delinquent.

"So where is he being a playboy?"

"Who, Habib?"

"Habib or Khaleed, what's the difference?"

"At Tadmor."

"*Palmyra?*" I spat the Roman name at him.

"Palmyra, yes."

He had told me right then. That really was the desert. The nasty geographical feature of Syria that being a fastidious type I had sworn to avoid. I had heard quite enough stories from my late brother the soldier about scorpions, thirst, warlike tribesmen, deadly infections from thorn prickles, and men raving as their brains boiled in their helmets from the heat. Festus had told a lurid tale. Lurid enough to put me off.

Perhaps we were talking about entirely the wrong family.

"So answer me this: does your young Khaleed have a girl-friend?"

The dope in the shirt looked guarded. I had stumbled on a scandal. Not hard to do. It was the usual story after all, and in the end he admitted it with the usual intrigued glee. "Oh yes! That's why Habib has gone to fetch him home."

"I thought it might be! Daddy does not approve?"

"He's furious!"

"Don't look so worried. I know all about it. She's a musician, one with a certain Roman elegance but about as high born as a gnat, completely without connections, and penniless?"

"That's what they say. . . . So do I get the money?"

"Nobody promised any money."

"The message for Habib then?"

"No. You get a large reward," I said, loftily giving him a small copper. "You have your free ticket to see the half-naked dancers. And thanks to you inflicting this scandalous story on my delicate earlobes, I now have to go to Palmyra to give the message to Habib myself."

Act Three
Palmyra

Late summer at an oasis. Palm and pomegranate trees cluster taste-
fully around a dirty-looking spring. More camels are wandering
about as a disreputable caravan arrives upon the scene. . . .

SYNOPSIS: *Falco*, a cheeky low-life character, appears in the gracious city of Palmyra with a troupe of *Traveling Players*. He dis-
covers that *Sophrona*, a long-sought runaway, is having an affair
with *Khaleed*, a rich ne'er-do-well whose father is furious; Falco
will have to resort to trickery if he is ever to sort things out.
Meanwhile, danger threatens from an unexpected quarter as the
drama onstage becomes more lifelike than the players had bargained for. . . .

Fifty-five

My brother Festus was right about the dangers. But Festus had been in the Roman legions, so he had missed a few quaint customs. For instance, in the desert everything is based on "hospitality" to strangers, so nothing comes free. What Festus left out were little matters like the "voluntary contribution" we found ourselves needing to make to the Palmyrenes who offered us their "protection" across the desert. It would have been fatal to cross without an escort. There were rules. The chief man in Palmyra had been charged by Rome to police the trade routes, paying for his militia from his own well-stuffed coffers as befitted a rich man with a civic conscience. The chief man provided the escort, therefore, and those who enjoyed the service felt obliged to show immense gratitude. Those who rejected the service were asking to be set upon.

The regular protection squads were waiting for us a few miles north of Damascus, where the road divides. Helpfully loafing at the wayside, as soon as we took the right-hand turn for Palmyra they offered themselves as guides, leaving us to work out for ourselves the penalty for refusing. On our own we would make an easy target for marauding tribesmen. If the tribesmen didn't know we were there, the rejected escort would soon point us out. This protection racket must have operated in the desert for a thousand years, and a small theater group with unwieldy baggage was unlikely to thwart the smiling tradition of blackmail. We paid up. Like everyone else, we knew that getting to Palmyra was only one part of our problem. Once there, we wanted to be able to come back.

I had been to the edge of the Empire before. Crossed the boundary, even, when I had nothing better to do than risk my life in a foolish mission. Yet as we headed eastwards deep into Syria, I had never experienced quite such a strong feeling that we were going to stare out at unknown barbarians. In Britain or Germany you know what lies over the frontier: more Britons or Germans whose nature is just a touch too fierce to conquer and whose lands are just too awkward to enclose. Beyond Syria, which itself becomes a wilderness a mere fifty miles inland, lie the unconquerable Parthians. And beyond them roll legendary tracts of unexplored territory, mysterious kingdoms from which come exotic goods brought by secretive men and borne on strange animals. Palmyra is both the end of our Empire, and the end of the long road leading towards us from theirs. Our lives and theirs meet face to face in a market that must be the most exotic in the world. They bring ginger and spices, steel and ink, gemstones, but primarily silk; in return we sell them glass and Baltic amber, cameo gemstones, henna, asbestos, and menagerie animals. For a Roman, as for an Indian or Chinaman, Palmyra is as far as you can ever go.

I knew all this in theory. I was well read, within the limits of a poor boy's upbringing, though one with access to dead men's libraries when they came up in my father's auctions. Moreover, I had brought with me a strikingly well-read girl. There had never been limits on what Helena's father could provide for her. Decimus Camillus had always allowed her to ask for literary works (in the hope that once she had grabbed the new scroll box and devoured it in an evening he might saunter through the occasional scroll himself). I knew about the East because my own father studied the luxury trade. She knew because she was fascinated by anything unusual. By pooling our knowledge, Helena and I were forewarned of most things we encountered. But we guessed before we ever started that mere theory might not be enough preparation for Palmyra in reality.

I had persuaded the company to come with us. Hearing that finding Sophrona had suddenly become a possibility, many were curious. The stagehands and musicians were loath to let me leave them so long as our killer remained on the loose. The long desert haul offered us one last chance to drive him out from under cover. So, by a large majority, Chremes' cherished plan to trot sedately up to Emesa had been overturned. Even the giant watermills on the Orontes and the famous decadence of Antiochia failed to match the lure of the empty desert, the exotic silk markets, and a promise of solutions to our mysteries.

I was no longer in doubt that I was finding solutions. I had obtained an address in Palmyra for the businessman whose son had absconded with the water organist. If I found her, I was confident I would also find some way of restoring her to Thalia. It sounded as if Habib was already hard at that. If he successfully split her from her boyfriend, my offer of her old job back in Rome should come as welcome news.

As for the killer, I was sure I was close to him. Perhaps even in my own mind I had worked out who he was. I had certainly reduced my suspects to two. While I could accept that one of them might have gone unobserved up the mountain with the playwright, I still believed it was impossible for him to have killed Ione. That left only the other, apparently—unless somewhere I could nail a lie.

Sometimes, when we pitched camp among the rolling brown hills where the wind moaned over the sandy slopes so ominously, I sat and thought about the killer. Even to Helena I was not yet ready to name him. But more and more in the course of that journey I was allowing myself to put a face to him.

We had been told it was a four-day trip to Palmyra. That was the time our escort would have taken, by camel, unencumbered by cartloads of properties and the awkward stumbles and accidents of complaining amateurs. For one thing, we insisted on taking our carts. The Palmyrenes had tried strenuously to persuade us to abandon our wheeled vehicles. Our fear had been that this was a ploy to let their comrades pinch the wagons once we had parked them and left them behind. Eventually we accepted that the urgings were genuine. In return for our money they did wish to give a good service. Oxen and mules took far more time than camels to cross the wilderness. They carried less, and were subject to more stress. Besides, as our guides generously pointed out, at Palmyra we faced a punitive local tax on each cart we wanted to take into town.

We said that since we were not trading we would leave our carts at the city perimeter. Our escort looked unhappy. We explained that trying to load a camel with two extremely large stage doorways (complete with doors), plus the revolving wheel of our lifting machinery for flying in gods from the heavens, might be difficult. We made it clear that without our normal transport for our odd trappings we would not go. In the end they shook their heads and allowed us our madness. Escorting eccentrics even seemed to give them a sense of pride.

But their pleas had been sensible. We soon groaned at the

slowness of our journey as the wagons toiled along that remote highway in the grinding heat. Some of us had been saved from the painful choice between four days of agony in a camel saddle or four days of increasing blisters leading a camel on foot. But as the journey dragged on, and we watched our draft animals suffering, the swifter choice looked more and more like the one we should have made. Camels conserved moisture by ceasing to sweat—surely their only act of restraint in regard to bodily functions. Oxen, mules, and donkeys were as drained of energy as we were. They could manage the trip, but they hated it, and so did we. With care, it was possible to obtain sufficient water to exist. It was salty and brackish, but kept us alive. To a Roman this was the kind of living you do only to remind yourself how superior existence in your own civilized city is.

The desert was as boring as it was uncomfortable. The emptiness of the endless dun-colored uplands was broken only by a dun-colored jackal slinking off on private business, or the slow, circling flight of a buzzard. If we spotted a distant flock of goats, tended by a solitary figure, the glimpse of humanity seemed surprising among the barrenness. When we met other caravans the escorting cameleers called out to each other and chattered excitedly but we travelers hunched in our robes with the furtive behavior of strangers whose only common interest would be complaints about our escorts—a subject we had to avoid. There were glorious sunsets followed by nights ablaze with stars. That did not compensate for the days spent winding headgear ever more tightly against the stinging dust that was blown in our faces by an evil wind, or the hours wasted beating our boots against rocks or shaking out our bedding in the morning and evening ritual of the scorpion hunt.

It was when we reckoned we were about halfway that disaster struck. The desert rituals had become routine, but we were still not safe. We went through the motions of following advice given to us by local people, but we lacked the instinct or experience that give real protection.

We had drawn up, exhausted, and were making camp. The place was merely a stopping-point beside the road to which nomads came to sell skinfuls of water from some distant salt marsh. The water was unpalatable, though the nomads sold it pleasantly. I remember a few patches of thorny scrub, from which fluttered a startlingly colored small bird, some sort of desert finch, maybe. Tethered at odd points were the usual unattended solo camels with no obvious owner. Small boys offered dates. An old man with extremely gracious manners sold piping-hot herbal drinks from a tray hung on a cord around his neck.

Musa was lighting a fire, while I settled our tired ox. Helena was outside our newly erected tent, flapping rugs as Musa had taught her to do, unrolling them one at a time from our baggage, ready to furnish the tent. When the disaster happened she spoke out not particularly loudly, though the stillness and horror in her voice reached me at the wagon and several people beyond us.

"Marcus, help! A scorpion is on my arm!"

Fifty-six

"Flick it off!" Musa's voice was urgent. He had told us how to smite them away safely. Helena either could not remember or was too shocked.

Musa leaped up. Helena was rigid. In one hand she still clutched the blanket it must have scuttled from, terrified even to relax her fingers. On her outstretched forearm danced the ominous black creature, half a finger's length of it, crablike, its long tail reared in an evil curl. It was viciously aggressive after being disturbed.

I covered the ground between us on legs of lead. "My darling—"

Too late.

It knew I was coming. It knew its own power. Even if I had

been standing at Helena's elbow when it rushed out of hiding I could never had saved her.

The tail came forwards over its head. Helena gasped in horror. The sting struck down. The scorpion immediately dropped off.

Hardly a beat of time had passed.

I saw the scorpion run across the ground, darting rapidly like a spider. Then Musa was on it, screaming with frustration as he beat at it with a rock. Over and over came his furious blows, while I caught Helena in my arms. "I'm here—" Not much use if she was being paralyzed by a fatal poison. "Musa! Musa! What must I do?"

He looked up. His face was white and appeared tearstained. "A knife!" he cried wildly. "Cut where it stung. Cut deep and squeeze hard—"

Impossible. Not Helena. Not me.

Instead I pulled the blanket from her fingers, supported her arm, cradled her against me, tried to make time jump back the few seconds that would save her from this.

My thoughts cleared. Finding extra strength, I wrenched off one of my bootstraps, then fastened it tightly as a tourniquet around Helena's upper arm.

"I love you," she muttered urgently, as if she thought it was the last time she would ever be able to tell me. Helena had her own idea of what was important. Then she thrust her arm against my chest. "Do what Musa says, Marcus."

Musa had stumbled to his feet again. He produced a knife. It had a short, slim blade and a dark polished hilt bound with bronze wire. It looked wickedly sharp. I refused to think what a priest of Dushara would use it for. He was trying to make me take it. As I shrank from the task, Helena now offered her arm to Musa; he backed away in horror. Like me he was incapable of harming her.

Helena turned quickly to me again. Both of them were staring at me. As the hard man, this was down to me. They were right, too. I would do anything to save her, since more than anything I was incapable of losing her.

Musa was holding the knife the wrong way, point towards me. Not a military man, our guest. I reached over the blade and grasped the worn hilt, bending my wrist downwards to stop him slicing through my hand. Musa let go abruptly, with relief.

Now I had the knife but had to find my courage. I remember thinking we should have brought a doctor with us. Forget traveling light. Forget the cost. We were in the middle of nowhere and I was going to lose Helena for want of proper expertise. I would never take her anywhere again, at least not without someone who could surgically operate, together with a massive trunk of apothecary's drugs and a full Greek pharmacopoeia. . . .

While I hesitated, Helena even tried snatching at the knife herself. "Help me, Marcus!"

"It's all right." I sounded terse. I sounded angry. By then I was walking her to a roll of baggage where I made her sit. Kneeling alongside I held her close for a moment, then kissed her neck. I spoke quietly, almost through my teeth. "Listen, lady. You're the best thing in my life, and I'll do whatever I have to do to keep you."

Helena was shaking. Her earlier strength of will was now fading almost visibly, as I took control. "Marcus, I was being careful. I must have done the wrong thing—"

"I should never have brought you here."

"I wanted to come."

"I wanted you with me," I confessed. Then I smiled at her, so her eyes met mine, full of love, and she forgot to watch what I was doing. I cut twice across the mark on her arm, making the two cuts cross at right angles. She let out a small sound, more surprise than anything. I bit my lip so hard I broke the skin.

Helena's blood seemed to dash everywhere. I was horrified. I still had work to do, extracting what I could of the poison, but at the sight of those bright red gouts welling up so fast I felt uneasy. Musa, who had no part in the action, fainted clean away.

Fifty-seven

Squeezing the wound had been hard enough; staunching the blood proved frighteningly difficult. I used my hands, always the best way. By then people had come running. A girl—Afrania, I think—was handing me ripped cloths. Byrria was holding Helena's head. Sponges appeared. Someone was making Helena sip water. Someone else gripped my shoulder in encouragement. Urgent voices muttered together in the background.

One of the Palmyrenes came hurrying up. I demanded if he carried an antidote; he either failed to understand, or had nothing. Not even a spider's web to salve the wound. Useless.

Cursing myself again for lack of forethought, I used some general ointment that I always carry before binding up Helena's arm. I told myself the scorpions in this area might not be fatal. The

Palmyrene seemed to be jabbering that I had done well with my treatment. That made me think he must reckon it was worth trying. He was nodding madly, as if to reassure me. Swallowing my panic, I tried to believe him.

I heard the swish of a broom as someone angrily swept the dead scorpion out of sight. I saw Helena, so pale that I nearly cried out in despair, struggling to smile and reassure me. The tent cleared suddenly. Unseen hands had rolled down the sides. I stood back as Byrria started helping Helena out of her blood-soaked clothing. I went out for warm water and a clean sponge.

A small group was quietly waiting by the fire. Musa stood in silence, slightly apart from them. Someone else prepared the bowl of water for me. Once again I was patted on the back and told not to worry. Without speaking to anyone I went back to Helena.

Byrria saw that I wanted to look after Helena alone; she discreetly withdrew. I heard her voice, chivvying Musa. Something in my head warned me that he might be needing attention.

While I was washing her, Helena suddenly started to collapse from the loss of blood. I laid her down and talked her back to consciousness. After a while I managed to get a clean gown over her head, then made her comfortable with cushions and rugs. We hardly spoke, conveying everything we felt by touch.

Still white-faced and perspiring, she watched me cleaning up. When I knelt down beside her she was smiling again. Then she took my hand and held it against the thick pad of bandages, as if my warmth were healing.

"Does it hurt you?"

"Not badly."

"I'm afraid that it will." For some time we stayed there in complete silence, gazing at one another, both now in shock. We were as close as we had ever been. "There will be scars. I couldn't help it. Oh my darling! Your beautiful arm . . ." She would never be able to go bare-armed again.

"Lots of bangles!" murmured Helena practically. "Just think what fun you're going to have choosing them for me." She was teasing, threatening me with the expense.

"Lucky stroke!" I managed a grin. "I'll never be in a quandary what to bring you for your gift at Saturnalia. . . ." Half an hour beforehand I had never expected us to share another winter festival. Now she was somehow convincing me that her tenacity would bring her through. The fast, painful throb of my heart settled back to nearly normal as we talked.

After a moment she whispered, "Don't worry."

I would have a lot more worrying to do yet.

She stroked my hair with her good hand. Occasionally I felt her tugging gently at the worst tangles among the uncombed curls that she had always said she loved. Not for the first time I vowed that in future I would keep myself barbered, a man she could be proud to be seen talking to. Not for the first time I dropped the idea. Helena had not fallen in love with a primped and pungent man of fashion. She had chosen me: a decent body; just enough brains; jokes; good intentions; and half a lifetime of successfully concealing my bad habits from the women in my life. Nothing fancy; but nothing too dire either.

I let myself relax under her fingers' familiar touch. Soon, through calming me, she put herself to sleep.

Helena still slept. I was crouching beside her with my face in my hands when a noise at the tent's entrance roused me. It was Musa.

"Can I help, Falco?"

I shook my head angrily, afraid he would waken her. I was aware that he picked up his knife, hesitantly taking it from where I had dropped it. There was one thing he could do, though it would have sounded harsh and I managed not to say so. A man should always clean his own knife.

He disappeared.

*　　*　　*

A long while later it was Plancina, the panpipe-player, who came to look in on us. Helena was still drowsing, so I was called outside and fed a huge bowl of the stagehands' broth. Even in the most isolated places, their cauldron was always put on the boil as soon as we stopped. The girl stayed to watch me eat, satisfied with her good deed.

"Thanks. That was good."

"How is she?"

"Between the poison and the knife cut, only the gods can help her now."

"Better sprinkle a few pints of incense! Don't worry. There's plenty of us ready to help pray for her."

Suddenly I found myself in the role of the man with a sick wife. While I was nursing Helena Justina, all the other women in our party would be wanting to act like my mother. Little did they know that my real mother would have knocked them aside and briskly taken charge while I was left with only drink and debauchery to keep me occupied. Still, Ma had had a hard lesson in men, being married to my pa. I didn't have to wonder what my mother would have done with Plancina; I had seen Ma put to flight plenty of floozies whose only social error was being too sympathetic towards me.

"We've been talking to the escorts," Plancina told me confidentially. "These things are not fatal in this country. But you'll have to be careful about infection in the wound."

"Easier said than done."

Many a fit adult had been terminally stricken after what seemed a minor accident. Not even imperial generals, with the full panoply of Greek and Roman medicine at their disposal, were immune to an awkward graze or septic scratch. Here we were surrounded by sand and dust, with grit working its way everywhere. There was no running water. Indeed there was barely water enough to drink, let alone to clean wounds. The nearest apothecaries must be in Damascus or Palmyra. They were famously good—but days away.

We were talking in low voices, partly to avoid disturbing my lass as she slept, partly from shock. By now I was desperately tired and glad of somebody to talk to.

"I'm hating myself."

"Don't, Falco. It was an accident."

"It should have been avoidable."

"Those little bastards are everywhere. Helena just had terrible luck." Since I was still looking glum, Plancina added with unexpected sympathy, "She was more careful than anybody else. Helena did not deserve this."

I had always taken the panpipe-player for a sassy piece. She had a loud mouth, a ferocious turn of phrase, and liked to wear skirts that were slashed from hem to armpit. On a Spartan maiden dancing her way around a redware vase this daring fashion looks the height of elegance; in real life, on a plump little wind-instrument-player the effect was simply common. I had had her down as one of those girls who have an immaculately presented face, with nothing behind the eyes. But like most girls, dashing men's misconceptions was what she did best. Despite my prejudice, Plancina was extremely bright. "You notice people," I commented.

"Not as dumb as you thought, eh?" She giggled, good-humoredly.

"I always took you for the clever one," I lied. It came out automatically; I had been a carefree womanizer once. You never lose the knack.

"Clever enough to know a few things!"

My heart sank.

For an informer, talking privately like this in the lee of quite a different situation can sometimes produce evidence that turns over the whole case. Plancina seemed all too eager for an intimate chat. On a better day I would have seized the chance.

Today I had totally lost the will to proceed. Solving mysteries was the last thing I wanted to bother with. And so, since Destiny is an awkward slut, today she had brought the evidence to me.

I managed to avoid groaning. I knew that Plancina was going to talk to me about Heliodorus or Ione. All I wanted was to wish them, and their killer, at the bottom of the Middle Sea.

If Helena had been sitting out here she would have kicked me for my lack of interest. I spent a few moments reflecting dreamily on the wonderfully curved ankle with which she would lash out—and her power to inflict a memorable bruise.

"Don't look so miserable!" Plancina commanded.

"Give it a rest! I'm heartbroken. I'm off duty tonight."

"Might be your only chance." She was bright all right. She knew how fickle witnesses can be.

This reminded me of a game I used to play in the army with my old friend Petronius: speculating which we liked better, bright girls who just looked stupid, or stupid ones who looked passable. On the whole neither kind had looked at either of us when we were twenty, though I used to pretend that I did all right and I reckon he had conquests I never knew about. He certainly turned into a sly reprobate later.

Shock must have plunged me into homesickness. I was off again into a reverie, now wondering what Petronius would have to say about me letting Helena get hurt like this. Petro, my loyal friend, had always agreed with the general view that Helena was far too good for me. As a matter of course he took her part against me.

I knew his views. He thought I was completely irresponsible taking a woman abroad, unless the woman was dismally ugly and I stood in line for a huge legacy if she was struck down by pirates or plague. According to what he called good old-fashioned Roman rectitude and I called blind hypocrisy, Helena should have been locked up at home with a twenty-stone eunuch as bodyguard, and only permitted to venture outside if she was going to see her mother and was accompanied by a trust-worthy friend of the family (Petro himself, for example).

"Do you want to talk or not?" Plancina virtually yelled, grow-ing indignant at my daydreaming.

"I was always the type who liked to run away," I muttered, fumbling the old repartee to the surface.

"Kiss and flee?"

"Then hope to get caught and kissed again."

"You're no fun," she complained. I had lost the knack after all. "I don't think I'll bother."

I sighed gently. "Don't be like that. I'm upset. All right—what are you telling me?"

"I know who he was," Plancina admitted in a hollow tone. "The bastard! I know who Ione was favoring."

I let the fire leap a few times. Some moments do need savor-ing.

"Were you and Ione friends?"

"Close as crumbs on a loaf."

"I see." This was a classic. The two girls had probably vied bit-terly for men friends, but now the survivor was going to split on the villain. She would call it loyalty to her dead friend. Really it was simple gratitude that it was Ione who had picked the wrong man. "Why are you only telling me this now, Plancina?"

Maybe she looked abashed, or maybe she was just brazen. "It's nice and quiet and dark. I've got an excuse to snuggle up out-side your tent and look as if I'm just consoling you."

"Very cozy!" I commented, in a gruff mood.

"Get off, Falco. You know the situation. Who wants to end up very wet and absolutely dead?"

"Not in the desert," I carped tetchily. "This bastard likes to drown people."

"So what's it worth?" Plancina asked frankly.

I feigned shock: "Is this a request to negotiate?"

"It's a request to be paid! You're an informer, aren't you? Don't you people offer cash for information?"

"The idea," I explained patiently, "is that we obtain facts by our skill and cunning." I left out theft, fraud, and bribery. "Then in order that we can make a living, other people pay *us* for those facts."

"But it's me that knows the facts," she pointed out. Not the first woman I had encountered who had brilliant financial acumen even though she never went to school.

"So what facts are we discussing, Plancina?"

"Are you getting paid to find the killer?" She was persistent, this one.

"By *Chremes*? Don't be silly. He calls it a commission, but I know that louse. No. I'm doing this out of my superlative moral sense."

"Drop dead, Falco!"

"Would you believe civic duty then?"

"I'd believe you're a nosy bastard."

"Whatever you say, lady."

"What a ghoul!" Plancina was fairly good humored with her insults. I reckoned she was intending to come clean without an argument. She would not have broached the issue otherwise.

There is a ritual in these exchanges, and we had reached the nub at last. Plancina pulled down her skirt (as far as this was possible), picked her nose, stared at her fingernails, then sat up to tell me all she knew.

Fifty-eight

"It was one of them clowns," she said.

I waited for more. Gradually I ceased expecting it. "Is that your story?"

"Oh, you want the dirty details?"

"I'd like some, at any rate. Don't shock me; I'm a shy floret. But how about, which one of them it actually was?"

"Gods, you don't want much, do you?" she muttered darkly. "You're supposed to be the informer. Can't you work it out?"

I thought she was playing me up. It was time for *me* to shock her. "Maybe I can," I said dourly. "Maybe I already have."

Plancina was staring at me. I saw a look of panic and fascination cross her face. Then she shivered. She dropped her voice abruptly, even though we had already been talking quietly. "You mean you know?"

"You mean you don't?" I returned. A neat turn of phrase, though it meant nothing.

"Not which one," she admitted. "It's horrible to think about. What are you going to do?"

"Try and prove it." She made a face, stretching the fingers of both hands suddenly. She was afraid of what she had stumbled into. "Don't fret," I said calmly. "Your Uncle Marcus has jumped in piles of donkey shit before. Nobody will have to know you said anything, if that's worrying you."

"I don't like the idea of meeting them."

"Just think of them as men you're stringing along. I bet you can do that!" She grinned, with a flash of wickedness. I cleared my throat. "All I need is whatever you do know. Tell me the story."

"I never said anything because I was scared." All her confidence was evaporating. That did not necessarily mean she had nothing useful to say. The ones to watch are those who come bursting with definite answers. "All I really know is that Ione was having a fling with both of them."

"Where does Afrania fit into this? I thought she was Tranio's pet?"

"Oh yes! Afrania would have been livid. Well that was why Ione was doing it; to put one over on Afrania. Ione thought she was a silly cow. And as for Grumio . . ." Plancina's flood of recollections trailed off for some reason.

"What about him? Did he have another girlfriend too?"

"No."

"That's a short answer. Is there a long explanation?"

"He's not like the others."

This surprised me. "What are you saying? He really likes men? Or he doesn't know how to get on with women?" I stopped short of the more disgusting alternatives.

Plancina shrugged helplessly. "It's hard to say. He's good company; they both are. But none of us like to get involved with Grumio."

"Trouble?"

"Nothing like that. We all reckon he never has much time for it."

"For what?" I asked, innocently.

"You damn well know what!"

I conceded that I knew. "He talks about it."

"That means nothing, Falco!" We both laughed. Then Plancina struggled to enlighten me. "He probably is normal, but he never bothers much."

"Too conceited?" I guessed.

"That's it." I swear she was blushing. Some girls who give the impression they are ready for anything are strangely prudish in conversation. She made herself try to elaborate: "If you had anything to do with him, you'd feel he would be sneering at you behind your back. Then if he did anything, he wouldn't want to enjoy it." No good at it either, probably.

"That's interesting." Discussing another man's impotence—or even his indifference—was outside my sphere. I remembered that the night I went to dinner with Chremes and Phrygia I had seen Plancina herself being entertained at the Twins' tent. "You've had dealings with the clowns yourself. I saw you drinking with them both one night at Abila—"

"Drinking is all there was. I got talked into it by another girl. Phrosine has her eye on Tranio."

"Popular fellow? So you drew the straw for Grumio?"

"Not likely! I went home. I remember what Ione used to say about him."

"Which was?"

"If he could do it, and if he did enjoy it, nobody else got any fun."

"Sounds as if Ione had some practice." I asked how she had

come to know such intimate details if Grumio rarely involved himself in sex.

"She liked a challenge. She went after him."

"So what exactly was the situation there?" I recapped. "Ione was sleeping with both Tranio and Grumio, Tranio on the side, and Grumio perhaps under protest. And were there plenty of others?"

"No one important. She'd stopped bothering with the rest. This is why I said it must be one of the clowns. She told me she had her hands full, what with trying to get at Tranio without Afrania noticing, and then having to use all her tactics to lure Grumio into anything. She said she was ready to chuck it all up, go back to the village she came from in Italy, and vamp some dumb farmer into marriage."

"A lesson to you," I commented. "Don't wait too long to retire, Plancina."

"Not in this bloody group!" she agreed. "I haven't been any help, have I?"

"Don't think that."

"But you still don't know."

"I know enough, Plancina." I knew I had to work on the clowns.

"Be careful then."

I thought little of her warning when she gave it. I watched her leave, carrying the soup bowl she had brought me. Then, with the eerie ability the clowns had to turn up just when they were on my mind, one of them came sauntering to my tent.

It was Grumio. On my guard, I was ready for most things, though not for what was about to transpire. I was certainly not ready to accuse him of anything. My bets were still on Tranio anyway.

Grumio parried with a few casual questions about Helena and

then asked, "Where's Musa?" He sounded so casual I knew that it mattered.

"I've no idea." I had forgotten about him. Maybe he was being entertained by Byrria.

"That's interesting!" exclaimed Grumio, knowingly. I had a feeling of being teased and spied upon, as if I were being set up for one of the Twins' practical jokes. Taking advantage of a man whose much-loved girlfriend had been stung by a scorpion would be just like them. I even felt anxious in case another attempt had been made on Musa's life.

Deliberately showing no further interest, I swung myself to my feet and made as if I were going in to see Helena. Grumio failed to enlighten me. I waited until he left. With a sense of unease I called Musa's name. When there was no answer, I lifted the flap on his part of our shared tent.

It was empty. Musa was not there. Nothing was there. Musa, with all his meager property, had gone.

I had believed him to be homesick, but this was ridiculous.

I stood, unable to take in what was happening, staring at the bare ground in the empty tent. I was still there when footsteps hurried up behind me. Then Byrria brushed against me as she pushed me aside to look.

"It's true!" she exclaimed. "Grumio just told me. There's a camel missing. And Grumio thought he saw Musa riding off back the way we came."

"Alone? Across the desert?" He was a Nabataean. He would be safe, presumably. But it was incredible.

"He had talked about it." I could tell the girl was unsurprised.

Now I was feeling really grim. "What's going on, Byrria?" Whatever their strange relationship, I had had the impression that Musa might confide in her. "I don't understand!"

"No." Byrria's voice was quiet, less hard than usual, yet

strangely dull in tone. She seemed resigned to some dire fatality. "Of course you don't."

"Byrria, I'm tired. I've had a terrible day, and my worries about Helena are nowhere near over yet. Tell me what has upset Musa!"

I realized now that he had been upset. I recalled his anguished face as he beat the scorpion to death in such a frenzy. I remembered it again later, when he came to offer help—help I had curtly refused. He had looked withdrawn and defeated. I was not an idiot. It was a look I didn't want to see, but one I recognized.

"Is this because he's fond of Helena? It's natural, when we have lived so closely as friends."

"Wrong, Falco." Byrria sounded bitter. "He was *fond* of you. He admired and hero-worshiped you. He had much deeper feelings for Helena."

Stubbornly I refused to accept what she was saying. "He didn't have to leave. He was our friend." But I was long accustomed to Helena Justina attracting followers. Helena's devotees came from some strange walks of life. The very top, too. A quiet, competent girl who listened to people, she attracted both the vulnerable and those with taste; men liked to think they had privately discovered her. Their next mistake was discovering that privately she belonged to me.

As I stalled, Byrria reacted angrily: "There was no room for him! Don't you remember today when you were looking after Helena? You did everything, and she wanted only you. You know he would never have told either of you how he felt, but he could not bear being no use to her."

I breathed slowly. "Don't go on."

Finally, too late, our misunderstandings unraveled. I wondered if Helena knew. Then I remembered the night we had entertained Byrria. Helena would never have joined me in teasing either Musa or Byrria if she had understood the situation. The actress confirmed it, reading my thoughts: "He would have died of shame if she had ever found out. Don't tell her."

"I'll have to explain where he is!"

"Oh you'll do it! You're a man; you'll think up some lie."

The wrath with which the girl had just spoken was typical of her contempt for all things masculine. But her earlier bitterness brought another thought to me: "And what about you, Byrria?"

She turned away. She must have been able to hear that I had guessed. She knew I meant no harm to her. She needed to tell somebody. Unable to prevent herself, she admitted, "Me? Well what do you think, Falco? The only man I could not have—so naturally I fell in love with him."

My own heart ached for the girl's distress, but frankly I had far worse on my mind.

I found out that Musa had already been gone for hours. Even so, I would probably have ridden after him. But with Helena lying so ill, that was impossible.

Fifty-nine

Despite my efforts to keep the poison from entering her bloodstream, Helena soon had a high fever.

There was a small Roman garrison at Palmyra, I knew. Another we had left behind at Damascus. Either might contain somebody with medical knowledge. Even if not, the troops would have tried out the local physicians and would be able to recommend the least dangerous to consult. As an ex-soldier, and a Roman citizen, I was ready to use my influence to beg for help. Most frontier garrisons were an abusive bunch, but mentioning that Helena's father sat in the Senate should encourage the career-conscious. There was always a chance, too, that among the battered legionaries I might find some ex-British veteran I knew.

I reckoned we needed a doctor as soon as possible. At first, it had not seemed to matter which way we went; soon I wished we had turned back to Damascus. That was nearer to civilization. Who could say what we were heading towards instead?

Helena lay helpless. Even in lucid moments she hardly knew where she was. Her arm gave her increasing pain. She desperately needed rest, not travel, but we could not stop in the wilderness. Our Palmyrene guides had adopted that annoying trait in foreigners: looking deeply sympathetic while in practice ignoring all my pleas for help.

We pressed on, with me having to do all the driving now that Musa had decamped. Helena never complained—quite unlike her. I was going frantic over her fever. I knew how badly her arm hurt, with a burning pain that could be caused by the cuts I had had to make, or by something worse. Every time I dressed the wound it looked more red and angry. To kill the pain I was giving her poppy juice, in melted honey drinks since I distrusted the water. Phrygia had produced some henbane to supplement my own medicine. For me, the sight of Helena so drowsy and unlike herself was the worst part. I felt she was going a long way from me. When she slept, which was most of the time, I missed not being able to talk to her properly.

People kept coming up, as if to check on us. They were kind, but it meant I could never sit and think. The conversation that stays in my mind most clearly was another involving Grumio. It was the day after the accident, in fact. He turned up again, this time in a most apologetic mood.

"I feel I let you down, Falco. Over Musa, I mean. I should have told you earlier."

"I could do with him," I agreed tersely.

"I saw him ride off, but hardly thought he could be leaving you permanently."

"He was free to come or go."

"Seems a bit odd."

"People are." I may have sounded grim. I was feeling drawn.

After a hard day on the desert road, with no hope of reaching the oasis yet at the dire pace we were traveling, I was at a low ebb.

"Sorry, Falco. I guess you're not feeling talkative. I brought you a flagon, in case it helps."

It was welcome. I felt obliged to invite him to stay and share the first measure with me.

We talked of this and that, of nothing in particular, and of Helena's progress or lack of it. The wine did help. It was a fairly ordinary local red. Petronius Longus, the Aventine's wine expert, would have likened it to some off-putting substance, but that was just him. This was perfectly palatable to a tired, dispirited man like me.

Recovering, I considered the flagon. It was a handy size, about right for a packed lunch if you were not intending to do any work afterwards. It had a round base covered in wickerwork, and a thin, loosely plaited carrying string.

"I saw one like this at a scene I'll not forget."

"Where was that?" asked Grumio, disingenuously.

"Petra. Where Heliodorus was drowned."

Naturally the clown expected me to be watching him, so instead I stared into the fire as if gloomily remembering the scene. I was alert for any twitches or sudden tensions in him, but noticed none. "These are about the most common kind you can get," he observed.

It was true. I nodded easily. "Oh yes. I'm not suggesting it came from the same vintner, in the same basket of shopping." All the same, it could have done. "There's something I've been meaning to ask you, Grumio. People have been wishing on me the idea that Heliodorus was killed because of his gambling habits."

"You asked Tranio about it." I was interested to hear they had conferred.

"So I did. He lost his temper," I mentioned, now turning a calm stare on him.

Grumio cradled his chin, looking reflective. "I wonder why that could be?" He spoke with the light twist of malice I had heard from him before. It was hardly evident—could have been an unfortunate mannerism—except that one of the times I had heard it was when he was entertaining the crowd at Gerasa by hurling a knife at me. I remembered that rather clearly.

I stayed calm. "The obvious reason is he had something to hide."

"Seems a bit *too* obvious, though?" He made it sound like a question I should have thought of for myself.

"There has to be some explanation."

"Maybe he was afraid you had found out something that looked bad for him."

"That's a good thought!" I replied brightly, as if I had been incapable of it myself. We were sparring here, each pretending to be simple. Then I let a growl slink back into my voice. "So tell me about you and your tentmate playing dice with the playwright, Grumio!"

He knew there was no point denying it. "Gambling's not a crime, is it?"

"Nor is having a gambling debt."

"What debt? Playing was just a lark from time to time. We soon learned not to bet seriously."

"He was good?"

"Oh yes." There was no hint that Heliodorus might have cheated. Sometimes I wonder how gambling sharks get away with it—and then I talk to an innocent minnow, and realize.

Tranio might know that Heliodorus had weighted his dice; I had wondered about that when I talked to him. So now I considered the interesting prospect of Tranio perhaps keeping this information from his so-called friend. Just what *was* the relationship between these two? Allies covering up for each other? Or a pair of jealous rivals?

"So what's the big secret? I know there must be one," I urged him, putting on my frank, successful-informer air. "What's Tranio's beef?"

"Nothing big, and not a secret." Not now, anyway; his friendly tentmate was about to land him in it without compunction. "What he was probably loath to tell you was that once, when he and I had been having an argument, he played with Heliodorus while I was off on my own—"

"With a girl?" I too could be disingenuous.

"Where else?" After my chat with Plancina, I didn't believe it. "Anyway, they were in our tent. Tranio needed a forfeit and placed something that wasn't his, but mine."

"Valuable?"

"Not at all. But as I felt like having a wrangle I told him he had to get it back from the scribe. Then, you know Heliodorus—"

"Actually, no."

"Oh well, his reaction was typical. The minute he thought he had something important he decided to keep it and taunt Tranio. It rather suited me to keep our clever friend on tenterhooks. So I let on that I was mad about it. Tranio went spare trying to put things right, while I hid a smile and got my own back watching him." One thing for Grumio; he possessed the full quota of the comedian's natural streak of cruelty. By contrast, I really could imagine Tranio taking the blame and becoming distraught.

"Maybe you should let him off now, if he's sensitive! What was the pledge, Grumio?"

"Nothing important."

"Heliodorus must have believed it was." So must Tranio.

"Heliodorus was so dedicated to torturing people, he lost touch with reality. It was a ring," Grumio told me, saying it with a slight shrug. "Just a ring."

His apparent indifference convinced me he was lying. Why should he do that? Perhaps because he didn't want me to know what the pledge really was. . . .

"Precious stone?"

"Oh no! Come on, Falco. I had it off my grandfather! It was only a trinket. The stone was dark blue. I used to pretend it was lapis, but I doubt if it was even sodalite."

"Was it found after the playwright died?"

"No. The bastard had probably sold it."

"Have you checked with Chremes and Phrygia?" I insisted helpfully. "They went through the playwright's stuff, you know. In fact we discussed it and I'm sure I remember them owning up quite freely that they had found a ring."

"Not mine." I thought I detected just a faint trace of irritation in young Grumio now. "Must have been one of his own."

"Or Congrio might have it—"

"He hasn't." Yet according to Congrio, the clowns had never asked him properly about what they were looking for.

"Tell me, why was Tranio afraid to tell me about this missing pledge?" I asked gently.

"Isn't that obvious?" A lot of things were obvious, according to Grumio. He looked remarkably pleased with himself as he landed Tranio in it. "He's never been in trouble, certainly not connected with a murder. He overreacts. The poor idiot thinks everyone knows he had a row with Heliodorus, and that it looks bad for him."

"It looks far worse that he hid the fact." I saw Grumio's eyebrows shoot up in a surprised expression, as if that thought had not struck him. Somehow I reckoned it must have done. Drily, I added, "Nice of you to tell me!"

"Why not?" Grumio smiled. "Tranio didn't kill Heliodorus."

"You say that as if you know who did."

"I can make a good guess now!" He managed to sound as if he were chiding me with negligence for not guessing myself.

"And who would that be?"

That was when he hit me out of the blue: "Now that he's skipped so suddenly," suggested Grumio, "I should think that the best bet is your so-called interpreter!"

I was laughing. "I really don't believe I heard that! *Musa?*"

"Oh, he really took you in, did he?" The clown's voice was cold. If young Musa had still been here, even innocent, I reckon he would have panicked.

"Not at all. You'd better tell me your reasoning."

Grumio then went through his argument like a magician consenting to explain some sleight of hand. His voice was level and considered. As he spoke, I could almost hear myself giving this as evidence before a criminal judge. "Everyone in the company had an alibi for the time Heliodorus was killed. So maybe, unknown to anyone, he had an outside contact at Petra. Maybe he had an appointment with somebody local that day. You say you found Musa in the close vicinity; Musa must have been the man you had followed from the High Place. As for the rest—it all follows."

"Tell me!" I croaked in amazement.

"Simple. Musa then killed Ione because she must have known that Heliodorus had some private connection in Petra. She had slept with him; he could have said. Again, the rest of us all have alibis, but wasn't Musa in Gerasa on his own that night for hours?" Chilled, I remembered that indeed I had left him at the Temple of Dionysus while I went off to make inquiries about Thalia's organist. I didn't believe he had been to the Maiuma pools in my absence—but nor could I prove that he had not.

With Musa no longer here, I could never ask him about it, either.

"And how do you explain Bostra, Grumio? Musa being nearly drowned himself?"

"Simple. When you brought him into the company, some of

us thought him a suspicious character. To deflect our suspicion, he took a chance at Bostra, jumped into the reservoir deliberately, then made up a wild claim that someone shoved him in."

"Not the only wild claim hereabouts!"

I said it, even though I had the inevitable feeling that all this could be true. When someone throws such an unlikely story at you with such passionate conviction, they can overturn your common sense. I felt like a fool, a bungling amateur who had failed to consider something right under my nose, something that ought to have been routine.

"This is an amazing thought, Grumio. According to you, I've spent all this time and effort looking for the killer when the plain fact is I brought him with me all along?"

"You're the expert, Falco."

"Apparently not . . . What's your explanation for the scam?"

"Who knows? My guess is Heliodorus was some sort of political agent. He must have upset the Nabataeans. Musa is their hit man for unwelcome spies—"

Once again I laughed, this time rather bitterly. It sounded weirdly plausible.

Normally I can resist a clever distraction. Since there certainly was one political agent among us, and he was indeed now acting as a playwright, Grumio's solemn tale had a lurid appeal. I really could envisage a scenario in which Anacrites had sent more than one disguised menial into Petra—both me and Heliodorus—and The Brother had schemed to deal with each of us in turn, using Musa. Helena had told me Musa was marked for higher things. Maybe all the time I had been patronizing his youth and innocence, he was a really competent executioner. Maybe all those messages to his "sister" deposited at Nabataean temples were coded reports to his master. And maybe the "letter from Shullay" he kept hoping to receive would not have contained a description of the murderer, but instructions for disposing of me. . . .

Or rather, maybe I should lie down quietly, with sliced cucumber cooling my forehead, until I got over this lunacy.

Grumio rose to his feet with a demure smile. "I seem to have given you a lot to think about! Pass on my regards to Helena." I managed a wry nod of the head, and let him go.

The conversation had been devoid of clowning. Yet I was still left with the sinking sensation that somehow the joke was on me.

Very neat.

Almost, as the grim jokester Grumio himself would have said, too obvious to be true.

Sixty

I was dismal now. It felt like a nightmare. Everything appeared close to reality, yet was hugely distorted.

I went in to see Helena. She was awake, but flushed and feverish. I could tell by looking at her that unless I could do something, we were in serious trouble. I knew she could see I had problems I wanted to talk about, but she made no attempt to ask. That in itself was a depressing sign.

In this mood, I was hardly expecting what happened next.

We heard a commotion. The Palmyrenes were all exclaiming and shouting. It did not sound as though raiders had set upon us, but my worst fears leaped. I rushed out of the tent. Everyone else was running, all in the same direction. I felt for my knife, then left it down my boot so I could run faster.

At the roadside an excited group had clustered around a particular camel, a new arrival whose dust was still creating a haze above the road. I could see the beast was white, or what they call white in a camel. The trappings looked brighter than usual and more lavishly fringed. When the crowd suddenly spilled outwards so I had a clearer view, even to my untutored eye this was a fine creature. A racing camel, plainly. The owner must be a local chief, some rich nomad who had made several fortunes from myrrh.

I was losing interest and about to turn back when somebody yelled my name. Men in the crowd gesticulated to some unseen person who was kneeling at the camel's feet. Hoping this might be Musa returning, I walked up closer. People fell back to let me through, jostling close behind again as they tried to see what was happening. With bruised heels and a bad temper I forced my way to the front.

On the ground beside the splendid camel, a figure wrapped in desert robes was searching in a small roll of baggage. Whoever it was stood up and turned to me. It was definitely not Musa.

The elaborate headdress was pushed back from a startling face. Vivid antimony eye paint flashed while earrings as big as the palm of my hand rattled out a joyous carillon. All the Palmyrenes gasped, awestruck. They dropped back hastily.

It was a woman, for one thing. Women do not normally ride the desert roads alone. This one would go anywhere she wanted. She was noticeably taller than any of them, and spectacularly built. I knew she must have chosen her own camel, with expertise and taste. Then she had cheerfully raced across Syria unaccompanied. If anyone had attacked her, she would have dealt with them; besides, her bodyguard was wriggling energetically in a large bag she wore slung across a bosom that meant business.

When she saw me, she let out a roar of derision, before brandishing a little iron pot. "Falco, you miserable dumbhead! I want to see that sick girl of yours—but first come here and say a nice hello!"

"Hello Jason," I responded obediently, as Thalia's python finally forced his head out of his traveling bag and looked around for somebody meek whom he could terrorize.

Sixty-one

There were a lot of frightened men at this gathering, and not all of them were worried about the python.

Thalia shoved Jason unceremoniously back into his bag; then hung it around her camel's neck. With one bejeweled finger she stabbed towards the bag. Slowly and clearly (and unnecessarily), she addressed the assembled nomads: "Any man who puts a hand on the camel gets seen off by the snake!"

This hardly squared with what she had always assured me about Jason's lovable nature. Useful, however. I could see the Palmyrenes all inclined to my own nervous view of him.

"That's a gorgeous camel," I said admiringly. "With a gorgeous rider whom I never expected to meet in the middle of the desert." It seemed right, however. Somehow I felt more cheerful already. "How in the name of the gods do you come to be here, Thalia?"

"Looking for you, darling!" she promised feelingly. For once I felt able to take it.

"How did you find me?"

"Damascus is plastered with posters with your name on them. After a few days of desperately dancing for the rent, I spotted one." That's the trouble with wall posters: easy to write, but nobody ever rubs them out. Probably in twenty years' time people would still be calling at Herod's Theater trying to touch a man called Falco for cash. "The theater gateman told me you'd gone on to Palmyra. Good excuse to get a camel. Isn't he a cracker? If I can get another and race them, he'll wow those front-seat freaks in Rome."

"Where did you learn to race a camel?"

"Anyone who can do a twirl with a python can manage a ride, Falco!" Innuendo came swimming back with every stride we took. "How's the poor girlie? Scorpion, wasn't it? As if one nasty creature with a wicked tail on him is not enough for her . . ."

I hardly dared ask, but brought out the question: "How do you know about it?"

"Met that strange fellow—your gloomy priest."

"Musa?"

"Riding towards me like a death's head in a cloud of dust. I asked if he'd seen you. He told me everything."

I gave her a sharp look. "*Everything*?"

Thalia grinned. "Enough!"

"What have you done with him?"

"What I do with them all."

"The poor lad! Bit tender for you, isn't he?"

"They all are by my standards! I'm still holding out for you, Falco."

Ignoring this dangerous offer, I managed to extract more details. Thalia had decided that looking for Sophrona was a mission I might not manage. She had taken a whim to come east herself. After all, Syria was a good market for exotic animals; before the racing camel she had already bought a lion cub and several Indian parrots, not to mention a dangerous new snake. She had been earning her way by displays of her famous dance with the big python, Zeno, when she noticed my posters. "So here I am, Falco, large as life, and twice as exciting!"

"At last. My chance to catch your act!"

"My act is not for faint hearts!"

"All right, I'll skulk out the back and mind Jason. So where's the snake you dance with?" I had never even seen this legendary reptile.

"The big fellow? Following on slowly. Zeno doesn't like disturbance. Jason's more versatile. Besides, when I tell him he's going to see you, he comes over all silly—"

We reached my tent, thank Jupiter.

At the sight of Helena I heard Thalia suck in her breath. "I've brought you a present, sweetie, but don't get too excited; it's not a new man." Thalia produced the little iron pot again. "Small but incredibly powerful—"

"As the alter boy promised!" quipped Helena, perking up. She must have been reading her scroll of rude stories again.

Thalia had already lowered herself to one mighty knee and was unbandaging Helena's wounded arm as gently as if she were tending one of her own sick animals. "Giblets! Some slapdash butcher made a mess with his cleaver here, sweetheart!"

"He did his best," Helena murmured loyally.

"To mangle you!"

"Lay off, Thalia!" I protested. "There's no need to make me out to be the sort of thug who'd knife his girl. Anyway, what's in your magic jar?" I felt obliged to show some caution before my lass was anointed with a strange medicament.

"Mithridatium."

"Have I heard of that?"

"Have you heard of gold and frankincense? Compared with this they're as cheap as cushion dust. Falco, this potion contains thirty-three ingredients, each one expensive enough to bankrupt Croesus. It's an antidote for everything from snakebites to splitting fingernails."

"Sounds good," I conceded.

"It had better be," growled Thalia, unscrewing the lid with relish, as if it were a potent aphrodisiac. "I'll spread it all over your lady first—then I'll tell you what you owe me."

I declared that if mithridatium would help Helena, Thalia could smooth on the stuff an inch thick with a mortar trowel.

"Listen to it!" marveled Thalia confidentially to her patient. "Isn't he ridiculous—and don't you just love his lies!"

Helena, who had always found that her spirits rose with any chance of mocking me, was already chortling healthily.

When we drove on towards Palmyra I had Thalia alongside like a spectacular outrider, galloping away in wild loops from time to time to exercise the racing camel. Jason enjoyed a more leisurely journey in a basket in the back of my cart. The Syrian heat had proved almost too much for him. He lay virtually inert, and whenever we could spare any water he had to be bathed.

"My python's not the only reptile in your group," Thalia muttered furtively. "I see you've got that know-all comic Tranio!"

"Do you know him?"

"I've met him. Entertaining is a small world when you've been doing it as long as me, and in some funny places too. Tranio used to appear at the Vatican Circus. Quite witty, but thinks far too much of himself."

"He does a good tug-of-war. Know his partner?"

"The one with the hair like a pie dish and the sneaky eyes?"

"Grumio."

"Never seen him before. But that's not true of everybody here."

"Why; who else do you know?"

"Not saying." Thalia grinned. "It's been a few years. Let's wait and see if I'm recognized."

I was struck by an intriguing possibility.

Thalia's thrilling hints were still engaging Helena and me when our long ride reached its end. We had been driving at night, but dawn had now broken. With the stars long gone and the sun strengthening, our party was weary and longing to break the journey. The road had grown more winding, twisting upwards through more hilly country. The caravan trail finally emerged onto a level plain. We must now be at midpoint between the fertile coast far away on the Mediterranean and the even more remote reaches of the River Euphrates.

Low ranges of mountains ran to the north and behind us, serrated by long dry wadis. Ahead, disappearing into infinity, stretched flat tawny desert covered with rocky scree. To our left, in a stony valley, stood square towers that we later learned were multiple tombs for wealthy families. These kept their lonely vigil beside an ancient track overlooked by the sheltering hills. On the bare slopes, a shepherd on a donkey was herding a flock of black-faced sheep. Closer to, we began to perceive a shimmer of green. We sensed expectation among our nomad guides. I called to Helena. As we approached, the effect was magical. The haze rapidly acquired solidity. The moisture that rose off the saltpans and lakes quickly resolved into fields surrounding large swaths of date palms and olive and pomegranate trees.

At the heart of the huge oasis, beside an energetic spring with supposedly therapeutic waters (like Thalia's dance, not for the fainthearted), stood the famous old nomad village of Tadmor, once a mere camp in the wilderness, but now the fast-growing Romanized city of Palmyra.

Sixty-two

If I say that in Palmyra the revenue officers take social precedence over members of the local government assembly, you will see their preoccupations. A welcoming city, in fact one that welcomed its visitors with a tariff of taxes on goods entering its territory, continued the happy greeting by relieving them of some hefty rates for watering their caravans, and completed the process by exacting a little something for the treasury for every camel, donkey, cart, container, or slave that they wished to take back out of the city when they left. What with the salt tax and the prostitution tax, staying there was clear cut too: the very staples of life were nobbled.

The Emperor Vespasian, a tax collector's grandson, was running Palmyra with a light hand. Vespasian liked to squeeze the fiscal sponge, but his treasury officials had grasped that they had little to teach the efficient Palmyrenes. Nowhere I had ever visited was so concerned to strip all comers of their spending money, or so adept at doing it.

Even so, long-distance traders were coming here with caravans the size of armies. Palmyra sat between Parthia in the east and Rome in the west, a semi-independent buffer zone that existed to enable commerce. Tariffs aside, the atmosphere *was* a pleasant one.

Historically Greek and governed now by Rome, it was packed with Aramaic and Arabian tribesmen who had only recently been nomads, yet it still remembered periods of Parthian rule and looked to the East for much of its character. The result was a mixed culture unlike anywhere else. Their public inscriptions were carved in Greek and a strange script of their own. There were a few massive limestone buildings, constructed on Syrian plans with Roman money by Greek craftsmen. Around these monuments were spread quite large suburbs of blank-walled mud-brick houses through which meandered narrow dirt lanes. The oasis still had the air of a massive native village, but with signs that sudden grandiosity was liable to break out all over the place.

For one thing, the people were unashamedly wealthy and enjoyed showing off. Nothing had prepared us for the brightness of the linens and silks with which every Palmyrene of any standing was adorned. The rich weaves of their cloth were unlike any produced further west. They liked stripes, but never in plain bands of color. Their materials were astonishing feasts of elaborate brocaded patterns, studded with flowers or other dainty emblems. And the threads used for these intricate weaves were dyed in spectacular varieties of purples, blues, greens, and reds. The colors were deep and warm. The hues in the streets were a dramatic contrast to any public scene in Rome, which would be a monochrome of scarcely modulated grades of white, broken only by the vibrant purple bands that designate high status.

The men here would have looked effeminate in Rome. It took some getting used to. They all wore tunics laden with splendidly embroidered braid; beneath were swathed Persian trousers, again richly hemmed. Most men wore straight-sided, flat-topped hats. Female dress consisted of conventional long gowns, covered by cloaks caught on the left shoulder by a heavy brooch. Veils were routinely worn by all women except slaves and prostitutes. The veil, ostensibly protecting the ownership of a strict father or husband, fell from a tiara or turban, and was then left loose as a frame to the face, allowing the owner to manipulate its folds attractively with one graceful hand. What could be glimpsed behind the pretense of modesty were dark curls, chubby chins, huge eyes, and strong-willed mouths. The women were broad in the beam and all wore as many necklaces, bangles, rings, and hair jewels as they could cram on; no wench with less than six neck-chains could be considered worth talking to. Getting them to talk might be difficult, however, due to the looming presence of jealous menfolk and the fact they all went about with dogged chaperones.

Philocrates did very quickly manage to make the acquaintance of a creature in lavish pleats of azure silk, crushed under eight or nine gold necklaces from which dangled an array of pendants set with pearls and polished glass. Her arms were virtually armored with metal bracelets. We watched her peep at him entrancingly from behind her veil, only one lovely eye revealing itself. Maybe she was winking. Shortly afterwards we were watching *him* being chased down the street by her relatives.

There was supposed to be a theater, so while Chremes tried to find it and find out whether rude Roman vagabonds like us could appear there, I set off to discover the missing girl, Sophrona. I had asked Thalia whether she wanted to come with me.

"No. You go and make a fool of yourself first, then we'll put our heads together once you know what the situation is."

"That's good. I had thought that with you in Syria I was going to lose my fee."

"You can't lose what you never earned, Falco. The fee is for getting her back to Rome. Don't waste your ink on an invoice until she's off the boat at Ostia!"

"Trust me." I smiled.

Helena laughed. I touched her forehead, which at long last was cooler. She was feeling much better. I could tell that when she gaily explained to Thalia, "It's sweet, really. Poor Marcus, he likes to convince himself he has a way with girls."

I leered like a man who should never be allowed out alone; then, feeling fonder than ever of Helena, I set off into town.

I seemed to remember hearing that this Sophrona was a beauteous bit of stuff.

Sixty-three

It had seemed best to deal with Thalia's task quickly, before Chremes called upon my services as his luckless author. Besides, I was happy to pack in some sight-seeing.

If you visit Palmyra, go in spring. Apart from the cooler weather, April is when they hold the famous processions at the great Temple of Bel. In any other month you get sick of people telling you how wonderful the festival is, with its minstrels, its palanquins of deities, and its lengthy processions of garlanded animals. Not to mention the subsequent bloodletting. Or the breakdown of social order that inevitably follows serious religion. The festival (to be regarded askance by a sober Roman, though it sounded good fun to me) must have been taking place about the time Helena and I were planning our trip. It offers the only chance of seeing open the mighty portals that hold back the public from the triad in the inner sanctuary, so if you like gaping at gods or at fabulous stonework, April is a must. Even then it's a slim chance, due to the secrecy of the priests and the vast size of the crowds.

In August you can only wander around the immense court-yard like a water flea lost in Lake Volusinus, being told by every-one what a treat you missed earlier. This I did myself. I sauntered between the altar and the lustral basin, mighty exam-ples of their kind, then stared sadly at the closed doors in the immensely high and opulently decorated entrance porch. (Carved monolithic beams and stepped merlons, in case you wanted to know.) I had been told that the inner sanctum was an architectural wonder. Not much use for adding tone to your memoirs if it's shut.

The other reason for not going to Palmyra in August is the un-bearable heat and brightness. I had walked all the way across town from our camp outside the Damascus Gate. I strolled from the Temple of Allath—a severe goddess guarded by a ten-foot-high lion with a jolly countenance, who sheltered a lithe gazelle—to the far end of town where the Temple of Bel housed the Lord of the Universe himself, plus two colleagues, a moon god and a sun god, named Aglibol and Yarhibol. The profusion of deities honored in this city made the twelve gods of Roman Olympus look a meager picnic party. As most of the temples in Syria are surrounded by huge open-air courtyards that act as suntraps, each of Palmyra's hundreds of divinities was baking, even inside his darkly curtained-off adyton. However, they were not as hot as the poor fools like me who had risked marching about the city streets.

The sulfurous springs were low in their cistern, the gardens surrounding them reduced to sticks and struggling succulents. The odor of hot therapeutic steam was no match for the pervad-ing wafts of a city whose major imports were heady perfume oils. Brilliant sunlight zinged off the dirt roads, lightly poached the piles of camel dung, then wrapped its warmth around thousands of alabaster jars and goatskin bottles. The mingling fragrances of heated Oriental balms and fine oils choked my lungs, seeped into my pores and hung about the crumples of my robes.

I was reeling. My eyes had already been dazzled by tottering piles of bronze plaques and statues, endless bales of silks and muslins, the deep shine of jade and the dark green glimmer of Eastern pottery. Ivory the size of forest logs was piled haphazardly alongside stalls selling fats or dried meat and fish. Tethered cattle awaited buyers, bellowing at the merchants selling multicolored heaps of spice and henna. Jewelers weighed out pearls in little metal scales as casually as Roman sweet-sellers toss handfuls of pistachio nuts into wrapping cones of remaindered songs. Minstrels, tapping hand drums, intoned poetry in languages and measures I could not begin to comprehend.

Palmyra is a mighty emporium; it depends on helping visitors secure contracts. In the packed streets even the busiest traders were prepared to stop and hear about my quest. We could understand each other's Greek, just about. Most tried to point me where I should be going. Once I had been marked as a man with a mission, they insisted on helping. Small boys were sent running to ask other people if they knew the address I was looking for. Old fellows bent double over knobby sticks tottered up twisting lanes with me to check possible houses. I noticed that half the population had terrible teeth, and there was a bad epidemic of deformed arms. Maybe the hot springs were not all that medicinal; maybe the sulfuric spring water even caused these deformities.

Eventually, in the center of town, I found the home of a well-to-do Palmyrene who was a friend of Habib, the man I sought. It was a large villa, constructed with no windows on the outside walls. Entering through a door with an exuberantly carved lintel, I found a cool, rather dark courtyard with Corinthian columns surrounding a private well. A dark-skinned slave, polite, but firm, made me wait in the courtyard while he consulted within several times.

My story was that I had come from Rome (no point pretending otherwise) as a connection of the girl's. Since I hoped I looked fairly respectable, I assumed her boyfriend's parents would be eager to check any faint possibility that their prodigal Khaleed had fallen for someone acceptable. Apparently not: despite my best efforts I failed to acquire an interview. Neither the Palmyrene who owned the house nor his guest Habib appeared in person. No attempt was made to deny that Habib was staying there, however. I was informed that he and his wife were now planning to return to Damascus, taking their son. That meant Khaleed currently lived here too, probably under duress. The fate of his musical pickup remained unclear. When I mentioned Sophrona, the slave only sneered and said she was not there.

Knowing that I was in the right place, I did what I could, then stayed calm. Most of an informer's work consists of keeping your nerve. My insistent efforts would have caused a commotion. Sooner or later young Khaleed would hear of my visit and wonder what was up. I guessed that even if he had been gated by his parents he would try to contact his lady love.

I waited in the street. As I expected, within half an hour a youth shot outside, glancing back furtively. Once he was sure nobody from the house was following, he set off fast.

He was a short, thickset lad of about twenty. He had a square face with heavy, flyaway eyebrows; they almost met in the center of his brow, where a tuft of hair grew like a small dark diamond. He had been in Palmyra long enough to be experimenting with Parthian trousers, but he wore them under a sober Western tunic in Syrian stripes and without embroidery. He looked athletic and good humored, though not very bright. Frankly, he was not my idea of a hero to run off with—but I was not a daft young girl hankering for a foreign admirer to lure her away from a job she was lucky to have.

I knew Sophrona was daft; Thalia had told me.

The young man kept up a rapid pace. Luckily he was heading west, towards the area where my own party was staying, so I was not too dispirited. I was starting to feel exhausted, though. I wished I had borrowed a mule. Young love may not notice draining heat, but I was thirty-two and ready for a long lie-down in the shade of a date palm. I wanted a good rest and a drink, after which I might manage to interest myself in a bit of fun with Helena, if she stroked my brow temptingly enough first. Chasing this sturdy playboy soon lost its appeal.

The increasing nearness of my tent beckoned. I was ready to peel off from the breakneck gallop. A fast sprint through the Thirteenth District in Rome is bad enough in August, but at least there I know where the wineshops and public latrines are. This was torture. Neither refreshment nor relief was available. And all in the cause of music—my least favorite performing art.

Eventually Khaleed glanced back over his shoulder, failed to spot me, then picked up even more speed. Turning off the main track, he dashed down a twisting lane between modest little houses where chickens were running freely along with the odd skinny goat. He plunged inside one of the houses. I waited long enough for the youngsters to start panicking, then I dived after him.

Unlike Habib's friend's villa, there was a simple rectangular doorway in the mud-brick wall. Beyond lay a tiny courtyard: no peristyle columns; no well. There was bare earth. A stool had been kicked over in one corner. Wool rugs hung over an upper balcony. The rugs looked clean, but I sensed the dull odors of poverty.

I followed the anxious voices. Bursting in on the couple, I found Khaleed looking tear-stained and his girl pale but definitely stubborn. They stared at me. I smiled at them. The young man beat his brow and looked helpless while the girl shrieked unpleasantly.

The usual scenario, in my experience.

"So you're Sophrona!" She was not my type. Just as well; she was not my sweetheart.

"Go away!" she screamed. She must have deduced I had not come all this way to announce an unexpected legacy.

She was very tall, taller even than Helena, who sweeps a stately course. Her figure was more scrawny than I had been led to expect, reminding me vaguely of somebody—but certainly not Helena. Sophrona was dark, with straight hair tied fairly simply. She had enormous eyes. They were a mellow brown with immensely long lashes, and could be described as beautiful if you were not too fussy about eyes revealing intelligence. She knew they were lovely, and spent a lot of time gazing up sideways; somebody must once have admired the effect. It failed with me. It made me want to chop up her chin and tell her to stop the deplorable pose. There was no point. No one would ever train her out of it; the habit was too ingrained. Sophrona intended to be pictured one day on her tombstone with this irritating expression, like a fawn with a head cold and a bad case of jitters.

She was about twenty, disreputably unveiled. On her long frame she wore a blue dress, together with ridiculous sandals and too much soppy jewelry (all tiny dangly animals and rings of twisted silver wire worn right on her knuckles). This stuff would be fine on a child of thirteen; Sophrona should have grown up by now. She did not need to grow up; she had the rich man's son just where she wanted him. Playing the kitten had achieved it, so she was sticking with what she knew.

"Never you mind who she is!" cried Khaleed, with spirit. I groaned inwardly. I hate a lad with spirit when he has his arm around a girl I'm intending to abduct from him. If he was already trying to defend her from a stranger whose motives might be perfectly harmless, then prying her free once I had made the situation clear posed even worse problems. "Who are you?"

"Didius Falco. Friend of the family." They were complete amateurs; they did not even think of asking me which family. "I see you're in love," I told them pessimistically. They both nodded with a defiance that would have been charming, if it had not been so inconvenient. "I believe I know some of your history." I had been called in to end unsuitable matches before, so I came prepared with a winning approach. "Would you mind telling the story, though?"

Like all youngsters with no sense of moral duty, they were proud of themselves. It poured out: how they had met at Thalia's menagerie when Habib had visited Rome, accompanied for educational purposes by his adolescent boy. Khaleed had been cool at first, and obediently went home to Syria with Papa. Then Sophrona had thrown up everything to follow him; boys from rich families appear so romantic. Somehow she made it to Damascus, neither raped nor drowned on the journey. Impressed by her devotion, Khaleed had happily entered into a secret liaison. When his parents found out, the pair ran off here together. Spotted and recognized by his father's friend, Khaleed had been extracted from their love nest and was now about to be dragged home to Damascus, where a suitable bride would be found for him fast.

"Oh how sad!" I wondered whether to bop Khaleed on the head, swing Sophrona over my shoulder, and make off with her. A neat trick, if you can pull it—which I had been known to do with shorter women, on my home territory, when the weather was cooler. I decided against playing the man of action here. That left me to use the more sophisticated skills of a Roman informer: blatant lies.

"I understand your problem, and I sympathize. I think I may

be able to help you. . . ." The babes fell for it eagerly. I was accepted as the classic clever trickster without needing any alibi for or explanation of my role in Palmyra. I could have been the worst pimp in Corinth, or a foreman recruiting forced labor for a Spanish copper mine. I began to understand why slave markets and brothels are always so full.

I scrounged in my purse for some of the tokens we used when we gave away free seats. I told Khaleed to look out for wall posters advertising a performance by Chremes and company; then to bring his parents as a filial treat. Sophrona was to attend the theater on the same night.

"What are you going to do for us?"

"Well, it's obvious what you need. Get you married, of course."

The wild promise could prove a mistake. Thalia would be furious. Even if I could achieve it—most unlikely—I knew Thalia had no intention of seeing her expensively trained product yoked to a brainless boy somewhere at the end of the Empire. Thalia dreamed only of providing Rome with high-class entertainment—entertainment she herself both owned and controlled.

You have to do your best. I needed to gather all the parties together somewhere. On the spur of the moment it seemed the only way to ensure everyone came.

If I could have told them just what kind of night out at the theater it was going to be, there would have been no doubt they would turn up.

Free tickets wouldn't have been necessary either.

Sixty-four

It was so late when I returned to camp that Helena and Thalia had despaired of me and were already eating. Chremes and Phrygia happened to be there too. Since they had dropped in casually, the manager and his wife were holding back from tucking in, though I knew Helena would have asked them to help themselves. To spare them the embarrassment of wanting more than they liked to take, I cleaned up all the food bowls myself. I used a scrap of sesame bread to load all the remains into one pot of cucumber relish, which I then kept as my own bowl. Helena gave me a snooty look. Pretending to think her still hungry, I lifted a stuffed vine leaf from my laden dish and set it on a plate for her. "Excuse fingers."

"I'm excusing more than that!" she said. She ate the vine leaf, though.

"You have a crumb on your chin," I told her with mock severity.

"You've a sesame seed on your lip."

"You've a pimple on the end of your nose—"

"Oh shut up, Marcus!"

The pimple story was untrue. Her skin was pale, but clear and healthy. I was just happy to see Helena with her fever gone, looking well enough to be teased.

"Good day out?" queried Thalia. She had finished her dinner before I arrived; for a big woman she ate sparingly. More of Thalia consisted of pure muscle and sinew than I liked to contemplate.

"Good enough. I found your turtledoves."

"What's the verdict?"

"She's as exciting as a used floorcloth. He has the brain of a roof truss."

"Well suited!" quipped Helena. She was surreptitiously fingering her nose, checking on my pimple joke.

"It will be Sophrona who is holding them together." I could see Thalia thinking that if this were the case, she only had to prise Sophrona off, and her troubles were over.

I reckoned Sophrona would be difficult to loosen from her prey. "She really means to have the rich boy. I've promised to get them married." Best to own up, and get the storm over as soon as possible.

A lively commotion ensued among the women of my party, enabling me to finish my dinner in peace while they enjoyed themselves disparaging me. Helena and Thalia were both sensible, however. Their indignation cooled rapidly.

"He's right. Yoke them together—"

"—And it will never last!"

If it did last, they would have outwitted us. But evidently I was not the only person here who felt so cynical about marriage that the happy ending was ruled out.

Since one person present was the person I intended to marry as soon as I could persuade her to sign a contract, this was worrying.

Chremes and Phrygia had watched our domestic fracas with a distant air. It struck me they might have come with news of our next performance. If it needed two of them to tell me about the play, that boded harder work than I wanted at this stage of our tour. Since Palmyra was likely to be the end of our association, I had rather hoped for an easier time, zonking the public with some little number I had long ago revised, while I relaxed around the oasis. Even perhaps laying before the punters Helena's perfect modern rendition of *The Birds*. Its neo-Babylonian flamboyance ought to appeal to the Palmyrenes in their embroidered hats and trousers. (I was sounding like some old sham of a critic; definitely time to resign my post!)

With Chremes and Phrygia remaining so silent, it was Helena who brightly introduced the subject of booking a theater.

"Yes, I fixed something up." A hint of wariness in Chremes' tone warned me this might not be good news.

"That's good," I encouraged.

"I hope you think so. . . ." His tone was vague. Immediately I began to suspect I would not agree with him. "There is a little problem—"

"He means a complete disaster," Phrygia clarified. A blunt woman. I noticed Thalia regarding her sardonically.

"No, no!" Chremes was blustering. "The fact is, we can't get the civic theater. Actually, it's not up to our usual standards in any case—"

"Steady on," I said somberly. "Apart from Damascus, we've mainly been playing at holes in the ground with a few wooden benches. This must be pretty rough!"

"Oh I think they have plans to build something better, Falco!"

"Everywhere in Syria has plans!" I retorted. "In twenty or

thirty years' time this province will be a theatrical company's dream of sipping ambrosia on Mount Olympus. One day they'll have perfect acoustics, majestic stage architecture, and marble everywhere. Unluckily, we cannot wait that long!"

"Well, it's typical!" Chremes gave in. He seemed even more despondent than me tonight and set off on a catalogue of miseries: "We have the same situation everywhere—even in Rome. The performing arts are in a steep decline. My company has tried to raise standards, but the fact is that legitimate live theater will soon not exist. We'll be lucky if plays are performed as readings by bunches of amateurs sitting round on folding stools. All people want to pay money for nowadays are mimes and musicals. For a full house you have to give them nude women, live animals, and men sacrificed on stage. The only part that is guaranteed success is bloody *Laureolus*."

Laureolus is that rubbish about the brigand, the one where the villain is crucified in the final act—traditionally a way of creating free space in the local jail by dispatching a real criminal.

Helena intervened: "What's wrong, Chremes? You normally look on the bright side."

"Time to face facts."

"It was time to face facts twenty years ago." Phrygia was even more gloomy than her hated spouse.

"Why can you not get the theater?" Helena persisted.

Chremes sighed heavily. "The Palmyrenes are not interested. They use the theater for public meetings. That's what they *say* anyway; I don't believe it. Either they don't enjoy entertainment or they don't fancy what we're offering. Being rich is no guarantee of culture. These people are just shepherds and cameleers dressed up in lush brocade. Alexander was supposed to have come here, but he must have thought better of it and passed them without stopping. They have no Hellenic heritage. Offering a Palmyrene town councilor the chance to see select Greek or Latin comedies is like feeding roast peacock to a stone."

"So what now?" I asked when the tirade finally ended. "Are we all trooping back across the desert to Damascus without speaking a line?"

"If only that were true!" remarked Phrygia under her breath. More than ever she seemed to be nursing some immense grudge. Tonight it was even making her incapable of being constructive about her beloved company.

Maybe that was because after all its vicissitudes, the company was finally cracking up. Chremes turned to me. His bluster was leaving him. "There was a bit of bother today among the lads and lasses." At first I assumed he was coming to me for help, in view of my success at turning around the stagehands' and musicians' strike. I was wrong, however. "The worst is, Philocrates has given notice. Having no stage available here is more than he can take."

I laughed briefly. "Don't you mean he's depressed by the lack of available women?"

"That doesn't help!" Phrygia agreed sourly. "There is some suggestion he's also upset because a certain party accused him of causing past events—"

"The certain party was me," I admitted. "Just stirring. He can't have taken it seriously."

"Don't believe it!" Thalia put in. "If Philocrates is the dot with the itchy piece and the big opinion of himself, he's shitting elephant plop." She missed nothing. She had only been with us a few days, but already knew who was a real poser.

"He's not the only one anxious to leave, Falco." Phrygia sounded ready to give up herself. So was I, come to that. "A whole mob are demanding their severance pay."

"I fear the troupe is falling apart," Chremes told me. "We have one last night together, however." As usual he rallied with a flourish, though an unimpressive one. His "last night" sounded like some grim party where your creditors turn up, the wine runs out, and a bad oyster dramatically lays you low.

"Chremes, you said you had failed to get the theater?"

"Ah! I try never to fail, Falco!" *I* tried to keep my face neutral. "There is a small Roman garrison," Chremes informed me, as if he had changed the subject. "Not very visible in the neighborhood, perhaps, though I believe that may be policy. They are here to undertake road surveys—nothing to which the Palmyrenes could take exception."

"If the roads are heading out to the Euphrates, the Parthians may balk." I had answered the political point without thinking. Then I guessed what the manager was saying and I groaned. "Oh, I don't believe this. . . . Tell us the worst, Chremes!"

"I happened to meet one of their officers. He has placed at our disposal a small amphitheater which the troops have built for themselves."

I was horrified. "Dear gods! Have you ever attended a garrison theater?"

"Have you?" As usual he dodged.

"Plenty!"

"Oh I'm sure we can manage—"

"You're ignoring the little matter of having no front stage," Phrygia gloatingly broke in, as she confirmed the unsuitable venue Chremes had accepted. "A performance in the round. No fixed scenery, no exits and entrances, no trapdoors from below, and nowhere to hide the lifting machinery if we want to do flying scenes. Giving our all to an audience of bullies, all screaming for obscenities and supplying them if we don't—"

"Hush!" Helena soothed her. Then her common sense broke through. "I do see it may be hard to keep soldiers happy for a whole play . . ."

"Torture!" I rasped. "If they only chuck rocks, we'll be lucky."

"This is where you come in," Chremes informed me eagerly.

"I doubt it." I was planning to load the oxcart and turn back to Damascus that night. "I think you'll find this is where I back out."

"Marcus Didius, listen. You'll be pleased by our idea." I doubted that too. "I've discussed this with the company and we all feel that what we need to hold the soldiers' attention is something short, light, dramatic, and above all, different."

"So what?" I asked, wondering why Helena suddenly giggled behind her stole.

Chremes for his part appeared to be blushing. "So we wondered if you were ready to let us rehearse your famous ghost play?"

That was how my elegant creation, *The Spook Who Spoke*, came to receive its sole performance on a hot August evening, in the Palmyra garrison amphitheater. If you can think of worse, I'd be intrigued to hear it. The soldiers, incidentally, only turned out at all because they had been told one of the support acts was a suggestive snake dancer.

They got more than they bargained for. But then, so did we all.

Sixty-five

One problem we faced was that as a result of all the derision people had poured on my idea, most of the play was not even written. All writers must know that sinking feeling, when the goods are demanded in the firm expectation of a delivery you know is impossible. . . . But by now I was so professional that the mere lack of a script left me undeterred. We wanted the drama to have speed and bite; what better than to improvise?

I soon knew that my play would not have to carry the entire evening: Thalia's traveling sideshow had caught up with us.

I first noticed something new when a lion cub appeared in our tent. He was sweet but ungainly, and so boisterous it was frightening. Investigation revealed extra wagons. One of them consisted of two large carts fixed together, on top of which loomed a massive structure shrouded in skins and sheets. "Whatever's that?"

"Water organ."

"You haven't got an organist!"

"You're fixing that, Falco."

I cringed. "Don't back that bet with money. . . ."

Among the new arrivals were one or two seedy characters from Thalia's troupe in Rome. "My dancing partner arrived too," Thalia said: the famous snake she called "the big one."

"Where is he?"

"In charge of my keen new snakekeeper." She sounded as if she knew something the rest of us had missed. "Want to see?"

We followed her to a wagon on the far side of camp. The lion cub gamboled after us. "What does keeping the snake entail?" Helena inquired politely as we walked, keeping an eye on the cub.

"Catching mice, or anything bigger, then poking them into the basket, preferably still alive. A large python needs a lot of lunch. Back in Rome, I had a gang of lads who brought rats to me. They liked to watch things being swallowed. We had some trouble once when there was a spate of lost cats in the Quirinal lanes. People wondered why their pet pussies kept disappearing. . . . Zeno ate a baby ostrich once, but that was a mistake."

"How can you swallow a whole ostrich by mistake?" I laughed.

"Oh it wasn't a mistake to Zeno!" Thalia grinned. "Fronto was owner of the circus then. He was livid." Fronto's menagerie had a history of creatures finding unfortunate meals. Fronto himself had become one eventually. Thalia was still reminiscing. "Apart from losing the feathers, watching the long neck go in was the worst bit . . . and then we had Fronto creating. We could hardly pretend it hadn't happened, what with the lump slowly gliding head first down inside Zeno, and the legs still sticking out. And of course they don't always do this, but just to make sure Fronto couldn't forget the loss, he spat out the bits that had once been the bones."

Helena and I were still gulping as we climbed into the wagon.

The light was dim. A large rectangular basket, worryingly knocked about and with holes in it, stood in the back of the cart. "Bit of trouble on the journey," Thalia commented. "The keeper's trying to find the baby a strong new cradle. . . ." I refrained from asking what the trouble had been, hoping the damage had resulted from ruts in the desert road rather than delinquent activity from the giant snake. Thalia lifted the lid and leaned in, affectionately stroking whatever the basket contained. We heard a sluggish rustle from deep within. "That's my gorgeous cheeky darling. . . . Don't worry. He's been fed. Anyway, he's far too hot. He doesn't want to move. Come and tickle him under the chin, Falco."

We peered in, then hastily withdrew. From what we could see of the big sleepy python, he was immense. Golden coils half as thick as a human torso were looped back and forth like a huge skein of loom wool. Zeno filled the basket, which was so big it would take several men to move it. Rough calculations told me Zeno must be fifteen to twenty feet long. More than I wanted to think about, anyway.

"Phew! He must be too heavy to lift, Thalia!"

"Oh I don't lift him much! He's tame, and he likes a lot of fuss, but if you get him too excited he starts thinking he'll mate with something. I saw a snake run up a woman's skirt once. Her face was a picture!" Thalia cackled with raucous laughter. Helena and I smiled bravely.

I had been leaning on a smaller basket. Suddenly I felt movement.

"That's Pharaoh." Thalia's smile was not encouraging. "Don't open the basket, Falco. He's my new Egyptian cobra. I haven't tamed him yet."

The basket jerked again and I sprang back.

"Good gods, Thalia! What do you want a cobra for? I thought they were deadly venomous?"

"Oh yes," she replied offhandedly. "I want to liven up my stage act—but he'll be a challenge!"

"However do you manage to dance with him safely?" Helena demanded.

"I'm not using him yet!" Even Thalia showed some wariness. "I'll have to think about it on the way home to Rome. He's gorgeous," she exclaimed admiringly. "But you don't exactly say 'Come to Mother!' and pick up a cobra for a cuddle . . . Some operators cut out their fangs, or even sew their mouths up, which means the poor darlings starve to death, of course. I haven't decided whether I'll milk his venom before a performance, or just use the easy method."

Full of foreboding, I felt obliged to ask: "What's the easy method?"

Thalia grinned. "Oh, just dancing out of range!"

Glad to escape, we jumped down from the wagon and came face to face with the "keen new snakekeeper." He had his sleeves rolled up and was dragging along one of the company costume trunks, presumably intended as the big python's new bed. The lion cub rushed up to him, and he rolled it over to scratch its stomach. It was Musa. Knowing Thalia, I had half expected it.

Musa looked unexpectedly competent as he dodged the big flailing paws, and the cub was ecstatic.

I grinned. "Surely the last time I saw you, you were a priest? Now you're an expert zookeeper!"

"Lions and snakes are symbolic," he answered calmly, as if he was thinking of starting a menagerie on the Petra High Place. I did not ask about him leaving us. I saw him glance diffidently at Helena, as if ensuring she was making a good recovery. She still looked pale. I slung an arm around her. I was not forgetting how serious her illness had been. Maybe I wanted to let it be known that any cosseting she needed would come from me.

Musa seemed rather withdrawn, though not upset. He stepped up to the wagon where the snakes were kept and lifted something from a peg in the dark interior. "Look what I found waiting for me at a temple here, Falco." He was showing me a hat. "There is a letter from Shullay, but I have not read it yet."

The hat was a wide-brimmed, round-crowned, Greek-looking number, the sort you see on statues of Hermes. I sucked air through my teeth. "That's a traveler's headgear. Have you seen it before—traveling very fast downhill?"

"Oh yes. I think it was on a murderer that day."

It did not seem the moment to tell Musa that according to Grumio he was the murderer himself. Instead I amused myself remembering Grumio's absurd theory that Musa was some high-powered political agent, sent out by The Brother on a mission to destroy.

Musa applied his contract killer's skills to clearing up a pile of lion dung.

Helena and Thalia set off back to our tent. I dallied behind. Musa, who had been grappled by the cub again, looked up long enough to meet my eyes.

"Helena has recovered, but she was very sick. Sending Thalia with her mithridatium helped a lot. Thanks, Musa."

He disentangled himself from the fluffy, overactive little lion. He seemed quieter than I had been dreading, though he started to say, "I want to explain—"

"Never explain, Musa. I hope you'll dine with us tonight. Maybe you'll have good news from Shullay to tell me." I clapped his shoulder as I turned to follow the others. "I'm sorry. Thalia's an old friend. We let her have your section of the tent."

I knew that nothing had ever happened between him and Helena, but I was not stupid. I didn't mind how much he cared about her, so long as he honored the rules. The first rule was, I did not expose Helena by letting other men who hankered after her live in our house. "Nothing personal," I added cheerily. "But I don't care for some of your pets!"

Musa shrugged, smiling in return as he accepted it. "I am the snakekeeper. I have to stay with Zeno."

I took two strides, then turned back to him. "We missed you. Welcome back, Musa."

I meant that.

Returning to Helena I happened to pass Byrria. I told her I had been to see the big python, recommended the experience, and said I was sure the keeper would be pleased to show her his menagerie.

Well, you have to try.

Sixty-six

That night I was sitting outside our tent with Helena and Thalia, waiting for Musa to turn up for dinner. We were approached by Chremes and Davos, together with the long, gawky figure of Phrygia, apparently on their way to dine at one of their own tents. Chremes stopped for a discussion with me about an unresolved problem with my play. As we talked, with me paying as little attention as possible to the manager's fussing, I overheard Phrygia muttering to Thalia: "Don't I know you from somewhere?"

Thalia laughed gruffly. "I wondered when you would ask!"

I noticed that Helena applied herself to a tactful chat with Davos.

Phrygia looked tense. "Somewhere in Italy? Or was it Greece?"

"Try Tegea," stated Thalia. She had on her sardonic look again.

Then Phrygia gasped as if she had been poked in the side with a spindle. "I need to talk to you!"

"Well I'll try and fit you in some time," Thalia promised unconvincingly. "I have to rehearse my snake dance." I happened to know she claimed *never* to rehearse her dance, partly because of the danger it entailed. "And the acrobats need a lot of supervision. . . ."

"This is cruelty!" murmured Phrygia.

"No," said Thalia in a tone that meant to be heeded. "You made your decision. If you've suddenly decided to change your mind after all these years, the other party deserves some warning. Don't push me! Maybe I'll introduce you after the play. . . ."

Chremes had given up trying to interest me in his troubles. Looking frustrated, Phrygia fell silent and allowed her husband to lead her away.

I was not the only one who had overheard the intriguing snatch of conversation. Davos found some excuse to dally behind, and I heard him say to Thalia, "I remember Tegea!" I felt Helena kick my ankle, and obediently joined her in pretending to be very busy laying out our meal. As usual Davos was being blunt. "She wants to find the baby."

"So I gathered," Thalia returned rather drily, tipping her head back and giving him a challenging stare. "A bit late! Actually, it's not a baby anymore."

"What happened?" Davos asked.

"When people give me unwanted creatures, I generally bring them up."

"It lived then?"

"She was alive the last time I saw her." As Thalia informed Davos, Helena glanced at me. So Phrygia's baby had been a girl. I suppose we had both already worked that out.

"So she's grown up now?"

"A promising little artiste," Thalia said grittily. That too was no surprise to some of us.

Seeming satisfied, Davos grunted, then went on his way after
Chremes and Phrygia.

"So! What happened at Tegea?" I tackled our companion innocently when the coast was clear. Thalia would probably have
said that men are never innocent.

She shrugged, pretending indifference. "Not a lot. It's a tiny
Greek town, just a blot on the Peloponnese."

"When were you there?"

"Oh . . . how about twenty years ago?"

"Really?" We both knew exactly where the conversation was
leading. "Would that have been about the time our stage manager's
wife missed her famous chance to play Medea at Epidaurus?"

At this, Thalia stopped playing at being unconcerned and
burst into guffaws. "Get away! She told you that?"

"It's common currency."

"Common codswallop! She's fooling, Falco." Thalia's tone was
not unpleasant. She knew most people spend their lives delud-
ing themselves.

"So are you going to give us the real story, Thalia?"

"I was just starting out. Juggling—and the rest!" Her voice
dropped, almost sadly. "Phrygia play Medea? Don't make me
laugh! Some slimy producer who wanted to get his hand up her
skirt convinced her he could swing it, but it would never have
happened. For one thing—you should know this, Falco—
Greeks never allow women actresses."

"True." It was rare in Roman theater too. But in Italy actresses
had done mime plays for years, a vague cover-for striptease acts.
In groups like ours, with a manager like Chremes who was a
pushover for anyone forceful, they could now earn a crust in
speaking parts. But groups like ours never took part in the ancient Greek mainland festivals.

"So what happened, Thalia?"

"She was just a singer and dancer in the chorus. She was drifting about with grand ideas, just waiting for some bastard to con her into believing she would make the big time. In the end, becoming pregnant was a let-out."

"So she had the baby—"

"That's what tends to happen."

"And she gave it away at Tegea?"

By now this was fairly obvious. Only yesterday I had seen a tall, thin, slightly familiar twenty-year-old who I knew had spent her childhood fostered out. I remembered that Heliodorus was supposed to have told Phrygia that her daughter had been seen somewhere by someone he knew. That could be Tranio. Tranio had appeared at the Vatican Circus; Thalia had known him there, and he presumably knew her troupe, especially the girls if his current form was indicative. "I suppose she gave it to you, Thalia? So where is the child now? Could Phrygia need to look in somewhere like Palmyra, I wonder. . . ."

Thalia tried just smiling knowingly.

Helena joined in, saying quietly, "I think we could tell Phrygia who her baby is now, Marcus."

"Keep it to yourself!" commanded Thalia.

Helena grinned at her. "Ooh, Thalia! Don't tell me you're considering how you can cheat Phrygia."

"Who, me?"

"Of course not," I weighed in innocently. "On the other hand, wouldn't it be a nuisance if just when you'd found your valuable water organist, some tiresome relation popped out of the rocky scenery, dying to tell the girl she had a family, and keen to whisk her off to join quite another company than yours?"

"You bet it would!" agreed Thalia, in a dangerous tone that said she was not intending to let Sophrona meet such a fate.

Musa turned up at that moment, allowing Thalia to shrug off the Phrygia incident. "What kept you? I was starting to think Pharaoh must have got out!"

"I took Zeno for a swim at the springs; he didn't want to be brought back."

My mind boggled at the thought of trying to persuade a giant python to behave himself. "What happens when he gets his own ideas and starts playing up?"

"You grab his neck and blow in his face," Musa told me calmly.

"I'll remember that!" giggled Helena, glancing teasingly at me.

Musa had brought with him a papyrus, closely written in the angular script I vaguely remembered seeing on inscriptions at Petra. As we sat down to eat he showed it to me, though I had to ask him to translate.

"This is the letter I mentioned, Falco, from Shullay, the old priest at my temple. I had sent to ask him if he could describe the man he saw coming down from the High Place just before we saw you."

"Right. Anything useful?"

Musa ran his finger down the letter. "He starts by remembering the day, the heat, the peacefulness of our garden at the temple . . ." Very romantic, but not what I call evidence. "Ah. Now he says, '*I was surprised to hear somebody descending from the High Place so rapidly. He was stumbling, and falling over his feet, though otherwise light of step. When he saw me, he slowed up and began whistling unconcernedly. He was a young man, about your age, Musa, and also your height. His body was slim. He wore no beard. He wore the hat. . . .*' Shullay found the hat later, cast aside behind rocks lower down the mountain. You and I must have missed it, Falco."

I was thinking fast. "It doesn't add much, but this is very useful! We have six possible male suspects. We can certainly now eliminate some of them on Shullay's evidence alone. Chremes, and also Davos, are both too old and too heavy to fit the description."

"Philocrates is too small," Musa added. He and I both grinned.

"Besides, Shullay would certainly have mentioned if the man was quite so handsome! Congrio may be *too* slight. He's so weedy I think if he had seen Congrio, Shullay would have made more of his poor stature. Besides, he can't whistle. That leaves us," I concluded quietly, "with only Grumio and Tranio."

Musa leaned forwards, looking expectant. "So what are we to do now?"

"Nothing yet. Now I'm certain it has to be one of those two, I'll have to identify which one we definitely want."

"You cannot interrupt your play, Falco!" Thalia commented reprovingly.

"No, not with a rapacious garrison screaming for it." I applied a competent expression that probably fooled no one. "I'll have to do my play as well."

Sixty-seven

Rehearsing a half-written new play with a gang of cocky subversives who would not take it seriously nearly defeated me. I failed to see their problem. *The Spook Who Spoke* was perfectly straightforward. The hero, to be played by Philocrates, was a character called Moschion—traditionally the name of a slightly unsatisfactory youth. You know the idea—trouble to his parents, useless in love, uncertain whether to turn into a wastrel or to come good in the last act.

I had never decided where the action should take place: some district no one ever fancies visiting. Illyria, perhaps.

The first scene was a wedding feast, an attempt to be controversial after all those plays where the wedding feast happens at the end. Moschion's mother, a widow, was remarrying, partly in order to allow Tranio to do his "Clever Cook" routine and partly to let the panpipe girls wander around deliciously as banquet entertainment. Amid Tranio's jokes about rude-shaped peppered meats, the young Moschion would be complaining about his mother, or when nobody had time to listen just muttering to himself. This portrait of dreadful adolescence was, I thought, rather finely drawn (it was autobiographical).

Moschion's grumbles were halted by a shock meeting with the ghost of his dead father. In my original concept the apparition was to have popped out of a stage trapdoor; in the amphitheater, where this effect would be impossible, we planned to tow on various chests and altars. The spook, chillingly realized by Davos, would conceal himself there until needed. It would work, so long as Davos could avoid getting cramp.

"If you do, don't let it show, Davos. Ghosts don't limp!"

"Stuff you, Falco. Order someone else about. I'm a professional."

Being a writer-producer was hard work.

The ghost accused the widow's new husband of having murdered her old one (himself), leaving Moschion in anguish about what to do. Obviously the rest of the play concerned Moschion's frustrated efforts to get the ghost into court as a witness. In the full-length version, this play was a strong courtroom drama, though the garrison was getting a short farce where Zeus nipped on in the last scene to clear everything up.

"Are you sure this is a comedy?" queried Philocrates haughtily.

"Of course!" I snapped. "Have you no dramatic instinct, man? You can't have spooks leaping about with lurid accusations in tragedy!"

"You don't have ghosts in tragedy at all," Chremes confirmed. He played both the second husband and also the funny foreign doctor in a later scene where Moschion's mother went mad. The mother was Phrygia; we were all looking forward to her mad scene, despite Chremes uttering disloyal thoughts that he for one would not be able to spot any difference from normal.

Byrria played the girl. There had to be one, though I was still slightly uncertain what to do with her (man's eternal predicament). Luckily she was used to minimal parts.

"Can't I run mad too, Falco? I'd like to dash on raving."

"Don't be daft. The Virtuous Maid has to survive without a stain on her character so she can marry the hero."

"But he's a weed!"

"You're learning, Byrria. Heroes always are."

She gave me a thoughtful look.

Tranio and Grumio doubled up as various silly servants, plus the hero's worried friends. At Helena's insistence I had even devised a one-line part for Congrio. He seemed to have plans for expanding the speech: a typical actor already.

I discovered that one of the stagehands had been sent to buy a kid, which was to be carried on by Tranio. It was certain to lift its tail and make a mess; this was bound to appeal to the low taste of our anticipated audience. Nobody told me, but I gained the definite impression that if things were going badly Tranio had been ordered by Chremes to cook the cute creature live onstage. We were desperate to satisfy the raw ranks from the barracks. The kid was only one distraction. There was also to be lewd dancing by the orchestra girls at the start of the evening, and afterwards a complete circus act that Thalia and her troupe would provide.

"It'll do!" Chremes pompously decided. This convinced all the rest of us that it would not do at all.

I wore myself out drilling the players, then was sent away while people practiced their stunts, songs, and acrobatics.

Helena was resting, alone in the tent. I flopped down alongside, holding her in the crook of one elbow while I stroked her still bandaged arm with my other hand.

"I love you! Let's elope and keep a winkle stall."

"Does that mean," Helena demanded gently, "things are not going well?"

"This looks like being a disaster."

"I thought you were an unhappy boy." She snuggled closer consolingly. "Kiss?"

I kissed her, with half my mind on it.

"Kiss properly."

I kissed her again, managing three quarters of my attention. "I'll do this, fruit, then that's the end of my glorious stage career. We're going home straight afterwards."

"That's not because you're worried about me, is it?"

"Lady, you always worry me!"

"Marcus—"

"It's a sensible decision which I made some time ago." About a second after the scorpion stung her. I knew if I admitted that, Helena would rebel. "I miss Rome."

"You must be thinking about your comfortable apartment on the Aventine!" Helena was being rude. My Roman apartment consisted of two rooms, a leaky roof, and an unsafe balcony, six stories above a neighborhood that had all the social elegance of a two-day-old dead rat. "Don't let an accident bother you," she added less facetiously.

I was determined to haul her back to Italy. "We ought to sail west before the autumn."

Helena sighed. "So I'll think about packing. . . . Tonight you're going to sort out Thalia's young lovers. I won't ask how you plan to do it."

"Best not!" I grinned. She knew I had no plan. Sophrona and Khaleed would just have to hope inspiration would strike me later. And now there was the additional complication of Thalia wanting to hide the facts of Sophrona's birth.

"So, Marcus, what about the murderer?"

That was a different story. Tonight would be my last chance. I had to expose him, or he would never be brought to account.

"Maybe," I reflected slowly, "I can somehow draw him out into the open in the course of the play?"

Helena laughed. "I see! Undermine his confidence by affecting his emotions with the power and relevance of your drama?"

"Don't tease! Still, the play is about a murder. It might be possible to work on him by drawing succinct parallels—"

"Too elaborate." Helena Justina always pulled me up sanely if I was flitting off into some rhapsody.

"We're stuck then."

That was when she slipped in cunningly, "At least you know who it is."

"Yes, I know." I had thought that was my secret. She must watch me even more closely than I realized.

"Are you going to tell me, Marcus?"

"I bet you have your own idea."

Helena spoke thoughtfully: "I can guess why he killed Heliodorus."

"I thought you might! Tell me?"

"No. I have to test something first."

"You'll do no such thing. This man is deadly dangerous." Resorting to desperate tactics, I tickled her in various places I knew would render her helpless. "Give me a clue, then." As Helena squirmed, trying not to give in, I suddenly eased off. "What did the vestal virgin say to the eunuch?"

"I'd be willing if you were able?"

"Where did you get that from?"

"I just made it up, Marcus."

"Ah!" I was disappointed. "I hoped it might be from that scroll you always have your nose in."

"Ah!" Helena said as well. She put on a light voice, avoiding particular emphasis. "What about my scroll?"

"Do you remember Tranio?"

"Doing what?"

"Being a menace, for one thing!" I said. "You know, that night soon after we joined the company in Nabataea, when he came looking for something."

Helena obviously remembered exactly what I was talking about. "You mean, the night you came back to the tent tipsy, brought home by Tranio, who annoyed us by hanging about and groveling in the play box?"

"Remember he seemed frantic? He said Heliodorus had borrowed something, something Tranio failed to find. I think you were lying on it, my darling."

"Yes, I wondered about that." She smiled. "Since he insisted that his lost object wasn't a scroll, I didn't feel I needed to mention it."

I thought of Grumio telling me that ridiculous story about his lost ring with the blue stone. I knew now I had been right to disbelieve the tale. You would never hope to find so small an item in a big trunk crammed with many sets of scrolls. They had both lied to me about it, but the famous gambling pledge that Tranio gave away to Heliodorus should have been obvious to me long ago.

"Helena, do you realize what all this has been about?"

"Maybe." Sometimes she irritated me. She liked to go her own way, and refused to see that I knew best.

"Don't mess about. I'm the man of the household: answer me!" Naturally, as a good Roman male, I had fixed ideas about women's role in society. Naturally, Helena knew I was wrong. She hooted with laughter. So much for patriarchal power.

She relented quietly. This was a serious situation, after all. "I think I understand the dispute now. I had the clue all along."

"The scroll," I said. "Your bedtime read is Grumio's inherited humor collection. His prized family asset; his talisman; his treasure."

Helena drew a deep breath. "So this is why Tranio behaves so oddly sometimes. He blames himself because he pledged it to Heliodorus."

"And this is why Heliodorus died: he refused to hand it back."

"One of the clowns killed him because of that, Marcus?"

"They must both have argued with the playwright about it. I think that's why Grumio went to see him the day he stopped Heliodorus raping Byrria; she said she overheard them arguing about a scroll. Various people have told me that Tranio tackled the bastard as well. Grumio must have been going spare, and when Tranio realized just what he had done, he must have felt pretty agitated too."

"So what happened at Petra? One of them went up the mountain to make another attempt to persuade Heliodorus to relinquish it, actually meaning to kill him?"

"Maybe not. Maybe things just went too far. I don't know whether what happened was planned, and if so whether both clowns were in on it. At Petra they were supposed to have drunk themselves unconscious in their rented room while Heliodorus was being killed. One of them obviously didn't. Is the other lying absolutely, or was he really made completely drunk by his roommate so that he passed out and never knew his companion had left the room? If so, and the first deliberately held back from drinking to prepare an alibi—"

"Then that's premeditation!" Helena exclaimed.

It seemed to me that if Grumio were the culprit but Tranio still regretted giving away the pledge, that could make Tranio willingly cover for him at Petra, and might explain Tranio's feeble attempt to make Afrania lie about his own alibi at Gerasa. But Grumio had a whole crowd of people to vouch for him when Ione was killed. Had Afrania been lying to me all along, and was Tranio Ione's killer? If so, were events at Petra the opposite way around? Did *Tranio* kill Heliodorus, and *Grumio* cover up?

"This is all becoming clearer, but the motive seems extravagant." Helena was looking worried for other reasons. "Marcus, you're a creative artist." She said it entirely without irony. "Would you be so upset by losing a batch of rather old material that you would go so far as to *kill* for it?"

"Depends," I replied slowly. "If I had a volatile temperament. If the material was my livelihood. If it was *mine* by rights. And especially if the person who now possessed it was an evil-mannered scribe who would be bound to gloat about using my precious material. . . . We'll have to test the theory."

"There's not going to be much opportunity."

Suddenly I reached the end of my tolerance. "Ah cobnuts, sweetheart! It's my debut tonight; I don't even want to think about this anymore. Everything will be all right."

Everything. My ghost play; Sophrona; finding the killer; everything. Sometimes, even without grounds for optimism, I just knew.

Helena was in a more sober mood. "Don't joke about it. It's too grave a subject. You and I never make light of death."

"Or life," I said.

I had rolled to pin her beneath me, carefully keeping her bandaged arm free of my weight. I held her face between my hands while I studied it. Thinner and quieter since her illness, but still full of searching intelligence. Strong, quizzical eyebrows; fine bones; adorable mouth; eyes so dark brown and solemn they were making me ferment. I had always loved her being serious. I loved the madcap thought that I had made a serious woman care for me. And I loved that irresistible glint of laughter, so rarely shared with others, whenever Helena's eyes met mine privately.

"Oh, my love. I'm so glad you've come back to me. I had thought I was losing you—"

"I was here." Her fingers traced the line of my cheek, while I turned my head to brush the soft skin of her wrist with my lips. "I knew all that you were doing for me."

Now that I could bear to think about what had happened with the scorpion, I remembered how one night when she had been tossing with fever she had suddenly exclaimed in a clear voice, "*Oh, Marcus!*", as if I had entered a room and rescued her from some bad dream. Straight after that she had slept more quietly. When I told her about it now, she was unable to recollect the dream, but she smiled. She was beautiful when she smiled that way, looking up at me.

"I love you," Helena whispered suddenly. There was a special note in her voice. The moment when the mood between us altered had been imperceptible. We knew each other so well it took only the faintest change of tone, a slightly increased tension in our bodies lying together. Now, without drama or prevarication, we were both wanting to make love.

Everywhere outside was quiet. The actors were still rehearsing; so were Thalia and the circus performers. Within the tent a couple of flies with no sense of discretion were buzzing about against the hot goatskin roof. Everything else lay still. Almost everything, anyway.

"I love you too. . . ." I had told her that, but for a girl with exceptional qualities I did not mind repeating myself.

This time I did not have to be asked to kiss her, and every atom of my concentration was being applied. It was the moment to find the jar of alum wax. We both knew it. Neither of us wanted to disturb the deep intimacy of the moment; neither of us wanted to draw apart. Our eyes met, silently consulting; silently rejecting the idea.

We knew each other very well. Well enough to take a risk.

Sixty-eight

We did our best to search the soldiers at the gates. We managed to confiscate most of their drink flagons and some of the stones they were planning to hurl at us. No one could stop large numbers of them peeing against the outside wall before entering; at least that was better than what they might do inside later. Syria had never been a fashionable posting; dedicated men applied for frontier forts in Britain or Germany, where there was some hope of cracking foreign heads. These soldiers were little more than bandits. Like all Eastern legions, they turned to salute the sun each morning. Their evening fun was likely to be slaughtering us.

Their commander had offered us military ushers but I said that was asking for trouble. "You don't control legionaries by using their mates!" He accepted the comment with a curt, knowing nod. He was a square-faced career officer, a sinewy man with straight-cut hair. I remember the pleasant shock of running into someone in authority who realized it would be useful to avert a riot.

We exchanged a few words. He must have been able to see I had a more solid background than scribbling light comedies. However, I was surprised when he recognized my name.

"Falco? As in Didius?"

"Well, I like having a reputation, but frankly, sir, I did not expect my fame to have reached a road-building vexillation in the middle of the desert, halfway to bloody Parthia!"

"There's a note out, asking for sightings."

"A warrant?" I laughed as I said it, hoping to avoid unpleasantness.

"Why that?" He looked both amused and skeptical. 'It's more *Render assistance; agent lost and may be in difficulty.*'"

Now I really was surprised. "I was never lost! Whose signature?"

"Not allowed to say."

"Who's your governor in Syria?"

"Ulpius Traianus."

It meant nothing much then, though those of us who lived to be old men would see his son's craggy mush on the currency. "Is it him?"

"No," he said.

"If it's a short-arsed flea called Anacrites from the political bureau—"

"Oh no!" The garrison commander was shocked by my irreverence. I knew what that meant.

"The Emperor?" I had long stopped respecting official secrecy. The commander, however, blushed at my indiscretion.

The mystery was solved. Helena's father must be at the back of this. If Camillus had not heard from his daughter for the past four months, he would wonder where she was. The Emperor, his friend, was not looking for me at all but for my wayward lass.

Oh, dear. Definitely time I took Helena home again.

The commander cleared his throat. "So are you? In difficulty?"

"No," I said. "But thanks for asking. Ask me again when we've played to your mob here!"

He did invite Helena to a seat in the tribunal, a nice courtesy. I agreed, because he seemed far too straight to start fingering her, and I reckoned it was the one place a respectable woman would be safe that night.

Helena was furious at being sent out of the way.

The house was full. We drew about a thousand soldiers, a group of Palmyrene archers who had served in Judaea with Vespasian and learned about Roman spectacles, plus a few townspeople. Among them were Khaleed and his father, another short, stumpy Damascene. Facially, they did not much resemble each other, apart from a slight similarity in hairlines. I joked to Thalia, "Khaleed must take after his mother—poor woman!" Then his mother turned up (maybe they had left her to park the chariot), and unfortunately I was right: not exactly a model of feminine beauty. We gave them front-row seats, and hoped nothing too hard would be thrown at them by the soldiers behind.

Sophrona had arrived earlier, and I had made her accompany Helena as a chaperone. (We kept the girl out of sight of Thalia, in case Sophrona realized what was planned for her and tried to do another flit.) What did happen, of course, was that the family of Habib soon spotted Sophrona in the ceremonial box alongside the garrison commander and Helena, who was in full regalia as a senator's daughter, resplendently dressed in new Palmyrene silk, with bronze bracelets to the elbow. My lady was a loyal soul. As it was my play's first night, she had even brought out a tiara to peg down the necessary veil.

The family were impressed. This could only help. I had not

worked out exactly how I would solve their troubles, but after three months submerged in soggy dramas, I was full of crass ideas.

The amphitheater was small by theatrical standards, and ill equipped for creating dramatic effects. It had been built for gladiatorial fights and wild-beast shows. There were two gates made from heavy timber balks at opposite ends of the ellipse. The arena had two arched niches on its longer sides. In one, our stagehands had draped a statue of Nemesis with garlands; the musicians were crouching under her skirts. The other niche was to be used as a refuge for actors exiting. Around the arena ran a wooden protective barrier, several yards high. Above it was a steeply raked bank with tiers of wooden benching. The commander's tribunal, little more than a plinth with a couple of thrones, was on one side.

That atmosphere was vibrant. Too vibrant. The troops were restless. Any moment now they would start setting fire to their seats.

It was time to diffuse the kind of trouble we could not stop by stirring up the audience even more with music and dancing girls. In the tribunal the commanding officer politely let drop a white scarf.

Thalia appeared at my side as I stood in the gateway listening to the orchestra begin its first number.

Afrania and Plancina jostled up, huddling in stoles. They wore headdresses and Palmyrene veils, but only bells and spangles beneath the stoles. Thalia took Plancina, who was nervous, under her accommodating wing. I talked with Afrania.

"This is the night, Falco!" Within the amphitheater our girls had been glimpsed. Boots began drumming rhythmically. "Juno! What a gang of turds."

"Give them your best; they'll be like kittens."

"Oh, I reckon they're animals all right."

Plancina ran on, doing things with a set of castanets it was hard to believe were possible. "Not bad!" Thalia commented.

Soon Plancina was working up a frenzy of applause with her panpipe dance. She writhed well. Afrania dropped her stole, grabbed her musical instrument, then, while I was still blinking, she bounced out, virtually naked, to join the dance.

"Wow!"

"She'll do herself a mischief with that tibia," growled Thalia, unimpressed.

Not long afterwards the stagehands started clustering around the gate with the props we would be using for *The Spook Who Spoke*. Soon the actors came out from the dressing tent in a tense group. Musa appeared at my elbow.

"Your big night, Falco!"

I was sick of people saying that. "It's just a play."

"I have my work too," he said, rather drily; he was looking after the kid that Tranio was to cook. It struggled valiantly in his arms, trying to run away. Musa also had charge of Philocrates' mule, which was to be ridden in a journey scene. "And tonight," he said, with an almost eerie satisfaction, "we shall identify our murderer."

"We can try." His calm attitude disturbed me. "Domestic livestock seems a comedown for you. Where's the big snake?"

"In his basket," replied Musa, with the faintest of smiles.

The music ended. The orchestra came off for a drink while the girls raced at speed for the dressing tent. Soldiers poured out for an interval pee, even though we had not planned to allow them an interval. I had been a soldier; I was not surprised.

The actors had seen it all before. They sighed, and stood back from the entrance until the crush had galloped by.

I could see Tranio approaching for his first scene as the busy cook. He looked preoccupied with his coming performance, and I reckoned I might be able to shake him if I asked the right question unexpectedly. I was weighing up my moment to beard him, when Congrio tugged at my sleeve. "Falco! Falco! This speech I have—" Congrio's "speech" was one line; he had to enter as a household slave and announce that the Virtuous Maiden had just given birth. (In plays, virtuous maidens are not *that* virtuous. Don't blame me; this is the tradition of a soiled genre. Your average theatrical juvenile sees rape as his first step to marriage, and for some reason your average comic heroine goes right along with it.) Congrio was still complaining. "It's boring. Helena Justina told me I can fill it out—"

"Do whatever you like, Congrio."

I was trying to move away from him. Tranio was standing some distance apart, getting his wig on. Just as I freed myself from Congrio and his maundering anxiety, a gaggle of heavies from the garrison blocked my path. They sized me up. They despised actors, but I was being taken as more promising bait. Evidently I looked tough enough to have my head kicked in.

I had no time to distract them with genial banter. I leaped straight through the group of hooligans, pounding off on a lengthy detour, then, as I swerved back towards Tranio, I ran into a little fellow who was swearing that he knew me: some lunatic who wanted to discuss a goat.

Sixty-nine

"Hello, this is a bit of luck!"

I had been stopped by a tiny chap with one arm cut off at the elbow and a hopeful toothless grin. Being trapped was unusual; normally I'm much too smart for street hustlers. I thought he was trying to sell me something—and I was right. He wanted me to have his goat.

My play was starting. I could hear Ribes playing a delicate introductory melody on the lyre.

Before I could buff aside the man who had stopped me, something made me think again. The loon looked familiar.

His companion seemed to know me too, for it butted me in the kidneys as familiarly as a nephew. It was a brown-and-white patched billy goat, about waist high, with a sad expres-

sion. Both its ears had nervous tics. Its neck had a queer
kink.

I knew about this goat. The owner made some hopeless claim
that it had been born with its head facing backwards.

"Sorry—" I tried to make off.

"We met at Gerasa! I've been trying to find you!" the owner
piped.

"Look, friend; I have to go—"

He looked downcast. They made a gloomy pair. "I thought
you were interested," protested the man. The goat had the sense
to know I just wanted to escape.

"Sorry?"

"In buying the goat!" Dear gods.

"What made you think that?"

"Gerasa!" he repeated doggedly. A dim memory of viewing
his beast for a copper or two in a mad moment came floating
back. A more terrible memory—of foolishly discussing the
beast with its owner—followed rapidly. "I still want to sell him.
I thought we had a bargain. . . . I came looking for you that
night, in fact."

It was time to be blunt. "You've got the wrong idea, friend. I
just asked you about him because he reminded me of a goat I
once owned myself."

He didn't believe me. It sounded weak only because it was the
truth. Once, for very complex reasons, I had rescued a runaway
nanny from a temple on a seashore. My excuse is, I was living
rough (I was doing a job for Vespasian, always prone to leave me
short of tavern fees) and any companion had seemed better than
none at the time.

I had always been a sentimental type. Now sometimes I let
myself indulge in conversations with owners of peculiar goats
just to show off my former expertise. So, I had talked to this
man in Gerasa. I remembered he had told me he wanted to sell
up and plant beans. We had discussed what price he wanted for

his quaintly angled exhibit, but I had never had any intention of rejoining the goat owners' guild.

"Look, I'm sorry, but I like a pet who looks you in the eye."

"Depends where you stand," the menace persisted logically. He tried to edge me into position behind his billy's left shoulder. "See?"

"I've got a girlfriend now; she takes all my energy—"

"He draws the crowds!"

"I bet he does." Lies. As a sideshow the goat was completely useless. He was also nibbling my tunic hem, despite his disability. In fact, the crooked neck seemed to place him more readily in line with people's clothes. The last thing I needed was a series of domestic writs for damaged skirts and togas.

"What was yours called?" demanded the owner. He was definitely mad.

"What? Oh my goat. She didn't have a name. Growing too familiar only leads to heartache on both sides."

"That's right . . ." The goat owner could tell I understood his problems. "This is Alexander, because he's great." Wrong. He was just terrible.

"Don't sell him!" I urged, suddenly unable to bear the thought of them parting. It seemed to me this couple of deadbeats depended on each other more than either realized. "You need to know he has a good home. If you're going to retire from the road, take him with you."

"He'll eat the beans." True. He would eat everything. Goats actually tear up plants and shrubs by the roots. Nothing they come near to ever sprouts again. "You seemed like a good sort, Falco—"

"Don't bet on it."

"He has his funny ways, but he repays affection. . . . Still, maybe you're right. He belongs with me." I had been reprieved. "I'm glad I've seen you again; it's cleared my mind." I pulled

Alexander by the ears, almost regretfully. Obviously a connois-
seur of quality, he tried to eat my belt.

I was leaving them when the long-faced goat owner suddenly
asked, "That night in Gerasa, did your friend ever find his way
to the pools?"

Seventy

"What friend?" If we were talking about Gerasa, I didn't need to ask what pools.

I was trying to keep things light, while all the time my sense of oppression grew. I hate murder. I hate murderers. I hate running up against the need to name one of them. Very soon now it was going to be unavoidable.

"He was in your company. When I came to offer you the goat, I asked him where you were. He said you'd gone into town, and in return for that he asked me directions to the pools of the Maiuma."

"What did he look like?"

"Blow me if I know. He had no time to stop; he was dashing off on a camel."

"Young? Old? Tall? Short? *Can you see him here now?*"

The man looked panicky. Unused to describing people, he was fumbling for anything to say. It was no use pressing him. Not even with one possible murderer—Tranio—standing ten feet from us waiting to go onstage. The witness was unreliable. Too much time had passed. Now if I offered suggestions he would agree with them instantly to escape his quandary. This loon held the answer to everything, but I would have to let him go.

I said nothing. Patience was my only hope. Alexander was slyly consuming the sleeve of my tunic; seeing it, his owner biffed him between the ears. Striking the goat's head reminded him of something: "He wore a hat!" I had heard that before.

While I was catching my breath, the goat's owner voluntarily described the Gerasa specimen. "It was one of them knitted things, with a flopped-over top."

That was nothing like the wide-brimmed, round-crowned Greek hat that Musa had been sent from Petra by Shullay. But I knew where I had seen this. "A Phrygian cap? Like the sun god Mithras wears?"

"That's right. One of them long floppy ones."

Grumio's collection cap.

So Ione's killer was Grumio. I had given him an alibi myself, based on the bad premise that I had seen him several times in the same place. I never dreamed that in between he might have galloped off somewhere else.

Looking back, my confidence had been ridiculous. Of course he had taken a break from his act. He could never have sustained that sparkling performance all night. If he had stood on that barrel for the whole evening, by the time Musa and I returned from the Temple of Dionysus he would have been hoarse and completely exhausted. That had not been his condition when he dragged me up for abuse and the near-fatal "accident" using my own knife. He had been alert, in control, exhilarated, *dangerous*. And I had missed the obvious.

Grumio had done two turns on the barrel. In between, he had ridden to the pools and killed the girl.

Had he acted alone? And had he killed Heliodorus too? It was hard to work out. My mind was a mess. Sometimes it is better to have twenty suspects than a mere two. I wanted to consult Helena. Unluckily I had trapped her in the commander's private box.

I walked to the arena entrance. Grumio was no longer there. He and Chremes had slipped into the arena ready to make their entrances from one side. They were hiding in one of the niches. Davos was concealed onstage, ready to pop out as the ghost. The rest of the cast had been waiting for me.

Ribes was still enjoying himself with the lyre. Luckily Syrians liked minstrels. Ribes fancied himself rotten, and since no one had signaled him to end the overture, he was working it up in frenzied improvisation.

Tranio was by the gate. I walked up to him casually. "You'll be glad to know I found Grumio's ring."

"His ring?"

"Blue stone. Could be lapis; might just be sodalite. . . ." He had absolutely no idea what I was talking about.

"As I thought—he even lied about that!" I grabbed Tranio by the elbow and yanked him closer.

"What's the game, Falco?"

"Tranio, I'm trying to decide whether you're foolishly loyal—or just a complete fool!"

"I don't know what you mean—"

"It's time to stop protecting him. Believe me, he's tried quite happily to implicate you! Whatever you think you owe him, forget it now!"

Other people were listening: Thalia, Musa, many of the cast. Tranio's eyes flickered towards those present.

"Let them hear," I said. "We can do with witnesses. Own up. What was the pledge you gave to Heliodorus, then had the row about?"

"Falco, I have to go on—" Tranio was panicking.

"Not yet." I gripped his costume by the neck and jerked it tight. He could not tell whether I was really angry, or just playing him along. "I want the truth!"

"Your play, Falco—"

"Stuff my play."

For a moment I felt things were getting away from me. Help came from an unexpected quarter: "The pledge was a scroll." It was Philocrates who spoke. He really must be worried that he would be blamed for the crimes himself. "It was Grumio's; his collection of terrible old jokes."

"Thanks, Philocrates! All right Tranio, you've got some fast answers to provide! First, were you really with Afrania the night Ione died?"

He gave up. "Yes."

"Why did you ask her to pretend otherwise?"

"Stupidity."

"Well that's honest! And were you conscious or in a stupor in Petra the afternoon Heliodorus was killed?"

"Paralytic."

"What about Grumio?"

"I thought he was the same."

"Are you certain he was?"

Tranio dropped his eyes. "No," he admitted. "I passed out. He could have done anything."

I let go of him. "Tranio, Tranio, what have you been playing at? If you are not the killer, why protect the man who was?"

He shrugged helplessly. "It was my fault. I'd lost him his scroll."

I would never entirely understand it. But I was a writer, not a performer. A comedian is only as good as his script. A writer never has to grieve too long for lost material. Unluckily for the reading and viewing public, writers can easily rattle off more.

I despaired of Tranio. In the arena Ribes had been covering the unexpected pause with his rapid plectrumming but the audience was tired of it. I could see he was starting to feel desperate as he wondered why Tranio was failing to enter. I took a swift decision. "We'll have to discuss this later. Get out onstage. Don't warn Grumio, or you'll be arrested too."

Released from my furious grip, Tranio pulled on a sparse two-tone wig, then strode in through the gate. Free members of the cast, together with Thalia, Musa and myself, all crowded around to watch.

Looking out at ground level, the elliptical space seemed immense. Musa and Thalia stared at me curiously as I wondered what to do. Onstage, Tranio began carrying on as the hectic cook. He seemed to be safely sticking to his lines. Soon he was berating the less sophisticated Grumio, playing a farm boy who had brought meat for the feast. Chremes rushed on to give them orders, made some jokes about voracious women wanting sex night and day, then rushed off again.

To one side, Philocrates as my hero, Moschion, interjected adolescent bile, sitting on a costume basket covered in a blanket to represent a couch. Davos, the ghost, was concealed in a portable oven. From time to time he leaned out to address Moschion—the only person who could "see" him. The ghost then became worried because Tranio was about to light a fire in the oven: sophisticated stuff. You can see why I had been proud of it. Not that the play mattered to me now. I was about to confront the killer; I had bile in my mouth.

Being set on fire was nothing to what I intended for Tranio for frustrating my inquiries. As for Grumio, I noted with relish that in provincial locations criminal executions usually take place in the local arena. I glanced up at the garrison commander. I wondered if he held the right to award the death penalty. Probably not. But the governor, Ulpius Traianus, would.

Davos let out a terrific shriek, which most characters onstage ignored. Clutching the seat of his ghostly robe, he ran off through the gate as if alight. The crowd really loved seeing a character in pain. The atmosphere was excellent.

"Falco, what's going on?" Davos exclaimed. While squashed in the oven he had had more reason than most to notice the long pause before we began.

"Crisis!" I said tersely. Davos looked startled, but evidently realized what sort of crisis it must be.

Onstage, Phrygia and Byrria had appeared from the far gate entrance. They were shooing away the two "slaves" in order to have a sly chat in the kitchen about young Moschion. Tranio and Grumio ran off, according to my stage directions, in opposite directions; fortuitously, that put them one in each side niche, unable to confer.

Moschion was hiding behind the oven so he could overhear his mother and girlfriend discussing him. It was meant to be a very funny scene. While the women tossed wit around, I breathed slowly to calm down.

Soon, however, the clowns were back onstage again. Suddenly I began to worry that I had misjudged Tranio. I had made a mistake.

I muttered to Musa, "This isn't going to work. . . ."

I had to choose: whether to stop the performance in midscene, or wait. We had a large group of unruly soldiers who had paid for a spectacle. If they were disappointed, we could expect a riot.

My fears were well founded. "You're going to catch it!" the Clever Cook warned the Country Clown as they bantered onstage. This was not in the script. "If I were you I would leg it while you can!"

Davos, quicker-witted than most people, grasped the point and muttered, "*Shit!*"

Tranio's exit was back into the side niche, but Grumio came our way. Maybe he thought Tranio had just been improvising lines. At any rate, he was still in character.

Musa glanced at me. I decided to do nothing. In the play, Philocrates was discovered hiding by his mother, had a quarrel with his girlfriend, and was exiled to the country for the usual complicated plot reasons. My drama moved fast.

Philocrates left the stage and arrived among us looking uneasy. I gave him a discreet nod; the play would continue. I noticed Thalia grab Davos by the arm. I saw her mouth in his ear, "Next time you're onstage, give that Tranio a thump!"

Musa went forward to hand Grumio the reins of Philocrates' mule, ready for the next scene. Both Philocrates and Grumio had flung on traveling cloaks; it was a very quick costume change. Philocrates as the young master swung on to his mule. Grumio for one was paying little attention to those of us standing around.

Just as they set off back onstage for a short scene journeying to a farm, Musa stepped forward again to Grumio. Grumio, leading the mule, was on the verge of passing into view of the audience. Quite unexpectedly, Musa rammed a hat upon his head. It was a wide Greek hat with a string beneath the chin. I saw Grumio go pale.

The hat was bad enough. But my faithful accomplice had devised a further trick: "Don't forget to whistle!" Musa commanded cheerfully. It sounded like a stage direction, but some of us knew otherwise.

Before I could stop him, he clapped the mule on its rump, so it skidded out into the arena, dragging Grumio.

"Musa! You idiot. Now he knows we know!"

"Justice must be done," said Musa calmly. "I want him to know."

"Justice won't be done," I retorted, "if Grumio escapes!"

On the far side of the arena, the other gate gaped wide. Beyond it a clear vista of the desert was stretching endlessly.

Seventy-one

I saw Grumio glance back at us. Unluckily for him, the sturdy figure of Philocrates was holding forth on the mule so there was no chance of bringing the scene to a premature end. Moschion had a lengthy speech about women, which Philocrates enjoyed giving. No wonder. The character was an ignorant bastard; the speech based on himself.

Spinning around, I gripped Davos by his arm. "I'll need your help. First, Musa! Get around to the end of the amphitheater, and if it's not too late, slam those gates shut!"

"I'll do that," said Thalia quietly. "He's caused enough trouble!" She was a girl for action. She ran for a camel left outside by one of the audience, and within seconds was haring off in a cloud of dust.

"Right, Davos. Go up the back of the arena, and down the

steps to the tribunal. Whisper to the commander we've got at least one killer out there, and possibly an accomplice." I was not forgetting Tranio, currently holed up in a side niche. I had no idea what he might be planning. "Helena's there. She'll back you up. Tell the man we're going to need some arrests."

Davos understood. "Someone will have to fetch that bastard offstage. . . ." Without hesitation, he threw his stage mask at a bystander, stripped off his white ghost's costume, and dropped it over my head. Wearing only a loincloth, he ran off towards the commander. I was given the mask.

I found myself shrouded in long folds of material that flapped strangely on my arms—and in darkness. The ghost was the only character we were playing in a mask. We rarely used them. I knew why the minute I had this one rammed over my face. Suddenly excluded from half of the world, I tried to learn how to look through the hollow eyes, while scarcely able to breathe.

A bothersome presence was grabbing my elbow.

"He's guilty then?" It was Congrio. "That Grumio?"

"Get out of my way, Congrio. I've got to confront the clown."

"Oh I'll do that!" he exclaimed. The certainty in his tone carried a familiar echo of Helena's brisk style. He was her pupil, one she had clearly led astray. "Helena and I have thought up a plan!"

I had no time to stop him. I was still trying to master my costume. Adopting a curious spring (his idea of great acting, apparently), Congrio raced into the arena ahead of me. Even then I still expected to hear the one line I had written for him: "Madam! The young lady has just given birth to twins!"

Only he did not say the line.

He was not playing the part I had written him, but the traditional Running Slave: "Gods above, here's a pickle—" He ran so fast he caught up the travelers on their mule. "I'm wearing myself out. Moschion turned out of doors, his mother in tears, the roast on fire, and the bridegroom furious, and now this girl—

hold on, I'll tell you all about the girl when I get around to it. Here's a pair of travelers! I'll stop for a chat with them."

Then, as my heart sank further than I had ever thought it could, Congrio began to tell a joke.

Seventy-two

Congrio had climbed up on a model of a rock for a better view. "Hello down there! You look glum. Would you like cheering up? Here's one I bet you haven't heard." Philocrates, still on the mule, looked furious. He liked to know where he was with a script, and hated minions anyway. Congrio was unstoppable.

"A Roman tourist comes to a village and sees a farmer with a beautiful sister."

I noticed that Grumio, who had been about to tug the mule's reins, abruptly stopped, as if he recognized the joke. Congrio was revelling in his new power to hold an audience.

"'Ho there, peasant! How much for a night with your sister?'

"'Fifty drachmas.'

"'That's ridiculous! Tell you what, you let me spend a night with the girl and I'll show you something that will amaze you. I bet I can make your animals talk. . . If not, I'll pay you the fifty drachmas.'

"Well the farmer thinks, 'This man is crazy. I'll string him along and agree to it.'

"What he doesn't know is that the Roman has been trained as a ventriloquist.

"The Roman reckons at least he can have a bit of fun here. 'Let me talk to your horse, peasant. Hello, horse. Tell me, how does your master treat you then?'

"'Pretty well,' answers the horse, 'though his hands are rather cold when he strokes my flanks. . . .'"

As Congrio rambled on, I could just make out through the mask that Philocrates looked stunned, while Grumio was seething furiously.

"'That's wonderful,' agrees the farmer, though he isn't convinced entirely. 'I could have sworn I actually heard my horse speak. Show me again.'

"The Roman chuckles quietly to himself. 'Let's try your nice sheep then. Hello, sheep! How's your master?'

"'Not too bad,' says the sheep, 'though I do find his hands rather cold on the udder when he milks me. . . .'"

Philocrates had assumed a fixed grin, wondering when this unplanned torture was going to end. Grumio still stood like bedrock, listening as if he could not believe it. Congrio had never been so happy in his life.

"'You're convincing me,' says the farmer.

"The Roman is really enjoying himself now. 'I knew I would. I'll do one more, then your sister's mine for the evening. Hello, camel. You're a lovely-looking creature. Tell me—'

"Before he can go any further, the farmer jumps up furiously. 'Don't listen to him! The camel's a liar!' he shrieks."

Someone else was jumping up.

With a cry of rage, Grumio flung himself at Congrio. "Who

gave it to you?" He meant his scroll of jokes. Helena must have lent it to Congrio.

"It's mine!" The bill-poster was taunting Grumio. He sprang down from the rock and leaped about the stage, just out of reach. "I've got it and I'm keeping it!"

I had to act fast. Still wearing the ghost's costume, I entered the ring. In the vain hope of making the audience believe my appearance was intentional, I waved my arms above my head and ran with a weird loping gait, pretending to be Moschion's paternal phantom.

Grumio knew the game was up. He abandoned Congrio. Spinning around, he suddenly grabbed Philocrates by one smart boot, gave a wrench of his leg and pulled him off the mule. Not expecting the assault, Philocrates crashed to the ground horribly.

The crowd roared with appreciation. It was not funny. Philocrates had fallen on his face. His handsome visage would be ruined. If only his nose was broken, he would be fortunate. Congrio stopped cavorting and ran to him, then pulled him towards the side niche, from which Tranio now emerged, also looking shocked. Together they carried the unconscious actor from the ring. The crowd were thrilled. The fewer cast members left still upright, the more delighted they would be.

Ignoring the rescue of Philocrates, Grumio was trying to mount the mule. I was still stumbling over the long hem of my costume, half blind in the mask. I struggled on, hearing the crowd's bursts of laughter, not only at my antics. Grumio had not reckoned with the mule. As he swung one leg to mount, the animal skittered sideways. The more he tried to reach the saddle, the more it veered away from him.

Amusement soared. It looked like a deliberate trick. Even I slowed up to watch. Hopping in frustration, Grumio followed the mule until they actually came face to face. Grumio turned to approach the saddle again, then the mule twisted, shoved him in the back with its long nose, and knocked him flat. Whinnying with delight at this feat, the mule then galloped from the scene.

Grumio was an acrobat. He had landed better than Philocrates and was on his feet straightaway. He turned to follow the mule and escape on foot—just as Thalia had the far gate swung closed against him. Designed for keeping in wild beasts, it was far too tall to climb. He spun back—and met me. Still dressed as the ghost, I tried to fill enough space to block his exit the other way. The gateway behind me gaped open at least twelve feet wide, but members of the company were pressing into it, eager to see the action. They would not let him through.

It was him and me now.

Or rather, it was more than that, for two other figures had emerged. For the last scene in the arena it would be him and me—plus Musa and the sacrificial kid.

Ensemble playing of the finest quality.

Seventy-three

I wrenched off the mask. Its flowing gray locks, made from rough horsehair, caught in my fingers. Shaking it free with some violence, I hurled it away.

Blinking in the torchlight, I saw Helena standing up in the tribunal, talking urgently to the commander. Davos was leaping down the steps towards the front, taking the treads three at a time. The Palmyra garrison must have some troops who were not quite the dregs; soon there was a flurry of controlled activity at one end of a row.

A long way behind me, Musa stood with the kid in his arms. He was crazy; a Nabataean; from another world. I could not understand the idiot. "Back off. Get help!" He ignored my shout.

I gathered the ludicrous folds of the costume and stuffed them in my belt. The crowd suddenly fell so completely silent that I could now hear the flames on the bitumen torches that stood around to light the stage. The soldiers had no idea what was happening, but they knew it was not in the program. I had a bad feeling that *The Spook Who Spoke* was turning into something they would talk about for years.

Grumio and I were standing about fourteen feet apart. Scattered around were various props, mostly items left as hiding places for the ghost: the craggy rock; the beehive oven; a wicker laundry trunk; a couch; a huge ceramic pot.

Grumio was enjoying it. He knew I would have to take him. His eyes were flashing. His cheeks were flushed hectically. He looked drugged with excitement. I should have known all along he was one of those tense, arrogant killers who destroy life coldly and never recant.

"This is the killer from the High Place," stated Musa, publicly indicting him. The bastard coolly started whistling.

"Give up." My voice was quiet, addressing Grumio. "We have evidence and witnesses. I know you killed the playwright because he would not return your missing scroll—and I know you strangled Ione."

"*'Now she's dead, which takes away some of the problem. . . .'*" He was quoting *The Girl from Andros*. The sheer flippancy enraged me. "Don't come any closer, Falco."

He was mad, in the sense that he lacked humanity. In every other sense he was as sane as me, and probably more intelligent. He was fit, athletic, trained to do sleight of hand, keen-sighted. I did not want to have to fight him—but he wanted to fight me.

A dagger was in his hand now. My own knife came from my boot into my grip like a friend. No time to relax, however. He was a professional juggler; if I came too close I was likely to find myself weaponless. I was unarmored. He, casting aside the cloak from his costume, was at least protected by the leather apron of a stage slave.

He crouched, feinting. I stayed upright, refusing to be drawn.

He snarled. I ignored that too. I started circling, weight secretly on the balls of my feet. He prowled too. As we spiraled gently, the distance between us reduced. On the long-benched galleries, the soldiers started a low drumming of their heels. They would sustain the dreadful racket until one of us was done for.

My body felt stiff. I realized just how long it was since I had exercised in a gymnasium. Then he came for me.

The fight was fierce. He had nothing to lose. Hate was his only incentive; death now or later the only possible prize.

One thing was pretty obvious: the garrison enjoyed gladiators. This was better than mere comedy. They knew the knives were real. If someone got stabbed, the blood would not be cochineal.

Any thought that the officer in charge would send men in to help me faded early. There was a group in armor at each gate now, but they were just standing there for a better view. If anyone from the theater company tried to rush on and assist, the soldiery would hold them back and call it keeping the peace. Their commander would know his best hope of maintaining order was to allow the contest, then either praise me or arrest Grumio, whoever survived. I was not taking bets; nor was the officer, I guessed. Besides, I was an imperial agent. He would expect a certain standard of competence, and if I failed to find it, he probably would not care.

Things began stylishly. Cut and slash. Parry and thrust. Balletic moves. Soon choreographed into the usual panic, heat and mess.

He tricked me. Dismayed, I fled; rolled; threw myself at his feet as he ran at me. He leapfrogged over me and dodged behind the laundry basket. The soldiery roared. They were on his side.

He was safe. I had to be more cautious.

I grabbed the spook's mask and flung it at him. Ever the juggler, he caught the thing and sliced it at my throat. I was no longer there. He spun; glimpsed me, so he thought; felt my knife rip the back of his tunic; but managed to slide out of it.

I pursued. He stopped me with a tornado of whipping strokes. Some bastard in the audience cheered.

I kept my head. I had been the unfavored man before. Plenty of times. Let him think he had the crowd. Let him believe he had the fight. . . .Let him jab me in the shoulder as the ghost's robes untwined around my feet and tripped me up.

I got out of that. With an ungainly clamber I straddled the wicker basket, flopped over it and just found time to thrust the folds of dragging material back in my belt. I stopped thinking pretty thoughts. Stuff strategy. Best just to react.

Stuff reacting. I wanted to finish it.

Grumio suspected the trip had thrown me. He was coming for me. I grabbed his knife arm. The dagger flipped across to his other hand: an old trick, and one I recognized. He stabbed up at my ribs, only to gasp as my knee hit his left wrist and cheated him of his intended blow. Now I was the one who was laughing while he looked stupid and yelled.

Taking advantage of his lapse in concentration, I fell on him. I had trapped him on top of the laundry basket. It lurched wildly as we struggled. I slammed Grumio's arm against the lid. I pinned him to the basketwork. I managed to press my own arm down onto his throat.

He looked thinner, but was as strong as me. I could find no better purchase. I knew that any minute he would fight back and it would be my turn to be hammered. Desperate, I rammed his body against the prop, so the whole basket skidded forwards. We both fell.

Grumio scrambled up. I was coming after him. He hurled himself across the basket as I had done earlier, then turned back. He withdrew the wedge from the clasp and pulled up the lid in my face.

The lid dropped open, on my side. Grumio had dropped his dagger but made no attempt to retrieve it. The thunder of boots from the soldiers stilled. Grumio stood transfixed. We both stared at the basket. There was an enormous snake looking out at Grumio.

The thud of the lid had mobilized the reptile. Even I could tell it was disturbed by the blaze of the torches, the strange setting, the violent shaking it had just experienced. Slithering restlessly, it swarmed out of the chest.

A gasp ran around the amphitheater. I was gasping myself. Yard after yard of diamond-patterned scales ran from the basket to the ground. "Keep away!" Grumio yelled at it. No use. Snakes are nearly deaf.

The python felt threatened by the clown's aggression; it opened its mouth, showing what seemed to be hundreds of curved, needle-sharp, backward-pointing teeth.

I heard a quiet voice. "Stand still." It was Musa. The keen snakekeeper. He seemed to have known what the chest contained. "Zeno will not hurt you." He sounded like some competent technician taking charge.

Thalia had told me pythons do not attack humans. What Thalia said was good enough for me, but I was not taking chances. I remained quite motionless.

The kid, still in Musa's arms, bleated nervously. Then Musa moved steadily past me towards the huge snake.

He reached Grumio. Zeno's tongue flicked rapidly through the side of his mouth. "He is just taking your scent." Musa's voice was gentle, yet not reassuring. As if to free himself for dealing with the python, he set down the kid. It leaped forwards. Tottering towards Grumio on fragile legs, it looked terrified, but Zeno showed no interest. "I, however," Musa continued quietly, "already know you Grumio! I arrest you for the murder of the playwright Heliodorus and the tambourinist Ione." In Musa's hand had appeared the slim, wicked-looking blade of his Nabataean dagger. He was holding it with its point towards Grumio's throat;

it was merely a gesture, though, for he was still several feet from the clown.

Suddenly Grumio sprang sideways. He grabbed the kid, and threw it towards Zeno. The kid let out a pitiful bleat of terror, expecting to be bitten and constricted. But Thalia had once told me that snakes in captivity can be choosy. Instead of cooperating, Zeno executed a smooth about-turn. Plainly unhappy, he doubled up on himself with an impressive show of muscle and tried to leave the scene.

The great python sped straight into a group of stage scenery. Hitching strong loops of himself around whatever he encountered, almost deliberately he knocked things flying. The big ceramic jar crashed over, losing its lid. Zeno wound himself around the stage oven, then curled up on top of it, looking superior, as the contraption bowed beneath his enormous weight. Meanwhile, Grumio had gained ground on both Musa and me. He seemed to have a clear run to the exit and began to spring away from us.

From the overturned jar something else emerged. It was smaller than the python—but more dangerous. Grumio stopped in his tracks. I had started to pursue him, but Musa exclaimed and gripped my arm. In front of Grumio there was now another snake: a dark head, a banded body, and as it reared upright to confront him, a golden throat beneath the wide extension of its sinister hood. It must be Pharaoh, Thalia's new cobra. He was angry, hissing, and in full threat display.

"Retreat slowly!" Musa commanded in a clear voice.

Grumio, who was nearly ten feet from the reptile, ignored the advice. He seized a torch and made a sweeping gesture with the burning brand. Pharaoh made what was obviously a mere feint. He expected respect.

"He will follow movement!" Musa warned, still unheeded.

Grumio shook the torch again. The cobra let out a short, low hiss, then darted across the whole distance between them and struck.

Pharaoh moved back. Slamming down at body height, he had bitten the leather apron Grumio wore in costume as a slave. The leather must be snakeproof. It would have saved the clown's life.

But his ordeal had not ended. As he was struck that first ferocious blow, Grumio, terrified, staggered and then tripped. On the ground, he instinctively scrabbled to get away. Pharaoh saw him still moving, and rushed forwards again. This time he struck Grumio full on the neck. The downward bite was accurate and strong, followed by a fast chewing movement to make sure.

Our audience went wild. A kill onstage: just what they had bought their tickets for.

Epilogue
Palmyra

Palmyra: the desert. Hotter than ever, at night.

SYNOPSIS: *Falco*, a playwright, not in the mood to play the hired trickster, finds that as usual he has set everything to rights. . . .

Seventy-four

Something told me that no one was ever going to ask me what happened about Moschion and his ghost.

Musa and I emerged from the arena badly shaken. We had seen Grumio collapse in shock and hysteria. As soon as the cobra retreated by stages from his vicinity, we crept forward cautiously and dragged the clown to the gates. Behind us the crowd was in uproar. Soon the python was maliciously destroying props while the cobra watched with a menacing attitude.

Grumio was not dead, but undoubtedly he would be. Thalia came over to look at him, then caught my eye and shook her head.

"He'll be gone before dawn."

"Thalia, should somebody catch your snakes?"

"I don't suggest anyone else tries!"

She was brought a long, pronged implement and ventured into the arena with the bravest of her people. Soon the cobra had been pinned down and reinstalled in his jar, while Zeno rather smugly returned to his basket of his own accord, as if none of the chaos should be blamed on him.

I stared at Musa. Clearly he had brought the python to the arena, ready for Thalia's act after the play. Had it been his idea to take the basket onstage as a dangerous prop? And had he also known that Pharaoh was in the ceramic jar? If I asked him he would probably tell me, in his straight way. I preferred not to know. There was little difference between what had happened today and subjecting Grumio to the delays of a trial and almost certain condemnation *ad bestias*.

A group of soldiers pulled themselves together. They took charge of Grumio, then, since the commander had told them to arrest all possible culprits, they arrested Tranio too. He went along with a shrug. There was hardly a case to answer. Tranio had behaved unbelievably, but there was no law in the Twelve Tables against sheer stupidity. He had given away the precious scroll of stories, failed to retrieve it, then allowed Grumio to carry on undetected long after he himself must have known the truth. But if he really thought that his own original mistake equated with Grumio's crimes, he needed a course in ethics.

Later, while we were waiting for the convulsions and paralysis to finish Grumio, Tranio would admit what he knew: that Grumio, acting alone, had lured Heliodorus up the mountain at Petra, making sure no one else knew he had gone there; that Grumio had been walking closest to Musa when he was pushed into the reservoir at Bostra; that Grumio had actually laughed with his tentmate about various attempts to disable me—letting me fall off a ladder, the knife-throwing incident, and even threatening to push me into the underground water system at Gadara.

When Helena and I finally left Palmyra, Tranio would remain in custody, though much later I heard that he had been released. I never knew what happened to him afterwards. It was Congrio who was to become the famous Roman clown. We would attend many of his performances despite those harsh critics at the Theater of Balbus who dared to suggest that the great Congrio's stories were rather antique, and that somebody should find him a more modern scroll of jokes.

Life would have to alter for several of our companions. When Musa and I first left the arena, Philocrates, in great pain and covered in gore from a glorious nosebleed, had been sitting on the ground waiting for a bone-setter. He looked as if he had a fractured collarbone. His nose, and probably one of his cheekbones, had been broken in his fall. He would never again play the handsome juvenile. I tried to encourage him: "Never mind, Philocrates. Some women adore a man who has a lived-in face." You have to be kind.

Once she had ruled out any hope for Grumio, Thalia came to help mop up the drips of blood on this casualty; I swear I heard her trying to negotiate to buy Philocrates' comic mule. The creature would be knocking people over regularly in Nero's Circus when Thalia returned home.

I myself was temporarily in trouble. While Musa and I were hanging on to each other getting our breath back, a familiar voice stormed angrily: "Didius Falco, if you really want to kill yourself, why not just get run over by a dung cart like everybody else? Why do you have to attempt your destruction in front of two thousand strangers? And why do I have to be made to watch?"

Magic. I was never so happy as when Helena was berating me. It took my mind off everything else.

"May as well sell tickets for the fight, and help you pay for my funeral—"

She growled, dragging the ghost's costume up and over my head to give me air. But it was a gentle hand that wiped my perspiring brow with her own white stole.

Then we were rushed by the Habib family. They had burst from their seats to tell us what a wonderful evening we had invited them to share—and to stare hard at Helena's lanky chaperone. I left the next part to the women. Helena and Thalia must have planned it in advance, and while Helena was taking her up into the tribunal, Sophrona must have been instructed to go along with it.

Helena hugged the girl, then cried to the Habib family gratefully, "Oh thank you for looking after her—I've been searching all over for the naughty thing! But now she's found and I can take her back to Rome with me to her proper life. I expect you realized she was from a good family. Such a talented musician, but wicked to run away to be on the stage, of course. Still, what can you expect. She plays the instrument of emperors. . . ."

I was choking quietly.

The Habib parents had weighed up the quality of Helena's jewels, some of which she must have been buying quietly from Nabataean caravans and Decapolis markets while my back was turned. They had seen the commanding officer treating her with extreme respect, since he knew that Vespasian himself wanted her whereabouts reported on. Now Khaleed put on a beseeching look. His father was salivating over their apparent good luck. Sophrona herself, like most girls, found she could easily slip into the appearance of being better than she was.

Khaleed's mother suggested that if the girl had to leave Syria, maybe the young couple could be married first. Helena then proposed that Khaleed should spend some time in Rome improving himself among the nobility. . . .

"Isn't that nice?" uttered Thalia, with no apparent trace of irony. Nobody but me seemed to entertain any notion that once in Rome the forceful Thalia would persuade Sophrona that her best interests lay not in settling down, but in her public career as an organist.

Discussion was avoided because of a rumpus in the amphitheater. Denied a full program, the angry soldiers had started to tear up benches from the ramps.

"Jupiter! Better stop this! How can we distract them?"

"Easy." Thalia grabbed hold of the young lady. "Now you're nicely sorted out, Sophrona, you can do something in return. Buck up! I didn't bring it all the way from Rome just to let mosquitoes breed in the water tank. . . ."

She signaled to her staff. With a speed that astonished us they lined up around a large low carriage. Calling some of Chremes' stagehands to help them, they wheeled it to the gate, counted three, then ran out across the open space. The audience stilled, and quickly resumed what was left of their seats. The shrouds dropped from the looming item. It was a hydraulus.

When levered off its carriage, the water organ stood over twelve feet high. The upper portion looked like a gigantic set of syrinx pipes, made partly of bronze, partly of reed. The lower part was formed from an ornamental chest to which bellows were attached. One of Thalia's men was pouring water carefully into a chamber. Another was attaching a footboard, a huge lever, and a keyboard.

I saw Sophrona's eyes widen. For a few moments she managed to hide her eagerness, performing a brief pageant of reluctant maidenhood. Helena and the rest of us went along with it and pleaded with her to take the stage. Next minute she was bounding out to give orders to those setting up the instrument for her.

It was obvious that playing the organ mattered. I decided I ought to introduce Sophrona to Ribes. Our moody lyre-player seemed like a young man who might be done a power of good by a girl with wonderful eyes who could talk to him about music. . . .

Thalia grinned at Davos. "Going to help me pump her bellows?" She could make the simplest question sound cheeky. Davos accepted the dubious invitation like a man, even though Thalia had a glint that promised even harder work for him afterwards.

A decent fellow. I reckoned he would cope.

Just as they were about to leave us to provide Sophrona's support onstage, Phrygia called Thalia back. She had teetered up, her long gangly figure balancing precariously on platform heels. She was waving at the equally tall figure of Sophrona.

"That girl . . ." She sounded anguished.

"Sophrona? She's just a waif I inherited with Fronto's circus." The narrowing of Thalia's eyes looked unreliable to anyone who wasn't desperate.

"I hoped my daughter was here. . . ." Phrygia was not giving up.

"She's here. But maybe after twenty years alone she doesn't want to be found."

"I'll make everything up to her! I can offer her the best." Phrygia gazed around wildly. Only one other female in our circle was the right age: Byrria. She snatched at the younger actress hysterically. "We took you on in Italy! Where were you brought up?"

"Latium." Byrria looked calm, but curious.

"Outside Rome? Do you know your parents?"

"I was an orphan."

"Do you know Thalia?"

I saw Thalia wink at Byrria. "Obviously," said Thalia quietly, "I never told your daughter a famous actress was her mother. You don't want girls getting big ideas."

Phrygia threw her arms around Byrria and burst into tears.

Thalia shot me a look, one of calculation and amazement at what fools would believe when their eyes should tell them different. Then she managed to grab Davos and escape into the arena.

"Everything is going to be wonderful from now on!" Phrygia

cried to Byrria. Byrria gave her the doubtful grimace of the usual ungrateful daughter who wants to make her own life.

Helena and I exchanged a glance. We could see the young actress considering what to do as she recognized her amazing luck. Out in the arena, Sophrona had no idea she was being displaced; she was being given plenty of options anyway. Byrria's determination to gain a place in the world had never been in doubt. She wanted a career. If she played along with Phrygia's mistake, she could not only demand good acting parts, but without a doubt she would sooner or later end up in command of the whole company. I reckoned she would be good at that. Loners can usually organize.

What Chremes had told us about the death of live theater would probably not count. He had been despondent. There was still scope for entertainers, certainly in the provinces, and even in Italy if they adapted to the market. Byrria must know she had been offered the chance of her life.

Chremes, who appeared to need more time than his wife to consider his position, gave Byrria an embarrassed smile, then led Phrygia away to join most of our company, who had collected inside the gate of the amphitheater. They were eagerly waiting to judge Sophrona's keyboard skills on the fabulous instrument. Byrria dallied behind with Musa, Helena, and me. On the whole, I thought Chremes' position was a good one. If he kept his head down he could keep his wife, find himself promoting a popular and beautiful young actress, and probably have peace at home.

Davos, I thought, might soon want to be leaving the company.

If Davos joined forces with Thalia, there seemed a possibility that Sophrona might have lost a mother, but gained a father here today.

I lurched to my feet. "I'm not a great fan of sonorous music." Especially after a nerve-racking physical experience. "Don't let me spoil the fun for anyone else, but if none of you mind, I've had enough of this." They all decided to come with me back to camp.

We turned away. Helena and I had our arms tightly around one another as we walked, in a sad and contemplative mood. Musa and Byrria were strolling in their normal manner, straight-backed, solemn-faced, side by side in silence and not even holding hands.

I wondered what would become of them. I wanted to think they would now find a quiet corner together and come to terms. Since it was what I would have done myself, I wanted them to go to bed.

Somehow I doubted that would happen. I knew Helena shared my melancholy feeling that we were watching a relationship fail to materialize.

Musa would return to Petra; Byrria would be well known in the Roman theater. Yet they were obviously friends. Maybe she would write to Musa, and he to her. Maybe I ought to encourage it, one link at least to smooth the path to Nabataean assimilation into the Empire. Cultural contact and private friendship forging bonds: the old diplomatic myth. If he could overcome his urge to run a menagerie, I could see Musa becoming a grand figure in Nabataea. If Byrria became a major entertainment queen, she would meet all the Empire's men of power.

Perhaps one day in the future, when Byrria had exhausted her dreams, they would meet again and it might not be too late.

We had walked some distance. Dusk had long given way to night. Beyond reach of the arena torches we had to pick our way with care. The great oasis was peaceful and mysterious, its palms and olive trees reduced to vague dark shapes; its homes and public buildings lost in their midst. Above our heads myriad stars plunged through their endless rota, mechanical yet heart-tugging. Somewhere in the desert a camel brayed its preposterous call; then a dozen others started harshly answering.

Then we all paused, and turned back for a moment. Awestruck, we had reacted to an extraordinary sound. From the place we had left sounded a resonance unlike anything any of us had ever heard. Sophrona was playing. The effect astonished us. If she was Phrygia's true daughter I could see exactly why Thalia wanted to keep the information to herself. Nothing should be allowed to interfere with such a remarkable talent. The public deserves to be entertained.

Around Palmyra, even the beasts in the merchants' caravans had ceased their cacophonous calls. Like us, they stood stock still, listening. The reverberating chords of the water organ rose above the desert, so all the camels were stilled by a wild music that was even more powerful, even louder, and (I fear) even more ridiculous than their own.

Footnotes

Archaeology

The first century is a patchy period in our knowledge of the eastern Mediterranean. The Emperors Trajan and Hadrian took a keen interest in the region, visited it, and initiated much new town planning. Many spectacular Roman remains in Jordan and Syria, therefore, including existing theaters, date from the Second Century. Information about what may have existed in A.D. 72 is so sparse that the writer of fiction must use intelligent invention. The location of some Decapolis towns has yet to be conclusively established. I have used the most widely accepted list, choosing the most convenient of several sites for Dium, and assuming that Raphana and Capitolias are the same place.

Political History

Nabataea was peacefully annexed by Trajan and became the Roman province of Arabia Petraia in A.D. 106. Bostra became its chief city and the trade routes were shifted east, away from Petra. This may have been a suggestion from an imperial agent, possibly one made under a previous emperor and which Trajan found filed in the Palatine archives.

Literature

Scholars are still hoping to discover a manuscript of *The Spook Who Spoke*. This lost comedy by an unidentified first-century author (conjecturally identified as M. Didius?) had only one recorded stage performance, but is believed by some to be the prototype for *Hamlet*.